Echoes of
An Uncivil War

Visit JamesRyanBooks.com

ECHOES OF
AN UNCIVIL WAR

BY

JAMES RYAN

This book I dedicated to…
My sister, Liz, who encouraged me to write this novel
My wife and son, who always support me
My extended family, the Roman's and Richhart's
My friend and editor, Gail
All of my dear friends in Ohio and Tennessee that made this book a
reality

<h1 style="text-align:center">Preface</h1>

Echoes of an Uncivil War started as notes about a forgotten time. Then I visited my childhood home near Rogersville, Tennessee. It, too, is forgotten, but sits in the most beautiful land that I have ever seen-East Tennessee. The more I wrote, the memories flooded back. Many good, many bad. While going through the difficult times of my life in my head, I decided to share some of them with those around me. I soon realized that every single person has some sort of difficulty in their lives. Some worse than others. I continued to write and as I researched for Echoes, I became captivated with the atrocities that our nation carried out on the Native Americans who lived here before us. Forcing them from their homes and relocating them to land already owned by other tribes became the groundwork for centuries of difficulty for them. While they are a proud community, they have endured what can only be descibed as persecution in their own land. This persecution has caused alcoholism to run rampant within those communities. I watched alcoholism take my mother, father, and brother. I can only imagine what our Native American brothers and sisters have gone through. Echoes is a fictional novel, but much of the storyline happens every day. I tried to honor the Cherokee Nation and respect those with difficulties in their lives. If you would like to help those in need, visit Horseshealingheartsusa.org and ask how you can help. Please enjoy this novel.

James Ryan

Chapter 1 –

1973, "No One Lives Forever"

Tad slowly woke. Confused and rubbing his eyes, he thought that he heard crying in the kitchen. He looked at his brother sleeping next to him. Shaking Brett, Tad asked, "Hey, is mom crying?"

Brett pushed him away, without even opening his eyes. Tad glanced around, climbed out of his bed slowly, and proceeded to the doorway. While standing in the doorway, he could see his father, Wally, sitting at the breakfast table, his head down, and shaking it from side to side, telling himself, "no, no, no". This all seemed very strange.

Not really sure how long he stood there, Tad, still confused, wondered why his mother didn't wake them. She normally came to their room every morning, caressed them gently, and they would wake to her singing a few notes from a song. Tad also noticed that his baby sister, Liz, wasn't in the kitchen nor with May May.

Tad slowly crept into the kitchen and to his mother's side. He wrapped his arms around her warm legs and asked. "What's wrong mommy?"

Kneeling down to pick him up, a warm tear fell from her nose onto his forehead. A strange feeling came over Tad. One that he'd not felt before. A feeling that something was very wrong.

As Mary, Tad's mother, picked him up, she hugged him, and said, "Punkin, Uncle Cliff passed away last night."

"Uncle Cliff", as Tad and Brett knew him, came over to the O'Banion house often. Wally worked for Cliff, and people rarely saw them apart. Cliff, the founder of Camelot, began developing this small resort in East Tennessee, north of Rogersville, just two years prior. When Cliff came over to the O'Banion's, he and Wally would talk "business" and drink scotch until they were laughing loudly, and their cigarettes filled the ashtrays. It was quite normal for them to talk about Camelot until late in the evening,…and sometimes early into the morning hours. Mary would eventually join them to give her perspective on "How they were mistaken".

Cliff never imagined how much Wally and Mary would play into his endeavors but felt their influence daily. They both proved to be more valuable than anyone could have imagined. The children, however, just saw Camelot as a "fun place to live", and Cliff Lafferty was just "Uncle Cliff".

"Mommy, I don't understand", Tad said.

She hugged him tightly and tried to speak, but nothing came out. She wiped away more tears and sat down on a chair. Lifting him onto her lap, she looked him in the eyes and said, "Honey, Uncle Cliff died. He's in heaven now. We can't see him, but he can see us. Cliff was in an accident last night and he didn't make it."

Still confused, Tad said, "So Uncle Cliff won't bring us candy anymore?"

"Oh, for Christ's sake!" Wally barked out, as he stood and walked out of the kitchen.

Tad never talked about it, but sometimes Tad thought his father seemed "nice". Other times, especially at night, not so nice. Brett said it was when their father drank "adult drinks" that Wally appeared the "meanest". Today, Tad thought his father was indeed "mean", and he wasn't drinking. This just added to the confusion for Tad.

Chapter 2 –

"The Vision of a King"

Cliff had envisioned "Camelot" many years ago but never imagined that it would be in East Tennessee. He didn't actually find this little "gem". Nancy, Cliff's wife, did. They traveled often, and Nancy found this "little antiquated hotel" while talking with a local during breakfast one day in 1968. Cliff and Nancy decided to check it out, and they ended up staying at "The Manor" hotel every time they traveled through the area called Pressmen's Home.

When the Laffertys stayed in Camelot, Nancy loved their walks down to the lake. So, after she passed, Cliff wanted to remember her and, to his surprise, much of the land around Pressmen's Home was available. Cliff purchased almost 3,200 acres. The hotel, the church, the old tradesmen's buildings, the stables, the livestock barn, and all the surrounding acreage, with a plan to develop the area into a nice resort, and get-away cabins for those wanting to live the "resort life".

Cliff thought the location was perfect, and this type of resort was becoming quite popular. Small lots that would be affordable by many "middle-income" families. They would have all the "niceties" of a resort. Golf, tennis, swimming pool, and horseback riding, without the exorbitant price tag of a high-end club. A theme that had previously worked well for Cliff.

The area, known as Pressmen's Home for over eighty years, had in fact been the headquarters for The Pressmen's Union until they became a part of The Teamsters Union in the sixties. In its heyday, roughly 3000 full and temporary residents walked the grounds of Pressmen's Home campus. The church housed parishioners who came from as far away as Jonesborough.

Pressmen's Home was a rather large campus for the time. A six-story tradesmen's building, a four-story administrative building, with dormitory, and cafeteria. The campus included the grand hotel that overlooked a thirty-acre lake. Built in 1899, "The Manor" hotel had been the perfect resting place for many affluent travelers, working their way west, from the coast, to St. Louis, Indianapolis, and Nashville. The hotel hosted the likes of Buster Keaton, Mae West, and Houdini, who performed his famous "water escape" in its very own theater.

After the Pressmen's Union moved to Washington D.C., in 1967, the union offered the trade and administrative buildings to the state of Tennessee, a move that the local community regretted approving. The state quickly took advantage of the sanitarium. The Union had previously used it for members with tuberculosis, but the state began to use it for patients with mental conditions, marking the beginning of decline for Pressmen's Home. The locals tell of many instances when patients would wander off. Some returned, with notable trauma to their mental condition, and some, seemingly, were never found. Pressmen's Sanitarium quickly became known as a place you did not want a family member entering.

For the short time that Pressmen's Sanitarium existed, travel through the area came to a crawl, as no one wanted to stay at a hotel right across from a sanitarium. The church went from 300 parishioners to less than ten and eventually closed the doors. The hotel eventually closed to travelers and remained open only to board the medical personnel for the sanitarium.

In the late sixties, The Medical Society began a campaign to dissolve sanitariums and asylums, deeming them unfit and cruel. This movement quickly closed the sanitarium at Pressmen's Home, and thus the whole campus went into a state of desertion.

"The Manor" reopened in 1968 and had only been open for a couple of months before the Laffertys' initial visit, only to close again in 1970, a month after Nancy's death. Knowing how much Nancy loved the place, Cliff became "hell-bent" on purchasing and reopening "The Manor".

Having already been successful in creating resorts in Florida and South Carolina, Cliff was always looking for that "gem". The happy memories of Nancy at The Manor "sealed the deal" in his mind. Pressmen's Home included the perfect mix of a relaxing atmosphere, a grand hotel, the beautiful lake, land for homes, and an ideal location for a golf course and clubhouse. He knew he could create this "clubhouse" from a large livestock barn, just an eighth of a mile down the road. This project was well underway by the time the O'Banions joined Cliff.

Not far from Camelot was a bustling little "historical community" named Rogersville. The "center" of Hawkins County, it offered all the amenities that "resort owners" might need. Grocery stores, restaurants, and various downtown shops.

Though "The Manor" hotel needed much work, it had once appeared "grand" at one time, and Cliff envisioned it that way again. He believed that his five-to-six-year plan was a bit aggressive, but doable. All he had to do was to convince the locals that Camelot was a "good thing", and he knew the county and state would follow suit. He had done it before…he would make Camelot a reality.

By the time Cliff convinced Wally to join him, Cliff had already developed the golf course and transformed the old livestock barn into what was becoming an impressive clubhouse. It mimicked a castle in many ways. He removed the dome roofs of the grain silos and cut crenels into the top of them, which gave them the appearance of battlements. The lower level, which was originally the "dairy parlor" and open stalls became offices and an extravagant meeting room. He'd been in the process of turning the upper level, the old hay mow, into a restaurant, bar, dance hall when Wally and Mary came on board. The "golf pro-shop" at the lower entry led out to a large stone patio with a fountain that spewed water from a miniature stone castle replica. To the surprise of most, Cliff's convincing the county board, and state, to rename this little area "Camelot" officially made the resort come alive.

Most folks thought Cliff's imagery of the "castle clubhouse" to be a tribute to the folklore of King Arthur and the knights of the "round table". But, in reality, Cliff meant it all as a salute to the Kennedy family, and all that they represented. Cliff, a conservative democrat, considered the Kennedys to be true royalty in the United States. All of the tragedies that befell the Kennedy family deepened Cliff's desire to salute them…not to mention that Nancy Lafferty greatly resembled J.F.K's wife, Jacqueline.

Although Cliff's ideas and vision were tantamount to those of any extraordinary entrepreneur, Cliff realized he needed help. He had achieved quite a bit, but there were just too many things to do. Cliff needed someone who could focus on selling the atmosphere of the resort, and ultimately the lots around the golf course and lake. Most of his recent acquaintances comprised of project managers and contractors from previous ventures. Not the talent to help him sell. He needed a "salesman" with the ability to appeal to the right people. Cliff thought long and hard. "Who has the talent and capability to join me?"…his thought fell to one acquaintance from Cincinnati, Ohio…Joseph Wallace O'Banion…AKA Wally.

When Cliff met Wally, Wally was an executive with a radio station in Cincinnati. With a strong reputation for "sealing the deal", Wally's personality tended to "set the hook" with every sales encounter. Everyone who met Wally seemed to enjoy his company and perspective. Pondering what needed to be done, it appeared obvious to Cliff that Wally might be the perfect candidate to take Camelot to the next level. Cliff knew Wally had "vision" and his young wife was rumored to be quite the visionary in her own right. Getting Wally to Camelot could be tough, Cliff thought, but he'd manage. Cliff devised a plan that Wally would surely not turn down.

Timing was everything for Wally; he wasn't expecting what was coming. His achievements and connections in the world of broadcasting seemed vast. He spent many years developing these relationships and enjoyed it.

Originally from Pittsburgh, Pennsylvania, Wally had joined the Army and fought in the South Pacific, during World War II. After the war, he returned to Pennsylvania and married his high school "sweetheart". Over the next ten years, his family life seemed perfect, happily fathering four children. But he felt himself "diving deep" into the world of broadcasting, which eventually pulled him to Ohio.

Sadly, the stress of this new passion fractured his relationship with his wife, and a tumultuous divorce completed his departure from the Keystone State. Leaving an ex-wife and four children behind was tough at first, and guilt set in hard. So, Wally filled his days, and nights, with a focus on success in broadcasting. He was "a natural", hitting the commercial sales and advertising side hard during the day and often working his customer base well into every evening. Wally thrived in advertising. Being good at it, he enjoyed the camaraderie, especially in this day and age when radio and television were on "the rise". Wally's advertising knack garnered him a reputation that "fast-tracked" him everywhere he went.

It wasn't long before he caught the eye of a young singer from Dayton, Mary Margaret. Mary studied music in Cincinnati and was once dubbed Lawrence Welk's "Champagne Lady", touring with him to all the local events. Ohio's runner-up for the Miss America Pageant in 1959, Mary became a popular socialite between Dayton and Cincinnati. It was not hard for Wally to charm his way into Mary's heart. He was debonair and often "turned a blonde's head" in his late-night escapades with customers and friends. While she'd already been "smitten" with him, eventually his eyes focused on Mary Margaret.

They married with an elaborate wedding in Cincinnati, Ohio. It had all the glitz and glamor of a movie star wedding in Bel Air, with an outdoor reception, next to the pool at The Preston Fieldhouse Hotel in Cincinnati. Several famous acquaintances were in attendance. James Garner, the actor who portrayed Brett Maverick; Jonathan Winters, the comedian who hailed from Dayton; and Bob Braun, a radio and TV personality from Cincinnati. All friends of Wally's, from radio and television. Mary, dressed in an sequin-encrusted wedding dress, and Wally in a black tuxedo, they spent their extravagant evening carousing, laughing, and dancing. Before the night ended, Jonathan Winters had people in tears from laughter, and someone tossed Wally into the pool twice.

Mary loved the "limelight", possibly more so than Wally did. She and Wally seemed to receive invitations to every event or gala in and around Ohio. At times, when Mary felt "in the spotlight", she would sing one of her favorite cover songs. Many of their "friends" played the piano. Other times she'd charm the band to play for her, just as Wally had charmed her. After singing something by Rosemary Clooney, or maybe Patsy Cline, she'd always finish the song and look at Wally. He'd wink, and she'd cup her hands together to thank everyone as they applauded her performance. The nights would go on, the smoke would fill the rooms, and the alcohol would flow like the river outside the club. Wally was always there until the last cigarette was lit, and the last drink thrown back, with his beautiful wife by his side.

Wally really was on the "Fast-track". Cleveland, then Columbus, then Cincinnati, all advertising positions in broadcasting, until he accepted his next challenge with an up-and-coming resort called Hide-Away-Hills in a rural Ohio community. He had "free rein" to work his magic. Within one year, he turned this resort into one of the most sought-after resort locations in the Midwest.

While Mary loved her "limelight", she also wanted a family. The fact that Wally already had four children didn't sway her one bit. Wally was a bit more apprehensive, though. But "the seducer" became "the seduced", and Mary won him over. Growing up in Dayton with two brothers of her own, three children sounded perfect to her. Brett was born in 1965, then Thadeus, three years later. But then, Ocean Breeze Condominiums offered Wally a lucrative position in Florida.

It was a similar situation as Hide-Away Hills, help a struggling resort "gain traction". But this time the location offered promise of the opportunity for Wally to open his own advertising agency, something that he, and Mary, grew to desire.

Moving to Florida and finding a multi-level condominium building with small shops and offices on the main level was the perfect setting. Wally and Mary jumped at the opportunity to open their advertising agency there, and soon *The Agency* was born. Wally split his time between Ocean Breeze and *The Agency*, while Mary focused on *The Agency*.

Wally again "waved his magic wand", and his approach seemed to be a magnet for those looking to invest in resort dream-homes, and parties at the clubhouse. Wally and Mary gladly hosted the parties with "themes" like "Bond night", "Maverick night", and the often popular "Sinatra night" where everyone pretended to be a mobster for the night. As always, Wally closed the night by being the last one out the door. But Mary's nights were ending earlier since she was pregnant with their third child, which Mary was sure was a girl. Soon, Ocean Breeze was as "happening" as every other resort that Wally touched.

The Agency grew, but not like Wally imagined. There was strong competition, and *The Agency* needed large cash reserves in order to cover ongoing expenses before they could invoice for jobs completed for clients. This, coupled with the need for Mary to work less and less, required them to be a bit more selective in the clientele. Choosing jobs that had fewer expenses and decent return took Wally to Mississippi, where he originally planned to stay for just a few months. Mary didn't want to travel because of the pregnancy and stayed in Florida until Wally called, saying, "I need you".

Mary replied, "I'm going to need help too. I think I'm gonna need a nanny."

To which Wally replied, "Not a problem. This client has just doubled in size, and we now have twice the advertising work to do. I'll have Tommy, my assistant here, help to find somebody around here. I'll come back this weekend to get you and the boys."

"Okay honey. How are we going to get everything we need to Jackson?" Mary asked.

Wally reassured Mary, "Again, not a problem, they're letting me use their limo to come and get you. All you need are clothes for you and the boys. You'll be riding in "style". I already have a short-term contract on an apartment".

So, Mary packed the boys up, and moved into the apartment in Jackson, Mississippi. She helped *The Agency* from the apartment when she could.

As their little family grew, it seemed that Wally was home less and less. Up at nine A.M. and home after midnight. Almost every day. He appeared to be burning the candle at both ends. Mary learned not to be up when Wally came home. He was loud, and sometimes quite obstinate. He didn't really "make good" on the "nanny", but sometimes Tommy would come over and help out. Mary didn't like Tommy one bit. Before long, the "few months" didn't appear to have an end in sight. Mary didn't like this either. She didn't like Jackson, she didn't like Tommy, and she didn't like the way Wally treated her. She let him know it when he appeared sober, and he seemed genuinely sorry. But Mary felt that this was all going to change soon.

As Mary lay sleeping in the hospital bed, she woke to Wally holding her hand and a healthy little girl in his arms. Mary winced from the pain of the incision, a horizontal cesarean across her belly. She had hoped for a natural birth, like Brett, but the doctors thought it wouldn't be possible since her womb had already been compromised with Tad three years earlier.

Mary slowly scooted up in the bed and asked, "What'd you decide?...her name?"

Wally looked down at the baby and back at Mary. "Lizabeth, I think she should be Lizabeth. People always say that you look like Elizabeth Taylor and let's give her a name befitting a star."

With that, he gently handed sweet little Liz the new mother of three. Mary got her "wish". For a moment, it seemed life couldn't get much better.

"Are the boys with May May?" Mary asked.

"Of course, where else would they be?" Wally replied.

As Mary stayed preoccupied with her new "bundle of joy", Wally talked about their latest ads and mentioned that he was working with a local producer to make a television commercial.

"Did you hear me?" Wally said.

"I'm sorry, what?" Mary replied.

"I said we're going to make our first television commercial!" Wally exclaimed.

With that, Mary's face lit up, and she proclaimed, "Honey, I don't know when I'll be ready for a commercial."

Wally broke out in laughter. "Mary Margaret!, you don't have to be the star. I'd rather have your input in all other aspects of it. We have a storyline and script, but I want you to look it over after you feel a little better. Has the doctor said when you'll be coming home?"

Mary lifted little Liz, winced again, and gently laid her in the arms of a nurse who had just walked in. "They said five days. They said Liz will stay in the nursery or with me until then. Do you think you'll be okay with the two "hellions" until then?" She said with her eyebrows raised.

Wally laughed, "Thank god for May May. Tommy has been helping out too."

"Tommy?" Mary exclaimed. "The whole time I was back in Florida, and you were talking about how much Tommy was helping you, I didn't realize that "Tommy" was a woman!"

Wally got defensive in his posture. "Okay, easy there, Honey. "Thomila" has been a big help, and she's a bit young for you to be jealous of, don't you think? Listen, I don't want you getting worked up over nothing. I'll let you rest, …but I got an interesting call today that I wanted to tell you about. It was from an investor in Tennessee. He's asking if we want to come to Camelot."

Mary interrupted, "Camelot, isn't that in Massachusetts?"

Wally laughed. "Different kingdom, honey. This guy, Cliff, he says he needs Merlin's magic, and he thinks that's me." Wally said with a grin.

Chapter 3 –

"The Dreadful Morning" Camelot, 1973

"Wally, stop! Tad doesn't understand." Mary exclaimed.

Wally just continued walking through the foyer and out the door. Tad was still on Mary's lap. Looking confused, he began to cry. Mary pulled him close to her and tried not to cry herself but couldn't hold back. After a few moments, both of their tears dried up. Mary sat Tad on the kitchen chair by himself and returned to the breakfast she'd started an hour earlier. May May came to her side and helped while Tad played with a Matchbox car.

The sunlight streamed through the kitchen window, which was still wet from the storm the night before.

Tad spoke up. "The lightning was loud last night. It woke me some. It crashed and crashed and sounded as if it was right outside our window". Zooming his car across the table, it rolled off and struck the floor. May May picked it up and returned it to Tad and then gave him a kiss on the forehead.

"Chil, dat's thunder dat makes the noise. Lightnin is just da flash, like a bub". May May said and kissed him again.

May May had become part of the family. She was good to them all, and always referred to the children as "her babies".

Wally found Mabel May Jackson in Hattiesburg, Mississippi, the home of The University of Southern Mississippi. The ad listed "Grama Needs Her Babies". After a brief phone call, Mabel offered to take a bus to Jackson and showed up at the apartment with a suitcase.

After meeting Wally, Mary, and the kids, she simply said. "I be sleeping in da room wit da baby. I need fi'ty dollars a week, and deese babies is mine. I don't wan no scuff bout how I take care of em. Day be safe. Don you worry."

The children took to May May immediately, and they were quick to show her as much love as she showed them. Before long, they went to May May for everything. She would hold them tight and stroke their hair with her dark hand. It was obvious to Wally and Mary that the children felt safe with May May, which set their minds at ease as well. May May's favorite place was sitting on the couch, Brett on one side and Tad on the other. Little Lizabeth was in the porta-crib right in front of them. May May, who had never owned a television, watched the shows with wide-eyed wonder. Occasionally, after Wally and Mary returned from an evening social event, they'd try to pick one of the children up and May May would bark, "Mister(or Miz) O'Banion, dat's not a good idea! You been out drinking and you is NOT gonna drop one my babies!". "Now you'uns get on to bed and let me do my job."

As Tad sat eating French toast, just a mere thirty minutes after hearing about "Uncle Cliff" untimely death, he seemed perfectly content. That was until Brett walked out of the boy's bedroom.

Mary asked, "Do you want some French toast?"

Brett replied, "Yes, please." As he rubbed his eyes and yawned, he walked over and hugged Mary's leg, just as Tad had done thirty minutes before him.

Brett looked up at her and said, "There was a crash or something out on the golf course. I could see it in the rain. There were fire trucks and a big tow truck. I watched it for a while, but it was hard to see cuz it was raining so hard."

Tad asked, "What's a tow truck?"

Mary seemed eager for the moment to end as she had just calmed from Tad's reaction.

Just then, Wally walked back in. He took his car keys off the wall and said, "I have to go to the clubhouse to see what needs to be done.", then out the door he went. No "goodbye", no kiss on the forehead, just out the door.

Mary took Brett into the family room to tell him the news. In the kitchen, May May remained seated, feeding Liz, glancing at Tad.

"No!" Brett cried and ran out the door that Wally had just left through.

Mary walked back into the kitchen and looked at May May. "Miz O'Banion, le' him be. I'll go check on him in a bit. Let's get Tad and Liz finished up and den I'll go find him." May May said.

After a little while, May May left. She returned carrying Brett, his cheeks red with dried streaks running down them. May May set him in the dining chair and patted him on the head as she walked back to prepare his breakfast. "Miz O'Banion, I got des babies. You go on and get ready. Mister O'Banion gonna need you."

***

Later that morning, Brett and Tad walked down to the golf course. The boys inspected the large ruts cut deep into the turf like little investigators. The boys deduced that Cliff's car created ruts as it rolled over, and emergency vehicles created others. Random pieces of the car trim and broken glass scattered across a narrow section of the fairway. Off to the side, in the rough, Brett found a small, wet paper sack. He reached in and pulled out two packs of "Sugar Babies", …the very candy that Uncle Cliff brought them every visit. Just then, a voice called out.

"Hey boys, ya'll need to clear out. We gotta get this cleaned up and re-sodded". It was Buddy from the stables.

Brett looked up from the bag and asked, "Buddy, you know who died last night?".

Buddy, looking a bit surprised, said, "Nope. All I know was there was a bad accident and me and Nick gotta get it cleaned up before anyone can golf on it. Otherwise, Mister Lafferty is gonna tan somebody's hide. So, you boys best get on outta here for I tell Pop."

"Pop", the elderly man that ran the stables, was often feared by some of the young men for his steadfast demeanor. Employing five, including the two teenagers, and young Brett, Pop had become an anchor in Camelot. No one seemed to know how long he had been there, they all knew it was a long time. Rumors were that he had been a cowboy from "out west", and settled in East Tennessee sometime in the fifties.

"It was Uncle Cliff", Brett blurted out.

"Wait, what?...It wa..was Mister Lafferty? Oh shit!" Buddy said as he stood with his mouth agape.

***

The following week seemed strange in "The Kingdom of Camelot". May May took care of the children at the house in Camelot, while Mary and Wally went to the funeral in South Carolina. May May tried to keep the boys busy, but Camelot seemed "desolate", with very little transpiring. A few contractors kept working, but most had stopped once they heard of Cliff's passing.

When Mary and Wally returned from the funeral, all of Camelot appeared quite solemn. Wally seemed pretty busy for a few days and then came home early one day. Wally walked in and asked May May to "bring the children in and sit down". Mary stood over by the window, looking out. The look on her face, one of sorrow, but also of contempt.

Wally started, "listen all, we're moving", He paused. "Believe me, I wish it made sense to stay. But Cliff didn't plan for a way, for someone to take over… and I learned a hard lesson myself. None of this was in writing". He waved his hand in a circle, meaning the Camelot Resort. Ironically, Tad thought he looked like the man called Merlin in the picture book Mary had bought them in Rogersville.

One might think that the children were too young to understand, but the sorrow on their faces showed clearly. For the O'Banion's and for the place that they called "home", something felt "lost". They enjoyed living in Camelot, and the realization of leaving it gave them all a strange feeling. It felt like "unfinished business" for everyone. It would be years later when Mary would explain to them why they had abruptly left Camelot behind, and why she didn't agree with Wally's decision.

Wally's agreement with Cliff was only guaranteed "with a handshake". Wally's job was to do what he had done so many times before — turn Camelot into a thriving resort that people would want to flock to. They had already sold almost every one of the eleven hundred lots. The old hotel was well on its way to being restored, with plans for a patio and pool to be installed in the spring of seventy-four. The lake now had floating docks. Dredged and stocked with multiple game fish, the "owners" could fish the lake any time they wanted. There was talk of refurbishing the old church and even turning one of the Pressmen's Home buildings into a grocery store. Wally and Mary had even shot a commercial with many familiar faces. Brett "riding the barrels", Pop yelping cowboy commands, just like John Wayne in "The Cowboys", golfers on the greens, and of course, Mary, showing off the clubhouse. Wally anticipated they would eventually put the agreement in writing for "Merlin's Magic," but they had never gotten around to it. Sadly, King Arthur had died. He had no heirs. So, it was time for Merlin to move on.

Chapter 4 –

"Heading to Pigeon Forge"

Wally had a temporary U-Haul hitch mounted to the limousine. He figured he would use the limousine until someone, most likely a lawyer, asked for its return. The U-Haul trailer was being loaded up by Buddy and Nick… Pop watched solemnly. "I'm contacting a few friends over in Pigeon Forge for you, Wally."

Loading a box in the trailer, Wally stopped and looked up at Pop. "For what, Pop?"

"Brett should keep riding. He's good, you know. He gets it fast. Not like these damn kids who grow up round here." Pop said with a smile.

Still holding a box and looking at Pop, Wally tried to explain, "Yeah, I'll have to see about that. It may not be so convenient over there. Hell, Brett walked to the stable every day. You and the boys watched him like he was one of your own. I appreciate that Pop… but it'll be different there." Wally stated.

Pop looked down for a moment and then back up. "How bout you let him stay here? At least for a while. Or, maybe he could come back during the summers and stay." Pop said, with his head cocked to the side.

"Pop, this isn't a movie about a bunch of boys you turn into cowboys. And besides, you know Mary won't go for that." Wally replied as he turned to put the box in the trailer.

"I hear ya Wally. But, if there's any chance that I can keep the stable, I need good help. Brett is young, but he is good help…And I can teach him to ride…Jus think about it Wally." Pop requested.

Wally acknowledged him with a nod and went back into the house.

"Hey Nick, have you seen Tad?" Mary asked.

"Yeah, I saw him running across the golf course with that dog, towards Pressmen's Home." Nick replied.

Mary stopped packing, walked to the open front screen door and looked out. "Taddy?" She called out, waited a moment, and called again. She closed the screen door and turned back to Nick. "Hmm, Nick, how long ago was that?" she asked.

"Oh, prolly twenty, thirty minutes ago. Do you want me to find him?" Nick asked.

"No, thanks Nick, I'll head over that way myself. I think I know where he might be." Mary said as she walked out the door and headed down the hill.

The Pressmen's Home Trade building was a fifteen-minute walk from the O'Banion's house. Mary was just coming to it when she saw Tad walking her way.

"Where've you been sweety? You saying goodbye to Moon Dove?" Mary asked.

Tad slowly strode towards Mary. "Yeah, she's very sad that I'm leaving. Most of the time, it's hard for me to understand her, cuz she talks funny. But today I understood everything she said. She said that she saw Uncle Cliff go with the Great Spirit, and she said she was sorry that he's gone. I can tell she's sad." Tad explained.

As Tad caught up with his mother, she kneeled down and wiped away a couple of tears. "Honey, I think Moon Dove with be with us in Pigeon Forge, don't you?" she asked.

"No Mom, she has to stay here. She can't leave. She told me that!" Tad said as he stared at his mother intently.

"I think that you'll find that Moon Dove joins you quickly in Pigeon Forge, sweetheart. Now let's get back to the house, we're almost ready to leave." Mary said as she picked Tad up and headed back.

***

Back at the house, the trailer was completely loaded. May May and Liz were already in the car. Poochie jumped right in and lay on the floor. Wally was explaining some things to Pop. Pop looked concerned and kept shaking his head.

"Everything is going to be fine Pop. That lawyer in Rogersville has lived here all his life and he knows how to handle this." Wally said with a smile.

"Now, you just said that you don't trust the Judge, Wally. What makes you think that damn lowyer is any better?" Pop claimed.

"There's not much I can do, but I'll tell you what Pop...I'll call that lawyer in a couple weeks, and make sure everything is going as planned. You should be able to keep The Stables. He already knows that." Wally reassured him.

Tad climbed in the back with May May, Brett, Liz, and Poochie. Mary took her spot in the front passenger seat. Wally shook the hands of Pop, Nick, and Buddy, then slid in the driver's seat, lit a cigarette, and started the limo. Driving away, Wally looked across the golf course with a grimace, then slowly wiped away a tear. Camelot was now forlorn.

***

One month later…

"Hey Hon, this is Wally O'Banion. I was partners with Clifford Lafferty, and I want to see how his estate is going." Wally said to the paralegal.

"It's not Mister O'Banion, I'm afraid Eugene Blackwell has passed. He had a heart attack three weeks ago. The judge says that everything is going to be in abeyance until someone can pick up where Eugene left off with it." The paralegal replied.

"What the hell does that mean?" Wally said as he looked at the phone.

"Mister O'Banion, do you know if there was a will beyond the one that you brought us. The one you brought us was over five years old and did not convey any of Camelot. This will eventually end up in Probate and the judge will have to go through it. Unfortunately, I don't see that happening any time soon. It could go on for months, possibly years." She said bluntly.

Wally looked at Mary, mouth slightly open, as he hung up the phone. "Oh shit, Camelot is crumbling." He said with an astonished look.

Chapter 5 –

"West Point Military Academy Graduation"

October 1826

As Commandant Worth lowered his sword and raised his right hand to salute the class of 1826, the cadets, in unison, all raised their right hands to their brows to salute in return. Then a volcano of noise erupted, as forty-one cadets cheered with thunderous shouts and applause. The cadets tossed hats with red plumage into the air, and five cannons bellowed into the Hudson.

After fifteen to twenty minutes of congratulations, but what only seemed to be a moment to the cadets, an honor guard of junior cadets and the drum corps began an "eagle drums" serenade that brought the crowd to a hush. As they watched the honor guard pass them, they all stopped and put their right hands over the left side of their lapels. They stood there, with hats lying all around. Some shed tears. Some just look elated, as they'd spent the last four years studying to be the best soldiers the United States trained. Most cadets received appointments to various forts, encampments, and even existing engagements with the "savages" that continued to hinder development of this new nation. A few of the cadets had requested further study at medical and naval schools. There were forty-one graduating cadets. Almost double that of 1825.

As the honor guard, West Point Band, and junior cadets marched by, one young cadet, Jefferson Davis, made eye contact with his graduating friend Albert Sidney Johnston. Jefferson mouthed, "I have something for you later", to which Albert replied with a wink and salute.

After the parade passed, Albert looked for the one man who had been by his side for the last four years, William Blackwell. Across the melee of cadets, he spied Will.

"Hey Will!" Albert exclaimed as he saw Will shoving one of his fellow cadets and playfully throwing punches at each other's chests and then laughing.
Will turned and looked up toward Albert.

"Hey, we're meeting Jefferson later. He says he has a surprise." Albert explained.

Laughing, Will replied, "Well it better not be any of that crappy-ass Irish whiskey that he stole from the Commandant's kitchen last time!"

With that comment, Albert quickly looked toward the Commandant, who had thankfully left the field.

"Well, what do you think my brother? We did it." Will said to Albert as the crowd seemed to separate into groups of friends. "Eighth in class, not bad for a nasty ole bedbug from Kentucky."

Albert grinned, "Ha, ha. Well at least this bedbug will always have a bed to return to in Kentucky. How many times did the damn savages burn down your homestead in Tennessee? Four or five?"

"Actually, it was only two times, my asshole friend. But we got the best of them. They will NOT have a third go at it since Adams signed the Creek Cede. Now, we just gotta get rid of the Cherokee and Chippewa, and all will be right." Will replied. "Mother and Father have things under control in Hawkins County, now. Rumor is that the Cherokee are going to Kentucky anyway!"

They both laughed and walked arm and arm towards the south barracks for a bit. Suddenly Albert stopped. "Oh shit! I have to go to the Commandants quarters."

***

Growing up in Virginia and then Tennessee, Will's family had issues with the indigenous Native Americans, often referred to as "Indians", and sometimes "savages" by those that disliked them. The Creek and Cherokee inhabited this portion of "America" for hundreds of years, but the American settlers were given the land to "homestead" and given free rein to build the towns that now flourished. The natives were not so friendly at first, but quickly realized that they needed to find ways to cooperate. Still, some small tribal factions fought the "American Advancement".

Attacking in stealth, and even at night. These small tribes often cause chaos for the homesteaders. Will believed that they were brutal and barbaric. He and his family had lost many friends to the Indians. Just one year before he came to West Point, Indians raped his own sister and threw her over a cliff. Will developed a strong hatred towards all Native Americans, no matter what tribe, and always referred to them as "savages". Albert, on the other hand, had a decent relationship with many of the tribes in and around Kentucky. But he certainly understood where his friend developed his hatred. Two different worlds separated by the Cumberland Gap.

***

Commandant Worth came to West Point in 1824 and wanted to make changes right away. He felt he was a man of honor and wanted to instill this philosophy in each of the cadets. So, in the last two years that Will and Albert were cadets, some of the curriculum changed.

Commandant Worth required more studies of how "honorable war" often succeeded. Gone were the days of having roundtable discussions of how the Indians used a much different tactic. Gone were the days of discussing how to reduce the loss of life on a battlefield. While they didn't necessarily agree with the changes to the curriculum, Albert and Will adjusted. Albert more than Will.

Besides the curriculum changes, there were rumors that Commandant Worth had wanted the cadet uniforms to return to blue instead of the pewter. Worth believed the pewter was a "volunteer" uniform and did not accurately represent the Military Academy's finest. The pewter being a result from the lack of indigo that was required for the blue uniforms. Commandant Worth had just recently been able to convert the cadets back to his prestigious "blue" uniforms.

Another "tradition" that Commandant Worth began in eighteen 1824 was that he would invite the top ten cadets of the class to his quarters immediately after the graduation ceremony. They would sip brandy or whisky, as the Commandant would award each of the cadets with their "orders". The "orders" were requests by current officers in the Army and Navy. The Commandant would assign the orders to each of the cadets, based on his analysis of their aptitude and abilities. The cadets rarely got their desired appointment, although they always showed appreciation for Commandant Worth's assignment. He would start at tenth in the class and make his way up to first in the class. While all cadets would leave West Point with the rank of Second Lieutenant, there were variations of that rank, and distinctions that Commandant Worth could award as well.

***

On this October evening, Albert showed up almost ten minutes late and immediately heard his name. Albert stepped forward as Commandant Worth exclaimed, "Cadet Albert Sidney Johnston. Your achievements at West Point have been exemplary. Your astuteness in studies and acumen have shown you to be one of the best here at The Military Academy. The only thing holding you back may be the company that you keep." Chuckles were heard around the room. All knew that the Commandant referred to Will and Jefferson.

The Commandant continued, "None the less, you've excelled and will be awarded the rank of Brevet Second Lieutenant. I may have had the hardest time with your assignment, Johnston. The Corps of Engineers wanted you badly."

Albert's heart almost leaped from his chest, as this distinction usually only goes to the top two or three cadets. "But I thought better of you", Worth said. "And you will serve in the Second United States Infantry, in the concerted effort to move Stockbridge West" Worth claimed. "I am sure that your expertise will be honed, and I look forward to see how your commendations stack in the years to come. It is my honor to present these orders Brevet Second

Lieutenant Johnston". Albert's heart sank. Stockbridge was the effort of the United States to move Indians west.

Being early in the effort, these were trying times for the U.S. Army. But today, most Indian tribes had resigned to the fact that their best chances for survival were to follow the Stockbridge effort to move them west, or accommodate the homesteaders as much as possible, with hopes of not being sent west.

This was not what Albert had hoped for, but he knew better than to show it. He smiled and thanked Commandant Worth, then looked at the audience as the next cadet was called.

In reality, the Army gave all West Point graduating cadets the rank of Second Lieutenant. Commandant Worth thought it was a bit more befitting for him to "award" the top of the class their rank and enjoyed the honor of awarding some with the commission of "Brevet". Originally used during the Revolutionary War for officers who joined from other countries. It was a "distinction" given to recognize that they fought "above the norms" without promoting their rank. Eventually, the Army adopted its distinction.

After awarding ranks and orders to all ten of the "top-of-class", Worth called for a toast.

"Gentlemen, you have all proven yourselves worthy to be soldiers. One day, I hope to see all of you become officers of the highest rank. I believe that you all have the ability. It has been my honor to command you in the easiest battle that you will ever be part of. Go forward and represent the United States Army and Navy with honor and dignity". Worth concluded. Afterward, all broke into their "Oath of Allegiance".

While Worth enjoyed the camaraderie, he specifically did not like the "Oath of Allegiance", as their oaths were cited to their respective states, not the United States Military. Worth thought this to be a gross contradiction, after spending four years training to be a United States soldier. As each cadet left, he saluted Commandant Worth, shook his hand and went out into the night.

Albert made sure he was last. He contemplated what he was about to do — request another assignment. But as he approached Worth, a big smile came across Worth's face, and after the salute, Worth actually embraced Albert. "Albert, my son, I feel you are not happy with your orders. But let me tell you, some very important people requested you to be at the Second Infantry. I really think that you will go far, so please do your best and prove me correct", Worth explained.

"Oh, …and I have something for you". Worth walked over to the cellarette, opened it, and pulled out a bottle of Kentucky Bourbon Whisky. He walked back to Albert and handed it to him with both hands. He then said, "Please don't drink that Irish Whisky that Jefferson finds lying around. Go, and make me proud!" he touted.

Albert knew that anything he might say would probably only look bad in the eyes of the Commandant. As he walked away, the Commandant called out, "Oh, and Albert, please tell William to stop by and see me in the morning before he leaves."

***

Walking across the fortress grounds and towards the South Barracks, Albert thought, "That was strange, he knows that I'm seeing Will tonight, and what could he want with Will in the morning? Surely, he will not deny his appointment to Nashville for medical school?"

By the time that Albert got to the barracks, Will was gone. Will's Faro box was still there. So, they were not playing cards. Which meant only one thing…Will and Jefferson were going to drink until they were "piss drunk" and undoubtedly end up in The Hudson…again. "Damn those guys", Albert thought. "They were supposed to wait for me. At least Will was."

Feeling the need to circumvent their revelry before they both ended up in front of Worth for discipline, which could certainly ruin their careers, or worse, Albert quickly changed from his dress uniform and into his blue chevrons and gray trousers. Before he walked out, he stopped and looked around. Some graduates had already pulled their curtains for the night, and a few looked up at Albert. With a quick flip, he jokingly saluted. Most laughed, but a few threw a shoe at him. Out the door, and gone he was.

Albert knew a shortcut to Duck Island that most did not. Duck Island wasn't really an island, at least not most of the time. It was a small peninsula on the east bank. During the Revolutionary War, soldiers fortified it with artillery. As West Point grew, the small island became less needed and eventually it just became a place for cadets "to get away". On Albert's route, he was not seen by any sentries. Then again, they all knew him, and would have let him through, anyway. But at least nobody would report him… unless they stopped him with a bottle of Kentucky Bourbon Whisky. He wasn't so sure about Will and Jefferson. They knew the "secret" route, but they rarely seemed to care if anyone reported them. To this very day, Albert did not know why Worth allowed either of them to get away with even half of the shenanigans that they got into.

Coming down the hill, Albert called out, "You two should probably stop kissing now!"

"Ha, Ha" Jefferson replied, and as Albert approached, Will jumped out with his sword "at the ready".

As Albert jumped backward, his hands went up, and the bottle of whisky flew from them in an arc. As the bottle spun in the air, Albert's eyes grew. The spinning bottle came down from its apex as Will snatched it like a snake handler. Will turned the bottle, inspected the label, pulled the cork and breathed in the "burned caramel" smell of Kentucky Bourbon.

Albert exploded. "What the hell is the matter with you William Edward Blakwell! You damn near ruined a bottle of the Commandant's finest whisky!"

Will laughed and replied. "Sir Albert Sidney Johnston, I was merely intent on inspecting the spoils of your soiree with the fine gentlemen of the Upper Class. The fact that you cannot handle your liquor is a testament that Jefferson and I have taught you nothing here at The Academy!".

Jefferson felt the need to interrupt. "Can't handle his liquor. Now that was funny! Bring that bottle over here and let's have a toast."

The three of them were still laughing as Jefferson poured the whisky into the three tin cups he had set on a big rock. They all raised their cups.

"To the finest men that I have ever served with". Albert proclaimed.

"And to the finest ladies that we have not met yet!" Will exclaimed.

With that, all tipped their cups and swallowed down the fine whisky that the Commandant had graciously offered. They all sat against the rock and took turns pouring and toasting.

Before long they were down to the last toast, and Albert said, "Gentlemen, I propose we hold this last toast for another day. When we are together again. Whether it be on a battlefield or enjoying each other's company, as we watch our grandchildren play in the field."

Both Will and Jefferson replied, "Here, here". So, they raised their cups to their mouths and finished the Kentucky liquor.

"Will, can I ask you a question?" Albert slurred.

"Certainly, Albert." Will replied.

"After your family settled in Hawkins County, your brother died, and then the natives brutally accosted and killed your poor sister. Of everyone in the graduating class, hell, maybe in this academy, you have the biggest reason to want to serve and oust the Indians from our lands. So, my dear friend, why are you not going to active duty, and instead choosing to go to Nashville to study medicine?"

Will sat looking out over the Hudson River.

Jefferson was sitting on the ground, back to the rock, and knees bent. He looked over at Will. "Albert, William has a calling that is much higher than either of us. It's a calling that will take him to places and responsibilities, of which I cannot comprehend. I'm certain that we will grow to appreciate William for everything that he will do and become."

Jefferson continued. "While a part of him was lost down there in Tennessee, it is very obvious that he has a "drive" to reach new heights, and I'm sure that he will never forget sweet Cecilia. His vengeance will come, but not in the way of normal men with a sword and gun. William's vengeance will come in much different ways. It may be by how many soldiers he can put back into battle, or it may even be with the stroke of a pen…when he becomes the

Governor. Either way, don't fool yourself into not understanding William's motives. He's as cunning as they come, and I personally know that his path is going to be great."

Will finally turned his head away from his stare at the river and looked at Albert. His facial expression clearly showed that Jefferson had answered for him.

They looked at each other for a moment. Then Albert spoke first. "Well Will, I guess your "squire" has spoken for you. I'm uncertain how Jefferson became so astute in just two years, but he obviously "has a knack for gab.""

Will started laughing and said, ""Squire"? Where'd you drum that old term from?"

Albert smiled. "Oh, it's from days gone by, but it seemed to fit. Will, I'm going to miss you."

"And I, you." Will replied.

With that, Will walked over to Jefferson and extended his hand. Albert did the same, and they pulled Jefferson to his feet.

Jefferson wobbled and spoke. "Well gents, I'll hold down the fort for the next two years. But then, I'll need both of you. So, please keep your scalps, and know that I'm coming to save you."

Will and Albert joined arm and shoulders with Jefferson, and they started back to camp, both supporting him, so that he could somewhat walk.

Halfway back, Albert blurted out. "Oh Will, I have almost forgotten... Commandant Worth asked to see you in the morning, before you leave. Do you wish I join you? If I do, he may go easy on you…well, for whatever it is that you did."

Will laughed and said, "No Albert. Worth's probably just going to give me a better bottle than he gave you!".

Arms broken free, they all laughed. Jefferson stumbled towards his barracks as Will and Albert watched. Both of them seemed genuinely impressed that he might make it. Then Albert and Will walked together to theirs.

***

The next morning, all the graduating cadets, now "officers", assembled their things into their wooden "lockers".

Will woke early and had already packed when he pulled his curtain open. From across the room, one graduate, Theo, directed a comment to Will and Albert. "Hey you guys, Lieutenant Perkins came by last night to hand out our sword knots. He asked where you two were. I told him I wasn't sure but most likely at another discipline meeting with Commandant Worth. He rolled his eyes and said to give you these". Theo handed each of them a cord with short tassels. They both accepted them.

Will walked over to his locker and laid the "knot" on top of it.

"That had better be there when I get back, or someone is gonna know what it's like to be run through." Will claimed, referring to the term of pushing one's saber all the way through the torso of a man.

As Will walked to the doorway, he stopped and looked back. This was the last time that he would see these men together. They had roomed together for the last four years. All of them were merely eight feet away from each other. Only separated by velvet curtains. He knew so much about all of them. It seemed so strange that he was going to do this all over again. Well, not quite; it would be different in Nashville. He decided right there that he would focus solely on his studies and become the best surgeon in the "New America".

***

Will knocked on Commandant Worth's door. Worth attended to the door himself, which surprised Will. As Worth opened the door fully, Will asked, "Sir, where's Adam? Did you graduate him too?"

"No, no, no, William. I asked Adam to assist in tending to the horses. He'll make his way back…or I will *graduate* him!" They both laughed.

"Come in, William. Please come over to my desk and sit down." The Commandant asked.

Will stepped in, closed the door, and did as instructed.

Sitting down, Will looked at Worth with inquiring eyes. "Sir, last night,… Albert used a term that surprised me,… and I'm sure it surprised Jefferson as well. Albert referred to Jefferson as my "squire". Is there something that I've missed with Albert?"

"No" Worth replied. "No, while I wish it were the case, Albert was not invited, as you and Jefferson were. But I am truly glad that you asked about it. Because,… I have something for you."

Worth stood and walked over to what appeared to be a chest of drawers. While looking like a chest of drawers, it actually opened up to form a desk that one would stand at, often referred to as a "Butler's Chest". He pulled one of the small desk drawers all the way out and reached back into the cavity that the drawer came from. He pulled another smaller wooden drawer-box out, then removed a small key from his pocket. Unlocking and opening the wooden box, Will watched. His eyes grew wide. Worth then removed one of several gold coins from the box and slid it into his pocket. He locked the drawer-box again, and returned both to the chest, the hidden one and the normal desk drawer. He closed the butler's chest and came back to the table.

He addressed Will. "William, please stand and give me your hand."

Will did as requested.

Worth then pulled the gold coin from his pocket and placed it in Will's hand. Worth folded Will's fingers over the coin. "William Edward Blackwell, you have been a squire of the Knights of Wisdom for over five years. I believe it is why you are here and why you are going to Nashville. In Nashville, you will be knighted. This coin is your passage. It must be protected with your life, if need be. You will know the day, time, and person of contact. You and only you will know this."

Commandant Worth paused. "My son, I cannot tell you how important your mission has become. Godspeed, and may Wisdom blow your sails."

William opened his hand to inspect the coin. The image of an owl with spread wings on one side, and a crested shield on the other. There were Latin words inscribed on each side. He closed his other hand over it, as if to pray, and looked at Worth.

While Worth was a tall man, and most had to look up to him, suddenly Will felt as though he was looking eye-to-eye with Worth. He ached and felt nauseous. But also, somehow, he felt invincible.

Will sat back down in the chair and began. "Commandant, I don't know what to say. Yeah, I questioned why you chose me to go to Nashville. But I never thought that I'd see knighthood until I was an old man."

Worth had also sat down. He set his hands on the table and interlocked his fingers. "My son, I am not your Commandant. I never was. We are brothers with a higher cause. I know that your heart was telling you to be the next General Jonathan Sevier. Especially, considering your home being so close, and your own realization the Sevier's heroic actions."

Worth continued, "But you have surpassed all desires that I had for a protégé. You played your part, here at the academy, so well that one day, we may well have Albert in the *Wisdom*,…and he doesn't even know it. I cannot tell you, William, how proud I am of you. In Nashville, by train, you'll be but a mere day's ride from your home. Perhaps, you'll be able to visit a few times?"
With that, Worth gave a wink.

After a long pause, Worth continued. "Will, you alone decided to travel down the path of this growing education of doctors, surgeons, and apothecaries. I just pointed you in the direction. But I certainly see it as a wise choice. The education that you shall bring to battle will save countless lives… We've had many a discussion about anatomy. Oh, and the ones that were about the female anatomy? Why, we'll keep those to ourselves!"

They both laughed.

"But son, Nashville is where you will learn so much more,…and it is the center of the Wisdom. I'm not only asking you to continue your studies, I'm also asking you to commit yourself whole-heartedly to the Wisdom." Worth concluded.

Except for the brief laugh, Will had been sitting there, listening to Commandant Worth, with the gold coin in one hand, fingers clamped over it. He then opened that hand, stood, slid the coin into his watch pocket and saluted Commandant Worth.

Worth stood and smiled. Instead of a salute, Worth reached out and embraced the young lieutenant.

Will returned the embrace for a moment and then stepped back. "Thank you, Sir" Will expressed.

With an enormous smile, Worth replied, "No, Thank You Will. Godspeed and safe travels."

With that, Worth walked to the door and opened it. Will walked out and down the path, as Commandant Worth watched him.

Chapter 6 –

Nashville, Cumberland Medical Academy July 1828

Will had just finished listening to a lecture by Doctor Ronan Kelly, one of the Cumberland Medical Academy's founders. Kelly, along with Doctor D.T. MacGarock, had purchased approximately twenty acres along the north side of Nashville, with the purpose of establishing a medical school. Choosing the name "Cumberland" because the land sat right up against the Cumberland River, which circled around the city, the two founders had put everything they owned into creating the new school.

The campus seemed well-funded beyond the founders' means, with new buildings constantly under construction. Will assumed that Kelly and MacGarock, had come from "Irish money". Both seemed highly educated, and each spoke with a brogue that often made it challenging understand.

Will was walking back to his room at the "Student Residence" when he heard his name called aloud.

"William!"

It was Sarah Beth Carver.

Sarah Beth's father, Doctor James E. Carver, was a lecturer at the school as well. She and her father lived on campus, as did many of the educators. Moving to the campus the same month that Will arrived, they had traveled from Cincinnati, Ohio, where Doctor Carver previously practiced medicine. Originally from The Village of Black Rock, New York, where Carver was an assistant to Joseph Ellicott while attending medical school. They had been surveying a new town that would eventually become Buffalo. Ellicott and his brother Andrew were instrumental in surveying and platting Washington, D.C. Both, high-ranking Freemasons.

"William Blackwell! You promised me a tour of the city three weeks ago, and I have yet to have seen your company." Sarah Beth proclaimed as she hustled by Will's side.

"Miss Carver, I am very sorry, but the studies do seem to take much more of my time than you could imagine. The lecturers here at Cumberland don't seem to want us to have any free time. Especially, Doctor Carver, my dear." Will said with a smile to Sarah Beth.

Smiling to herself and blushing a bit, Sarah said, "Well, I will be having a stern conversation with Doctor Carver about this! How is a young lady to have any courtship when all of the available bachelors are too busy studying to watch me walk across the campus? Do you know how many times that I put on my nicest silk dress, shawl, and bonnet, walked across this campus, only to arrive back to our quarters without a single gander by one of you silly students?"

Will replied, "That'd be twelve times in the last six months…that I know of."

Sarah made a light fist and punched Will in the chest. "William Blackwell, you let me do that and not once have you come to my side. And! You are correct too! You've seen me every time?" Sarah questioned.

"Well, my desk does face the window to the courtyard." Will sighed. "It's just that I figured by the time I got my coat and hat on you'd already have a gentleman by your side. Me, not being a gentleman, I figured I wouldn't have a chance with the most beautiful lady in Nashville."

With this, Sarah Beth grabbed Will's arm and stopped them both from walking. She stepped to be directly in front of him.

"First William Blackwell, if you are no gentleman, then I am no lady. So, the next time I put my finest on, I fully expect to see you come running out to the courtyard for a stroll…and second, thank you for the compliment…Oh, and knowing exactly how many times I did that. Whoa, I believe I may be smitten". Sarah Beth exclaimed as she fanned her face with her hand.

Will was always confident, sometimes boisterous, and never without words. But at that moment, his mouth opened, and nothing came out. Before he could even think of what to say, Sarah Beth tipped up on the balls of her feet and gave Will a kiss on the cheek. She then turned and ran towards the Carver quarters.

After a few strides, she stopped, turned, and said. "Oh, and that tour of the city?"

Will felt an exhilaration that he'd never felt before. He blinked and replied. "Um, Saturday?"

Sarah Beth cocked her head, put a finger to her chin and replied, "Isn't that the day that Doctor Carver gives his six-hour lecture?"

Will gave a chuckle. "Yeah, it is, but I think that I've come down with something. I'll come by right after the lecture starts".

With that, Sarah Beth winked, turned and skipped off, like a little girl.

Will was back at his desk in his room. Having trouble thinking about anything but Sarah Beth, he tipped back in his chair. Closing his eyes and turning his head towards the ceiling, he could see her. Sarah Beth was quite beautiful. Will was not making that up. She was quite tall for a woman of the time. Standing probably just an inch or two below Will's six-foot stature, she had blonde hair, light freckles on her cheeks, and the bluest eyes Will had ever seen. He wasn't sure, but he believed her age to be sixteen to eighteen years old. The perfect age for courtship. He was sure that no "gentleman" had come to her side in the courtyard, all those times, because her father was one of the primary lecturers. He could probably have anyone expelled that he wanted. Will didn't care. All he could think about was Sarah Beth kissing him on the cheek. He tingled, and it felt like his heart might leap from his body. He smiled and couldn't wait for Saturday.

***

Doctor Carver's lecture on the "Devil's Concoctions" began at nine o'clock. Sarah Beth began dressing the minute her father went out the door. She had even curled her hair by the time there was a knock on the door. Most women would don a wig, but not Sarah Beth. She loathed them. Although the effort of curling one's hair was troublesome, she wanted to. She wanted to impress Will with her natural hair and not some "wig". She was just putting on some "finishing touches" when there was another knock.

Will was nervous. He picked some flowers right out of the courtyard and knocked on the door. He wasn't sure how much time had passed, but it seemed like it was an eternity. He knocked again, and the door opened.

"William Blackwell! Would you please give a lady time to get to the door?" Sarah Beth exclaimed.

"I'm sorry, my lady, I was afraid that you'd already gone for the day. Oh, these are for you." Will clamored as his heart began beating and he felt faint.

"My Lady??, Why I didn't think that you were a gentleman. I must have the wrong suitor at my door." Sarah Beth stated as she took his hand, pulled him in and closed the door.

She took the flowers from him and stepped into another room that Will assumed was her bedroom. He waited by the door and worked to calm himself. Surprisingly, he calmed quickly. A skill that had gotten him out of many "jams" at West Point.

When Sarah Beth returned, she had put on a bonnet. Will watched her walk towards him, and she looked him in the eyes all the way across the room. When she reached him, he noticed that they were standing "eye to eye". She apparently had boots with heels that made her taller.

Sarah stopped in front of Will and said, "Cat got your tongue?"

He chuckled and replied. "Nope, just still trying to get over how beautiful you are. And Sarah Beth,… it's just Will. Not William, or William Blackwell, just Will".

Sarah Beth stepped back and looked him over. Stepped to each side of him, looking him up and down. Will had dressed in the best suit he owned. He also wore a vest and hat. He kept looking straight ahead, trying to figure out what she was doing.

While at his side, she drew closer to him. Grabbing one shoulder and raising herself closer. So close that he could feel her breath on his ear. "Well Will, it's just Sarah".

She whispered in his ear. Then she gave him a kiss on the cheek, stepped back and said, "Shall we?"

At that, Will immediately raised his arm and opened the door.

They walked arm in arm across the courtyard. Both of them thinking, "What if someone sees us", and then both smiling. Because neither of them really cared. Being "smitten" does this.

The downtown was a mere twenty-minute walk from the medical campus. Will had been there many times since he had arrived in Nashville. He had seen it grow already.

As they walked the streets, arm in arm, Will told Sarah what he had learned about the city. As he talked, she would often look right at him intently. At first, he found this odd. As he got used to it, he enjoyed it. It gave him the feeling that she was really enjoying their conversation.

They stopped at a few stores. There were trinkets and even a dress that Sarah claimed she liked. Will wanted so much to buy them for her. But the little money that he had was a stipend that he received from the government, and a small bag of gold coins that would randomly appear on his desk.

Will believed that Commandant Worth had made sure the government recognized William Blackwell's "assignment", and apparently The Knights of Wisdom as well. He was reasonably sure that he was the only student at Cumberland who received such recognition. The stipend that Will was awarded from the government was barely enough to pay for his clothes and some food, so there was no way he could afford gifts for Sarah. He thought about the gold coin in his watch pocket and quickly dispelled that thought.

At one point, in one particular shop, Sarah saw the look on Will's face as she picked up a candlestick. She quickly set it back down and said, "Will, I know what you're thinking."

Will laughed, "Sarah, there is no way that you know what I am thinking!"

She reached out and grasped the front of his coat with both hands. She pulled him close and whispered so that others could not hear, "You see me admiring the baubles, dresses, and such, and you want to buy them for me, but you know you cannot afford them right now. But what you don't know is that someday I will want the things, but until that time, the only thing that I want is your company. Today we play like we have money, Okay?"

Will shook his head. "How, how could you know?" he stuttered.

Just like at the Carver quarters, she pulled herself close to his ear and whispered, "Because I can read your mind". Then she pecked him on the cheek, turned and said, "Let's go. I want to walk for a bit."

Will and Sarah walked the downtown area for quite some time. They shared some bread from a bakery, and as they walked, Will felt so alive. Being with Sarah was a feeling that he had never experienced before.

But something bothered Will. He got a strange feeling that they were being followed. Will swore he had seen the same three men at different times on their walk. He even thought that the men appeared to be swapping coats and hats with each other. So, whenever Will would see them, they had a different appearance. Will kept up with the conversation with Sarah but also watched for the strange men.

During their walk, Will saw an alley and quickly said, "Let's go down here".

Sarah shrugged her shoulders and said, "Sure".

As they walked down the alley, they noticed doorways and openings to saloons and brothels. Women from the brothels would be out front, mostly drinking. But, as Will and Sarah walked by, one particular gal barked out, "Hey baby, how bout you come in and let me show you what a real woman can do?"

Sarah stopped Will, released his arm, walked over to the offensive woman, and said, "Listen, Baaaby. My man would never want to leave my bed for yours. In fact, it takes everything in him just to leave my bed for his job. Therefore, you can be certain he won't come in there!"

The woman looked at Will, and Will gave her a cock of his head, and an overly fake smile.

As Sarah was walking back to Will, the woman barked out, "Hey honey, you sound as though you're already a "Soiled Dove". There's room for you here. Listen, you might be surprised how much you'd like it. Maybe we could teach each other a thing or two. Hey, stop! I'm not hustling…Not now!"

Will and Sarah kept walking away, both grinning from ear to ear.

As the two continued to walk arm in arm, making their way back towards the medical campus, Will had not seen the *three mysterious men* since he and Sarah had ducked into the alley. This made him feel better, but he was still curious why they appeared to be following them.

The afternoon was quite warm, and Will asked if Sarah minded if he removed his coat.

Sarah replied, "Of course not". She moved behind him to help him take it off. She folded it in half and allowed him to grasp the collar so that he could hold it over his free shoulder. They again looped arms and continued walking.

"You did that like a professional, back there", Will said.

Sarah smiled and replied, "I always help daddy with his jacket."

Will paused and then said, "I meant at the brothel. I appreciate your chivalry, but you didn't have to say anything. We could've kept walking."

Sarah stopped them both and turned to Will. "Will, I'm telling you. I can read your mind, and you can lose that thought right now! What I said to her was telling that woman "hands off!". I just got your attention two days ago, and I be damned if I'm going to lose it!...to a brothel, no less. Whatever you are reading into exactly what I said, Stop!... I am a virgin and will be to the day I choose to be otherwise. What I said was just to put that whore in her place! Do you understand me, William Edward Blackwell?"

Will smiled, "Uh Oh, I think I have a "bad name" now…Sarah, are you really mad at me?". He said with a grin.

Sarah smiled. "Yes, I am mad at you. I've given you four kisses now and not a one from you!"

With that comment, Will slowly cupped his hands on Sarah's cheeks, leaned in and gave her a kiss on the lips. He didn't want it to stop. As he began to pull away, she pulled him back for another.

They broke without a word, locked arms and began to walk quietly. At one point, Will could feel Sarah almost skipping… again, like a little girl. Apparently, this girl got what she wanted after all.

Chapter 7 –

"The Plan"

Spring of 1973, Camelot, Tennessee

Mary was picking through the copper printing plates, looking for specific images. She and Tad had been at the tradesmen's building all morning, and she finally felt like she might have enough of them to fill in the framed insets on the bar front. Mary had been using the copper printing plates in all kinds of places around Camelot. They covered the coffee tables in Cliff and Wally's offices; they adorned the library at The Manor, and now Mary was accenting the ballroom bar with them. They looked so nice when displayed, and the nostalgia of them coming from Pressmen's Home just seemed awfully appropriate.

Mary called out, "Tad, honey, tell Moon Dove that you'll have to visit with her at another time. I've got to get these over to the clubhouse, so the contractors can get them on the bar."

The limo's rear suspension was almost bottomed out as Mary put the last few plates in the trunk. Tad came scurrying up, put his little hand on the door handle and pushed the button hard with his thumb. He was proud that he could open the big limousine doors because even Brett had trouble getting them open. They were heavy, and it took every ounce of strength for Tad to pry them open. But he could.

Sitting in the rear-facing middle row, Tad started playing with the rear radio. Camelot being in a valley, it was hard to pick up stations. So, what Tad heard mostly was just static. But nonetheless, just playing with a radio seemed interesting to Tad. Every once in a while, Tad would tune in to a local channel. A tune from George Jones would come in loudly, and Mary would bark out, "Leave it there!"

When Mary got into the car, she turned from the front seat and checked on Tad. He seemed content. She wondered, "What did Moon Dove have to say today, Tad?"

Tad looked up, paused, and cocked his head. "Um, she was happy. I brought her my hurt turtle, Willow. He's still there. They're playing snd Moon Dove said she can make him better."

Now Mary paused, got a perplexed look and said, "How did you get your turtle here Tad?"

"I put him on the floor of the car before we left. He rode over with us." Tad said, looking up with a grin.

Mary shook her head and started the limousine. As they were pulling away, Mary said, "Do we have to pick up Willow later, or does he get to stay all night?"

Tad replied, "Nah, Moon Dove said that he can stay with them. She said that he would need to stay some to get better."

"Them? Now there's a "them"?" Mary exclaimed and rolled her eyes. As they drove the short distance to the clubhouse, Mary thought, "The imagination of this kid is wild. I don't remember having imaginary friends who had more imaginary friends. I had better tell Wally, before he thinks that our son "has lost it"." She smiled, and in some ways, was glad that Tad had such a good imagination. There were no other children of his age in Camelot. At least not yet. Brett was almost always at The Stable, so Tad liked to hang out with his mother most of the time. She tried leaving him at home with May May. But he would just end up wherever Mary was anyway. Right now, all of Camelot was "within walking distance". It was pretty much an open golf course, with mountain ridges on each side. The separated main road split all of it evenly. Tad was safe anywhere here, and everybody knew him anyway, including an imaginary Indian girl named "Moon Dove".

Wally walked into the main ballroom. He stopped and watched the contractors. They reminded him of carpenter ants, hustling around methodically. He admired what he was watching. Mary sure had a knack for the extravagant. What was once a hayloft now had a finished floor; all the trusses and beams had been stained in a dark mahogany color. Scaffolds extended towards the peak of the ceiling. Almost thirty feet up were contractors and electricians, mounting and wiring enormous "candelabra looking" light fixtures that Mary had picked up in Rogersville.

She had taken church pews from the old Pressmen's Home church and had them refinished. They were now along any "open" wall space available. She bought ten "high top" tables, and twenty "low" tables that were stacked in one corner. Wally could already imagine this room "set" for dinner and dancing. The tables draped in white cloths, the bar stocked, patrons everywhere, laughing and mingling about.

Wally smiled and thought, "This is definitely going to be the most extravagant room that we've done."

He looked across the room at the colossal project transforming. A bar, over thirty-five feet long, almost encompassed an entire far wall. Carpenters were busy mounting the copper printing plates that Mary had already adorned throughout much of the clubhouse. The printing plates gave the face of the bar a mosaic-like appearance with multiple hues of copper, and even some of antique green. From anywhere in the ballroom, the bar just "invited" you over. Mary had also done this to the library at The Manor, and Cliff loved it.

As Wally stood there admiring Mary's ingenuity, Cliff walked up behind him.

"I'll tell you what Wally. That woman, she really sure can make something out of nothing." Cliff boasted. "But then again, It's also looking a bit like a church, don't you think Wally?"

Wally chided, "Not many churches have bars and giant fireplaces, Cliff. When she gets done with this place, you won't even be able to tell it was once a barn. I'll bet you that people will think that it was a castle all along."

Cliff laughed, "Yeah, I'll be the only one with a Castle in Tennessee,… or a fifteen-foot-wide fireplace, that's for sure. This place is really exceeding all of my expectations. Heck, I was ecstatic just to have the big round table she found for my office. I now have a round table for my nights." Cliff again giggled.

Wally looked at him and laughed. "You know that was a square table to begin with." Cliff looked puzzled.

Wally continued. "Mary picked up that square table in Jonesboro, had it taken to a carpenter who made it round. Then she asked if the carpenter could in-lay the mahogany "spokes" that you see today. You're right, Cliff. She can make something out of nothing, for sure."

Cliff just shook his head in astonishment. "How are things going up a The Manor?" Cliff asked.

"You really need to go up there with Mary. She's really doing the same thing up there. It's looking good. The den and library look great. The lobby looks good. Well, except one thing right now…Mary had the guys stack all of the beds in the lobby, and she's going to have them hauled off to the dump." Wally explained.

"What's up with that, Wally?" Cliff quizzed.

"Well, she says the beds are too old. Even the newest ones are "old" according to her. She says that the "The Magic Fingers" machines wouldn't be a "good look" for us. She's probably right, so fair warning,…She's going hit you up for all new beds." Wally replied.

"Ya know Wally, eventually I'm gonna run out of money. With Mary, and you, especially when you talk me into doing things like buying three Cadillac limousines. Heck, I should've bought Mary an old pickup truck. I constantly see her using one limo to haul stuff around about every other day." Cliff complained with a smile.

Wally smiled with that little *Irish grin* and said, "Maybe you should let her use your convertible Eldorado? I'll bet she can get more in that than the limos!"

Cliff's brow went up, and his eyes opened. "Hell no!" Cliff replied. "That convertible. She's my baby. I always promised Nance I'd get her one. Unfortunately, I pinched those pennies too hard when she was alive, and she never got to see it. But I named her Nancy, and I'll have her till the day I die! Even if the O'Banion's put me in the poorhouse!"

"Well, I'll tell you what Cliff, if you really need money. I'll buy one of those limousines from you, after I sell all of these lots! How about that?" They both started laughing.

Wally continued. "About that, I want to talk about some ideas that I have to get people in here. Is the bar open in your office?" Wally boisterously chimed.

"Always! Let's go." Cliff said, and they headed towards the stairway.

Upon reaching Cliff's office, Cliff went to a small bar table, turned over two glasses, and poured a generous amount of Scotch into each.
Walley set his briefcase on the "round table" and popped the briefcase open. He pulled out a ruffled legal pad, with pages and pages of notes, and set it down. Then he pulled out two maps and laid them out. One map was of Camelot land as it was "today" and the other was of Camelot completely subdivided. It had the planned roads and outlined all the lots for the homes, cabins, and condominiums.

Cliff came over and sat down beside him. "This is different than I submitted to the county, or state, last year. Have you talked to anyone there?" Cliff questioned.

"Yes, I have." Wally replied. "The zoning board for Hawkins County is just two people and they said that this will not be a problem. They actually like it, and will present it to the state." Wally explained.

"How the heck did you pull that one off? I had a hell of a time getting the first round through." Cliff asked.

Wally grinned. "Hear me out Cliff, and try not to laugh." He paused. "The Barnum and Bailey Circus is coming in two weeks, and I kinda promised that the two of them could borrow our limousines to take their first-grade students to the show. Both of them have "first graders", at the same school in Rogersville, and the idea just kinda came to me while we were talking about the latest events in Hawkins County." Wally explained.

Cliff laughed so hard he had to set his drink down and put his hand on the table. Leaning over, he said, "Do you mean to tell me you used a circus to get these new plans through?"

"And your limos." Wally replied.

"Done!" Cliff cried, holding his belly and laughing.

After the two of them finally stopped laughing, Cliff stood upright and took a better look at the new plans. "Wally, are all of these lots on the original property, or am I buying more land?" Cliff inquired.

"Yes Cliff, …and No." Wally replied.

"How many?" Cliff quizzed him.

"Your original plan had fifteen hundred lots. This is just over two thousand." Wally said, with an inquisitive look back at Cliff.

Cliff stood tall and stated, "I have two questions Wally. One, will this fly with the county? And two, how are we going to sell almost seven hundred more lots?"

Wally walked over to the bar, replenished his scotch, turned around, and took a big drink. All the while, Cliff stared at him intently. "Cliff, this plan has over twenty-five percent more profit, and I promise you I will get this passed with the county and state."

"Even if you could, how are we going to sell twenty-two hundred lots?" Cliff sternly asked.

Wally again turned and replenished his scotch. But this time, when he turned around, he was grinning from ear to ear. Cliff laughed, "Let me guess?...You have a plan!...Another circus?"

Wally went to his briefcase and pulled out some documents. As he laid them out on the table, Cliff thought he had better replenish his own drink because he was sure Wally would make it a "double" if he let him.

Wally started in, "Listen, we did this before,… at Hide Away Hills. It'll cost some money, but it will floor you how many people will come, and how many buy. We'll schedule two big events for this year. One will happen in about a month or two depending on when we can get this young man in here, and the other will be in the summer. After them both, I'll have one half to three quarters of the lots sold."

Cliff stared at the documents and then back at Wally. He paused for a moment and looked up at the ceiling. He appeared to be "going through the numbers in his head". Cliff slowly lowered his head and stopped, looking right at Wally before he spoke. "If you are actually able to pull that off, we'd have the money to put the pool in at The Manor and start the work on the grocery! And that's with the road and property developments rolling too! Wally, this would be massive! Tell me more."

Cliff's curiosity had Wally rolling with what he did best,…sell.

"Cliff, there's kid from California. His name's John Denver. He's an up-and-coming folk singer. Hell, he's already been on the radio, and we think we can get him here."

Wally flipped the legal pad to a sketch of a promotional flyer. "We can get him here, and invite a thousand, fifteen hundred, maybe two thousand, just to hear him sing. It'll be a big event,…and we'll sell!" Wally touted.

Cliff looked perplexed, rubbed his chin and headed over to the bar. As he was pouring another drink, he looked at the wall and spoke. "What makes you so sure that you can get him here to Camelot, Wally?"

Then, that Irish grin came across Wally's face. "Cliff, John's father was in the Army Air Corps, and was a pilot, just like me. While I didn't know Dutch, John's dad, we have a common friend in Colonel James Taggert. I also understand that John has become quite "the pilot" on his own."

Wally had moved over to the leather couch. He sat on the edge of the couch cushion and continued. "Mary and

I have been knocking this around for a week. We have a lot of ties back to this kid. Mary has already reached out to Bob Braun, a friend of hers in Cincinnati. Bob just interviewed Denver last month, and is willing to contact Denver's agent. I, on the other hand, will get a hold of my buddy, the Colonel, who will reach out to Dutch… we're going to let them fly a Thurston Teal and land our lake."

"A what?" Cliff exclaimed.

"A Thurston Teal. It's a seaplane, a flying boat, and I'm fairly certain that neither of them has ever flown one. It's a very rare plane. Only a handful of pilots, in the entire world, have flown one, and I happen to have a friend, in Ohio, who has one."

Cliff's perplexed look never changed. "Of course you have a friend, who has a plane, that I've never heard of, to fly a singer, that I've barely heard of, to land on my lake, for a *shindig* that will make me a shit-ton of money. I, for the life of me, cannot figure out where you and Mary come up with this shit!"

Cliff walked over and sat on the armrest of the couch.

Wally spoke up. "It's really kind of simple. This kid will be in Nashville in six weeks. Don't laugh,…I have a friend who will charter Denver and Dutch from Nashville to Knoxville, where my buddy, from Ohio, will be waiting for them with the Teal. They'll fly in here Saturday morning, have a mid-day concert, and fly back to Knoxville before dark."

Wally stood. "We'll invite people Friday, Saturday, and Sunday. We can have some locals sing on Friday and Sunday. I'll borrow some stands from the Hawkins County school district, and we'll have Pop put together some rodeo events….and, and, by bringing Denver's dad along, I don't think that he'll want a thing for compensation beyond flying a Thurston Teal. Mary'll make sure that a few of the rooms are ready at The Manor, just in case they want to stay. Which, of course, would be even better!"

"I'm telling you, Cliff! It'll work. One to two thousand visitors,…hell, it could be five thousand…to Camelot!" Wally touted.

"Wally, how are you NOT at ABC, NBC, or CBS?... Never mind, I don't want to know, because I'm sure you have friends there. You might be crazier than Big Chief, over in Pigeon Forge, but let's do this. I'll let Jean know to get you whatever you need." Cliff conceded.

"Big Chief?" Wally looked puzzled.

"Oh, he's this Indian guy who owns all the land along 321, in Pigeon Forge." Cliff explained. "Nance and I stopped to see him every time we went to Gatlinburg. That might be the next place we go with your crazy ideas. There could be even more money there, if we could get Big Chief to sell. I'll have to take you over there one day. He's a "hoot". Comes out in full "Indian attire", with the big feather head-dress and everything. He's even got black bears as pets."

"You know what Wally? Could you and Mary meet me at The Manor after dinner to show me how things are coming there,…and talk about the pool plans? I think that I'm going to run into Rogersville and have a talk with Fisk about our line of credit." Cliff inquired.

"Sure Cliff, but the Denver weekend is only ONE of the two big events that we've come up with." Wally explained. "There's more."

"Oh boy, I can't wait to hear the next." Cliff roared as he stood and picked up their glasses.

"No, No. The next one is pretty simple. It would be another weekend event, but "invite only", and we'll hit every doctor, lawyer, politician, and wealthy person in Hawkins

County. We'll invite them to see Camelot Saturday and Sunday, but Saturday night will be a "Costume Ball". Dress attire mandatory. Bring your spouse and dress as your favorite actor, character, or mobster." Wally explained.

"Another?" Cliff asked as he rose and raised his glass towards Wally.

"No, …thanks." Wally replied.

As Wally watched Cliff pour himself another drink, Jean Ranier, Cliff's longtime assistant, walked in.

"Mister Lafferty? Don't forget that you have a lunch meeting with Brooks Brothers about the roads, sewer, and water. Should I tell them that you'll be late?" Jean asked as she noticed his state of insobriety.

"Yeah, cancel the meeting today. Schedule one for tomorrow morning. Ten AM. Oh, and take over the new plans that Wally has right there. That oughta get them going. Tell them they're "almost" approved. Right Wally?" Cliff slurred.

"Jean, tell them I'll have them approved within two weeks. They may not believe it, but it'll get done. Oh, and one or two council members from Hawkins County will be calling you to borrow all three limos for a field trip. Can you have someone clean them up?...and you'll need to call Mary to get "her's". Thanks Hon!" Wally said with a wink.

Jean blushed and smiled. As she was walking out the door, she shot a look back at Wally and smiled again. She was an attractive woman. Blonde and thin, she looked fabulous in a dress, but often just wore blue jeans and a flannel shirt. Wally couldn't understand why Cliff didn't have "eyes" for her. But then again, Nancy was the "light of his life". So, Wally was fairly certain that Cliff hadn't gotten over Nancy yet. "Maybe, one day." Wally thought.

"A costume ball, huh? With movie stars and mobsters? You gonna have your friends like Garner and Jack Ruby attend?" Cliff asked with a grin.

"If Jack was alive, I'd invite him. He'd buy twenty lots…and he'd have been the "life" of the party, that's for sure. It still kills me they let him die in there." Wally said, as he looked down at his hands, folded together, as if in prayer.

"Ya know Cliff, Tommy and I went over and saw him at the Texas State Penitentiary, just one month before he died. He told me he knew he was sick. Even before he shot Oswald. Otherwise, he might not have done it. Yeah, he sure loved Jack,-" Wally said, referring to John F. Kennedy.

"We all did Wally, we all did." Cliff interrupted, and raised his glass.

"To Camelot", Cliff toasted.

Wally, without a glass, nodded. "To Camelot." He replied.

"Wally, you mentioned *Tommy*. Is Jean still sending checks to her?" Cliff asked.

"I believe so. I haven't spoken to Tommy in a little while. But the last time I did, she thanked me. I should probably call her soon. Thanks for reminding me." Wally said.

Cliff furrowed his brow. "You need to figure that situation out before Mary finds out. But, I'll confirm it with Jean. Listen, since I'm not meeting with Brooks Brothers today, how about you run to the bank with me. I'm going to need a larger line of credit, and you would be the right person to explain why. You up for a *field trip* of our own?" Cliff asked.

Wally stood, walked over and took Cliff's drink from his hand. "Sure." Wally said. "But I'm driving. Maybe we can catch lunch in Rogersville. Hey, we can pop in and see if

Robert, or Betty, are free and you can *officially* offer the limos."

Wally gathered everything and put it back into his briefcase. Cliff grabbed his coat from the coatrack, reached in the pocket, pulled out the keys to his convertible El Dorado, and threw them to Wally.

Wally reached out and caught them without looking. Cliff saw this and thought. "I think that man might actually be *magic*". Together, they walked out the door.

***

They drove to Rogersville on Tennessee 70. Wally knew Cliff preferred it over sixty-six. Mainly because there were a whole lot fewer turns,…and Cliff had a bad habit of taking up more than his lane on the sharp ones. Cliff drove fast too. Mary and Jean fussed at him on multiple occasions to "slow down", especially on Pressmen's Home Road. Today, Wally was driving, and Cliff was just "taking it all in". Since it was a nice, sunny day, Cliff made sure that they dropped the top before they left.

As Cliff looked around, he saw Wally's profile. The man looked like Clark Gable. Wally had slightly silver hair, combed over and slightly back. A popular men's hairstyle for many decades. Cliff remembered the day that Wally and Mary first arrived at Camelot. They pulled up to the clubhouse in a Cadillac not much older than Cliff's. He remembered Wally opening the door for Mary and her stepping out in a calf length fitted dress and shawl. Her dark hair pulled back, held in place with a band. Anyone could have mistaken her for Elizabeth Taylor,…and Wally for Clark Gable.

Cliff thought about the costume party that Wally claimed they'd done before. He was sure he knew who they would dress up as. Cliff enjoyed their company. Their interests aligned, and Wally could hold his own until late at night. Mary could too, for that matter. They were entertainers, and much more.

Wally parked on the street, one block down from the courthouse. Cliff had closed his eyes halfway there, but he quickly perked up when he felt them backing into a spot on the street.

"Did ya doze off there, Cliff?" Wally inquired.

"Na, not really. Just thinking a little deeper about your crazy ideas for selling property. How'd you come up with these ideas of having a shindig to promote the sale of properties?" Cliff asked.

They had exited the car, and Wally was stepping onto the sidewalk. He looked at Cliff and replied, "Arthur, if Merlin told you all of his secrets, you might not need him anymore."

"That's it, I'm King Arthur. It's perfect!" Cliff exclaimed. "I'm assuming that you'll be bringing Miss Taylor, Mister Gable?" Cliff joked.

Wally laughed as he set his briefcase down, pulled open the bank's front door and used the other hand to gesture Cliff in. "Your majesty, wealth awaits." Wally said with a grin.

They stepped into the bank, and Cliff was quickly greeted by the bank manager, Leonard Fisk. Leonard's family had been in the area as long as the Crocketts. Leonard claimed that his great-great grandparents were buried in Crockett Springs Park, along with Davy Crockett's grandparents. All of whom were killed by Indians in the late seventeen hundreds.

Leonard quickly asked, "Mister Lafferty, I wasn't expecting you. Did we have a meeting scheduled? Oh, and can I get you some coffee?"

Cliff looked back at Wally, who gave his approval for coffee. "Thanks Leonard, coffee would be fine, and no, we didn't have a meeting scheduled. I had just hoped you fit me in." Cliff explained.

"Louisa, could you bring a couple cups of coffee for Mister Lafferty, and Mister… oh, sorry, I didn't catch your name, Mister?" Leonard inquired as he ushered them into his office.

"Leonard, this is Wally O'Banion. He, and his beautiful wife, are my "right hand" at Camelot. He's actually the reason that we're here." Cliff said as he pointed towards Wally's briefcase.

"Nice to finally meet you Mister Fisk." Wally said, nodding and opening his briefcase.

Before Wally could get a copy of the plans out, Cliff interrupted. "Leonard, I'm going to need more money. We've changed the plans slightly, which will bring another couple hundred people to Camelot, and another couple hundred people to your bank."

Looking perplexed, Leonard replied, "Mister Lafferty, you paid cash for the property, and we gave you a line of credit, but you haven't touched it yet. If you're saying that you want a larger line of credit, we can do that, but I'm afraid that we may need a lien on the property in order to do so. We didn't do that with your existing line of credit because you are banking with us and we want to keep you here".

Wally was laying the plans on the banker's desk, but Cliff quickly pulled them away. "Fisk,…I'll be heading to Knoxville tomorrow to meet with Knoxville Central Bank. I'll be needing a check in the morning for the balance in my personal and Camelot accounts. Can you take care of that, Fisk?" Cliff rebuked.

Wally followed Cliff's lead and quickly put the plans back in the briefcase and stepped towards the door.

Leonard's face was pale. His mouth was open and eyes big.

Trembling, the banker quickly replied, "Ma,..Mister Lafferty, there's no need for that. I will approve whatever you need for the line of credit. Pla,..Please sit down and let's see how we can help. Mister O'Banion, please feel free to get those plans back out. I'd love to see them. In fact, I want to see which property Lucy and I would like. Can we do that Mister O'Banion?" Leonard hesitantly quizzed.

As Wally popped open his briefcase, Cliff looked agitated, and Leonard quickly waved Louisa to bring more coffee.

Wally spoke up. "Well, Mister Fisk, these properties are going fast. We're taking down-payments right now, until we get final approval from the county, which is expected any day. We do have a beautiful new area called Sir Lancelot Village. You can have the "pick of the litter"." Wally explained while pointing to a section of the map subdivided to the north of Pressmen's Home Road. Leonard's face immediately lit up.

"I can have any of these lots? They look a little small compared to most of them though. Are you saying that you have down payments for these bigger lots down by the clubhouse?" Leonard inquired.

***

When they got to the car, Wally watched a few cars pass by before stepping off the curb and rounding the front of the car. Then he stopped and spoke. "Cliff? Leonard's going to figure out that people haven't put down payments on those lots."

Cliff climbed into the passenger seat and stopped before he closed his door. " Hmm,… Good point." Cliff said as he paused, looking down.

He continued. "Not a problem! I've got it. I'll have Jean transfer a hundred and fifty thousand dollars from my NC State Savings account on Monday. That'll be more than enough to cover the "down payments". I'll have her explain that she accidentally put it in my NCSS account. Leonard will be tickled pink". Cliff touted.

Wally shook his head, put the key in, started the El dorado, dropped it in gear, and pulled away.

Halfway back to Camelot, Cliff startled Wally. "Oh shit, we were supposed to see if we could take the zoning board to lunch!"

Wally didn't even take his foot off the pedal and replied, "Nope, we're picking Mary up and celebrating. We just sold our first lot!"

Chapter 8 -

"Pulling it all together" – Camelot, Summer 1973

It had been an exhausting few months, but Camelot was just days away from having the first of the two events. Wally was sure they would catapult their resort into notoriety.

They had quietly secured the plan to bring John Denver and his father to Camelot. The two of them leapt at the opportunity to fly the Thurston Teal, especially with a little coercion from Wally's friend, Colonel Taggert.

Mary was relentless with the subcontractors. So much so that a few of them left,…only to return a week later. As it turns out, "the grass isn't always greener…". The ballroom was almost complete. The Manor's lobby was complete, and ten of the fifty hotel rooms were ready for guests.

Cliff had coordinated adding onto the outdoor-patio area, and had a temporary stage built on the backside of the clubhouse. He figured he would give Mr. Denver his choice of locations. John could perform outside or inside, as two stages were available.

Pop pulled seven bleacher-sets over from Rogersville. Since the school was closed for the summer, Wally convinced Robert and Betty to let him borrow them for a couple of weeks. Pop wasn't looking forward to moving them back on the "crooked" Route sixty-six, but Cliff had asked for Pop to have a small "rodeo" at The Stable, and Pop was ecstatic to oblige.

Knowing that Wally was the mastermind, Pop made sure that young Brett was going to perform in the "Rodeo". So, he had been training Brett almost every day. The barrel racing was going to be Brett's first event ever, and Pop was going to make sure his "cowboys" were ready.

Just two weeks beforehand, Pop had asked Wally and Mary's permission to take Brett to see the movie "The Cowboys". It was a John Wayne movie about an aging rancher who had lost all his ranch hands to the gold rush. In the movie, Wayne's character is forced to accept adolescent boys to help him drive his cattle four hundred miles to South Dakota. Pop took Brett, Nick, Buddy, and even Tad got to "tag-a-long". Leaving that movie, all the boys looked at Pop just as the "Cowboys" had done with Wayne.

Tad was upset, realizing that he was too young to take part in the "Cowboy events" and eventually ended up back down at the old tradesmen's Building, playing with his imaginary friend. Knowing that Tad was lonely, Mary didn't complain when he brought home an injured stray dog.

To Wally's disappointment, and without his approval, the O'Banions had adopted this stray, which Brett named "Poochie". Tad had found him lying in the field beside the tradesmen's building, with a small bullet hole in his leg. Tad claimed that Moon Dove had told him that the dog needed his help. So, Tad slowly coerced the mutt to follow him home.

Poochie was a Border-Collie mix and appeared grateful when May-May bandaged the leg and made a bed for the dog in the laundry room. He licked her dark skin, and she smiled.

May May knew the mutt was a "good dog" when she heard the yelping one afternoon. May May had just left Liz, now being called "Tizzy", in the hall to play while she went to start dinner. When she came a-hustling to see what was all the commotion, Tizzy had made her way to the laundry room, and had Poochie's injured leg pulled back over its head. The dog was yelping, but would not make a move to stop this little child. May May scolded Tizzy and gently returned the dog's leg to a comfortable position. Appearing to smile again, Poochie licked May May.

When Mary return, later that day, May May explained, "Dat dog's a protector." She claimed. "Tizzy tried him real good dis afternoon, an he shoulda bit her. But he didn't. When he better, he gonna be a good one. I'm telling you."

Mary looked curious, but was afraid to ask. "May, after we have this big weekend, do you want us to get you a bus ticket to Mississippi? You can go back and visit for a couple weeks. I know you haven't seen your family since you left."

May May stopped what she was doing. "Missus O'Banion, Don' take dis wrong, but you'uns need me. Dee's babies need me. You and Mister O'Banion aw'ways out doing som'tin, and tween yo jobs an dat damn liquor, you gonna get dee's babies hurt, if I ain't here. I don' need go back to Hattiesburg anytime soon. You'uns do yo thing, an let me watch for dee's babies. Days my family right now."

Seemingly offended, Mary rebutted, "Mabel, what the hell is that supposed to mean! You know we both love our kids, and we'd never do ANYTHING to hurt them!"

"I know you love dim, Missus O'Banion. But, yo may not even know if yo hurt dim. I'm here to help. Don' be mad at me. Dare my babies too. You fire me if you wan', but I ain't leavin." May May finished.

Mary paused, and thought, remembering that May May took care of the children more than she, and much more than Wally. She thought, "Calmer minds prevail", a saying that her father often said.

"I'm sorry May May. You're right,…and just know that the offer is out there…if you ever need to go home." Mary apologetically explained.

With that, May May headed back to the stove to finish preparing dinner.

After dinner, which Wally did not attend, Mary went back to the clubhouse to continue preparing for the weekend's events. When she and Wally returned late that evening, May May heard them. They were loud and boisterous. Contemplating intervention if they woke the children up, she sat up. Tizzy slept in her room and appeared undisturbed in her baby-bed. In the darkness, she saw a shape under the baby bed. She sat there until she saw one eye open from the shape. It was Poochie, the "Protector". May May smiled, lay back down, and listened until she finally heard the quietness of all, including Poochie, resting.

Chapter 9 –

"Take Me Home"

Friday's events were a hit. Pop had over two hundred attendants at the "Kick-off Rodeo". Pop's friend, Miles Boyd, brought in a couple "up-and-coming" riders that entertained the crowd. Brett, Nick, and Buddy performed "basic riding techniques" to close the show and allow all to walk over to a cookout at the "Castle" Clubhouse.

After the cookout, "The Possum Creek Revue" performed on the outdoor stage.

Cliff mingled about the crowd, taking notice of Wally and Mary. He watched them from afar. After a moment, he smiled. Noticing that they spent time with certain people, and eventually pointed to the clubhouse. Almost every time they walked away from someone, that person remained for a moment and then walked over to the stairway and eventually into the clubhouse.

Inside the clubhouse, Jean was ready for most of the people, but a few lines were beginning to grow. She excused herself and called some new friends. Every call was, "Hey, how you doing today? You wouldn't want to see a free concert tomorrow, would you, it's John Denver? I just need half an hour of your time to help us register people to Camelot. Sounds good, see you here." She was smart and could already see that she would need their help.

When the crowd dwindled to a few mingling about Friday night, Cliff went to Jean to check on sales.

"Hey there Miss Ranier, how'd it go tonight? I saw Wally and Mary working the crowd, so I started doing the same. Hopefully, we got a few to buy?" Cliff inquired.

"Cliff, you're not going to believe this,…over three hundred bought lots tonight. It could be four! I swear, I think that the give-aways, the can openers, blenders, and fishing rods that Mary went and got in Ohio brought half of the people over to the tables. I doubt that we'll have any left for Sunday. That was a genius move on her part." Jean concluded.

"I knew we sold quite a few, but you're right. That's crazy!" Cliff exclaimed. "I thought I was good at this, but I'm out of my league with those two. I'm guessing tomorrow might be huge. Are you ready?"

"Yes Sir. I'll have more than double the help. I just need to stay and get this place cleaned up for tomorrow." Jean clarified.

Cliff was shaking his head. "Jean, sweetheart. Pop's guys are cleaning up. It's late, and tomorrow's a big day. Please go home and get some rest."

Jean smiled at Cliff, and blushed. "If you say so, Boss."

Cliff was heading towards the bar when he stopped and turned. "Please don't call me that, Jean. In fact, please just call me Cliff."

He winked at her. She nodded and blushed again.

Jean was heading towards the door but stopped as Cliff continued towards the bar. She turned, smiled, and then sighed. She turned back and continued to the door. As she walked to her car, she was no longer smiling. In fact, her face was one of worry and concern.

*****

Cliff, Wally, and Mary watched the Thurston Teal circle and approach the lake. Watching the seaplane land its belly on water was impressive to all. The high-winged plane looked strange on the water. The fuselage in the water, like a boat, and the engine-propeller high above, like a periscope.

Seeing the round glasses as the canopy doors swung open, made Cliff's smile grow wider. He and Wally had walked out onto the dock and were watching what appeared to be John taxi the plane to the dock.

When close, a hand from behind the two front seats, reached up and tapped John on his shoulder. John focused on the cockpit, and the single engine shut down as the plane floated slowly to the dock.

Wally, never too shy to make immediate friends, shouted, "Perfectly landing there, John!"

"Thank you, Sir. I had quite a bit of help from my two co-pilots." John answered. "A little heavy for a hot June day, but sure was a lot of fun!"

John was referring to the weight on the plane. The cooler the day, the denser the air is, and the wings have more lift. This day was warm, so take-offs and landings tend to take more runway.

Wally and Cliff anchored the plane to the dock as John, Dutch, and the Colonel exited the plane. As Cliff and Wally introduced themselves, the Colonel checked the bow and stern lines. The plane was now considered "a boat".

After the Colonel checked the lines, he started up the dock, where three golf carts were waiting.

"Taggert! Good to see you!" Wally barked out.

"You too, my friend." The Colonel replied.

"What lies did you tell these fine gentlemen, on the way over from Knoxville?" Wally asked.

Now laughing, the Colonel pointed towards the plane. "No time to lie. These two have flown more planes than me, and that's all we got the chance to talk about. That boat right there makes over a hundred different aircraft for Dutch. He says that there are another ten to fifteen that he can't even talk about because he flew them out of Roswell Walker."

"Damn it, Taggert. Now, I have to kill you." Dutch retorted.

They all laughed and sped off in the golf carts. John's guitar sticking out of the back of the lead cart.

The clubhouse and grounds looked like an "anthill". There were people walking everywhere. A local band had just played on the patio stage, and groups of people were walking to and from The Stable. Mary was able to watch Brett compete in the barrel racing, just twenty minutes before the golf carts came pulling up.

John had removed his glasses, so he wasn't easily recognized, and he quickly blended in with his "southern draw". Every once in a while, he could catch someone looking at him as though they recognized him, but they couldn't quite "place him".

After introductions, they all went to Cliff's office, where Mary and Jean had prepared a spread for lunch. As they talked, Mary immediately moved closer to John.

"So, Mister Denver, I hear you sing folk, as well as country? You ever make your way out to Venice, to visit my friend Lawrence Welk?" Mary challenged.

"Please call me John, Ma'am…I was on the Smother's Brothers's show, and Tom Jone's, but I ain't been out to meet Mister Welk. I'd like to one day. If you know him, maybe you can get me an introduction?" John replied.

Mary grinned, cocked her head back, and then kept her head tilted as she said, "I'm sure I could, John. I know him. Sang with him in Dayton, and Cincinnati. I'd be glad to hook you two up." She boastfully replied, all the while knowing that the reality of her contacting Welk's agent was unlikely. But she wanted her "moment" to feel like she was a famous singer, that had "rubbed elbows" with the "greats".

Mary wanted to stay and talk with John, but knew that he had to perform shortly, so she called Cliff and Wally over. "John's got to go on shortly. You two need to give him the "lay of the land" and explain what we're doing here in Camelot." She turned to John. "We need you to "plug" Camelot a couple times, if you would."

"Sure thing, Ma'am. It was good talking to ya, and I'll be looking you up for that invite from Mister Welk. Many Thanks." John replied.

Mary smiled, shook John's hand, and left him to the two that needed him most…King Arthur and Merlin.

John Denver took the stage at one PM. He played and sang for an hour and a half. In between songs, he talked about his young life, and, of course, "plugged" Camelot, "and the beautiful setting of this little secluded resort", as he put it.

As his set was coming to an end, John stood and pulled the stool to the side of the stage. "I've got one more for you folks. Well, actually two, if I can get Lawrence Welk's very own Champagne Lady up here on the stage. Where you at, Mary? Come on up."

Mary fanned her face and waved to John, as though she didn't want to perform. But John saw her stepping forward and knew that he could get her on stage.

"Come on up Mary…and sing with me." John persisted.

Mary turned to look at Wally, Cliff, and Jean. They all flipped their hands, gesturing for her to go up on stage. All the while she slowly kept moving towards the stage and was instantly at the stair steps with John reaching down to give her a hand up.

She walked up to the center microphone and pulled it from the stand. John had taken a position behind her, next to the bass player.

Looking back at John, Mary was already performing. "Well John, you surprised me with this. I'm afraid that I'm not only out of my league with you, but you all won't know anything that I sing."

John smiled and shook his head. "Try us, Mary."

Mary looked at the drummer, bass, lead, fiddle, and then back at John. "How about Patsy? Walkin' after Midnight?" They all nodded in agreement.

Mary turned and began to bend her leg repeatedly. The motion of her leg was her metronome, and the band began to play. During the chorus, she walked over to John, and he joined her in singing the chorus. The audience swayed as Mary Margaret and John Denver performed this classic country song.

Cliff, Wally, and Jean were at "stage left". They all were mesmerized by the performance. At one point, Jean asked, "Can someone pinch me, I think I'm dreaming? Is Mary really up there singing with John Denver?"

"She's eating this up." Wally replied.

When they finished, there was thunderous applause. Mary clasped her hands together, bowed to the audience, and then to John. Then she held her arm out, palm open, towards the microphone stand, leading John back up front.

John stepped forward and bent to the microphone. "Ladies and gentlemen, Mary Margaret!" he re-introduced her. "Mary will be signing autographs for everyone that buys a property today. So, after my next song, hurry into the clubhouse and get you a part of Camelot, and Mary's autograph."

John paused, walked back to the band, and they all huddled around him. After a few moments, the band members nodded in agreement as the fiddle player handed his fiddle to John.

"This next song has been in my head for a bit. It's a bit rough, but we're gonna give it a go." He looked at the band and slapped his hand on his thigh. "Welllll, life on a farm is kinda laid back," he started.

Soon, the upbeat song had the entire audience clapping and belting out the chorus. The audience didn't know the song would soon be recorded and become a number one country hit.

Mary had hoped to see John before he left, but she was too busy signing autographs for all the new landowners at Camelot. She thought signing "Mary Margaret" on the backs of their land contracts was pretty cool at first. But it got "old" quickly. She laughed and said out loud, "Damn you, John." Jean laughed too.

John, Dutch, and the Colonel flew away, with Dutch at the wheel. Wally and Cliff watched from the dock. After they were out of sight, Cliff turned to Wally.

"You're a damn genius O'Banion!" Cliff exclaimed. "I don't know how many people are back there at the clubhouse, but I'm guessing over three thousand. Hell, they're parked in every field, for Christ's sake. I think we may have "struck gold" right here in Hawkin's County, Tennessee, my friend."

"And we're not done yet." Wally agreed. "Maybe, we need to be thinking about Pigeon Forge next?" Wally suggested.

By the end of the weekend, they had sold three-quarters of the lots in Camelot. Cliff, Wally, and Mary were celebrating in the ballroom when Jean walked up solemnly.

"Wally…I'm sorry… it's the Colonel." Jean said. "He went down flying back to Ohio."

Mary's hand went to her mouth. "John and Dutch?" she asked.

"They're fine." Jean explained. "It was on James' final leg back to Ohio. He was alone… I'm sorry Wally." Jean bowed her head, turned and walked back towards the stairwell.

Wally was looking down, then looked up at the ceiling. He paused, then walked around the bar, took a bottle of Scotch, and poured a whiskey-glass full. He raised it towards the West, and said, "To you, Colonel James Taggert. The Quiet Birdmen have another angel watching over us.", and he downed the Scotch.

Mary attempted to come to Wally's side, but he pushed her away. Cliff started to speak, but stopped. Wally walked across the ballroom floor, and out the door.

At three AM, Wally was still on the dock, looking towards the northeast. He was remembering that day in the South Pacific, when Taggert pulled Wally from that foxhole. Literally five seconds later, a motor round exploded in the hole. Wally certainly would have perished. "Taggert's the reason that I have a Purple Heart, and not a flag-draped coffin." He thought.

With the bright moonlight, he could see the Thurston Teal "wave" its wings as it flew away.

When he finally walked the short distance to their cottage, something caught his eye. It was a wolf. A red wolf… sitting by the old Pressmen's Trades building. He watched it as he walked, and it appeared to watch him, as well. What he did not notice was the pink hue coming from the building…or the other eyes watching him walk home.

Chapter 10 –

"Cowboys and Indians"

It was a few weeks before Wally seemed normal again. He had driven up to Ohio for the funeral of Colonel James Taggert. Mary did not go. Wally had asked her to stay behind, so she could continue to focus on the sale of the lots at Camelot.

They sold a few more lots over the coming weeks, but nothing like the weekend sale when John Denver performed. Remembering Mary's performance with Denver, Cliff asked her if she would consider singing on the ballroom stage. Possibly, routinely. She politely declined, feeling that her commitment should be to preparing Camelot. With the next big event being just six weeks away, there was much to do.

Mary had coordinated the finishing touches at The Manor hotel. She had hoped to complete all the guest rooms but knew she would fall short. Cliff had curtailed her budget on The Manor, as it was quickly draining his resources.

"Cliff, what is a hotel, with half of the rooms available? It's really just a bed-and-breakfast at that point. I can't replace The Manor's majestic appearance with ten thousand dollars." Mary insisted.

Cliff wrung his hands together. "Mary, Listen. You've done a fabulous job. It looks better than any time that Nance, and I stayed there. But that place is sucking me dry. Why refinish the ballroom there, when we have one here at the clubhouse. I'd much rather put that money towards a pool. Besides, you yourself said it would be cheaper. An indoor pool? The closest one to us would be Gatlinburg. Why don't we go that direction?" Cliff pleaded.

"Dammit, Cliff. Houdini himself performed in that ballroom. I was kind of joking about the pool. I didn't really think that you'd go that direction. What would Nancy want, Cliff?" Mary questioned.

Cliff threw his glass of Scotch. "Dammit Mary, I said NO! You've got ten thousand dollars to get a God Damn pool in there! Enough!" He barked.

Mary knew she had "crossed the line" with the "Nancy comment". She began placing the wood samples back into her canvas bag.

Cliff came to her side and placed them in as well.

"Mary, Listen, I'm sorry. I shouldn't have blown up like that." Cliff paused. "It's just that you've got to realize that there is a bottom to the well. And I'm getting close to the bottom. Let's spend the next two years finishing up here, and move on. Hell, If I had the money, we'd already be working that Pigeon Forge corridor. I think that place will explode." He claimed.

"Okay Cliff. It's your money." Mary said contritely.

"Hey, You and Wally have both been working your asses off. Do me a favor, why don't you, Wally, and the kids, go to Pigeon Forge for the weekend. There's an amusement park there called Goldrush Junction. The boys would love it. There're all kinds of rides. I'll have Jean book you guys a couple of adjoining rooms at the Howard Johnsons right on

321, down the street from the park. Whad'ya say?" Cliff challenged.

Mary smiled, as if she had won. Maybe not the battle that she had hoped to win, but she felt like she "won".

***

As they wheeled into Pigeon Forge, Wally immediately spotted the man he had come to see. Standing by the road, waving to passersby, "Big Chief" was exactly where Cliff said he would be.

Big Chief was the man Cliff was convinced owned much of the land around Pigeon Forge. Greeting Gatlinburg and Pigeon Forge visitors for years, Big Chief always had a huge smile. His small souvenir shop specialized in "Cherokee Indian" apparel, assorted Gatlinburg trinkets, and all kinds of "black bear" toys. He owned two black bears, kept in a pen on the property. Customers could see "Smokey" and "Yona" behind the souvenir shop almost every day.

"Hey boys! There's Big Chief. You guys want to meet him?" Wally asked Brett and Tad.

Mary, holding Tizzy, said she'd stay in the car, since little Liz was sleeping.

Wally pulled the limo into the gravel lot and came to a stop by the entrance to Big Chief's souvenir store. Wally exited the car and opened the rear limo door for the boys. Big Chief was quick to head their way from his post by the street.

Waving as he approached. "Osiyo, friends. I'm guessing that we have a few movie stars visiting our beautiful city?" Big Chief inquired.

Tad looked up at the Native American and eyed the large headdress. Pointing at the headdress, he asked the man, "Osiyo, What's that?"

As Tad continued talking to the Cherokee, Wally walked to the side of the store and began looking at the hillside. Brett, however, immediately saw what he wanted in the store window…a "Bowie knife".

Big Chief kneeled by Tad. "It is my "war bonnet". Because I am Big Chief, I get to wear it. You said "hello" well little man. Tohitsu?(How are you?)"

"Osada, nihina?(I'm fine, how about you?)" Tad replied.

"You know Tsagali, little man?" the Chief asked.

"You mean, the funny words? I know some. Moon Dove taught me some. I can understand her when she speaks it, but I can't always say it…and then,… sometimes…it just comes out." Tad explained.

Big Chief smiled. "Your friend, Moon Dove, is an excellent teacher. She is also named after a famous Indian Chief's daughter."

Tad squinted as the sun shone on his face. "That's her. Her father was an Indian Chief and went to Oklahoma." he claimed.

Big Chief stood up and took Tad's hand. They walked towards the store. "Oh, little man, Moon Dove was lost in the "Trail of Tears", many, many moons ago. Some say, when the wind howls, it is Moon Dove, crying for her father, and her tribe." Big Chief asserted.

"I think it's her. Her tribe is with her. I haven't seen them, but she says they're with her. I'm going to marry Moon Dove, when I grow up. She says that she will stay with me, if I save her, and her people." Tad boasted.

Big Chief laughed. "Let's go meet your family, little man." He instructed.

"It's Little Warrior. She calls me Little Warrior." Tad clarified.

Again, Big Chief laughed. Not realizing that Wally was still outside, Big Chief and Tad had stepped inside. The Chief walked Tad over to Brett, who was gazing at the "Bowie knife" that he'd seen from the front.

"Osiyo, Tohitsu?" Big Chief said to Brett.

"What?" Brett asked.

"He doesn't know the funny words." Tad clarified.

"That's a Bowie knife there, cowboy. You've got a few more years before your parents may buy that for you…but maybe a pocketknife? Where'd your dad go?" Big Chief inquired.

Brett pointed to the large front windows, where Big Chief saw Wally walking past, smoking a cigarette. Soon, he was coming through the front door. The little bell on the door rang. "Ring, ring".

Wally walked right to them. "These little tyrants bothering you, Big Chief?" He asked, with an outstretched hand. "Name's Wally O'Banion. I've been wanting to meet you. I work with Cliff Lafferty, from up above Rogersville." Wally disclosed.

"Oh Yes, I do know Mister Lafferty,…and his lovely wife, Nancy. I haven't seen them in quite a while. How are they doing?" The Chief questioned.

"Oh, Sorry, Big Chief. Nancy died a few years back. I'm sorry to be the one to tell you." Wally looked down, and back up. "Listen, Cliff and I are putting together a bit of an event, in a couple weeks. Why don't you come up, just the way you are? People would love it. A real Cherokee Indian." Wally suggested.

Big Chief stood tall. "Thank you for the invitation, Mister O'Banion, but I must pass. I don't drive,…and I have to stay here for "the boys". It's an agreement that I have with the city." He stated.

By now, Brett's patience had worn thin, and he tugged on Wally's arm.

"Oh bullshit, I'll come and get you. We'll put you up in The Manor. Hell, I'll talk to the city. I'm sure that I can get you a "pass"…or can't someone else watch the boys?" Wally challenged.

Brett continued to tug at Wally's arm.

Big Chief shook that big headdress. "Mister O'Banion, "the boys" are my black bear. Smokey is over six hundred pounds. And Yona isn't far behind him. I doubt it, but let me see. Maybe I can leave for a few hours. Call the store telephone next week, and have Samantha find me. Until then, you might want to take care of this little Indian, I think he's fixing to scalp you." The Chief jested.

Brett again reached for Wally's arm, but Wally pulled away. "What the hell is so important, Son?"

"Can I get that knife? I have money that Pop paid me." Brett asked.

Tad had walked away and was looking at a mannequin, just a row away. It was a mannequin resembling a young Native American woman. Wearing a deerskin dress. Sashed at the waist, she also wore a large beaded necklace. Tad was mesmerized.

Wally was smiling. "Brett, you always go "big", don't you? Just a bit too big, this time. How about we downsize? A pocketknife, or…Hey, Pop said you need a new buckle since you took "second" in the barrel races. How about that?" Wally contended.

Brett didn't look too happy that he was refused the Bowie knife, but the consolation was that he did "get something". Samantha was showing them some belt buckles when Big Chief found Tad by the mannequin.

"That Moon Dove, Little Warrior?" Big Chief asked.

"It looks like her, but it's not her. Moon Dove is prettier,…and she has a necklace with a red moon." Tad replied.

"Little Warrior, the next time you see Moon Dove, tell her Big Chief said "hello"… and can you ask who her father is? Can you do that?" The Chief inquired.

"I will, Big Chief." Tad answered as he realized his brother was getting a souvenir. Jealousy set in, and he made a beeline towards them.

Big Chief stood by the mannequin for a moment, looking perplexed and then followed.

After a contentious five minutes with the two boys fighting over "who" should get a souvenir, Wally was just about to "give in" when Big Chief interrupted.

"Little Warrior. It's okay, I have something for you." Big Chief walked behind the counter and pulled down a much smaller version of a "war bonnet", with colorful feathers, and a beaded headband. He waved Tad over. Cinching the junior headdress to its smallest position, the Chief placed it on Tad's head.

Wally was not happy about Tad's little tantrum. "Big Chief, it's okay, Tad doesn't need—", then Wally was interrupted.

Holding his hand up to Wally, Big Chief adjusted the headdress. "It is my gift to this Little Warrior." The Big Chief avowed.

"You are a good man, Big Chief. We've got to get going, but I will call in a couple weeks. We'd really appreciate it. Besides, Cliff and I want to talk to you about Pigeon Forge too." Wally said with a wink.

Wally paid Samantha for the belt-buckle,…and the pocketknife. As the trio walked out, Big Chief watched them leave. Standing by the counter, he whispered, "very strange". Samantha heard him and asked, "What's that, Big Cee?"

Big Chief kept watching as they pulled away. "That little boy. When I spoke with him, over by the mannequin…we talked in Tsagali. He spoke it perfectly. Except, he speaks a much older dialect. That dialect died off a hundred years ago." Big Chief divulged.

***

Not far down the road, the Howard Johnson's Motor Lodge beckoned the O'Banions. Jean had booked them adjoining rooms, so that the children could laugh and play in one, and Wally and Mary could relax in the other. There was a pool out front, Putt-Putt to one side, and a restaurant on the other. Conveniently, the restaurant shared a parking lot with a liquor store, which Wally stopped at first.

"Hurry up, Honey. Liz is waking up, and she'll want to eat right away. If not, Tizzy will be back." Mary pleaded.

Wally was in and out in no time. They started the limo back up and headed over to the Howard Johnson's. Wally pulled under the portico, and asked that everybody "stay put, while I get the keys".

By noon, they were poolside. The boys, running and jumping from the diving board. Mary, with her swimming cap, had Liz in a Styrofoam "floaty", wading in the pool. Wally was sitting at a poolside table, looking comfortable in a plaid swimsuit, drinking a scotch.

"Honey, if it's too hot at Goldrush Junction tomorrow, Tizzy and I may have to go back to the car some time during the day." Mary explained.

Wally looked up from his newspaper. "Well, I don't plan on spending the whole day there. We're driving into Gatlinburg later in the afternoon. Cliff says that we need to check it out. He said that we could probably spend most of a day in Gatlinburg. But we'll be back here, soon enough. I'll be back in a few minutes. I need to go back to the room to make a few calls. Watch those boys."

Mary held up a hand and then focused back on Liz. The boys just kept chasing each other, in and out of the pool.

Just as Mary was beginning to wonder about Wally, he came out of their room. Mary watched him walk across the parking lot. His "Irish Smile" in full "bloom". Then, just as he reached the poolside gate, he appeared "serious".

"Gotta make a quick trip back to see Big Chief, Mary." Wally informed her.

"Did you forget something?" Mary asked.

"No. We're going to talk about all of this land that he owns around here. You know Cliff would want me to take advantage of being here. I'll be back in a couple hours. Then we can walk over to the restaurant for dinner." Wally said.

Mary noticed Wally had put on a tan pair of trousers but still had on the light button-up shirt. She checked the boys. They were slowing down. She turned her attention back to little Liz.

By six-thirty, Wally had not returned. Mary had a drink herself and decided that the "kids" needed to eat. All three of them had taken a nap and were getting restless. Leaving Wally a note, she got the children dressed and they walked over to the restaurant.

Halfway through dinner, Mary saw Wally enter the front door of the restaurant. Not happy with him, she kept looking down until he came to the table.

"Hey gang, eating without me?" Wally asked as he looked for a chair to pull up.

"It's probably seven-thirty Wally! How long did you want them to wait?" Mary asked, noticing Wally's state of inebriation.

"As long as it God Damn takes!" Wally protested loudly.

"Yeah, you need to order something. You might want to get it to-go. We're about done, and the boys want to play Putt-Putt. You told them that you'd take them there after dinner." Mary laid on the guilt.

"They'll have to play Putt-Putt tomorrow. I'm relaxing for a bit." Wally stated as he looked at the menu.

Mary looked mad. She wiped Liz's face, stood and turned to the boys. "Take care of the bill, Wally. Come on boy's, I'll take you to the Putt-Putt." Mary picked Liz from the "hi-seat", grabbed her purse, and headed for the door.

***

Mary paid to play Putt-Putt herself, but she knew that she'd only be able to play a hole or two. Holding Liz with one arm, and swinging her putter with the other, Mary got a hole-in-one on the first hole. The boys enjoyed the game, and they even let Liz attempt to putt.

By the time they were walking back to the motel, it was close to nine o'clock. Coming past the pool, Mary saw Wally. He was lying in a sun chair,...and snoring. She diverted the children's attention from the pool and towards the street. Mary successfully kept the children from seeing Wally's unconscious state, then put them all to bed. They immediately fell asleep.

Mary had had enough. She needed to relax, so she made herself a drink and settled into bed with the television quietly showing "I Love Lucy".. She didn't know what time Wally came in, but he was in the bed next to her at seven AM. Still in his clothes from the trip to see Big Chief, Mary noticed something. A smell...perfume.

Brett and Tad enjoyed the trip to Goldrush Junction more than anybody else. The Country Fair Falls "log flume" ride soaked them all and the "Rebel Train" ride kept them on the edge of their seats. By two o'clock, the children were tired. Wally bribed each of the boys with a "Golden Horseshoe" to leave. Soon, they were heading towards Gatlinburg.

Having the limousine again proved to be an asset, as everyone in the back drifted to sleep.

Wally drove down Parkway, amazed at the number of visitors. He thought to himself, "Imagine getting just half the amount of people in a developed Pigeon Forge?". He was surprised to see how small the town actually was. To him, it seemed only a few blocks in length. He heard movement behind him.

"Uh, oh. The natives are restless." Wally claimed.

Sitting up, Mary asked, "Is this Gatlinburg?...What the hell?... There's a ski resort here?"

Wally chuckled deeply. "Yeah, it looks like they're building a tram to go up there. The next time we come, we'll stay here in town. You, and the kids would love to walk around here."

"You, and the kids?" Mary replied with extreme sarcasm. "Where would you plan to be?" she grilled.

Wally looked at Mary with that "Irish Grin" again. His eyes almost closed with the squint. "Oh Mare, I'll be here too. I just may have to have a meeting with Big Chief. That's all I meant." He winked.

Mary's blood was "boiling". They were heading back through the center of town, and Mary noticed a playground. "Pull over there. That playground. The kids can play, while we have a talk…and my name's not fucking MARE! I'm not a damn horse!" she demanded.

Wally had been in a "pinch" before and knew that it was better to play it "cool", than escalate the situation.

"Honey, I'm sorry. You're right. You are Mary Margaret O'Banion, and my wife. Calling you "Mare" was not meant to be an insult. Do you really want me to pull over to that school or should we head back to the motel and I'll take the kids to the Putt-Putt. You can relax, and we'll do dinner,…together." Wally proposed.

Mary was calming. "Relaxing" sounded good. A drink sounded good. She looked out the window as they drove by. "Pi Beta Phi Elementary School", the sign read. "That's an interesting looking school" she thought. "It looks newer than anything else here." Her mind wandered off as they continued to drive.

The brief trip back to Pigeon Forge was relaxing for Wally as well. He saw all but Brett sleeping. So, he lit a cigarette and enjoyed the scenery. The route through to Pigeon Forge has the north and southbound lanes separated by the Little Pigeon River. So, the drive is very pleasant. No oncoming traffic. Wally thought about Big Chief, and the possibilities in Pigeon Forge.

"Boys! How about some Putt-Putt?" Wally asked as the limo came to a stop.

Everyone woke.

Although Brett dozed during the last few miles, the words "Putt, and Putt" woke him instantly.

Mary was still mad, and the mere thought Wally offered to take "only the boys" angered her more. She wanted so badly to put Liz in Wally's arms and walk back to the room. But she thought for a moment… For Liz's sake, she was better with her mother.

Brett and Tad quickly joined Wally, heading to the Putt-Putt course. Wally showed them how to putt "correctly". Brett picked it up quickly, but Tad struggled.

Although he had trouble keeping up, Tad thought the first few holes were a lot of fun. Then, Wally and Brett made him feel like he was slowing them down. Before long, Wally and Brett were on the hole ahead of Tad. Frustrated, Tad hit the ball as hard as he could. It bounced and lofted…over the fence. Tad was not looking, but Wally and Brett were. The ball hit a customized van two rows out in the parking lot. The side door of the van slid open, and a long-haired man came out.

"What the fuck, man! Long-hair exclaimed.

"Tad! What the hell!" Wally shouted.

Wally handed his putter to Brett and headed for the parking lot.

Walking towards the long-haired man, Wally noticed that the man didn't even inspect the damage. He just started looking around.

Wally approached him. "Hey, bud. Sorry about that. One got away from my kid. Can I pay you a little something for it?" Wally asked.

Never looking at the dent, the man finally agreed to forty dollars, which Wally paid him. Then the man climbed back inside the van and pulled the door shut. Wally turned towards the boys. He was mad. Stomping over to Tad, he picked Tad up with one hand. Pulling his pants down with the free hand, Wally began spanking Tad on his bare rear. Wally spanked Tad as they walked back to the motel, carrying him with one arm, and spanking with the other. Brett followed far behind. By the time they got to the room, Tad was bawling profusely. Wally banged on the motel room door.

Thinking something was extremely wrong, Mary came quickly.

"What happened to him?" Mary asked as she took Tad from Wally's grasp.

"The little shithead fucking hit a car in the parking lot with a golf ball. That's what!" Wally retorted.

Mary, looking confused but ready to defend her child, hollered back. "It was an accident, Wally. Why'd you spank him?" She fumed as she carried Tad to his bed, Tad sobbing and choking back tears.

Mary didn't actually care how it happened. She just didn't like the fact that her child had been spanked, especially in public. Wally, on the other hand, was furious.

"We watched him do it! The little shithead did it on purpose." Wally accused.

"Wally!! If you call him "shithead", one more time, I swear you will not like the consequences." Mary sat on the bed, stroking Tad's arm.

Liz started crying from all the commotion, and Brett slowly crept into his bed.

Wally did not speak. He saw the bottle of scotch by the television and walked towards it.

"Leave it!" Mary barked. "And close the connector. We'll see you in the morning." She commanded.

Wally did as Mary asked. Mary soon heard the front door of the adjacent room open and then slam shut. She picked up Liz, walked over to the front window and pulled the curtain slightly to peek out. She thought that he surely was going for the limo, but he didn't. He walked out onto the sidewalk and began walking along 321. Once Mary lost sight of him, she went back to Tad.

With Liz on her lap, she asked, "Honey, you, okay?"

Tad replied, "Mom, they were leaving me. They were--"

"He was too slow, Mom." Brett interrupted.

Mary put her hand up. "Stop, Brett. He's three years younger than you. You need to help him, not leave him behind." She asserted.

"I was with Dad." Brett argued.

"So, you both were leaving him behind?" Mary sarcastically refuted.

Brett started to talk again, but again Mary held her hand up. "Listen, you had better find a heart for him, because you're sleeping with him tonight."

Mary went to the bottle of scotch. Looked at it, turned to walk away, and turned back. After filling a plastic motel glass, she picked up the ice bucket and started towards the door. "Do you kids want to eat at that restaurant that we did last night or do you want pancakes from down the street?" She asked.

"Pancakes!" they unanimously affirmed.

It appeared the "skirmish" was over, and all was "right" again. The rest of the evening remained uneventful. Even Mary felt a bit of relaxation, …and a little worried.

***

Leaving Pigeon Forge, they saw Big Chief outside of the souvenir shop, waving, as usual. Wally "tooted" the horn, and the kids waved as if nothing was wrong.

Once back in Camelot, Wally seemed to change. He was much more pleasant than he was over the weekend in Pigeon Forge, and possibly more so than in the few weeks beforehand. Mary decided it was best not to "rock the boat" and did not confront him over any of the Pigeon Forge events. They both focused on the upcoming costume ball.

The Camelot Costume Ball flyers were posted in and around Rogersville. Mary had even driven to Bean Station to post another batch, hoping to bring some "money" up from the Cherokee Lake region. Upon returning, Wally explained he had spoken with Big Chief, and that Big Chief did not believe he could attend the event. Wally contended, "I'm going to run down there tomorrow and try to change his mind."

Mary didn't meet Big Chief but knew that Wally wanted to be friendly to him. Wally also said that he was considering a change in their previous costume attire. Wally was now thinking of going as a "cowboy", and that Mary should go as an "Indian girl". He thought it'd be cute. But of course, the costumes would have to be perfect.

Mary contemplated Wally's suggestion. "Yeah, well, I'm not so sure I'd fit into that "Liz Taylor" dress anymore, honey. So, that might be a good idea. Do you want me to go with you?" She asked.

"No. You're needed here. I'll just run down there tomorrow afternoon, talk him into coming, and come right back. I'll pick you up a costume right there at his store." Wally insisted.

Mary pondered. She was quite busy…and she wanted to talk to Cliff about a new idea for The Manor. One that she really didn't want Wally to contradict her on. So, she agreed.

At noon the next day, Wally headed to Pigeon Forge,…and Mary headed to the clubhouse. She saw Jean hanging streamers. "Hey Sweetie, you seen Cliff?" Mary asked Jean.

"Oh, Hi Mary. Yeah, he's in his office. He just got back from the bank, so he might be a bit grumpy." Jean said, eyes looking up.

Mary went to Cliff's office. He was filling his scotch glass when she knocked on the door.

"Cliff? You got a minute?" Mary asked.

"Yeah, what's up?" Cliff inquired.

Mary walked in. "Well, I've been thinking about your indoor pool idea, and I had one contractor give me a "ballpark" quote. It was kinda high. So had him give me a quote for an outdoor pool, and that was half the price-"

"Of course." Cliff interrupted.

"If we did an outdoor pool,…aaaand refinished the kitchen, we could have a small restaurant in The Manor." Mary blurted out.

"But we already have a restaurant here." Cliff rebutted.

"Yeah, but wouldn't it be nice to have two restaurants in Camelot?" Mary proposed.

Cliff took a drink of scotch with his right hand and then lifted his left to his chin. Rubbing his chin, he appeared to be seriously contemplating Mary's idea. "How much would it cost?" He asked.

"Less than the indoor pool…for both." Mary boasted.

Cliff finished his drink and set it down. "Mary. I just came from the bank. We're doing pretty well, because of the last "sale event" that you and Wally pulled off. I'll make you a deal…If you guys can sell off the remaining lots,…or even get close, this weekend,…then I'll give you the money for your pool, and restaurant. How's that?"

"Done!" Mary turned and smiled as she walked out his office door. Another "win".

Mary was ecstatic. She had just won a battle and didn't even have to fight. She impressed herself and was already thinking about the little restaurant in The Manor. "What should it be called?" she thought. Realizing she was being a bit narcissistic, she thought, "Mary's Place? Mary Margaret's? Maggie's?"…that was it "Maggie's Place".

Mary woke up the following morning. She hadn't heard Wally come in last night, but thought that it might have been late, and maybe he had laid down on the couch.

She walked out into the living room. He was not on the couch.

He hadn't come home. She thought for a moment and then realized that he had probably slept at the clubhouse. It had happened once before when he and Cliff "worked" too late. Knowing that she had a nine o'clock meeting at The Manor, she soon dismissed any worries about Wally and began notes for the contractor.

Wally arrived at the clubhouse at eleven-thirty in the morning. He brought several "hanging garments" to Cliff's office and laid them down on the "Round table".

"Wally, I challenged your wife yesterday." Cliff proclaimed.

"Oh yeah? How'd you do that?" Wally inquired.

"She came up with another one of her crazy ideas. But it's not so crazy. She wants to put a restaurant in The Manor." Cliff continued.

"But we have a restaurant here." Wally refuted.

Cliff held up his finger. "That's exactly what I told her. But think about it. The one here at the clubhouse, only does sandwiches for the golfers, and then a small dinner menu. The one at The Manor could have a better menu, serve the hotel guests, and she says that she can do it for less than my "indoor pool" idea. We'd have to go back to an outdoor pool." Cliff explained.

"Hmm,…I see your point. Well, Mary's point, I guess. Hey, before I forget, If Mary asks, could you say that I slept on your couch, here,…last night?" Wally questioned.

Cliff sighed. "Pigeon Forge, again? Did you see the Chief?"

"Yeah, I did. He can't come. He won't leave for anything but groceries because of those damn bears. Have you ever seen him go into the cage with them? They're like big old teddy-bears to him. It's crazy. Anyway, we talked about the land a bit, and I picked up costumes for Mary and I." Wally revealed.

Glancing at the garments, Cliff looked perplexed.

Wally smiled. "I'm going to put these in my office, and head over to Pop's, to make sure he's ready for Saturday. Oh, you said that you challenged Mary. What was the challenge?" Wally asked.

Now, Cliff smiled. "I told her she could have her restaurant, and outdoor pool, if you two could sell all of the remaining lots Saturday."

Wally's smile got bigger. "She played you like a fiddle, Cliff. We'll sell them all. Guaranteed!" he avowed.

As Wally picked up the garments and walked out, Cliff raised his left hand to his chin, and rubbed, just as he had done when Mary was there. Were they confident or arrogant? Cliff wondered.

Saturday came quickly, and Mary absolutely loved the Native American dress Wally had gotten her. She had moccasins, a headband, and a single feather pointing to the sky. She put her hair in two braids. "What do you think, Hon?" she asked Wally.

"Perfect!" Wally replied.

Mary went to the boys' room. "What do you think kids?" She asked.

Tizzy was in the room with them. They all turned. "Mom! You look like Moon Dove!" Tad exclaimed.

"That's who I am tonight sweety. If anyone asks, I'll say that I'm Moon Dove. Do you think she'd be okay with that?" Mary inquired.

Tad curled his lip and raised his palms. "I guess. I don't know." He replied. He looked back down at the cars, and track that they were assembling. "It's not fair!" he muttered.

Mary approached Tad. "I know, Honey. Brett's only going for a little while, with the boys from The Stable. Pop wanted him there. When you're riding for The Stable, then you'll go too. Just a couple more years, okay?" She pulled him to her side and patted him on the back.

Mary gave Tad a kiss on the head, then walked over to Tizzy, and did the same. As she was walking to the door, she stopped and looked back at Brett. "May May is getting you ready at four. You go straight to Pop's, and don't get dirty. I'll see you at the clubhouse for dinner. When Pop brings you back, you listen to May May. No Lip, okay?"

"Yes, Mom. I got it." Brett insisted.

Mary wore her costume throughout the day. As the protocol stated, Jean also wore a costume. She was quite the attractive "medieval maiden". They both had the attention of many guests, as they hosted some of the games set up for them. All the games had incentives that gradually sold off every lot left in Camelot. Before five o'clock, Mary had fulfilled her promise to King Arthur.

Cliff, dressed as King Arthur, came up the stairwell to applause. He even had a broadsword that garnered the attention of many. He came to Jean's side, who many "dubbed" Guinevere. Jean blushed and waved away from herself.

The costumed guests arrived for the evening's soiree. A gorilla, a vampire, a Bavarian couple wearing Lederhosen. All sorts of extravagant attired guests slowly came in. Mary had hired a local photographer and prepared a place for the guests to have their photos taken. As dinnertime approached, Mary wondered about Wally. Where was he?

Wally had been mingling with the guests throughout the day. Dressed in his normal "business casual" attire, he greeted guests as they arrived. Many had asked, "what are you?", and he would reply, "I'm the Big Chief here." Mary just shook her head. Eventually Mary lost track of him and didn't see him as the evening approached.

Suddenly, a drum began to beat. One bartender had donned a twin-feathered headband, similar to Mary's. The man was dancing in circles and beating the drum that he held under one arm.

Then the chanting started, "Hey, Ya, Yah, Hey, Ya, Yah". It came from the office stairwell. As the chanting continued, Wally came up the steps. He was dressed just as Big Chief, war-bonnet to the floor. He danced over to the bartender with the drum…"Hey, Ya, Yah, Hey, Ya, Yah", as they danced around each other. Wally suddenly stopped, stood tall, and crossed his arms. "Big Chief is Here!" he proclaimed, as the room broke into applause.

Cliff walked up to Wally at the bar. "So Big Chief came after all?" He asked.

"Yeah, I guess so. He actually loaned this to me. I think he felt bad that he couldn't come. While Tommy was trying on Mary's costume, Big Chief came out with this for me. I was going to dress as a cowboy, but I couldn't pass this one up." Wally explained.

Cliff curled one cheek. "You might want to change that story, and not include Tommy, next time you tell it to anyone." He asserted.

"Yeah, sorry. Where is Mary? We should get our picture before dinner." Wally asked.

"Oh, you mean "The Real Merlin?" Cliff prided. "The woman sold the last lot an hour ago. She's already referring to The Manor restaurant, as "Maggie's", and says it'll be open in three months. I'll tell you what, Wally. You better get your shit straight. Cuz, I'm going to need you both, when we start building the cabins, and eventually move on to Pigeon Forge. Got it?" Cliff made his message clear.

Wally, looking humbled, replied, "I got it. I'm working things out. Can we celebrate?"

"By all means! Chris, a round on "The King" please!" Cliff announced.

A few close to them cheered, "All hail the King!"

Cliff smiled and poured down his drink. Wally did the same, turned and looked for his Indian princess.

Chapter 11 –

Nashville, Summer 1829

The pastor stood before them both. "Do you William Edward Blackwell, take this woman to be your lawfully wedded wife, to love, to cherish, and protect her, in sickness and in health, for rich or for poor, as long as you both shall live?"

William, holding Sarah's hand, answered, "I do."

The pastor then turned to Sarah. "Do you Sarah Beth Carver, take this man to be your lawfully wedded husband, to love, to cherish, and protect him, in sickness and in health, for rich or for poor, as long as you both shall live?"

Sarah smiled at Will's face. "I DO!" she announced.

The pastor looked up from the book. "As you have spoken these vows, in the house of the Lord, your commitment to each other, and to God, has been bound. I pronounce you, husband and wife. May God bless you both."

William and Sarah turned toward their guests. With their arms interlocked, the newly married couple smiled and took a bow. As the room applauded, Doctor Carver stepped forward. Extending a hand to Will, the professor said,

"William, I was beginning to wonder if any man would meet Sarah stringent expectations. I wish you all the best, my son."

"Thank You, Sir. With your permission, sir, I'd like to take Sarah to Hawkins County, to meet my parents." Will inquired.

Doctor Carver laughed. "Son, she's your princess now. Good luck with that." As he continued to laugh, he said, "Your studies will be here when you return. Don't be gone long, though. You can get behind quickly."

"Understood, Sir. We'll leave at first light, and we'll be back within a week. Thank you, sir." Will explained.

The professor's face changed. "Will, in uniform!…and I'll send three men with you. They'll be in uniform as well. They don't converse much. So, don't waste your time trying. They'll camp. Just give them a place to do so."

It was now that Will's demeanor changed. "Sir, I-." Abruptly interrupted by Doctor Carver holding up his hand. Carver gave Will a stern look. "It's for the both of you, Will. You are both too important to too many people. You'll find out soon enough, but your "calling" is close at hand."

Before Will could say another word, Sarah spun him and kissed him on the lips. Most of the small crowd of women around them laughed, with a few shaking their heads in disapproval. Sarah did it again. Will, believing that she did out-of-spite.

They finished the evening at the Carver's residence. Carver's servants had created a spread of roast leg-of-pork, cornbread, stewed turnip greens, and "Hoppin John", a rice and black-eyed peas mix. They served dinner on the lawn in front of the residence and drinks inside afterward. Knowing that Will and Sarah were leaving early, Doctor Carver conveniently shortened the celebration.

Before Will and Sarah retired to their new quarters, a few doors away, Doctor Carver called Will over to his side. Walking over to his new father-in-law, Will recognized the man next to him. He was tall and looked like he had worked on the railroad. His chest and shoulders were large. His legs filling his trousers fully. He was one of the men he remembered seeing that day in Nashville. One of the three that followed him and Sarah around town.

"Will, this is Corporal Stanfield Heath. They call him "Bear". He will be accompanying Sarah, and yourself, to Hawkins County. He'll meet you out front tomorrow with another trusted friend. There will be a third. But you may not see him until you reach Hawkins County. Trent'll be out in front of you. I know you are familiar with the natives. But I also know that you've had misfortune with them. Bear, Trent, and Michael, will make sure that you have safe passage. Godspeed, my son." The Professor proclaimed as he extended his hand.

Will shook both hands that were presented to him, then returned to his wife. Sarah looked impatient, but Will's mind was elsewhere. "Bear", Trent, Michael,… surely these were the three that Will recalled from downtown Nashville. But they changed clothes, or at least Will thought they had. "Are they all as big as Bear?" Will wondered. "Are they just soldiers, or something else?" "Why does it seem that they report to Doctor Carver?" Will's mind raced.

"William Blackwell!" Sarah exclaimed. "I have dropped my kerchief and you have yet to pick it up!"

Will looked down, and sure enough, there lay Sarah's kerchief. He bent down to pick it up. When he stood, he quickly noticed that one of Sarah's dress sleeves was off of her shoulder. As he attempted to pull it back up, Sarah stopped him. Confused, he looked at her face.

"My love, that happened when I dropped my kerchief. Would I get your attention, if I continue to drop my kerchief?" Sarah asked.

Will smiled. "You would, my dear. But let's not drop the kerchief here. Let us retire,…where you can drop your kerchief as many times as you like." Will grinned.

Walking away, they heard the light clapping of a few, and Sarah, once again, smiled from ear-to-ear.

The morning seemed to come quickly to Will. They had packed prior to the wedding, and Sarah had laid out their traveling clothes. Unfortunately, Tad was obligated to dress as the Professor requested. To his surprise, the uniform still fit him. With Sarah attempting to "fatten him up for the slaughter", he was sure that the trousers would not fit. They were tight, but manageable. Cinching his sash and placing his sword in the scabbard, he adjusted his hat and checked on Sarah.

"Dearest Sarah, can I help you with anything?" Will asked.

"Yes! Since you seemed to be so damn good at taking this off, can you help me get this corset on?" Sarah requested.

"Certainly, Love." Will replied. "And please just don a bonnet. We'll be traveling for two days and my family will love you anyway you arrive."

Before long, they were stepping out of their residence.

Waiting for them outside was Bear. He climbed down from the Brougham carriage and addressed Will. "Lieutenant, let's lose the hat. We're not in a parade. I suppose the rest is fine. I wasn't sure if you had one, so I bought you a side arm. Do you have a belt and holster?" Bear inquired.

Will looked the pistol over as he'd never held one. "No. I do not. The only weapon that we leave West Point with is our sword." Will replied.

"We'll get you one from the armory. Set your bags by your feet and step in." Bear instructed.

Will had been in an enclosed carriage only twice before. He helped Sarah into the carriage, and then he stepped in. Bear unbuttoned the leather window curtain and folded it down. He closed the door, and peered in. "Both of you, listen up. The Lieutenant is supposed to be in charge. But, if you want to stay alive, you need to listen to me. Do what I say, and when I say it. Do you understand?" Bear affirmed.

Will looked at Sarah, but she only looked at Bear. They both replied, "Yes."

Riding away from the campus, Will's mind again raced. "Why does a school have an armory? Why do Sarah and I get an escort to Hawkins County? What in the world is that uniform that Bear is wearing?" Will wondered.

Bear not only acquired a holster for Will, but he also put two rifles in the cab. Sarah looked at them with disgust. "Can those things just "go off?" she asked.

"No, Dear. They cannot. I suppose, if the hammer was back, it could, but I don't even think those are loaded. That leather bag has the balls and powder." Will said, to set Sarah's mind at ease. He knew they were loaded.

Michael rode up alongside them soon after they cleared Nashville. Will watched him ride. He was smooth. He indeed was large, just like Bear. His clothing resembled a United States military uniform, but he wore a leather hat with no markings. He appeared to have regulation gloves and boots that were almost "new". This seemed odd to Will, as most enlisted men did not receive "new" uniforms. As Will watched Michael, he noticed the man was constantly looking in all directions. He never focused "ahead". Will quickly realized that this was a good trait and wondered how one learns that "trait".

They rode throughout the day, rarely resting. When they did rest, Bear would water the horses, while Michael stood "watch". Ever vigilant, with his rifle carried with both hands. Sarah and Will were told to stay close to the carriage, which made Sarah nervous.

"Its okay sweetheart. These men obviously know what they are doing. I believe we are in excellent hands." Will reassured her.

At one point, Will noticed Bear pull a small object from his shirt pocket, then used it to reflect sunlight. Will then noticed that there was a flash from a ravine, almost a mile away. "Trent?" Will asked.

"Good." Is all Bear said.

Climbing back into the cab of the carriage, Will asked Sarah if she wanted a drink of water from a canteen. She quickly snatched the canteen. "Easy, Dear. We've still got a long way to go." Will explained.

Sipping slowly, Sarah quizzed Will, "Where will we stay tonight?"

Corking the canteen, Will sat next to Sarah. "Bear says we're staying with a friend near the Cumberland Mountains. He said that you will have a bed, but the rest of us will rest outside." Will looked out at Bear. "I've been watching our escorts. They handle themselves as well as any fighter I've seen. While some of their tactics seem unorthodox, They're quite resourceful. Hell, I watched Bear talk to Trent over a mile away! They communicate with mirrors. I know we are in good hands, Love."

Sarah looked out the window. "I hope so. Father says we are traveling directly through Indian territory. He says that there is a heightened danger with the homesteader's impending movement west. I mean, your own sister was killed. Are you frightened, Will?" Her voice was solemn and low.

"No, dear. The Cherokee are mostly passive. That's mostly who we would encounter. The Creek, on the other hand, can be a bit more barbarous. That's who killed Cecilia,…in South Carolina. Since moving to East Tennessee, my father says they have only had friendly encounters. He says they can be pushy, but not violent. We'll be fine, love." Will comforted Sarah, knowing that he was lying.

Arriving at the base of the Cumberland Mountain range gave Will some comfort. They came upon a small cabin. Standing at the front of the cabin was a man in woodsmen's clothing. Leather blouse and trousers, with a leather hat. Unlike most of the woodsmen that Will had met, he was clean-shaven. "Colonel Crockett, It's good to see you!" Bear called out.

The Colonel stayed where he was until Bear, Michael, Will, and Sarah approached him. "You have one more Bear?" the Colonel inquired.

"Yes sir. Trent is up top. He'll be down after a bit and Michael will go up. This one of your get-aways?" Bear asked.

The Colonel turned to look at the little cabin. "Yeah, one of 'em. When I come through, some are still standin', some ain't. Hell, I had one in Franklin County that a Cherokee chief took as his own."

Bear laughed. "I suppose, you got it back?" He asked.

The Colonel was shaking his head. "Naah! He kept better care of it, and now my visits to Franklin come with a home-cooked meal. He tries to make me sleep in his bed. But I always refuse because his damn wife is there, nude!"

He and Bear laughed. "Who do I have the honor of hosting tonight?"

Bear turned to introduce Will and Sarah. "Lieutenant William Blackwell, and his lovely wife Sarah. The Lieutenant is attending the medical school at the capital. William, Sarah, this is Colonel David Crockett."

William stepped forward to shake the Colonel's hand. "Blackwell. I know that name…and please, call me Davy. Bear and I met in the Tennessee militia, and he tends to think that he still reports to me. I now report to all of you. I'm Representative in the U S House, Tennessee, of course." Crockett explained.

Will instantly recognized the need to respect the man in front of him. "Representative Crockett, it is an honor to meet you sir. I know the name well. My family settled in Hawkins County. Just North of Rogersville, where I believe you have kin. I can't thank you enough for the resting place." Will asserted.

"It's nothing special, but it'll keep the rain off your head, and your lovely wife can stay warm tonight. Lieutenant, you can sleep inside, if you like. Bear, the boys, and I will stay out here. I don't expect anything tonight, but an Indian friend of mine, Redhawk, will probably be by at any time. He'll let us know of any local tribes that might be getting a bit rowdy." Crockett responded.

Will gave Crockett a perplexed look. "A bit rowdy?" he asked.

"Yeah. We've got many members of Congress that are pushing for this "Indian Removal Act". They're trying to make the tribes from here to Florida move into the Oklahoma Territory. It's hogwash, and I'm fighting it. Hell, there's already Indians in Oklahoma. So, some of the local tribes have heard of it, and they are a bit pissed. Wouldn't you be Lieutenant?" Crockett challenged.

Will frowned. "Sorry Representative, you're preaching to the wrong parishioner. The Creek raped and killed my sister. I have little sympathy for the savages. If alright with you, I'd just as soon stay out here with you guys." Will stated.

Crockett nodded his head and began walking towards a clearing. Climbing out of a creek bed, Will saw a Native American on horseback. Neither the Native American nor Davy Crockett seemed alarmed by the other. They met in the clearing, and the Native American climbed down from his horse. They both gestured as they spoke to each other. Will noticed the Native American pointing in different directions as they continued communicating.

Bear was unbridling the carriage horses, and Michael had already taken the saddle from his, setting it near a stone-circled fire pit. Will continued watching the U S Representative, and his visitor.

Suddenly, Sarah cried out, "William!". Will instantly pulled his pistol and ran into the cabin. In the corner of the cabin was a raccoon, just as startled as Sarah.

Bear, almost beating Will to the door, barked out. "Don't! Don't waste your ammo….or give anyone a reason to investigate." He had a large knife in his right hand. "Let's give him a free pathway to the outside. Come on over here." Bear explained as he pulled Will, and then Sarah, from the path. The critter instantly burst through the doorway, and out it went.

"Let me check the chimney first, but if you get a fire started, he'll leave you be." Bear offered.

Realizing that he'd just be "in the way" of Bear's attempt to make Sarah comfortable, Will went out to see if he could help Michael.

Michael had already prepared the fire pit and was using some flint rocks to strike a blaze. Crockett was coming back across the clearing, and the native was nowhere to be seen.

"What did he say?" Will inquired as Crockett came walking back.

"Oh, it's just as I suspected. There's rumors starting, and some are not happy. Redhawk says that some tribes are pretty mad. He says that they will not abide by the "white-man's law, and it's not even "law" yet. Besides, I'm not even sure that it would be legal. My colleagues and I are reviewing the "legal side" of it. Well, at any rate, it sounds like we don't have to worry about it tonight. Redhawk says that the only tribe that would bother us is around Sevier County. We'll be fine." Crockett assured them. "In fact, I'm going to hike up and bring Trent down. If you all want to get that fire prepped for a pot, I'll get something together when I get back."

***

Afraid to ask what was in the stew that Crockett and Bear had prepared, Will quietly ate. If asked though, he would have to admit that it was quite tasty. Will continued his inquiries about the local natives. His concern was mostly about his parents. But part of him desired to return to Hawkins County, and call it "home" one day. As the discussion carried on, Will became annoyed with Crockett's continued defense of the "Indians".

"Representative Crockett, you continue to claim that this land was the Indians land before it was ours. But yet they have no deeds to the land to prove ownership. In fact, they seem to migrate, at times, only to return to land after it has been claimed." Will argued.

"It's not ours to "claim", Lieutenant. This cabin is not mine. It belongs to the land. One day, the land may take it back. My point is,…if land has a tribe living on it, before we attempt to settle it… well then, that land, it's, well, it's theirs. Lieutenant Blackwell, I've spent more time than you can imagine out here in the wilderness. "Respect" is what allows visitors to survive. Whether it is the copperhead, the black bear, or the Native American, I just believe that they all need to be respected." Crockett concluded.

Defiantly, Will shook his head, stood to stoke the fire, and refuted, "Well, you obviously have not had you sister killed by the damn savages!"

Davy Crockett did not reply. He just sat on a log, looking at the flames.

***

Will awoke on the wooden porch. The sun was rising, and the birds sang. He looked for the others. Seeing no one, he stood up and adjusted his clothing. He knocked on the cabin door. "Sarah, it's Will. Probably oughta get up and get ready. These boys'll want to get going early." he instructed.

"Yes, dear. I'll need your help in about five minutes though." Sarah replied.

"Okay, I'm going to check on them." Will informed her.

Will walked out by the smoldering fire. Both Trent and Michael's saddles were no longer by the fire,…and their horses were missing. He suddenly heard a twig snap. Before he could turn around, he was pulled to the ground. Bear had a large knife at his throat. "If I'm Indian, or some other bad guy, I just killed you. You have to be vigilant Lieutenant!" Bear claimed.

As Bear lay on top of Will, he heard the click of a pistol beneath him. "The worst part of it would be you dying on top of me Corporal." Will whispered.

"Nice Lieutenant." Bear affirmed, as he lifted himself from the much smaller man. "We need to bridle-up and get going in the next ten minutes. Crockett, Trent, and Michael are all out in front of us. Crockett'll turn back soon, so we may pass him. By the way Lieutenant, Indians slaughtered Crockett's grandparents…not far from your home in Hawkins County. Just thought you should know." Bear commented, turning and heading for the horses.

Will stood for a moment contemplating what he had said the night before, then he started heading for the horses, until he heard Sarah call out. "William, I need you." Will turned back.

After assisting Sarah with her corset, Will stepped back outside. Bear had already bridled one horse and was working on the other. As Will attempted to help, Bear stopped him. "Lieutenant, I'm quicker by myself, thanks. Oh, and don't shoot the Indian that looks like Redhawk. Crockett asked him to help us to Rogersville."

"Why would he do that?" Will inquired.

"Because he was asked to." Bear replied sarcastically.

They traveled for about half an hour before they passed Crockett, heading in the other direction. Neither stopped. The representative nodded to Will as they passed and continued on.

Will felt remorseful. Sarah could tell. "William, what's wrong? You look as if you've done something wrong." Sarah quizzed.

"I'm afraid I have, my dear. I tend to disregard the opinion of others who I feel do not understand my cause. Whereas, I should listen and respect the causes of others. That man was nothing short of a protector to us, and I disrespected him by my own ignorance. I hope, one day, to meet him again. I owe him an apology." Will solemnly explained.

Sarah laid her hand on his and squeezed. She laid her head on his shoulder for comfort. Will sighed. "I would not have married you, If I didn't think you were a good man, William." Sarah encouraged. Again, Will sighed.

They passed through Jacksboro and Tazewell before reaching Rogersville by early evening, Trent and Michael riding beside them for the final half hour. Once in Rogersville, Bear asked if they needed to stop for any provisions. Will agreed, so they stopped at McKinney's Tavern and General Store.

"This is a quaint little town." Sarah exclaimed.

"Just a little less than an hour ride to my family's homestead. You'll soon meet my parents, and my little brother. They're gonna love you, my sweet." Will kissed her on the cheek. Sarah smiled.

***

Will noticed Trent and Michael disappeared during the short ride to the Blackwell homestead. He thought it strange. They were merely miles from his parents. Thinking they were well past any danger, he leaned forward. "Hey Bear?" Will inquired.

"Yes, Lieutenant?" Bear replied.

"Why'd Trent and Michael head out?" Will questioned.

"Look for Indians, Lieutenant." Bear claimed.

Will sat back for a moment, then leaned forward again. "But we're between Rogersville, and my home. Can there really be Indians, here?"

"Oh, there out there. You just can't see them. Never let your guard down, Lieutenant. That's when shit gets sideways." Bear explained.

Will sat back, looked out the window, and raised a brow. He continued looking and began to focus on the top of the ridgeline. He saw movement. Continuing to focus, he recognized the absolute calm. Then the shiftiness. A deer. Then he saw movement again. "What was that", he thought. It was coming down the mountain, right at them.

"Coming down the mountain, Bear! To your right!" Will cried out.

"That's Trent, Lieutenant." Bear said calmly.

Trent came riding up beside them. "Three, up top. 'Bout a quarter out. I'm dropping behind. Mike's pulling point. We're thinking Stoney Crest, Bear."

Starting into a slow gallop, Bear kept looking straight ahead. "Stoney Crest, it is Trent. You want another rifle?" Bear asked.

"Yeah." Trent replied.

"Lieutenant, hand Trent one those rifles." Bear instructed.

Will grabbed one of the rifles. "You want me to load it, right?"

"They're already loaded, Lieutenant." Bear clarified.

Will handed the rifle to Trent as they continued down the path. Trent tucked it behind him and pulled back on his reins.

Will looked back at a startled Sarah. "I thought you said-"

"Hush, hon." Will interrupted her. "Bear, where do you want me?" Will asked.

"Sit back, Lieutenant. Relax, and stay calm…but vigilant. It's the only thing that will get you through "the fight"…which I doubt we'll have."

Will sat back and thought about what Bear had said. He looked at Sarah. She was obviously nervous. He calmly put a hand on each of her cheeks and gave her a kiss. "It's all good, sweetheart. I promise."

***

The next twenty minutes seemed to last forever, but they reached the homestead safely. Bear pulled the carriage right up to the main cabin. The wheels of the carriage almost touched the crossboards of the porch.

Will's father came out and looked at Bear. "What the hell, son. Think you pulled up close enough!?" He barked.

"Father!" Will shouted. "Corporal Heath knows what he's doing. Please do not reprimand him. Oh, and good to see you, too."

Will stepped out and helped Sarah onto the porch. Sarah stepped down, and looked up at an elderly man, and a homely dressed woman. The man looked haggard. His face wrinkled and cracked, but with a twinkle in his eye that was quite noticeable. The woman was different, though. Her face was beautiful, her body tall, and thin. Although her dress was not, she held herself in an almost "regal" manner. She was much younger than her husband.

"Mother, Father, this is my wife, Sarah." Will boasted with a smile. "Sarah, this is Ezra, and Louisa Blackwell, my parents."

Sarah took Ezra's extended hand and curtsied. She then did the same to Louisa. "It is a pleasure to meet the fine parents of the man that has taken my heart." Sarah asserted.

The introduction went silent as Ezra and Louisa seemed entranced by Sarah's presence. Ezra finally broke the silence. "Come, come inside. Louisa will fix up Jonathan's room for you. I can fix up a bed for that big fella in the barn after a bit. You two sit down and have some tea. Are you hungry?"

Bear didn't even introduce himself. In fact, by the time Ezra shifted his attention to Bear, he was already guiding the carriage towards the largest barn. "Hey there, fella. I'll help you", Ezra called out. Bear held up a hand, showing that "he did not need help".

"That fella don't seem too friendly." Ezra declared.

Will smiled. "They're soldiers, Father. They do their job, and that's about it. You can offer, but they'll find their own place to rest. We'll stay for two or three nights, then head back to the Academy." Will explained.

"They?" Ezra inquired.

"Yeah, there's two more that'll eventually make their way down. They're on "sentry", watching for the Indians." Will confirmed.

Ezra looked out, though the valley, then up at the ridgeline. "If them boys are looking for trouble, they'll find it. The Cherokee seemed to get a little more raucous since The Creek been moving through. They leave us alone, though. Ma and I leave them corn, vegetables, and some moonshine out at the end of the valley. That seems to keep them "away"." Ezra touted.

"They'll stay away from them, Father. Besides, I don't think that the Indians want anything to do with them either. Come, let's go in. I want to visit with Mother and Sarah.

As Will and Ezra stepped into the cabin, Louisa was helping Sarah out of her corset. Ezra immediately covered his eyes. "Oh, Lord. I'll step outside." He proclaimed.

Sarah laughed. "Father. Have you never seen a woman, in her undergarments? I'm still completely covered, you know…and much more comfortable than in this darned dress." Sarah divulged.

Will was smiling too. "It's okay, Father. Sarah is a lady, but far from bashful. She'll not be offended, unless you are. Tell me Father, how is young Jonathan?" Will inquired.

"Jonathan is like you William. He's a workhorse. He's down at Mount Sterling right now, so you'll be in his room. Been kinda quiet around here, without him for the last week. He's down there helping to get some hay in. In order to make some money, he worked his ass off to get ours in early. He'll be back in a couple days, but I'm afraid that you'll miss him." Ezra explained.

Finally, climbing out of her dress, Sarah spoke. "How old is Jonathan?"

"Let's see, he'll be fifteen in a few months. Ain't that right, Ma?" Ezra asked his wife.

"Yes, dear." Louisa replied.

"Fifteen and already working on farms. Quite impressive." Sarah asserted.

"William was the same way. Up until he got that offer to West Point." Ezra contended. "He worked over at Jonesborough for three summers. Somehow, he impressed the right particulars and they took him away from us. I guess he did alright at West Point, though. Now over at a medical school? Ain't never had no doctor in the family. When you gonna actually be a "doctor", Will?" Ezra asked.

"Well Father, I have studies for another two years, but Sarah's father has me pulling double-duty. I thought that he was originally doing that, to keep me away from his daughter." Will chuckled.

"That's not true, William!" Sarah claimed.

Will was furrowing his brow at Sarah, then continued. "I may only have another year. But then, I've agreed to serve with the Army. I'm sure that I'll be placed, as a "surgeon", somewhere. I'm just not sure where that may be. Hopefully, near here. I heard that there is a fort up in Blountville. That'd be nice. Don't you think, Mother?"

"That'd make me quite happy, my son." Louisa agreed.

Bear, Trent, and Michael had settled into the barn. Each of them, taking shifts to "patrol". The trail through the valley was almost a mile and a half long. Staying on the trail was logical but went against their training. So, each would ascend the North ridge, walk along that ridge until the end of the valley. Then, they'd drop down and descend the south ridge, taking it all the way back to the homestead.

The Blackwell homestead was larger than most in the area. With the natural valley being flat, and protected from much adverse weather by the northern and southern mountain ridgelines that extended the length of the homestead property. The mountain ridgelines were a natural barrier to weather adversity, and provided beautiful views. Since serving in the Revolutionary War, Ezra had gotten most of the land through a Military Land Grant. The ground was quite fertile, with a large creek supplying endless water for the crops and livestock. Ezra, Louisa, and Will had dammed the creek on the northeast entrance to the homestead, which created a large pond. With the help of other locals, the Blackwells had a reasonably sized cabin, and two barns.

***

Bear returned from his patrol and shook Trent. "You're up, Trent. I got a small fire going out back. There's coffee on." Bear started to lay down on his wool blanket. "Oh, I ran into Redhawk on the south ridgeline. He says that he's staying until we go back. Take some of that bacon with you. I'm sure he'll eat it." Bear requested, eyes already closing. "All looked clear. Didn't see nuthin' but Redhawk."

Sarah woke up to the smell of bacon. Will had somehow snuck out before she woke up. She put on a light dress, house shoes, and tied her hair back. Stepping out into the main cabin, she saw Louisa at the fireplace.

"Can I help?" Sarah asked.

Louisa turned, but stayed kneeling. "Certainly, my dear. Can you mix the cornmeal and starter? Roll them into biscuits and place them in that "spider-skillet". I'll finish up this bacon. Oh, and dear. Thank you for saving our son. I was losing hope, but he has come home with the most beautiful and kind person ever." Louisa declared.

"Certainly, Mother. I'll get these made. By the way, I love Will more than you can imagine. I hope to give you many grandchildren, and I know they'll be beautiful too. Just like their grandmother." Sarah claimed.

Louisa smiled and turned the bacon.

After splitting logs, feeding the cows, pigs, and chickens, Will joined the family for the first meal of the day. "You know, I didn't expect you to come here and work all day, William." Ezra asserted.

"I know, Father. After I take some food to the boys, Sarah and I will take a long walk around the property. Maybe, we can all go into Rogersville, for a proper supper?" Will inquired.

"Proper!" Louisa exclaimed.

"William!" Sarah chastised.

Will's face had turned red with embarrassment. "I'm sorry, Mother. That did not come out right. What I meant to say was that I would like to take you and Father into town for supper. It may not be as good as yours, Mother, but I would like for Sarah and I to take you to dinner." He said apologetically.

Looking at Will intently, Louisa replied. "Not necessary, William, but we'll wait and see. Eat up. This young lady needs an escort around the homestead." She directed.

"I can take her." Ezra offered.

Louisa looked at Ezra with eyes wide and hands slightly raised. "Ezra, these two were just married. Will you let your son escort his own wife around property that will be theirs one day?"

Ezra shrugged his shoulders, returning to his meal.

Sarah looked at Will from across the table. Her slight smile made him do the same. Then Louisa followed. They immediately began to giggle. Ezra looked up and shook his head in confusion.

Will and Sarah brought food out to the barn for Bear, Trent, and Michael. Seeing the smoke from behind the barn, they approached and saw Michael drinking coffee from a tin cup. "Bear around?" Will asked.

Michael watched them walk his way. "He's sleeping. You need something?" He inquired.

"We have food for you guys." Will said as they set down the baskets. "Me and the Missus, are gonna walk the property. If that's okay?"

Michael was walking over to the baskets and took a knee. Not looking up, he said, "I assume you know the property. So far, the only Indian we've seen is Redhawk. He's hanging with us until we leave. You might see him…or Trent. Although Trent should be coming in at any time. So, you may see me. Thank you for the grub. You'll be safe. Enjoy your walk." Michael affirmed, as he rummaged through the fresh food.

Will and Sarah set out across the valley. Will explained the "lay of the land" and how he had hoped to return to build them a large home someday. Sarah smiled throughout Will's guide across the property. She enjoyed hearing his "hopes, dreams, and promises". They all included her and the many children that they hoped to have.

Circling back across the southern ridgeline, they saw Michael talking to Redhawk. They waved, but kept walking. Descending the ridgeline became cumbersome for Sarah. Her light dress helped, but nevertheless, it was cumbersome. There were small cliffs and "cuts" in the rock where sections of the cliffs had fallen away, leaving crevasses they had to jump over. "Where are you taking me, William?" Sarah challenged.

"To my secret place. A place that I used to go, when I was little." Will revealed.

Will guided her as they descended and eventually came to an opening in a cliff. "It's a cave William. How neat. Can we go in?" Sarah asked.

William grabbed Sarah by the hand. "Sure. It's straight for about twenty or thirty feet. After that, it turns. Then it gets real dark. We'll go inside the front of it. Come, let me show you."

They sauntered into the cave. It was bigger than she had expected. Probably ten feet wide, there were sections of rock lying on the cave floor, some as big as a sow. Sarah, holding William's hand tightly, slowly loosened her grip. After about fifteen feet, Sarah said, "Stop." She turned to Will, pulled him close, and kissed him.

***

At the cabin, having no intention of going to Rogersville, Louisa was preparing a few things for supper. Ezra was across the valley cutting up a dead tree.

Will and Sarah stepped into the cabin. Will walked to his mother and gave her a kiss on the cheek. Louisa smiled. "Did you two have a pleasant walk?" She inquired.

"We did. Sarah showed me where she wants us to build our home. The children can run between our house and yours. She says that she could already "see" them. Will boasted.

Louisa was facing Will by now and looking past him as Sarah poured a glass of water. "Well, that is a beautiful thought…and it looks to me like that might happen sooner than later." She claimed.

Will turned and chuckled.
Sarah, watching Will and Louisa chuckling at her said, "What are you two laughing at?"

Louisa was covering her mouth and starting to laugh harder. "My dear,…your entire backside is covered in coal dust. Come, lets' get you into one of my dresses." Louisa offered.

Sarah pulled on her dress and twisted her body. She grinned. "Oops", is all she said, and laughed, as well.

Louisa took her to the bedroom. After finding a different dress for Sarah to wear, Louisa instructed Will to take her down to the creek to get the coal dust from her arms and legs. Louisa said that she'd bring down the dress, a bucket, and some lye, so that they could wash up the dress. When Will and Sarah set out from the porch, Louisa called them back.

From the porch, Louisa gave each of them a kiss on the cheek. "I love you both! Just wanted you to know." Louisa stated, smiling the biggest smile that Will had ever seen on his mother.

***

They spent the next day, like the first. Helping with chores and taking "their walk" around the property, Louisa gave them a light blanket that she said she'd gladly wash instead of another dress.

The morning of the third day came too quickly for all. Even "the boys" had seemed to lighten up a bit. As they packed up the carriage and horses, Will noticed Bear's demeanor change. He concentrated and stopped being lighthearted.

As they all stood on the front porch, Louisa commented about the mounted Indian that she could see far across the valley. "I hope that's Redhawk." She didn't seem too concerned, as the Indian just sat, and watched them. She then turned to Sarah. "Sarah, dear, you are my daughter now. This is your home, any time that you wish to stay, it will be here for you. Nothing would make me happier than to see you two build a home here and let me help care for your little ones. Watch after this rascal that you married, my dear. He's a good one, but he's a rascal, nonetheless." They embraced.

"Son, not a day will go by where I won't think about you two. You be safe returning to your studies. We'll be here, when you can visit again." Ezra extended his hand. As he shook his son's hand, he continued. "Thank you, boys, for watching over my son and new daughter. May God watch over you always. I'm forever in your debt. If you ever need a place to stay, my home is yours." Ezra claimed, looking at Bear, Trent, and Michael.

Will walked over to his mother. "Mother, please tell Jonathan that we miss him, and we'll be back to see him. We love you all, so hold down the fort for us. We'll be back soon enough.

Trent and Michael had already mounted when Sarah and Will climbed into the carriage. Trent led them towards the Indian, and out of the end of the valley.

Chapter 12 –

"Two Roads" – Nashville, Spring 1930

"Lieutenant William Edward Blackwell, please approach the council." Doctor Carver instructed.

Will was standing in a long "gathering" room. Often used for lectures, today it had but one lone student, facing twelve administrators of Cumberland Medical Academy. The Chancellor, Academy Dean, Chair of Anatomy, Chair of Surgery, Dean of Medicine, Secretary of Faculty, and five assorted Professors, and Trustees. Doctor Carver was unanimously picked to present the title of Medical Doctor to Will.

He thought he would be nervous, standing before them. On the contrary, he was quite calm, and they noticed it.

Doctor Carver continued, "William Edward Blackwell, you have successfully completed the requirements outlined by this academy. In so doing, it is my honor to present to you,…your diploma. This document has been signed by the Chancellor, Dean, and faculty here. My son, and I believe I can call you son." Doctor Carver turned to his colleagues and snickered. A light laughter erupted, then quickly subsided. "William, we at Cumberland Medical

Academy, are very proud to have had your presence. A graduate of West Point, an exemplary student, and a fine young man. You are the epitome of what type of student had hoped would come our way. A "little bird" told me, upon graduation, you will join General Winfield Scott. Joining the General's Surgeon Corps will undoubtedly allow you to gain more experience. With that, William, I will give you the opportunity to speak."

Will stepped forward, removed his uniform gloves, then squeezed them with both hands. "Chancellor Kelly, Dean Thompson, Doctor Carver, and all my respected professors, and colleagues. It is my honor to be with you today. It has been my honor to study under all of you. When I came to Cumberland, I didn't know what to expect. In fact, I thought I was coming here for a completely different purpose. But I saw myself growing with this academy. The respect that I have for this institution is only surpassed by the love of my dear wife, Sarah. Today I stand humbly before you. While I may not have the experience that many of you have, I am an amalgamation of all of you. That said, I firmly believe that your experience has transcended to me, and I know I can be better than any single doctor out there today because I learned from all of you. I thank you colleagues for this gift. I will make you proud. Thank you." Will lowered his hands to his side.

There was a long pause. A few colleagues whispered disapproval of Will's speech. Finally, Doctor Carver spoke. "Doctor William Edward Blackwell, would you please step forward and sign your diploma?"

As Will did so, all applauded. A few stood. A few did not.

Doctor Carver walked back towards the residences with Will. "William, I must say, your speech roughed a few feathers."

"Oh, how so, father?" Will inquired.

"Well, some took your statements as you being better than them." Carver explained.

"Good. That's what I meant. If you think about it, it's true. If you study with a combination of the "best", you will be better." Will contended.

The doctor stopped walking. Putting his hand on Will's shoulder, he began, "Son, it doesn't work that way, and I think you know that. Listen, Sarah is going to Franklin tonight with my assistant, Lucy. Why don't you come over for dinner and a cigar?"

"Sure, Father. That sounds great. Six?" Will asked.

"Yes, William." Carver replied. The Doctor suddenly looked tense and hurried towards the residence. Will noticed it. He was beginning to notice a lot of things. It was something that Bear taught him…vigilance.

Will went home to Sarah. She was preparing for her trip to Franklin. "Well, it's official, my dear." Will asserted.

Sarah continued packing a light luggage duffle. "What's that, sweetheart?" She nonchalantly inquired.

"You really don't know?" Will asked.

Sarah stopped her packing, looked at Will, and cocked her head. "Oh, for goodness sakes, Doctor Blackwell. Do you really think I'm that ignorant? I've known longer than you, Mister know-it-all. I only wish that father would not have planned this trip for me. On the very day that my husband becomes a "doctor", no less. I only hope that I'll still be your first patient. I'll be back tomorrow evening, and I plan to be "ill". So please be prepared to work, Doctor Blackwell." Sarah stood grinning at him.

"Your father scheduled this trip?" Will asked.

Sarah again walked around the room, grabbing one item at a time. "Yes, yes. We've talked about it for a while. But then he suddenly planned it about two weeks ago.

Anyway, Love, I'm almost packed. Come over here and give me a proper goodbye, then get out of my way for five more minutes."

Will did as Sarah requested, kissing her, and then exiting the room.

Will waved as he watched the women leave in a carriage. He eyed the driver. A short, stocky man. Not the giant that he remembered the last time he visited Hawkins County. Will had not seen Bear, Trent, or Michael since their return. He was surprised because he thought they had started a friendship.

When Will returned to the residence, he noticed a letter lying on the table. From Sarah, Will read, "*My Love, Do try to behave yourself with father. I miss you already and will be home soon. I so look forward to the next chapter of our lives. I am so proud of you! There is a gift for you in the springhouse. Love, Sarah Beth*".

Will smiled. He then folded the letter and placed it in his pocket. He stepped out and walked to the springhouse. Walking down the steps, Will pushed open the creaking door. Even in the dark springhouse, Will could see the small cask of beer. He smiled again and thought to himself, "Later. After dinner, with Doctor Carver." He then returned to the residence, deciding to take a brief nap prior to dinner.

Arriving at Doctor Carver's residence promptly at six, Doctor Carver's servant, also named William, greeted Will, showing him to the library, where Doctor Carver sat. Doctor Carver stood and greeted Will. "William, welcome. Please come in and have a drink." The doctor insisted.

"Certainly Father." Will graciously accepted. "Father, May I ask you a question?" Will inquired.

Doctor Carver was pouring Will a drink. As he did so, Will noticed something that caught his attention. The bottle… He did not recognize the bottle. He had many a drink with the doctor, but this appeared to be something new. But then, the doctor topped off his own elixir with the same bottle. Will suddenly thought, "It's nothing. I notice too many things that are not important…thanks to Bear."

Doctor Carver walked over to Will. Handing him the drink, he replied, "Certainly, son. You know you can ask me anything. What's bothering you?"

Will took a drink and continued. "Do you know why I was brought to Cumberland?"

"I do, William. I personally believe that there were multiple reasons for your placement here and one of them is by God. I believe you were sent to meet my daughter. But that is not what you are asking, is it William?" The doctor challenged.

Will took another drink. His courage grew. "Sir, I did not expect to meet your beautiful daughter, and I thank God that I did. But I expected a camaraderie that never surfaced." Will explained.

Doctor Carver took a sip of his drink. "How do you know, William? Do we not have a camaraderie?"

Will took another sip of the flavorful liquid. He felt strange, almost in a state of extreme "focus". He looked down at the green color in his glass. The glass appeared tiny. He giggled. He thought, "Wow, if that was a chamber pot, I'd surely miss it". The room twisted. Colors began to merge.

"William, have you come to seek wisdom?" asked Doctor Carver.

Will looked at the doctor. His appearance seemed normal. "Wisdom? Yes, wisdom. That's exactly why I'm here!" Will affirmed.

The doctor took the "tiny" glass from Will's hand. "Well, you found it, my son."

***

Laying on the floor, Will awoke, feeling the cool stone floor beneath his legs.

"I need my letter. My letter from Sarah." Will thought. "Where am I?"

The room was dark and cold. Will touched his chest. He was shirtless. He touched his trousers. Trying to stand, he quickly dropped to his knees. He shook his head as he imagined seeing cloaked shapes enter the room holding candles, the last holding a long broadsword.

Will realized why he was here and dropped his head to acknowledge his understanding.

With three cloaked "knights" on each side of him, Will watched the one with the sword circle around them, and out of his sight.

"William Blackwell, have you come here of your own free will?" the voice asked.

"Yes." Will replied.

"Do you swear allegiance to The Knights of Wisdom?" the voice asked.

"I thought that I already did that." Will replied.

"If your answer is that you will always remain loyal to your prior promise, then you will receive that last rite of The Wisdom. Is this your desire?" the voice asked.

"I do swear to abide by all rites and promises to The Wisdom." Will claimed.

"Above all others?" the voice asked.

Will paused. He thought about this statement. "Surely this does not mean above my wife, or God?" he thought. "Think, Will, think. Oh, to hell with it!" He lifted his head. "YES!" he said.

Will suddenly felt the piercing of his skin as a blade snaked down his back. He wasn't sure how deep it was cutting, but it hurt. After it stopped at the base of his torso, he felt it again as the blade crossed his shoulder blades.

***

Two weeks later, Nashville, Cumberland Medical Academy Yard

Lieutenant Blackwell had said his "goodbyes". It was time for work. Appointed to the rank of First Lieutenant by Governor William Carroll, a close ally of President Andrew Jackson, Blackwell felt "honored". Understanding President Jackson's desire to oust the Native Americans, and further learning about Blackwell's past, Governor Carroll wasted no time in giving Will the promotion. He even made a slight insinuation that Blackwell could be looking at Captain, should his endeavors be "fruitful". Blackwell was to be a platoon leader and would assist in medical needs from time to time, a useful, but rare convenience that his men were glad to have.

Governor Carrol was present for the "send-off". "Lieutenant Blackwell, take good care of these men. The State of Tennessee thanks you for everything that you are about to embark on. Please give Colonel Taylor my regards. He's a good man. You will learn much from him. Godspeed traveling North." The Governor said.

Blackwell did not say a word, only tipped his head and trotted across the campus lawn. Corporal Trent Bettingham quickly strode up alongside him. Thirty-two soldiers stood at attention. Blackwell and Trent strode alongside the troops, stopping at the front of them.

Blackwell barked out, "Company,…Ahhhttention! Prepare to march!" He plodded his horse forward. "Forward!...March!" He belted out.

Trent allowed all the troops to pass him and then he kept his horse at a slow canter, behind them.

Sarah, standing far from her father, started to weep.

***

6 weeks later, Fort Armstrong, Illinois Territory.

As they approached Fort Armstrong, two soldiers intercepted them well before the gate. "Lieutenant Blackwell?" one asked.

Blackwell was walking beside his horse, with a sickly-looking soldier teetering in the saddle above him. "Yes, Private. Can you fetch the doctor, please? This man was bitten by a snake yesterday…and hurry!"

The soldiers appeared to have lost some of their "military" marching cadence, and a few even set down their rifles as they came to a stop.

Blackwell turned to them. "Company,…Attention!" The troops quickly assumed proper military marching positions. "Prepare to march!...Forward, March!" Blackwell commanded.

Entering the fort, one of the Army surgeons met Blackwell. He and Blackwell helped the soldier off Blackwell's horse. Lying him on the ground, Blackwell kneeled, pointing at the soldier's leg. "Doc, I believe I got most of the venom out. But he still took a good bite." Blackwell explained.

From behind Blackwell, a voice called out, "Looks like we have us another doctor. Huh, Doc?" the man declared.

Blackwell stood and turned. Before him was an Army Major, slender, and tall. He extended his hand. "Major

Jonathan Bliss, Lieutenant. Glad to receive you." The Major greeted.

"First Lieutenant William Blackwell, Sir…and yes, doctor, as well. This Company has been under my command for the last six weeks. They are fine men. I believe I am to turn these men over to your command. Please take good care of them, as we've already taken a liking to each other and I'd like to see them right." Blackwell told the Major.

Major Bliss turned to Blackwell's men. "Lieutenant Blackwell, you've got a bit of a rag-tag group here. I watched you marching in. If you want to call it "marching". I think that I'd like to leave these young men in your command for a bit. I would like to see a bit more regiment in them and expect you to train them so."

"Sir, I'd be honored to retain these fine-" Blackwell paused, as he heard a familiar sound of Trent's horse galloping up. He continued. "These fine men. We've already been to battle together and I respect them all. I apologize for their appearance, and I will certainly get them cleaned up."

The Major looked at Trent. "Corporal! Do you not march with your troops?"

Before Trent could speak, Blackwell interrupted. "Again, apologies, Sir. Corporal Bettingham was on reconnaissance, sir. He was, um, scouting, sir."

"Scouting?" The Major cried out. "Scouting,…like an Indian, Lieutenant? Why would he need to "scout" so close to our fort Lieutenant?"

This time, Trent interrupted, "Because there are fifty Sauk Indians gathered about a half mile to our east, sir!" Trent informed him.

Major Bliss looked surprised. "What? How can you be sure, Corporal?" He asked.

Trent looked straight ahead as he sat on his horse. "Because I saw them, sir. I don't believe they saw me. But they were painted, and war-bonneted. Not scouts, sir." He explained.

The Major suddenly turned. "Close the gate! Men to your posts! We may have uninvited visitors!" He barked. "Blackwell, You and your men eat,…rest. We'll talk more later. You're dismissed."

"Thank you, sir." Blackwell saluted, and Major Bliss did the same.

When Blackwell turned to address his men, he was immediately confronted by a Second Lieutenant, sword drawn, and pointing directly at Blackwell's face. "Lieutenant Blackwell, you scoundrel! Not even an invitation to the wedding!"

As the Second Lieutenant kept his sword raised, he heard the clicking of multiple rifles behind him. He slowly lowered his sword. "How is it you spend four years in medical school? Not a single battle, and now you out-rank me, William?"

Blackwell's face was one of pure happiness. "Jefferson Davis! Damn you! How the hell have you been?" Blackwell smiled.

Davis slowly turned and saw Blackwell's men lowering their weapons. "I'm impressed. These men are already prepared to be hung for treason… for you, William."

Blackwell addressed the soldiers. "At ease, men. This is an old friend. Men, you preformed phenomenally on our journey. Major Bliss asks that you remain under my command, for the time being. Lieutenant Davis and I will escort you to the mess hall. Then you will set up camp. I'm not sure where just yet, but we'll find out soon. Stay together and rest. Follow us, men!" Blackwell directed.

Lieutenant Davis waved them towards a building in the center of the camp. "Let's get your men fed." He announced. "William, you'll be living in the officer's quarters. Kind of like the old days, a curtain separating us. But two to a room. So, you are stuck with me!" He chuckled.

That evening, Jefferson and Will caught-up on the years that they'd been apart. Jefferson gladly shared his only Kentucky Bourbon bottle and made sure that his old friend, …and he, finished it. Will enjoyed the opportunity to talk about Sarah. But their conversation eventually took a darker tone as Will led them to discuss the eradication of the Native American Indians. Will allowed the hatred that he'd been harboring for years to be revealed. His hatred of the Native Americans had only grown. He told of a skirmish they had just three weeks earlier. He stopped abruptly, claiming that he "Must write a report for Major Bliss." They ended the night on a pleasant note, with Will toasting to "Jefferson, himself, Albert, and wisdom."

The following morning, Blackwell woke to a bugler and drum call. At first, he was a bit confused, then heard Jefferson rustling across the room. At "roll call", Blackwell took his place next to the other First Lieutenants, standing at attention. Major Bliss walked the officers, then asked them to roll call their troops. Each "sounded off". Blackwell added his soldier in the infirmary and finished with "all present and accounted for, Sir!"

After "roll call" the troops were excused to their duties. Major Bliss came to Blackwell. "Lieutenant, I want to speak to you a bit more about your knowledge of the Sauk Indians, and their habits. Would you please join me?" he asked.

"Yes, Sir. May I ask Corporal Bettingham to join us?" Blackwell returned.

"Does he need to be there, Lieutenant? He is a Corporal, after all." Bliss retorted.

"Sir, Corporal Bettingham knows Indians. He's my most trusted soldier…and to be honest, Sir, he should be a Sargent." Blackwell implored.

Major Bliss smiled, but with a slight smirk. "Very well. The two of you, meet me in my quarters in fifteen."

"Yes, Sir." Blackwell replied.

Blackwell quickly checked that his men were indeed busy with chores, then went to find Trent. Fourteen minutes later, they were at the Major's quarters.

Blackwell knocked. "Come in." He heard.

The Major's quarters were not large, but had a table and four chairs, which Blackwell had not seen in any quarters thus far. He noted the Major's bed was made and had a side table. There was a tall bureau along one wall.

"At ease, gentlemen. I want our meeting to be cordial. Please sit down." Bliss pulled a chair out from the table. "William, please tell me of your experience with the natives."

"Sir, my war experience with the natives is but a skirmish that we had a few weeks back. However, Corporal Bettingham and I had much time to talk. The Corporal has dealt with the natives for over ten years. He has been a member of the Tennessee Volunteer Militia and has learned much. I will speak for him and he can chime in as he sees fit. If that is alright with you, Major." Blackwell requested.

Bliss had taken a seat as well. "Gentlemen, inside these walls, you may call me John, and…yes, Bettingham may speak freely. Please tell me more."

Blackwell shifted in his seat. "Sir, um, John. Trent, Corporal Bettingham, has been using the native's tactics against them for many years. I have seen Trent in action, and his scouting is exemplary. He stays well ahead of us during our march and he notifies me of potential native adversaries with a mirror. We have a bit of a code that we've developed, and I can get his signal from afar. Furthermore, my company and I have developed a bit of an unorthodox reaction plan, when in danger. We take immediate cover, Sir." Blackwell explained.

The Major was listening intently but interrupted. "No different than any other attack. Correct?" Bliss inquired.

"Yes sir, it is. We stay hidden and flank from cover. The element of "surprise" is how the Indians have caught our troops with our pants down. We fight from cover,…at all times. The days of a "gentlemen's battle" are over. Sir, we've ambushed our own ambush. Because we know how to fight them." Blackwell explained.

Bliss continued to listen. "So, you've used this tactic in battle?"

Blackwell stood. "We have, Sir…and we obliterated them. We circled them before they even knew we were doing it."

"Interesting, William." Bliss stood. With his fingers rubbing his beard, he turned and walked towards the far side of the room. "Blackwell, If you can prove to me that this tactic works, I'll put you in charge of the effort to push them out. If you can get Blackhawk, and his band of rabble-rousers moved over to The Iowa Territory, I'll nominate you for Captain the next day."

Chapter 13 –

"The Uncivil War"

Successfully completing the challenge Major Bliss offered, Blackwell became Bliss' "go-to" for everything related to the abrogation of Native Americans. Blackhawk led his small tribe back across the Mississippi, and they appeared to be "on the run".

Trent Bettingham was subsequently promoted to Sargent and Blackwell nominated for Captain. Once approved by Congress, and assuming there was a vacancy at that rank, he would be promoted. Bliss, a bit disturbed by Blackwell's tactics but impressed, made good on his promise.

Blackwell's company routinely returned to the fort smeared in mud. Their faces and uniforms often hard to recognize by the fortress guards. The first time that Bliss saw this, he immediately summoned Blackwell. "In God's name, soldier, what is the meaning of the disheveled appearance of your company?" He asked.

"Just trying to blend in Major. If we're in our normal uniforms, we stick out like sore thumbs, Sir. Leaving our hats behind, and camouflaging our bodies allows us to travel quite a bit more stealthily. With your permission, Sir. I would like for a few of our men to dress for these missions in buckskin. It would really confuse the Indians, Sir." Blackwell explained.

Bliss looked perplexed. "You realize your requests defy all military protocols, Blackwell?"

"I do sir. But our tactics work. If we were fighting the British, I would agree with my Westpoint training. But we are fighting savages, who use tactics we've not seen." Blackwell contended.

"I'll consider it, Lieutenant. Get cleaned up for chow. Oh, something came for you." Lifting a letter from his desk, he presented it to Blackwell. "I believe it may be from your wife."

"Thank you, Sir. I believe that I'll read it in my quarters. Anything else, Major?" Blackwell added.

"Yes. I don't believe that you've met Colonel Taylor yet, William. He'll be coming through in the coming days. Have your men clean up before they return to the fortress. There's a God damn river right before you approach the gate. Use it! If Taylor sees your rag-tag company, he's liable to have both of us court-martialed." Bliss smiled at Blackwell. "Besides, I want to introduce you. You've got a lot in common. You're dismissed, Lieutenant."

Before Blackwell retired to his quarters, he met with Trent and asked him to explain to the men that they would be required to clean up in the river before coming into camp. Almost all of them were perfectly fine with this. Hell, who wouldn't want to get cleaned up immediately upon returning to camp?

Blackwell then went to his quarters, where Jefferson was quick to offer a "nip" from his latest acquisition, yet another Kentucky bourbon. After a brief discussion about the "hypocrisy of our government", Blackwell retired to his side of the room and removed the letter from his pocket.

Dearest William,

There are no words to describe how much I miss you. When I curl up at night, I always reach out, hoping to find you there. I am writing to you from Hawkins County. Father and I began to argue over the commitment that he bestowed upon you. I shall never forgive him and could not bear to see him daily. I hope you are not angry, but Bear brought me to your homestead, and your loving mother is treating me like her own. She seems happy that I am here. I finally met Jonathan, and he has also welcomed me into the family. Jonathan is often away helping others. He is a hard worker, even helping some of the Cherokee locals. They visit the homestead often and we have shared as much food as we can spare. There are rumors that the government is going to force them away. I hope that these are purely rumors, though. Father, Mother, and Jonathan all said to tell you they miss you as well. I long for the day that you ride into the valley, my love. I will be waiting. May God watch over you, my William.

All My Love, Sarah

Blackwell folded the letter, smiled, and removed his boots. William slept well that night.

Just a few days later, Colonel Zachary Taylor rode into Fort Armstrong. Bliss formally met him in the yard, then they hastily made their way to Major Bliss' quarters. Ten minutes later, Bliss also summoned Blackwell to his quarters.

Meeting Blackwell intrigued Colonel Taylor. "Congratulations are in order, Captain. I have been briefed on your endeavors and am proud to meet you. Please tell me more."

Listening intently to the new Captain, it was obvious that he had a strong distaste for the Native Americans, but yet he appeared to understand them. He knew their characteristics, their methods, and their reactions. He could "read" them better than anyone Taylor had ever met. At times, Blackwell sounded a bit brutal, but his techniques sounded effective.

"Captain Blackwell, I would like for you and your men, to join me in a campaign to the south. I think you would be well-suited for my assignment. There is another small tribe of Sauk who need to be moved, as Blackhawk's tribe was. They are about 20 miles south of here. I want to arrest them and move them to the Blackhawk camp. Are you up to this Captain." Taylor asked.

Blackwell saluted the Colonel. "Certainly, Sir. Sir, may I assume you approve of our approach and tactics. Accordingly, we won't be wearing proper military attire?"

Colonel Taylor chuckled. "Well Captain. You seem to know what you are doing. I'll reserve judgement for now, and tell you what I think after the campaign. You will be under my command, but I will allow you the freedom to "lead". I will instruct my men to support you, and your men. You have my permission to give commands to my men, with my presence and acknowledgement. If I disagree with any of your commands, I expect you will comply without complaint. Understood, Captain?"

Blackwell saluted. "Understood, Sir. How soon will we be leaving Sir?"

The Colonel returned the salute. "I will ride out and explain the campaign to my men. They are resting five hundred yards outside the fort. Just as soon as you and your men are ready, meet up with us. I'll send a trooper back to escort you to us."

Blackwell smiled. "Not necessary, Sir. We'll know where you are. My men track better than the Cherokee. We'll see you soon, Sir."

Within ten minutes, Blackwell and his men left Fort Armstrong.

When Captain Blackwell and his small company reached Colonel Taylor's three companies, south of the fort, Colonel Taylor regretted his decision. Blackwell was dressed in a deerskin blouse and gray trousers, as were a few of his men. The rest of them wore military uniforms that looked as if they had dragged behind a wagon for many miles. Some men had smeared charcoal on their faces. They resembled the very savages the campaign aimed to remove.

Making good on his word, Colonel Taylor mounted his horse. Riding up to meet Captain Blackwell, he asked. "Captain Blackwell, Do your men know how to march?"

"They do, Sir. This man riding with me is Sargent Bettingham. He will ride ahead. I will apologize now, as you will see some of my men taking off on their own. They will return, though. They are all trained to scout. At least four of them will randomly post to notify us of any ambush or flanking efforts." Blackwell explained.

"Very well, Captain. I will ride beside you." Taylor stated.

They were soon traveling south to Colonel Taylor's first Native American "battle". Taylor felt amazingly safe with Blackwell and his men, though he was slightly offended by their attire, he felt safer than he'd ever felt on any campaign. Watching Blackwell communicate with his scouts over a mile away amazed him.

*****

Three weeks later, Colonel Zachary Taylor, led by Captain Blackwell, and all thirty-one of Blackwell's company, returned to Fort Armstrong. Climbing down from his horse, Taylor walked over to Blackwell. "Captain, if I hadn't seen it with my own eyes, I wouldn't have believed it. Your men are quite impressive. Almost "savage", but quite impressive. I have one injured soldier, that you attended to yourself. Without your help, this campaign probably would have been twenty-five casualties. This was the bloodiest battle that I have seen to date. We will be returning to Fort Crawford tomorrow. If I can get Bliss to let you go, would you accompany us to Fort Crawford to discuss continued Indian removal. Jackson's insistence that we go after the Creek, Cherokee, Seminole, and Choctaw is growing. From what you've told me, this is in your neck of the woods. Please join us to discuss, Captain."

As Blackwell dismounted, Lieutenant Jefferson Davis approached. "What the hell are you doing Will? You were supposed to take me with you!" he challenged.

Laughing, Blackwell remarked, "Jefferson, you coot, this is Colonel Zachary Taylor. Under his command we just relocated almost two hundred Sauk to Blackhawk." Blackwell knew that by giving the credit to Taylor, he would gain favor and possibly diffuse any insult that Taylor may have felt by Jefferson's interruption.

Jefferson quickly stood at attention and saluted the Colonel. "Sorry, Sir" he exclaimed.

"It's okay Lieutenant, the Captain and I were just catching up on what was an outstanding campaign. Please introduce yourself." The Colonel asked.

While Blackwell went back to address his men, Jefferson did as instructed. "Second Lieutenant Jefferson Davis, Sir. Currently under the command of Major Bliss. But, If I may be so bold, always looking to improve myself with campaigns as well, Sir. I attended Westpoint with Lieutenant Blackwell, Sir."

Taylor's left eyebrow raised. "I think you mean Captain Blackwell? Not happy here with Bliss, son?"

"It's not that, sir. I greatly respect Major Bliss. It's just that I guess I'm jealous of my former roommate,

CAPTAIN, Blackwell, Sir" Jefferson quickly corrected himself, recognizing the admiration that Taylor had for Blackwell already.

Colonel Taylor smiled. "Well, I do appreciate an honest man. I'll see what I can do Lieutenant." Taylor turned and began to remove a few items from his horse.

The next morning at reveille, Major Bliss ordered Captain Blackwell and his men to accompany Colonel Taylor back to Prairie du Chien. Lieutenant Davis and one other Lieutenant were to accompany them as well, explaining that they would all get their new orders at Fort Campbell.

During the trip to Fort Campbell, Jefferson Davis watched Blackwell command his men in what appeared to be a very unorthodox military exercise. What Jefferson missed was that all of Blackwell's men were in standard military uniforms. He could clearly see them on the ridges and valleys, where they would normally be camouflaged. Davis took note that Colonel Taylor did not once question Blackwell's exercise, and appeared to give him free reign to the endeavor.

Riding into the gates of Fort Campbell, a young woman ran up to Colonel Taylor. "Father, I'm so glad that you are back!"

Colonel Taylor reached down and patted the young woman on the head. "It's good to see you too, Sarah." He exclaimed.

Jefferson was riding next to Blackwell. "Wow, who is that?"

Blackwell replied, "Looks to be the Colonel's daughter. I'd tread lightly there Jefferson."

The commanders spent the following months planning and discussing how to approach the impending campaign to rid the new frontier of the Native Americans.

Andrew Jackson's Indian Removal Act had been signed into law on May 28th, 1830. The "peaceful" action was much more like an "eradication". There was much argument between the tribes and the government.

The Colonel Taylor—Captain Blackwell duo wreaked havoc on the natives throughout the Mississippi River corridor, rounding up Sauk, Sioux, and Fox tribes throughout the rest of 1830 and on into 1831. Rumors began that Blackhawk was again gathering some of the ousted tribes, and making threats to return to the Illinois Territory. Blackwell squashed one such uprising in the fall of thirty-one, but Blackhawk seemed relentless.

***

The Blackhawk War – April 1832

Colonel Taylor met Captain Blackwell in the armory. Blackwell, just returning from scouting with a small group of his men, seemed quite irritated. "Sir, we're running into small bands of Blackhawk's men almost every day. I've got a hunch that something is brewing." Blackwell reported.

"Will, you know I respect your opinion. What's this "hunch" telling you?" Taylor inquired.

"Sir, I'd like to send a small squad of my guys over to watch Blackhawk's reservation for a few days. I'd like to allow Trent to pick his best four, go over there and not be seen. I've got a weird hunch Blackhawk may mount a retaliatory action our way. Do I have your permission, Sir?" Blackwell asked.

The Colonel wrung his gloves with both hands. "Proceed Captain. In the meantime, I'll send word to Colonel Davis of the Illinois Militia. He can send a company that we can use for appearance. We obviously can't ask for

Winfield's support unless we see proof that a battle is imminent. Since the day General Atkinson took command, he has doubted your course, Will. I want you to stay true, though. Let me deal with Atkinson. But I certainly do not want to be caught with my trousers down.

Trent left that evening, all five soldiers changing clothing a mile away from the fort, not unusual for them since General Atkinson took command. Atkinson was not enamored with Blackwell's stealth tactics. Taylor had his respect though, and he left him to make most of the daily decisions.

When Trent returned four days later, Blackwell's hunch appeared correct. Giving Taylor a "situation report" in the armory, Taylor appeared worried. "Will, this is going to get a bit "sticky" if Blackhawk really tries something. Atkinson is unprepared for this. The militia should be here in a week, but I don't know their capabilities. If I convince Atkinson to dispatch your company to assist his, do you think you can squash this rebellion?" Taylor asked.

"Colonel, the Sargent says they mostly stay in small groups. But he's seen enough to believe that Blackhawk has over a thousand men gathered. You and I both know that can be too much for us, or the militia. I would call for reinforcements, Sir." Blackwell explained.

Taylor pounded one fist onto the other. "This is about as frustrating as watching that damn Jefferson court my daughter. What if I sent you to talk to General Winfield?" Taylor offered. "While you're gone, I'll meet up with Colonels Dodge, and Henry of the militia. We'll have them set up camp outside of the fort and wait for your return."

"Sounds good, Colonel. I've met Winfield and I think he likes me. I'll convince him to send us help. We'll stomp this out, Sir. I promise." Blackwell assured.

Atkinson seemed indifferent to Zachary Taylor's explanation of the Blackhawk's recent activities. But he felt it was important for him to join Taylor in meeting the Illinois Militia.

***

Following day – Battle of Stillman's Run – May

By the time they reached Stillman's Run, the militia had already been decimated. Soldiers lay everywhere, many without their scalps.

Taylor quickly rode to Atkinson's side. "General Atkinson, we really need to fall back to the safety of the fort. They outnumber us greatly. They appear to have moved north, but they could circle back at any time. Let's take what's left of the militia's men and wounded. We can bury the dead near the fort. We can hunker down until Winfield and Blackwell return." Taylor explained.

General Atkinson was shaken by the image before him. "Why would he do this Taylor?"

Taylor stayed atop his horse and adjusted in his saddle. "Sir, Blackhawk feels wronged. In his mind, it doesn't matter that his people signed a treaty…and unfortunately, he's a warrior. We need Captain Blackwell back for a plan to take Blackhawk, and Winfield to hold our ground."

General Atkinson continued looking around at the chaos. Shaking his head, he commanded. "Colonel, I believe these heathens to be on the run. I want two detachments in pursuit, and I want to take this Blackhawk into custody. Do you understand me?" The General inquired.

"With all due respect, Sir…That would be a mistake." Colonel Taylor explained. "They are famous for ambushes. If there is anything that I've learned from Captain

Blackwell, it's that these people are never "on the run". They will disappear into the forest and pick us off one by one. I highly advise against any more fighting today, Sir."

Just then, a tall militiaman walked up to the General. "Sir, may we load the dead onto your wagons? I'd like to get out of here before they come back." The man asked.

Atkinson seemed taken aback. "What's your name son?" he inquired.

"Lincoln Sir, Second Regiment, Central Illinois Militia. We're hurt bad. Can we load our dead into your wagons?" The tall man replied.

Atkinson let out a long sigh. "Okay, Taylor. Have our men help with the wounded and dead. We'll do it your way. I'm heading back with a detachment. Let's give it a few days, and see what kind of plan the Captain comes back with."

The next day, Blackwell returned. Riding into the fort, he saw the triage tents and soldiers carrying shovels. He knew something was wrong and looked for Colonel Taylor. Seeing Taylor on the far side of the fort, Blackwell galloped towards him. "Colonel Taylor, what happened?" Blackwell asked.

"They ambushed the militia before we met up with them. Got 'em good William. By the time we reached them, there weren't but fifty men standing. Almost all of their officers were casualties." Taylor explained.

"My men, Sir?" Blackwell inquired.

"About half are deserters. I'm sorry William, I wouldn't have believed it, if I hadn't seen it with my own eyes." Taylor explained.

"They're not deserters, Sir. My bet is that they're tracking down the Sauk. They'll be back. No doubt, with a few scalps. They're an eye for an eye bunch, for sure." Dismounting, Blackwell continued. General Scott's held up.

His men are fighting cholera. I didn't want him bringing it here, so I asked him if he would work his way over to us, but to make sure that damn disease stays in Chicago. He agreed. He thought they might head this way by the end of the week. I'll help with the wounded. With your permission, sir, I'd like to send a small group of my men out to support the others…the ones that I know are not deserters." Blackwell finished.

Taylor was shaking his head. "William, we need every man to protect this fort. Besides, I really don't want another group of deserters." Taylor asserted.

"Sir, please. My men are not deserters. I promise you. They'll be back." Blackwell insisted.

Taylor was still shaking his head. "It's against my better judgement, Captain. But alright. You haven't steered me wrong yet. Send four men out. That's it." Taylor offered.

Blackwell wasted no time. Quickly, four of his men were riding out in tattered uniforms.

Blackwell worked on the wounded all night and into the morning. As he stepped out of the tent at daybreak, he heard a sentry call out. "Over a dozen men coming from the West. They appear to be Indians. Heading straight towards the gate!" The young man exclaimed.

Several men broke formation and quickly gathered their muskets. Captain Blackwell, Colonel Taylor, General Taylor, and Lieutenant Davis all jogged towards the blockhouse, next to the front gate.

Being the first to climb up, Blackwell raised his hand in the air and pumped his fist.

The second up was Taylor. "What the hell." He exclaimed.

Then Jefferson Davis. "Oh my God!"

Then General Scott. "For the love of God! What happened to them?" he asked. "Call the Surgeon! They need medical help."

"Open the gate!" Taylor barked.

Fourteen men walked in. Shirtless and covered in blood. The leader, Sergeant Bettingham, tossed a bloody bag to the ground. Blackwell didn't have to ask. He knew what was in the bag…vengeance.

"We got most of 'em sir. But we failed. Blackhawk got away. They'll be back though, so we better be prepared. I give 'em a few weeks, or a month to get their shit together. Then they'll be back." Trent stated.

General Scott's mouth was open. Looking at the blood-covered soldiers, he muttered, "We thought you were deserters."

Trent laughed. "Deserters! You kidding me? We went to take care of things, Sir."

Then Taylor spoke. "Sargent, you and your men, go get cleaned up. Get something to eat and we'll call reveille at…" He pulled a pocket watch from his uniform. "Nine o'clock… and whatever is in that bag, dispose of it, soldier."

Trent looked at the blood-covered Surgeon William Blackwell. "You look like you've been busy, Sir." Blackwell smiled, then nodded his head in approval. The bloody soldiers hustled back out of the fort, where they could bathe in the river.

Later that day, Blackwell, resting in his quarters, heard a knock. It was his friend Jefferson Davis. "Come in." Blackwell said, sitting up on his bed.

Jefferson stepped in with his head down. "I'm sorry Will. I thought it was good news. I read the letter." He walked over and handed the letter to his friend.

Dated four weeks back, the letter read:

Dearest Brother,

It is with a heavy heart that I must inform you that our mother was taken captive by the natives. I am currently trying to find them. I am very sorry to say they took Sarah too. They left father for dead, which he is not. He seems to be recovering, but he is broken. I'm not sure which tribe took them. Some believe it to be the Creek, some the Cherokee. I will do everything in my power to bring them back, my brother. I have many friends helping me. I'll send word once they are safely home. I am so very sorry.

Jonathan Blackwell

Blackwell stared at the floor, then crumpled the letter with one hand. He sat there for hours, just staring at the floor.

Jefferson had informed Colonel Taylor and General Atkinson of the situation with Blackwell's wife. They all knew the plight that she faced. Most of the kidnapped women were raped and found dead or never found at all. The Cherokee were not known to commit such acts, but this was a "trying" time for all Native Americans. The three of them discussed options, knowing that Blackwell would want to return to Hawkins County. As they discussed, there was a knock at the door.

"Yes." Atkinson called out.

Blackwell opened the door and stepped in. Dressed in his deerskin blouse and gray trousers, wearing a sash with a small knife and a pouch for his cartridge box, he set down his musket and stood at attention before the three of them.

"Sir, I respectfully submit my resignation as an officer of the United States Army." Blackwell said as he laid a letter upon the table.

General Atkinson picked up the letter and read it. He set it back down, stood, and walked to his bureau.

Reaching into the bureau, he pulled out something wrapped in cloth. He walked over to the table and unwrapped the object. It was a knife. A rather large knife. Atkinson lifted the sheathed knife with both hands and presented it to Blackwell.

"William, this was a gift to me from James Bowie. It's the very knife that disemboweled Norris Wright. James gave it to me when I saved his life in Texas. I can't imagine how many lives you have saved and I want you to have it. You need to put that resignation in your bureau, and I will make this promise to you, William. We will all go to Hawkins County together to find Sarah, and Louisa. But, we must finish our duties here first. I need you to be part of this effort, and we will bring it to an end as hastily as we can. Wait one week. If you still want to leave then, I will approve of it. Do you agree William?" Atkinson asked.

Standing at attention, Blackwell's expression did not change, but his mind was racing. After a long pause, Blackwell replied. "Together, Sir?" he asked.

"Yes, Son. Together. All three hundred and fifty of us." Atkinson replied.

"Why would you do that for me, Sir?" Blackwell inquired.

"Because you'd do it for any of us, William. I know you would…and remember William, there's strength in numbers." Atkinson pleaded.

Blackwell looked at Zachary Taylor and Jefferson Davis. They both nodded. "Very well, Sir. One week. I'll give it a week." Blackwell stated, then looked at the sheathed knife in his hand. "Thank you, Sir. Thank you all." Blackwell cast a glance at all three, then turned, and let himself out the door.

After Blackwell left, Jefferson spoke up. "Gents, you know his entire command will leave, if he does."

Taylor stood and agreed. "Yep"

"I don't want any part of a mass desertion, Gentlemen. We need to do everything in our power to keep the Captain from causing one. I want you to start a "rumor" amongst the ranks. I want it known that the minute General Scott arrives, we are heading south to Tennessee. Understood?" Atkinson affirmed.

Colonel Taylor and Lieutenant Davis confirmed with a nod of their heads.

Four weeks went by before they were notified that General Winfield Scott's troops were in route. Blackwell had stayed, although he no longer wore a United States Army uniform, nor did Sergeant Bettingham. They both wore their deerskin blouses and trousers daily. Blackwell's sash now had the large "Bowie knife" attached. Atkinson thought it better to leave the "negligence in dress" without reprimand.

Blackwell led countless patrols and engagements against the Sauk, Fox, and Kickapoo. It took some convincing by Atkinson, Taylor, and Davis, but Blackwell eventually took prisoners instead of killing those that surrendered. They took the prisoners to Jefferson Barracks in St. Louis, Missouri to be processed and eventually transferred to The Iowa Territory. In an untimely visit to one of his wives, Blackhawk found himself captured by Blackwell. No longer desiring any "credit" for his achievements, Blackwell asked his friend, Jefferson Davis, to escort Blackhawk to Prairie du Chien and then on to Jefferson Barracks.

Knowing that the Blackhawk War was ending, and that General Scott was in route, Atkinson chose to honor his word. General Atkinson returned command of Fort Armstrong to Major Jonathan Bliss. Atkinson and Taylor took two hundred soldiers, along with Blackwell and his men, and headed south to Tennessee.

Stopping in St. Louis, Atkinson and Taylor made a bold decision…Catching Lieutenant Jefferson Davis early the morning of their departure from St. Louis, General Atkinson approached him. "Lieutenant, it's against my better judgement, but I'm entrusting you with our families here in Jefferson Barracks. I want someone I trust staying here. I need Taylor, and it's obvious that Blackwell wouldn't stay. Colonel Taylor isn't pleased, so I ask that you be a gentleman. I have not explained this to Captain Blackwell, but our objective in East Tennessee is much bigger than he knows. While we will actively look for his wife, we are also under the orders of President Jackson to move all indigenous to the Oklahoma Territory. I will send for you once we settle in East Tennessee.

Davis was a bit surprised. He felt he owed it to his best friend to be by his side. Unfortunately, Atkinson stated it was "an order", so anyone who argued could face disciplinary action. Besides, he could stay and watch over the Colonel's daughter.

"I understand, Sir. I will protect both of your families with my life. Please send for us just as soon as you can General." Davis pleaded. "May I speak to William, Sir?" Davis asked.

"Certainly. I'll send him to you before we set off, Lieutenant." Atkinson replied.

Lieutenant Davis watched the soldiers prepare to march. His desire to be with them grew as the troops massed. A familiar voice startled him from behind. "Got a drink for an old friend?" Blackwell asked.

"Shit. You scared me Will! It's no wonder you take as many scalps as the indig's. You're probably quieter than they are." Davis exclaimed.

"It's the way you walk, what you wear, and being afraid of nothing, my friend." Blackwell explained.

"Will, I wanted to wish you well. Atkinson is leaving me here with he and Taylor's families. Well, and of course, because of Blackhawk. But I'll be by your side as soon as I can, brother…and I'll finally get to meet your Sarah." Davis avowed.

Blackwell laid a hand on Davis's shoulder. "My Sarah is gone, my friend. I feel it in my heart…or what's left of it. My job now is to gather up every single wretched savage and dispose of them in the Oklahoma Territory. I'm looking forward to it. You are more than welcome to join, but it will not be pretty. You might be best served to take care of that little lady. Godspeed brother. We'll meet again one day."

Neither of them said another word. Blackwell checked his knife, picked up his musket and walked over to his horse, behind Colonel Taylor. Swinging onto his horse like a Native American, he sat "high" in the saddle. General Atkinson cried out, "All men, Foooorward march!"

Davis watched them leave. He felt sick to his stomach. His friend had changed. He was a shell now. A heartless machine with one objective…kill.

***

The Trail of Tears

Atkinson, Taylor, and Blackwell began to fulfill President Andrew Jackson's request by moving the Cherokee, Creek, Choctaw, Chickasaw, and Seminole tribes to land in the Oklahoma Territory.

Though President Jackson requested that the process be "humane", it was often brutal. In particular, the Cherokee were not fully represented when the agreements with the United States government were signed. In fact, the United

States government was selective in which tribes signed the agreements and treaties but enforced them across all tribes. This was not well received by the many tribes with a misunderstanding of the agreements. For this reason, the Indian Removal Act that Andrew Jackson signed into law in 1830 was often not recognized. Unfortunately, the United States government did not see it this way and deemed the uncooperative tribes as an "illegal occupation".

Legal action didn't seem to work either. Cherokee Principal Chief, John Ross, sued the State of Georgia. The suit went all the way to the United States Supreme Court and Ross won. But Andrew Jackson's response was "try to enforce it". So, the Trail of Tears continued with over sixty thousand Native Americans being forced to move to The Oklahoma Territory. Thousands upon thousands died during the journey.

While small skirmishes abounded with all Native American tribes, the Seminole tribes were the most resilient, fighting hard through 1836 and 1837.

***

General Atkinson returned to Jackson Barracks to assist with logistics, while General Winfield Scott and now Captain, Jefferson Davis joined the effort against the Seminole. Colonel Zachary Taylor won what was to be the largest battle, the Battle of Okeechobee, in 1837. Major William Blackwell and his deadly band of unorthodox soldiers continued to break the tribes whenever they seemed to grow strong. Blackwell became quite feared by the Native Americans. They even gave him the nickname Nudoi, which meant "spirit of the dead"…or ghost.

After the Second Seminole War, Blackwell joined General Winfield Scott to, once again, assist in the removal of the Cherokee, Creek, and Choctaw.

Blackwell often visited his family's homestead. During one such visit his brother and father explained they had buried two mutilated female bodies, believed to be Louisa and Sarah. Blackwell doubted their find. I didn't feel right to him.

Sitting in the kitchen, Blackwell looked at the Bowie knife stuck into the table. The bedroom door opened, and Jonathan nearly leaped out of his clothes. "Good Lord brother! I didn't hear you come in. Did I not lock bolt the door?" Jonathan asked.

"It was bolted. Just as it probably was when Mother and Sarah were taken. Tell me again Jonathan how you found them?" The Major inquired.

"Really William? Must I relive this every time you come home?" Jonathan pleaded.

"Something does not seem right with what you told me. The Cherokee do not mutilate their captives. Many tribes do, but not the Cherokee. But you contend it WAS the Cherokee that took them." William grilled.

Jonathan sat in a chair across from the Major. "Dear God, William. Father did not eat for days. He was going to die. You needed closure as well." Jonathan wrung his hands together and appeared uncomfortable.

"What are you saying, Jonathan?" Blackwell questioned.

Jonathan sat with tears slowly rolling down his cheeks. "The Cherokee chief brought them to me. He had known Ma and Sarah were missing. He left them and expressed sorrow for our loss. But,…But they both had dark hair William." Jonathan dropped his head.

Blackwell jumped from his chair. Pulling the knife from the table, he pointed it at Jonathan and shouted, "You mean to tell me you buried two women in our cemetery, put my mother's name, and my wife's name on tombstones, all the while knowing that neither was actually them??!! Is the body in father's grave even him?" Blackwell berated.

"Yes, yes. Pa is in his grave…and I'm sure that he is with Ma now. Please, William. I'm so very sorry." Jonathan implored.

The Major sat back down and gave a long sigh. "I knew it. I could feel it all along. Something was wrong with your story, and I knew it." Blackwell paused. "It's not your fault Jonathan. It's not your fault. I'm the one that is paying for my sins. I've allowed hatred to cloud my mind. I'm the one who will pay for the hundreds of Indians that I've killed, and I'm sure that I'll burn in hell. But you, Jonathan. You can be better than I. You must wed and have children who can one day own this land. Teach your children to be strong, but wise. Teach them not to be like Uncle William." The Major smiled.

Jonathan was on his hands and knees in the bedroom doorway. "There is someone, William. From Jonesborough. Her name is Mary. I love her, and I'm going to ask for her hand. Please tell me I have your blessing?" Jonathan asked.

Blackwell walked over to Jonathan and set his hand on his shoulder. "You'll always have my blessings, brother." Blackwell walked out the door, leapt upon his horse, and galloped across the valley.

Jonathan watched him from the porch. "Hundreds?" His pale face saddened.

After relocating the Native Americans to Oklahoma, Major Blackwell spent some time in Richmond, Virginia and then returned to St. Louis, where his friend, General Henry Atkinson had died.

Without a war that interested him, Major Blackwell settled in St. Louis and became known as Doctor Blackwell. Practicing medicine and caring for his friend's widow, Mary Ann, and two sons. This seemed to be one way he could attempt to do something "good" in his life. Avoiding the advances of Mary Ann, Doctor Blackwell did nothing but care for the Atkinson family, which the boys eventually grew to respect. Doctor Blackwell co-sponsored both young men to the Military Academy and eventually moved Mary Ann to the Atkinson Estate in Louisville, Kentucky, where she could be with other family members.

Telling Mary Ann that he was returning to St. Louis seemed to break her heart. On the day he left, she asked for one thing from him… a kiss. It was the first kiss since he had last seen Sarah, so many years ago. Doctor Blackwell and Mary Ann embraced for five long minutes. When he returned to the carriage, Mary Ann called out, "I love you", but the Doctor did not reply. As pulled the carriage away, he cried.

Once back at St. Louis, his friend General Winfield Scott visited him. "William! How have you been?" Scott inquired.

"Why, if it ain't Ole Fuss 'n Feathers!...It's Doc, now sir. I've been good. I'm delivering babies, and sewing up the cuts and bruises of the loud-mouthed soldiers who think they can whip any townsman around. Back to wearing normal clothes feels good." Doctor Blackwell chuckled.

"I see that, William. You look good, I might add. I'll get to the point. We've got this little thing going on in Texas. Just as we get a treaty signed, someone else steps up and says "NO". On top of it all, the Comanche are a bit of a problem for us. Your name constantly comes up, and frankly, we could use your help. What do you say we put your old regiment back together, William?"

"I'm afraid not sir. I'm retired. Besides, who would deliver all of the babies? I'm honored by the request, but I'm done with the military. It's time for me to finish what I started here, then back to Hawkins County, to be buried in the family cemetery." Doctor Blackwell explained.

General Scott attempted one more time. "Your ole boys, Taylor, and Davis are commanding, and I heard an ole friend of yours, Albert Sydney Johnston is under Taylor's command. Come on, boy. It'll be like the ole days. What'ya say?" Scott was grinning.

"Albert? Under Zachary Taylor. Hmm…You sure are working me hard there, sir. But I must decline. I haven't been on a horse in three years. Not sure that I even know how to ride anymore. General, you already have the best. Please tell them all that I miss them, and you be safe out there. Oh, and here, I have something for you." Doctor Blackwell went to a storeroom and came out with a wooden box. "Take these and give them to your officers. They're tourniquets. Every man should carry one. Then some them boys might keep their damn legs!"

"Alright, William. If you change your mind, send word, and I'll personally come back here to get you. Be safe William!" Scott extended his hand to shake.

William reached out and grabbed Scott's enormous hand. "Godspeed, General. Godspeed." William offered.

After General Scott left, William felt better than he had felt in a long time. He had decided that he did not need to fight or go into battle. He thought of Sarah and smiled. "I am saving lives sweetheart. Not taking them." He whispered.

Doctor Blackwell practiced medicine in St. Louis for another five years, often visiting Jackson Barracks, where he could get the latest news about his friends. William was ecstatic to see Jefferson during one visit to the Barracks.

While visiting Jefferson in his temporary quarters, Jefferson commended William on his apparent physical and mental health. "I know those were some tough years for you William, but you look great! You seem happy. We'll soon all be retired, and I'll have to get some land in Virginia, maybe just north of Hawkins County, my friend. We'll open our very own Kentucky Bourbon distillery and grow old together. Sound like a plan, Will?" Jefferson asked.

"It does, dear friend. Maybe we can get Albert to join us as well." William offered.

As William was leaving, he stopped to look back at his friend one more time. Jefferson mimicked a shot glass in his hand and raised it. "To Wisdom, William."

William smiled. "To Wisdom, brother."

Chapter 14 –

"The Best Years"

The years stretched on, William yearned to return to Hawkins County. His mouth hung open in astonishment as he rode between the mountain ridges, gazing at the new structures near the valley's heart. William stopped counting at over two hundred head of steer.

Jonathan had two sons, Samuel and Thomas, with another child on the way. Jonathan's wife, Mary, was beautiful, with an uncanny resemblance to Sarah. William moved into the old homestead, which Jonathan had made many improvements to. He enjoyed the small cabin. From the front porch he could watch his nephews in the fields.

William opened a small doctor's office in Rogersville but only went there twice a week. The rest of the time he spent at the homestead, helping Jonathan expand the farm. Samuel was already fourteen, and could do almost anything that William could. Thomas was five and loved being with William.

William really enjoyed the next few years. Thomas affectionately called him "Doc". Jonathan was pleased to see them so close, as he never forgave himself for the loss of his mother and Sarah. William never spoke of either of them again. He didn't visit the cemetery either. He focused on his nephews.

***

Mary had their third child in 1856, with Doctor William Blackwell assisting her. He said that she had "the will of a thousand Cherokee warriors".

Thomas overheard William's comment and asked, "Doc, did you ever fight the Indians? Were they bad people?"

William struggled to answer. "Thomas, my boy. There are good and bad people in this world. Sometimes, situations can make people do bad things. What you need to remember is to always give people a chance to be good first. Then you can be good back to them." Will felt tears welling beneath his eyes as he realized what he had just said, and how he himself never followed his own words.

"William, something's wrong with Mary!" Jonathan exclaimed.

William returned and saw the amount of blood. "Okay, Mary, listen, I need to put my hand up there. You just gave birth, my hand will fit. I'm going to rub some Ergot on the inside. This should cause the blood vessels to constrict, Okay?" William rushed. "Jonathan, quickly make some Ergot tea for her, while I do this."

Mary turned pale and began to breathe shallowly. When Jonathan returned with the tea, William's hand was out, and he was packing her with gauze. "William! Is she going to be okay?" Jonathan implored.

"She'll be fine. I need you to get her to drink some of that tea before she passes out. Quickly!" William commanded.

Jonathan did as he was told. Mary drank most of the cup before she went limp in his arms. "William! Is she dying??!!" Jonathan screamed.

William stood and helped Jonathan lower Mary down. "She will not die, Jonathan. She is a warrior. Warriors don't die. I promise you, she will be fine."

William led his frantic brother over to a chair, forcing him to sit down. There, Jonathan watched as a calm Doctor Willliam Blackwell attended to his recovering wife. He watched the slow, methodical movements that William made. His hands appeared to move like water over her body. Jonathan couldn't tell if he was cleaning her body, or massaging her, but her color slowly returned.

Jonathan woke still sitting in the chair. Mary was awake, with William spoon-feeding her soup. He was confused. "Where was the blood? Where is the baby? Where are my sons?" he thought.

"You've been out for a while, brother. Everybody is fine. This lovely one gave you another son. It looks like that "Blackwell name" is going to be around for a while." William claimed.

"Wha,…what'd you do?" Jonathan asked.

As Mary lay back, William held the bowl in one hand and slowly patted her arm with the other. "You rest now warrior, you rest." William whispered softly.

"You saved my,…my li-" Mary tried to speak, before succumbing to the effects of the natural drug William mixed into the soup.

"She'll be fine, Jonathan. After many years of being around them, let's just say I learned a thing or two about "Indian medicine". She'll be out for a while. The baby is sleeping right over there, and the boys are outside." William nodded in each direction.

"While I'm forever grateful, William, I have trouble understanding how you can hate a race of people and yet use their own practices to save lives. It's quite hypocritical. Don't you think?" Jonathan inquired.

William bowed his head. "I honestly cannot defend my actions as a warrior. That was a different time for me. If I could take it all back, I would. But I can't brother. I can only make today "count", as it could be my last. That holds true for all of us."

William stood, walked over to his brother, and knelt next to him. "Jonathan…war is horrible. It forces a man to make decisions he would not normally do. I became part of that, and in some ways, I saved lives. I took lives in order to save lives. Then, it takes you over. You only see those that you feel you need to protect. Everyone else is just collateral damage. I never want to put that uniform on again. With any luck, I'll be on the right side of Hell."

Jonathan put his arms around William's head and pulled him close. After a moment, William pulled away from Jonathan to check on Mary. She was sleeping soundly.

William walked to the doorway and paused. "Watch her and the baby Jonathan. You need to think of a name for this little guy. I'm going to check on the boys and start some dinner. Call for me if there's anything wrong."

Jonathan came to Mary's side and spoke softly. "We had a name darling, but… I know of one better,…his name is William."

Doctor William Blackwell often claimed that the following few years were the best of his life. He watched Samuel grow into a man. While not as close to Samuel as he was to Thomas and Will, he admired Samuel greatly. Samuel was a large man for his age. Towering over them all, able to lift a wagon, while the others replaced a wheel, he was by far the best help around any farm.

On a summer day in 1858, William was helping Samuel harness the plow oxen when Samuel asked William a question that caught him off-guard. "Uncle, why did you not show any interest in Miss Bowman? When she came by the other day, she was obviously interested in you. But you politely ran her off. Aren't you lonely?"

William thought for a moment and answered. "Samuel, you are wise beyond your years, and I'm sure you'll meet a woman that will take your heart one day. That woman will be your "everything". She'll be the first thing that you think of when you wake, and the last thing you think of when you lay your head down. If that woman were to disappear from your life, you lose interest in replacing her. Maybe,…someday, I'll find a special woman again,…and I'll know right then and there, she's the one. Miss Bowman is not her."

"I think I understand, Unc. I hope you meet her again one day…that special woman." Samuel smiled.

William smiled. "Hey, why don't you come with me to town tomorrow? You can help me out at the office for a bit, then we'll go over and check out the new train station. With any luck, a train will come through. That sound like a good get-away?" Will offered.

"I'd like that, Uncle, but chasing them boys around Rogersville don't sound like fun to me." Samuel explained.

"Naaah! Just you and me, Samuel. The boys can stay here. Your dad was going to be here anyway." William clarified.

"Seriously?" Samuel questioned.

William's face lit up. "Sure. We'll go over and see ole' Davy Crokett's grandparents grave, and I tell you about the time that I stayed with him, in his cabin."

"You did not!" Samuel exclaimed.

"I did. But I'll tell you the story tomorrow, okay? Get this field plowed and call for me to help with the harness afterward." William affirmed.

The next morning, Samuel had all of his morning chores finished by sunrise. He had cleaned up and was sitting on William's porch when William came out.

William was pleased. "I suppose you have all-"

Samuel quickly interrupted, "Yep, all done. Woke Pa, told him. He said to go and have fun. But no amputations today."

William laughed. "Don't jinx me Samuel!...I haven't had to do that in years. Let's go harness up the wagon."

"I already did it Unc. We're ready to go." Samuel proudly said.

Still laughing, William reached in the cabin, picked up his doctor's case and started for the stables. "Well, I guess we'll be in early this morning. So, we can leave and fun early, right son?"

"Sure thing, Unc." Samuel replied.

Riding into Rogersville, William thought they would go by the new train station, just to see if there might be a train coming through.

"How does it work, Uncle?" Samuel asked.

"What? Do you mean, when do they come?" William replied.

"No. How are the trains driven? I watched one from Kettler's farm a week ago. I think the thing in the front is pulling it." Samuel explained.

William slowed the wagon. "That's correct Samuel. They ride on the tracks and have to stay on them. The different wagons are actually called cars, or coaches. The locomotive is in the front, and it runs off a boiler that is fueled by wood or coal. I think most of them are coal."

"You mean, like the coal that's in the old cave at the homestead?" Samuel asked.

"Wait, you mean that old cave has coal in it?" William acted inquisitively, even though he'd known this for years.

"Oh yeah. Every time I'd go up there and play, I'd come home covered in coal dust. I got a few ass-wuppins because of that place. But it goes way back in the mountain. You never been up there?" Samuel inquired.

"I have. But it was a long, long time ago. I came home with a bit of coal dust on me a time or two. You'll have to take me up there some time." William insisted.

"Sure thing, Uncle. Hey, that sign says "Next Train 10AM". You think we could come back and see it?" Samuel asked.

"Sure. Maybe we'll get a ticket and go somewhere. You wanna go to Knoxville, or Bristol?" William asked, leaning to his side and bumping Samuel's large shoulder.

Samuel laughed. As they rode away, Samuel turned around and continued looking at the train station. "Wow. That's crazy Unc."

Samuel spent the morning moving supplies from the General Store to the second story of "Doctor Blackwell's Medical Emporium". In St. Louis, the customers paid with cash. Here in Hawkins County, William learned he might have to trade something for his services. The second story had become a collection of things that William thought he might take to his grave. Silverware, quilts, small furniture, and even the goats on the farm came from customers needing "Doc Blackwell's" services. William was mighty glad that he had Samuel to help today. Now at fifty-five, his own body was aching daily.

At around nine-thirty, William called up to Samuel. "You ready to go to the train station Samuel?" he announced.

"Sure thing, Unc. I'll be down once I get all these plates packed." Samuel replied.

As Samuel was coming down the stairwell, he surprised William. "Hey Uncle? If they use coal to power those trains, could we actual sell them some coal?"

"Samuel, you're scaring me, son. I was already thinking the same thing. If it's not raining tomorrow, take me up to the old cave and let us take a peek. Now let's go have some fun." William proclaimed.

***

The two of them watched the train come into the station. William had seen the trains in St. Louis. Even rode one, just to say he did. Went to the next town, got off, and bought a ticket right back to St. Louis. But Samuel's mouth just stayed open. The large "Iron Horse" enamored him. During the train's stop, the conductor kicked them off of the train twice. Both of them laughing and the conductor shaking his head.

Afterward, William and Samuel went back to the Emporium. Samuel eventually stopped talking about the train and went back to organizing "stuff" upstairs. William was in his office when he heard the bell ring on the entrance door. When William came out of his office, Miss Emily Bowman was standing in the waiting room.

"Why Missus Bowman, you look like you're dressed for church. What can this ole' Doctor do for you today?" William inquired.

Emily Bowman wore what certainly appeared to be her "Sunday best". She had even donned a bonnet and parasol. "Well, I be. I was hoping you was in Doctor Blackwell. I have had the worst pain in my shoulder, ever since I toted ten buckets of water for Pa yesterday. Is there anything that you can do for it?" She asked.

"Sure, Missus Bowman, I can-" William was quickly interrupted.

"Emily, Doctor Blackwell. Please call me Emily… and it's Miss now. I think you know that I'm a widow. Been that way for almost five years now. May I call you William, Doctor Blackwell?" She asked.

William grinned. "How about Doc. Most my friends call me Doc."

"Well Doc, Pa was hurtin' so I told him I would get the water for the animals. 'Bout ten buckets in, I felt terrible pain in my neck and shoulder. It's been hurting ever since." Emily explained.

Doc looked her up and down. "Do me a favor Miss Emily, walk across the room and back."

Emily did as requested. William focused on her movements and tried not to notice her smile. When she returned, William asked her to sit on the examination table. He then helped her to lie down on her back. Palpating her neck, shoulders, and ribs, William assessed her condition. He walked to the end of the table with her feet and pushed her feet up, so they were perfectly perpendicular to the floor.

"Miss Emily, I do apologize if anything I do makes you uncomfortable. Shoes and clothing do add a bit of an obstacle when examining. May I remove your shoes?" William inquired.

"William, I mean Doc, you may. I am wearing an undergarment, so please do what you need to do. I'm not bashful anyway." Emily offered.

William blushed. "No, No, Miss Emily. I just want to see your bare feet, and compare them."

William unbuckled and removed Emily's shoes and laid them on the floor. He took one foot in each hand. Setting them side by side, he looked. "Miss Emily, I do believe that your spine is not aligned correctly. It was probably mis-aligned before you carried all that water, and you aggravated the situation. I need you relax, okay? I'm going to get your spine back where it should be, but it might scare you a little. Just try to stay relaxed." William clarified.

Emily shook her head in understanding. Then William positioned her in a bit of a contorted posture and, with one sudden jerk, her back made a loud popping sound. He then rolled her over to the other side of her body and did the same. Laying her back on her back, he palpated her ribs, shoulder and neck again. He then positioned himself over her head and quickly pulled on her head. "pop, pop, pop" went her neck. He again palpated. Then he went back to her feet, and examined them, as he had before.

"Okay Miss Emily, let me help you up and I want you to walk across the floor, as you did before. Can you do that for me?" William asked.

Emily purposefully remained quite limp while William helped her up, essentially forcing William to raise her by putting his arms around her. Once she stood on her own, her face "lit up". "Oh Lord, William! You've fixed me. No pain. Maybe a little sore, but no pain. How did you do that?" She questioned.

William smiled. "You're a good patient Miss Emily. Please walk across the floor for me."

Emily raised onto the balls of her feet and spun like a ballerina. Dropping back down, she walked slowly across the room and back.

"Perfect! Your look great." William expressed.

"Why, thank you, William. You look pretty darn good yourself." Emily replied.

William chuckled. "I apologize, I meant you gait. I mean…well. Oh, now you have me all flustered." They both laughed, then Emily reached out and hugged William.

"Thank you, Healer." Emily stated. She then picked up her shoes, walked over to a chair, and sat down to put them on. "What do I owe you William?"

"Nothing, Miss Emily. It was easy. Like I said, you're a good patient." William said as he walked over to his desk. "I recommend you come back next week, so I can make sure your back stayed aligned…unless you have pain come back sooner, then please call for me at the farm."

Emily stood, walked over to William's desk, leaned down and kissed him on the cheek.

"Paid in full" William exclaimed, and Miss Emily giggled.

Emily stopped halfway to the door and looked over her shoulder. "You'll be expecting an apple pie this week from me, William." She then helped herself out of the office.

As she turned outside of the Emporium and strode down the wooden walkway, William noticed a slight hop in her step. He closed his eyes; it reminded him of Sarah.

"What was that all about, Unc?" Samuel asked as he came down the stairs. "Was that more Indian magic?"

"No, No, Samuel. When I was at medical school, a fella came down from Canada and showed us how to do that. Everyone's backs get out of alignment and fixing it is usually pretty simple. Miss Emily's was easy to fix." William explained.

"Miiiiiiiss Emily?" Samuel smiled and raised his eyebrows at William.

"Oh, Stop Samuel. It's nothing, she's a patient, that's all." William rebutted and stood. "Show me what you've done upstairs before I pay you for the day."

After seeing how well Samuel organized the second floor, William paid him with two "half-dollar" coins. Samuel tried to give them back, but William would not accept them.

As William normally did, they stopped at the Post Office before heading back to the homestead. Riding home, William told Samuel his story of "Davy Crockett", embellishing a few parts. Samuel seemed amazed and asked questions all the way home. Crockett had become a local hero as a Tennessean and was often thought of as a martyr at the Battle of the Alamo.

After they put the horses away and attended to the evening chores, William thanked Samuel for the hard work. Samuel shook his head. "Thank you, Uncle! I had a great time today. I'd have paid a dollar for it!" he exclaimed.

Waving goodbye, William headed to his comfortable little cabin. Once inside, he removed an envelope from his breast pocket and laid it on the table. Preparing a pot of coffee, he looked back at the envelope. "Who do I know from Cincinnati, Ohio?" he thought. Pouring himself a cup of coffee, he sat down to read. William noted the envelope was addressed to Major William Blackwell and slowly opened it.

24, July, 1858

Greetings Major Blackwell,

Forces within "the system" are culminating, and soon something must be done. Those of us who are committed to a greater purpose understand that the Republic cannot exist without us. I write to you as a professor of Medical Studies at The Eclectic Medical Institute of Cincinnati, but we both serve a higher cause. I am asking for your assistance in this matter and beg your presence in Richmond, Virginia on 11, September, 1858. You will join my colleagues Colonel Jefferson Davis, Colonel Albert Johnston, and other notables. For the sake of Wisdom, please keep this invitation private.

Sincerely,

Doctor George W.L. Bickley KGC

William did not realize that he furrowed his brow. He looked up at the lantern, the only light in his tiny home. He stood, picked up the letter and envelope, opened the door of the pot-belly stove, and tossed them in.

The next morning, William and Samuel went to the "ole cave". William had not been there since his visits with Sarah. They inspected the walls of the cave. Samuel was right. There was much evidence of coal, and the cave went very far back. They even found another entrance, William not pointing out the yellow rock that he saw embedded in the second entrance wall.

They both "studied up" on extracting coal and contacted the East Tennessee and Virginia Railroad charter. Before they knew it, Jonathan and Samuel were coal miners. The first investment they made was a heavier wagon, and two Clydesdale horses, for their daily trips to Rogersville.

William visited existing coalfields near Knoxville. Meeting with engineers there, he learned how to create a mine "shaft" and "modern" ways to extract coal. Returning to Hawkins County, he shared this information with his brother and nephew. Soon they had a working coal mine, that supplemented their farming and Doctor Blackwell's Medical Emporium. The Blackwell Coalfield supplied E.T. & V. with coal often. The three of them worked their mine at their own pace. Some weeks they'd have three wagonloads. Some weeks, four.

On the morning of September ninth, William explained he needed to take a trip to Virginia. Samuel begged to go with him, but William explained it was a medical trip, and his "Partner" needed to stay and run the mine. Samuel was disappointed because he couldn't go on the train with his uncle but knew how important his uncle was.

William rode the train to Richmond on the tenth, meeting Jefferson at the station when he arrived. Seeing each other for the first time in many years, Jefferson stated Will must know of a secret elixir, because he appeared to have not aged. William did not agree and accused Jefferson of the same.

"Why am I here, my brother?" William asked.

Jefferson held his finger to his mouth. "There are spies. We must watch what we say. We'll talk more after a bit. Let's get you some dinner. Then we'll go to a place where there are no "eyes and ears. Tell me Will, how is life in Hawkins County? Johnathan?" Jefferson inquired.

As they walked, William told Jefferson about his small Medical Emporium, and their recent discovery of a coalfield on their property. He explained Jonathan had three young sons, and how one of them had the strength of two oxen.

Jefferson told of his eventual marriage to Sarah Knox Taylor and the sad demise that took her just three months later. Jefferson had retired from the military solely to marry "Knoxie" and had developed The Brierfield Plantation in Mississippi. Marrying again in 1845, Jefferson now had two children, with one "on the way". His second wife of thirteen years was back home, in Mississippi.

"How about you, Will? I hear that you never married again. You can't tell me you didn't meet someone who could have been the next missus Blackwell." Jefferson chastised.

"No, I'm afraid Sarah was the one. I've not met another." William thought of Miss Emily for a moment. "Besides, Jonathan's family is my family too. His lovely wife, Mary. Their beautiful children, Samuel, Thomas, and William are my life now. They make my happy little life complete." William concluded.

"I personally think that you could have used the company of a woman, but I certainly understand your feelings. I still miss my Sarah." Jefferson agreed. "I've reserved four rooms for us. The furthermost room should be safe to talk in. We'll have your meal brought up." Jefferson explained.

"Four?" William asked.

"Yes. You, myself, Albert, and a brother from Baltimore, Booth. John Booth. He's young but committed. He's working as an actor, but he has very good connections." Jefferson claimed.

That evening, William met John Wilkes Booth, a member of The Knights of the Gold Circle. Booth stayed in the hall, watching for "spies", while William, Jefferson, and Albert discussed why they were in Richmond. Jefferson explained that a somewhat secret "uprising" had started, and that there were quite a few "politicians" who supported such a conflict. Many politicians in the Carolinas, Virginia, Mississippi, Arkansas, Georgia, Louisiana, Texas, and William's home state of Tennessee disagreed with the current government's stance on slavery, state's rights, and other politics. George Bickley was the "head" of The KGC and was asking for the help of The Knights of Wisdom to overthrow the current government.

Hearing all of this, William appeared perplexed. His life felt pretty good right now. He didn't show it, but he had doubts about the intentions of this George Bickley. When he spoke, he was careful with his words. "So, the effort is just to research and bring the discrepancies to light, or is this going in a different direction?" William asked.

Looking as if he were preparing a speech, Jefferson walked across the room. "Will, we've actually been at this for many months. I had an actual heart to heart with Zachary during his presidency. He explained to me that there are factions within our own government that seem to run things "contrary to the will of the people". Power, land, and money seem to drive these factions and I truly believe that they took him out. I don't believe for one second he died the same as my Knoxie. I have gotten close to the Democratic party over the years. They are the closest allies we have. But even they have factions that are devious. Let's see what Bickley has to say tomorrow and hold our judgement. What do you say Will?" Jefferson concluded.

"I'll try to keep an open mind, my friend." Will replied.

"I say we fucking secede." Albert blustered. "We already have the numbers. We know which states will follow. We should already be giving Washington an ultimatum."

Jefferson, looking ever so understanding, held his hand up. "Now Albert, let's not get ahead of ourselves. We are here to meet with George Bickley. Our two societies have worked side by side for many, many years. Let's hear what he has to say and let me do the talking. Understood?" Jefferson asserted.

"Yeah, you are in charge." Albert agreed.

William watched Jefferson as he looked to the corner of the room, slowly rubbing his chin. It was then that he realized something that had not occurred to him before…Jefferson was very "high up" in the ranks of The Knights of Wisdom. William wondered why he himself was here. In the big picture, he was merely a soldier in the society. He didn't even realize he had been doing exactly what the KOW wanted him to do many years ago… and then there was the thing that he had never told anyone. That was the situation that eventually led to Sarah's demise. She did not want her father forcing The Wisdom on William, and if he hadn't, she may have stayed in Nashville and could be alive today. William struggled with that thought and his promise to The Wisdom. He knew he was a hypocrite for his growing animosity towards The Wisdom.

Albert exited the room, asked John Booth if he wanted to get a drink, and off they went.

Jefferson looked at William. "Nightcap, my friend?"

William saw his old friend's smile. "It's been a while, what'ya got?"

Jefferson walked to his overnight bag. "You know me…only the best Kentucky Bourbon".

They toasted each other, with William excusing himself after one small glass.

The next morning, they met downstairs, in a quiet bar, before heading over to meet Bickley at The Exchange Hotel. Jefferson asked that he and William go first, then Albert and John were to join fifteen minutes later. While William found all the secrecy kind of humorous, he realized he had spent many years working in the very same fashion. He suddenly recalled what the natives called him,…Nudoi, "the ghost".

Bickley had done similarly to Jefferson. He'd booked three rooms at one end of a hall. He even booked the same for the floor above, and below. Bickley wanted to be absolutely sure that no one was able to hear what he had to say. When he spoke, his voice was clear and decisive. William felt like a parishioner with the best evangelist speaking directly to him. Bickley spoke for over forty-five minutes before pausing. What bothered William the most was that this definitely sounded like a succession plan. Albert and John just smiled. But Jefferson, he challenged Bickley. In response, Bickley always seemed to have a plausible answer.

"Who's it going to be?" Jefferson asked.

"Abraham Lincoln, for sure." Bickley replied. "And that will be why we must move ahead. Lincoln will abolish any chance we have."

"And with the South?" Jefferson again inquired.

Bickley smiled. "There's Toombs from Georgia, Cobb, also Georgia, Alexander Stephens seems to be a favored,…and you, who has my vote."

William shot a glance at Jefferson. Jefferson sighed. "Georgia in December, George?"

"Yes, you should be there. We'll actually be meeting at the state capital in Milledgeville. I would expect a debate, as well. Would you choose William, or Albert as Vice?" Bickley challenged.

Jefferson looked at William and then Albert. Both of them raised their hands "in defense". "No, if this happens, it could be ugly. I would want both of these men as my first appointed Generals. What about John, George?" Jefferson asked.

John Booth stood and spoke. "Gentlemen, I'm a skilled actor. I've served the KGC in clandestine operations many times. My home is on the road. I play in every major city, so I may be the perfect spy. With the KGC, I can find

out anything. If I were you, I'd keep me right where I'm at."
He concluded.

After another twenty minutes of discussion, the five
of them stood and agreed to consider all that had been
presented. Jefferson bade Bickley a gracious farewell, and
out the door he went. William and Albert followed.

Walking back to their hotel, William could no longer
hold back. "Jefferson, if this is inevitable, I need time to
think. While I didn't know what to expect coming here, this
kinda caught me by surprise. I've settled down a bit. I'm also
a doctor that owns a coal mining business. I don't know that
I'm your General. Now Albert, I would follow him into any
battle." William articulated.

"I see that, William. I do not see that "fire" that I
saw twenty years ago. But you two are my most trusted
friends. I wouldn't go into battle without both of you. Think
about it, and by the way, owning a coal business when
locomotives have become the primary method to transport
troops, is a good business to be in." Jefferson explained.

William did not stay another night. Something
bothered him, and he felt the need to travel back to
Hawkins County. Having been able to catch an earlier train,
he drifted off during the ride. In his dream, he saw Sarah;
she was beautiful. Just the way he remembered her. Then he
saw himself slowly creeping into an Indian camp. He saw
Sarah bound to a tree, covered in bruises, and bleeding from
lashing wounds. He attacked one by one, taking out each the
savages with his Bowie knife. When he finished the last of
them, he turned to Sarah, but she faded away like an
apparition. He suddenly woke. Sweating profusely, he
breathed heavily. It had been a long time since he had
dreamed of Sarah.

Arriving a day before Jonathan expected him,
William figured he would stop by the post office and then

stop at the tavern to see if anyone was heading towards the homestead. If not, he would just stay at the Emporium for the night, and work the next day until Jonathan arrived.

At the post office, there was a letter for him. It came from Oklahoma, and the envelope was written in perfect script, which he thought was strange. He tucked it into his vest pocket as he headed to the tavern.

Once at the tavern, William found no one heading towards the homestead, so he went to the Emporium. Sitting at his office desk, he pulled the letter from his vest pocket, and cut it open.

Dearest William,

I hope this letter finds you well. I have struggled for many years now with the thought of writing you. But, I eventually thought it best that you know I am well, as was your mother. Know, William, that it felt as if my heart was ripped from my body that fateful day in 1832. But I learned to live again and I am now in the Oklahoma Territory. I am with child once again, and I know that this little girl will live a healthy life thanks to Running Bear. He treats us well and allowed me to name our first child William. I love him, dear William. He is a good man. He and Chief Red Moon saved Mother and me from the Creek. Chief Red Moon took your mother as his own and treated her well. She passed last year, but you have two stepbrothers here in Oklahoma. It is quite odd, this thing called "life". It gives us adversity, but then gives us unexpected happiness. I'm sure you've wed again, and I must say, I would love to see your children running and playing in that beautiful Hawkins County valley. William, please know that I am truly happy and I know that would make you happy. Know that I see a piece of you every day in this young man named William. I will always love you, William. I will always cherish our short time together.

Goodbye My Love,
Sarah Blackwell Running Bear

William dropped the letter, brought his cupped hands to his face, covering his mouth. One tear rolled down his face. Then, he slowly raised his hands and curled his fingers. He began to sob uncontrollably, then finally looked up to the ceiling and stopped. A coldness came over him, then anger. William struggled with the emotions that had just entered his body. He wanted Sarah back, but more so, he wanted retribution to the ones that took her from him.

William looked at the stairway to the second floor. Feeling himself rise and walk towards it, his adrenaline pumped. Finding the old chest was difficult, as Samuel had many quilts lying on it. Opening the old chest, his eyes gazed upon the things that he would need.

The moon glowed brightly. No longer needing a "ride", William Blackwell set out to make his way back to "the valley", his homestead. Dressed in buckskin garments, and carrying a large Bowie knife, Blackwell returned into the wooded abyss.

Chapter 15 –

"The Civil War"

"Samuel! We're not getting enough coal out of the mine. You either gotta pick it up son, or we're going to need help." Blackwell commanded.

"William! Samuel worked in that damn mine every day this week. What do you expect from him?" Jonathan asked.

"There's a storm coming, we need to store ahead. I want two weeks of supply in the barn. What do we need to do to get there?" Blackwell insisted.

Jonathan, shaking his head, refuted, "William, why? What storm? This seems silly. Three months ago we didn't even have the coal field income."

Realizing that he had an opportunity to appease Uncle William, Samuel offered a solution. "Actually Pa, I might know of a way. Remember my friend? The girl I told you about? She knows people that are looking for work. Keeping them together, would make them happy, and they'd probably take less wage, if I kept them together."

Blackwell grinned at Samuel. "Now you're thinking, son. How many you thinking we could put to work?" He asked.

"I'm just guessing,…maybe four, five, six? I'm going to see her after dinner and I can talk to her about it then. Are you thinking that we can sell more, Unc?" Samuel questioned.

"I'm sure those trains will be doubling their trips. I'm going to Milledgeville tomorrow to meet with the most important people in Georgia. If I come home with a contract for double or triple our current output, do you think you can make it happen, Samuel?" Blackwell challenged.

"I believe I can, Uncle. We'll have to build more timbers, but Pa can help me with that. I need to get a set on the entrance anyway." Samuel mused.

Jonathan was no longer shaking his head. "You two sound like damn businessmen! William, you're a doctor. Why are you even foolin' with this?"

"For our future, Jonathan. I see big changes coming and we just might be in the best position to take advantage of this great opportunity. When I was in Knoxville two days ago, the owner of E. T. and V. introduce himself to me. Ten minutes later, he introduced me to the owner of Memphis and Charleston Railways. When I finished talking talking with them, they thought we were as big as The Sewanee Coalfield. I say we hit it hard and make ourselves enough money to sit back and relax here in the valley. What'ya think, boys?" Blackwell asked.

After a resounding "Yes", Blackwell nodded and walked back to his cabin. He knew they didn't know what was coming, and if things played out the way he thought they might, The Confederacy would need all the surplus coal available. He had now been to three meetings and knew that secession was inevitable. There was even talk of a temporary Confederate president being voted in once the secession took place. Tomorrow, he would meet three of his closest friends in Rogersville, then on to Milledgeville, the capital of Georgia. Jefferson Davis, Albert Johnston, and Samuel Cooper were already en route. Davis, now the front-runner, expected to be voted provisional president of the Confederacy.

Blackwell sat by the fireplace that evening. Drinking from a bottle of Kentucky Bourbon, he contemplated how he would go to Oklahoma and exact revenge on the "savages" who took his wife and mother so many years ago. In his mind William Blackwell had again become the person who people feared. He felt adrenaline rush back into his body and couldn't wait for the smell of blood.

***

Spring 1860

The Blackwell Coalfield now employed six Native Americans, and one free Negro. The young female who Samuel had taken a "liking to" led the Native Americans. Moon Dove was the "friend" who he'd spoken about months before. William Blackwell did not like that his nephew was "courting" the young native, but he tolerated it because she had a powerful influence over the rest. When Moon Dove was present, the crew mined almost double the amount as when she wasn't present.

***

Summer 1860

With eight working hard, Blackwell Coalfield began to store coal in the barns and Jonathan farmed only what the nine of them needed. This freed up time for Jonathan to help with the coalfield. William and Samuel managed the mining company. Jonathan delivered coal to Rogersville every day. The Emporium was only open one day a week, but Doctor Blackwell often tended to medical needs from "the valley". Becoming somewhat reclusive, he had lost his desire to work the business in Rogersville.

After receiving the "cold shoulder" multiple times, Miss Emily no longer visited. William Blackwell focused his attention on other methods to acquire the resources he wanted. He became a self-centered opportunist who even his own nephew jokingly called "Ebenezer Scrooge".

***

Fall 1860

Blackwell had traveled to almost every state Jefferson thought would join the "Southern Cause". Blackwell, himself speaking on the lawn of many state capitals. Even Jefferson once asked him, "Am I going to be running against you, Will?".

"No, Jefferson. I just see how blind we were in our younger days. We worked hard to establish our sovereignty, and for what? So a bunch of damn politicians can ruin our very livelihood and economy. While I personally do not have any slaves, I see no reason why someone should lose something they paid good money for!" Blackwell explained.

"Well, don't forget Will,…I'm one of those "damn politicians". Although, you and I may see things the same way, if I didn't have my slaves, I wouldn't have a cotton business. At this point secession is inevitable…and it's damn near half the country wants to leave the Union. We'll get ours, you'll see." Jefferson claimed.

***

Winter 1860

Samuel approached his uncle. "Unc, I know you meant well with the purchase of the two slaves. But, it's causing some confusion with the others. You have them mining longer than the others. Oos says that Frederick, Enoli, and Tooantuh are leaving. They won't work where slaves are being used." Samuel contended.

Blackwell looked up from his medical journal. "Oh?...Well, I have an easy fix for that. I'll replace them all with slaves. How's that?" Blackwell argued.

Samuel sensed the hostility in Blackwell's tone, and he watched his uncle's demeanor slowly change over the last year. Thinking it best to calm the situation, he attempted to lighten the tone. "Listen, Uncle, I apologize, I didn't mean to complain. I'm just working to be fair to all. Oos says she knows four more natives who will mine tomorrow. We pay them well, so they don't normally say much. Is it okay if I tell Cufee and Juba that they will work the same time, and take the same breaks as the rest?" Samuel pleaded.

Blackwell calmed and admired the negotiation tactic his nephew exhibited. He liked it. Samuel had become a effective leader, as was Moon Dove. Blackwell's recent discussions at many events made him realize all negotiations required compromise. "I'll tell you what, Samuel, I know you like Moon Dove. "Oos", I think you call her. I'm going to Montgomery in two weeks. While I'm gone, you can turn my little cabin into a "bunkhouse" for Cufee, Juba, and any others who wish to stay. I don't expect my return for some time. Eventually, I hope to build a place at the other end of the valley. Cufee and Juba should be happy about that. But, when they are not in the mine, I want you using them around the farm, understood?” Blackwell asserted.

Feeling “the win”, Samuel was giddy. “Sure thing, Unc! Thank you. Oos will be so happy. Are you really going to be part of the new government?” He asked.

“I’ve told you very little, but Jefferson wants to make me a General in the Confederacy. I haven’t been a soldier for almost twenty years. Been a doctor for all that time. I’m not sure where I can best serve, but we’ll figure it out. Hell, maybe I’ll just be a politician!” Blackwell laughed.

***

February 9, 1861 – Montgomery, Alabama

The Confederacy unanimously elected Jefferson Davis as its provisional president. He immediately began assembling his cabinet from the initial six states that seceded, and Texas, which would secede before his inauguration. Davis’s cabinet would begin in Montgomery, the new capital of The Confederate States.

“William, I’ve chosen four Generals thus far, and you are obviously among them. Will you accept this responsibility?” Jefferson asked of Blackwell.

“Jefferson, I’ve thought a lot about this. I’ll do whatever you ask, but I left the military a long time ago. Is there a better place for me to serve? Your personal doctor?” Blackwell submitted.

“As have I, my friend. I thought perhaps you’d say something like that. I’m going to create a new cabinet position, and I believe you to be perfect for it. “Surgeon General” is the position. You would report to me and would manage all medical related topics for the Confederate States.

If war breaks out you may be asked to serve with the rank of General. What says you?" Jefferson inquired.

"Jefferson, I'd be honored," Blackwell replied, "and Albert?"

"He had a bit of the same argument, but he crushed the Later Day Saint rebellion in Utah, just four years ago. He's in California right now, but I expect to bring him aboard soon. Cooper, Lee, Beauregard, and Joseph Johnston have all agreed serve. I may need you as acting commander until I can decide who goes to the top. Can you do that for me, Will?" Jefferson challenged.

"Understood. I saw Bickley and Booth here. Are you appointing them, as well?" Blackwell asked.

"No, they serve the KGC, which will be an asset to our cause. They introduced me to this young man from Missouri, Frank James. I believe him to be the next generation of KGC. We should have a similar discussion regarding The Wisdom. Your nephews… have you considered?" Jefferson proposed.

"I have. All three of them seem to favor my ideals over their father's. Jonathan, I'm afraid may be a sympathizer. I'll bring Samuel to Montgomery for a bit. He has a native inamorata who is trustworthy. I'll work on him. Is The Wisdom represented well within this new government?" Blackwell questioned.

Jefferson stood to shake Blackwell's hand. "Yes, it is. An Indian girlfriend? Now that's ironic. Listen, I need to speak to a few others today, but join me for dinner tonight. You'll be pleased with how committed The Wisdom is to our cause.

As Blackwell left the office, he saw the gathering of notable socialites and politicians who he figured he would meet very soon. He saw George Bickley and thought that he should say "hello".

Extending his hand, Blackwell approached Bickley. "Greetings, George. I see you are in good company." Blackwell, acknowledged John Wilkes Booth, who was standing next to Bickley.

"General Blackwell. I AM in good company. Might I also introduce Alexander Franklin James." Bickley stated, waving an open palm toward a young man next to Booth.

Not extending his hand, but nodding, the young man made eye contact with Blackwell. "It's Frank, sir…and I was hoping to serve under you one day. Mister Booth has told me a lot about you. Says you're a just a doctor now?"

Blackwell pursed his lips. "I've been appointed Surgeon General, and acting commander of the Confederate Army,…Son."

"Oh, good. Then you are the right person for me to enlist under. If I get in today, could I be made an officer?" James asked.

Scoffing at the young man's brazenness, Blackwell spoke slowly. "Young man, enlisted soldiers are not officers. If you want to be an officer, you must graduate from one of our military academies,…A minimum of three years." Blackwell asserted.

James cocked his head. "That's just stupid. Why wouldn't you promote those that already know how to fight?"

Booth quickly interrupted, "Frank, General Blackwell is a graduate of Westpoint and served his country admirably. Show some respect."

"Sorry General. But keep me in mind when you run out of officers that can fight." James offered.

Blackwell acknowledged the young man with a nod. He shook John Booth's hand and patted Bickley on the shoulder. "We thank you and the K.G.C. for all of your support. Without your monetary support, I'm not sure that we'd be able to pull this off. Thanks, George." Blackwell said.

"We'll keep it coming, William. All causes need an excellent base, which we are happy to supply. Good day, General." Bickley concluded.

Blackwell moved around the room, shaking hands with many and eventually worked his way towards the front door. That night, Blackwell was introduced to a chapter of The Knights of Wisdom that he did not know existed. The Wisdom had infiltrated the highest levels of state government. He assumed it must be the same way with the Union, which made him realize that this secession had "teeth". He thought, "Someday those "teeth" will bite".

President Jefferson Davis spent countless hours and days discussing the Congress of the Confederacy with his provisional cabinet, including with William Blackwell, in his new position of Surgeon General.

The North quickly took issue with the secession of the Southern states. Abraham Lincoln was indeed voted into the Presidency and his response was to "call up" seventy-five thousand troops to "coerce" the southern states out of secession. The "call" had the opposite effect. As the seventy-five thousand troops were being deployed, Virginia, North Carolina, Arkansas, and Tennessee joined the South in secession.

Unfortunately, "the powder keg" was that the Union forces not only held Fort Sumter in the, now Confederate, State of South Carolina, but they also attempted to resupply the fort. Davis, and the Confederate Congress, saw this as provocation, deciding to attack the fort on April 12th, 1861.

Blackwell placed Brigadier General PGT Beauregard in charge of the campaign, which lasted thirty-four hours and ended when Union Major Robert Anderson surrendered to the onslaught from Beauregard.

An enormous victory for The Confederacy, the action prompted many Union officers to resign from the U.S. Army, notably Albert Johnston and Robert E. Lee. Both immediately joined the Confederate cause.

In July, The Confederacy achieved another victory at the Battle of Bull Run. General Blackwell, arriv by train with General Joseph Johnston and eight thousand reinforcement troops. Blackwell insisted on the use of the railroad, which proved to be the fastest way to move the troops.

In May of 1861, officials moved the Confederate capital to Richmond, Virginia. A move meant to bring the center of The Confederacy to the largest city in the "South". While Blackwell traveled throughout the south, he liked that the major rails, Virginia Central and East Tennessee & Virginia Railroads, were two of the fastest. He could travel to Rogersville in a day and a half. A trip he attempted monthly.

Samuel had visited Montgomery and was officially initiated into The Knights of Wisdom. He joined primarily out of respect for his uncle William, but he had a firm opinion that Abraham Lincoln would be the demise of America. When Blackwell told him about Lincoln calling up the seventy-five thousand troops to oust the South, Samuel immediately wanted to enlist in the Confederate Army. Catching Blackwell a bit "off-guard", he argued that Samuel's calling would be at another time. "Besides, son, we need you running the coalfield." Blackwell had insisted.

***

The Battle of Shiloh - April 1862

While technically having joined the Confederacy, Tennessee was a severely divided as a state. Being one of the most active states for skirmishes, the situation came to blows in April of 1862. The Union's General Ulysses S. Grant led two significant victories in Middle Tennessee. This allowed his troops to move south down the Tennessee River. With Grant in charge of the Union's Western Campaign, they had the potential of cutting off the western part of Tennessee, if successful, a major victory for the Union. Union General Don Carlos Buell had taken Nashville and was working his way south as well. In order to stop this movement, General Albert Sydney Johnston, who was in charge of the Confederate Western campaign, began his movement up from Alabama to meet with General PGT Beauregard and General Braxton Bragg. Between them, almost 60,000 confederate troops were under their command. They would meet up at Pittsburg Landing on the morning of April sixth. General Johnston commanded from the front lines, which proved to be his demise. Often seen far in front of the front lines General Johnston rallied his troops with a tin cup on his sword, rattling during battle. Soldiers claimed Johnston rode by them with blood noticeably dripping from his boot and bullet holes in his uniform. In the early afternoon, he rode back to the front line and slumped in his saddle. Soldiers lowered him to the ground and watched him quickly die as he bled out.

Surgeon General Blackwell arrived at the battle with over one hundred medical soldiers. Upon arrival, Blackwell saw the bodies, commanded his men to begin triage and asked for General Johnston. After hearing of Johnston's death, Blackwell asked to see him.

Stepping into General Johnston's tent, Blackwell removed his hat. They had laid Johnston on his cot and covered his body with a woolen blanket. There was still blood dripping to the floor when Blackwell dropped to one knee. "Damn you, Albert. This wasn't supposed to happen.

You were supposed to take me to Oklahoma! Why did you have to be the one up front? Why, Albert?" Blackwell pleaded.

Pulling the blanket back, Blackwell looked over Johnston's body. Probing the holes in his uniform he found only one superficial injury. That was until he removed the blanket from his legs. With one boot missing, Blackwell could see the trousers covered in blood. He lifted Johnston's leg. Probing from below, he found the bullet hole that caused Albert's death. His popliteal artery had been severed.

"Oh, Albert. Where was your damn tourniquet? I instructed all of you to carry them with you at all times. That would have saved your life. Damn you, my friend." Blackwell dropped his head.

Believing they had successfully defeated Grant in the bloodiest battle yet, General Beauregard did not realize that Buell had joined forces with Grant and on the morning of the seventh, battle raged once again. Eventually, Beauregard called for a retreat since he realized they were outnumbered.

Blackwell had already left, driving a wagon with his friend's body south towards safety. Eventually he arrived in New Orleans, where Blackwell asked that General Albert Sydney Johnston be buried with military honors.

Richmond mourned upon hearing of Johnston's death. President Davis traveled to New Orleans for the funeral of his friend. Giving what many believed was the most touching speech of his life, Davis gave a eulogy that had many weeping. "For we have lost the shining light, the guiding star of our army, and the Confederacy has lost the man who was to have been it's savior." Davis uttered.

After the funeral, that evening, a soldier came to Davis's quarters. "President Davis, The Surgeon General is here to see you."

"Of Course, Captain. Send him in." Davis replied.

A melancholy William Blackwell entered the den. Before he could speak, President Davis approached him with arms extended.

Embracing momentarily, President Davis quickly took the advantage to speak. "Will, we knew this was possible. Hell, it could have been you. I'm glad you were the one that could bring Albert home. I thank you for that Will."

Blackwell walked to the window and looked out. "This isn't his home, Jefferson. This is war, and we are all casualties. The day I left West Point, I was a casualty. The day Sarah married me…she, was a casualty. Nobody makes it home, Jefferson." Blackwell stated. He paused briefly, then spoke again before Davis could speak. "You know,…Albert was going to take me to Sarah. She's in The Oklahoma Territory."

Jefferson Davis already knew what his friend was going to say. He had heard of the "white Indian women"… those who had been kidnapped and eventually becoming part of the tribe.

"Probably not a great idea, Will. It's been too long. Did she ask for you?" Davis asked.

"No, just the opposite" Blackwell replied.

Thinking it best to change the subject, Davis addressed other issues. "Will, the damn Yanks cut Tennessee in half. We're amassing enough troops in Corinth to take it back. I want to put you in command of "the west". Can you do that for me, Will?" Davis requested.

As he had done so many times before, Blackwell wrung his hands together. Shaking his head, he looked up at Davis. "Jefferson, like I said, we are already casualties. I don't have any reason not to drive a spike right into Grant's heart. Give me two thousand men, and I'll get close enough to do it." Blackwell claimed.

"A suicide mission is not what I meant, Will. Losing you for Grant accomplishes nothing. You need some time to think. I'm going to grant you three weeks' leave, then I want you putting back together the "Wicked Nineteenth". You can pull any of your former soldiers to resurrect the Nineteenth. You will have my full support. I want to use the Nineteenth as a reconnaissance group solely. You'll be in command." Davis explained.

"Reconnaissance group!?" Blackwell contended.

"In two months, I'll send orders to Hawkins County. You'll most likely meeting up at Chattanooga. I'll put Bragg in charge of the Western Theater for now…Beauregard's a bit flaky. Head on back to Hawkins County Will and look for my orders." Davis offered.

Blackwell left New Orleans with a feeling of despair and disenchantment. He felt anger towards the one person who he thought was his dearest friend. His own ignorance had overtaken and he could not understand Davis's change of plans for him.

Upon reaching the valley, Blackwell was surprised to find that Jonathan, Mary, and little William had left. Samuel explained they had left the month before and planned to visit Mary's family in Northern Kentucky. They had not returned, so Samuel suspected they had stayed in Kentucky.

Apparently, Jonathan had been quite upset that William had purchased the slaves for the farm. He further contended that the mined coal was for the Confederate cause and not that of the Union. Jonathan believed this to be wrong and got even angrier when Samuel mentioned his desire in joining the Confederate Army or Tennessee Militia.

"And Thomas? How'd he get to stay?" Blackwell asked Samuel, inspecting the mounds of coal, now being kept in the largest barn.

"He ran off two weeks before they left. Ma and Pa assumed he joined the militia. He came back the day after they left. I still ain't got a straight answer out him. Don't say much at all. Oos and I been tryin'…but nuthin'. You just comin' through?" Samuel asked.

Blackwell looked toward the mine. "No, I'm on leave. My buddy Albert died, and Jefferson wants me to prepare to take Tennessee back from the "Yanks". If them damn reds are in my cabin, I'll set up my tent next to the house." Blackwell muttered.

"Hell, stay in Ma and Pa's room. Ain't no one in it. It'll be good to have you around for a bit. I want to hear about the war. I'm itchin' to go, but Oos says that I need to be here for the coalfield. Else, she's thinkin' that someone'll come in here and take it for themselves." Samuel explained.

Still looking up towards the mine, Blackwell added, "Yeah. She's right Samuel…and there's something else up there. If someone knew about it, they'd kill for it." Blackwell asserted.

"The gold?" Samuel asked.

"You know about the gold?" Blackwell quizzed.

"Yeah. Known about it for some time. Oos showed it to me. It's on the other side. She had walked all the way through the mine and saw it on the other side." Samuel disclosed.

Blackwell was now looking right at Samuel. "They haven't touched it, have they?"

"No. The coal means more to them than the gold. I went up and got a few nuggets. I figger'd you knew about it. So, I just got some pieces for you. They're at the house. Oos'll be down to make us dinner, in a bit. Why don't you come on over and get settled. I wanna talk." Samuel offered.

Blackwell smiled. "I'd like that Samuel. Maybe we can talk Thomas into helping me unload this wagon, and board the horses for the night. I gotta get it back to that new blacksmith in the morning."

That evening, Blackwell enjoyed himself more than he had any time since the war started. He told the boys about a few battles, watching their faces change as he explained the skirmishes in detail. Afterward, all three of them tended to the wagon and horses, while Moon Dove prepared dinner for the rest of the miners. William surprised Samuel by refusing help from Cufee and Juba.

After almost everybody had turned in, Blackwell poured a tin cup of bourbon, pulled a cigar from his satchel and sat down on the front porch. Pushing himself back with one foot, the creak of the front door startled him. Stepping out, Samuel noticed Blackwell reaching for a sidearm that was no longer present. "It's just me General." Samuel said, with a smile. He then pulled two nuggets from his pocket and held them up for Blackwell to see.

Blackwell set down the tin cup and held out his hand. Setting them in Blackwell's hand, Samuel said, "I think there's a good bit up there Unc,…I mean General."

Blackwell smiled at Samuel. "Tell me something, Son. What would you do with it?"

"I give it to the cause General." Samuel replied. "From what you've said, we need everything that we can get. We need to win this war, Sir."

Blackwell held out the nuggets for Samuel to take back. "Samuel, you never cease to amaze me. I wish you were my own, and I thank the Lord that he made you a Blackwell."

"I am, Uncle William…and damn proud to be by your side." Samuel avowed.

"Me too." A whisper sputtered. In the shadow of the open door, Thomas was standing.

"Is that my Thomas, I see?" William stated with a big smile. Out walked Thomas, wearing a Confederate kepi. The well-worn hat being too big for Thomas' thirteen-year-old head.

Samuel's eyes widened. "What the hell? You really did go join the militia, Thomas! How many them damn Yanks you killed boy!" Samuel quipped.

Blackwell immediately noticed something that he had seen all too often. Except this time, his heart nearly broke.

Thomas' head dropped, and his voice trembled. "J,-Just one,…I think." He muttered.

Blackwell lowered his tipped chair, stepped up and walked over to the trembling boy. Wrapping his arms around him, he patted his back. Suddenly, Samuel realized Thomas was telling the truth. He walked over and put his hand on Thomas' shoulder. They all stood there until Thomas stopped shaking.

Blackwell walked Thomas over to the chair he'd been sitting in, and sat Thomas down. "Son, I've been there…it's scary. It makes you sick. Just know that it's not your fault. You were just doing what you were ordered to do. I'm sorry that you had to go through that. You are a young man. But you are too young to go through that. We've talked enough about it tonight. But, I want you to come to me if you ever need to talk about it again. Do you understand me, Thomas? Come to me anytime that you need to talk."

Thomas looked up at William. "Yes Sir, Thank you, Sir". He stood and slowly walked inside.

After Samuel knew Thomas was back inside and out of ear-shot he looked at Blackwell.

"Daaaaaamn! I didn't expect that. That little shit's already got him a Yank. I'm jealous." Samuel shared.

"Don't be, Samuel. It's a heavy burden on your soul. Knowing that you've killed someone and may not go to heaven is not what you want." William insisted.

"But it's war, Uncle William." Samuel argued.

"You think that makes it right?...to take another man's life?" Blackwell paused. "Oh, I've gone through the effort of convincing myself that "war" is justifiable, and I'll be forgiven. But, it doesn't make it right,…and I know that I'm going to Hell for what I've done. When I go back, I'll do my best to save lives. But, inevitably, I know I will have to take them as well. Please Samuel, you and Thomas can do the most for The Confederacy from here. Don't get the desire to fight. You saw what it did to Thomas. Just stay here." Blackwell begged.

***

Over the next three weeks, Blackwell watched the miners go into the coal mine, then he'd head over to the other side of the mountain, where the old cave exited. At the place he'd seen gold rock years before, he'd spend a few hours there every day.

Packing the wagon, Samuel knew what was in the wooden ammo box. "Uncle William, I'll watch over Thomas. I really want to do more than just feed these damn "iron horses". But I will watch over him."

Placing his luggage in the wagon, Blackwell paused and looked down. "Samuel. You do not know how much you are doing for the war effort, and, between us, it might be worth while to quietly mine a bit of that gold. I'll be back in a month, or two. I'll stop to check in on you and the crew. You're a good man." He smiled. "I don't approve of your taste in women, but we'll leave that discussion for another time." Blackwell winked at him.

As the months went on, Blackwell recruited troops and settled in at Blountville, Tennessee. Nestled along the edge of the Appalachian Mountains, Blountville was a perfect place for Blackwell to amass troops. It was a primary stop on the rail that traveled to Rogersville and went on to Knoxville. In the other direction, it traveled to Richmond. So, Blackwell was prepared for the day when Davis would eventually call on him.

With a fair amount of Union skirmishes, Blackwell seemed to hold the territory well for the Confederacy, thusly protecting the rail route to Rogersville, and the gold that Blackwell filtered into the "Confederate cause". He had heard the stories of Frank James robbing trains, so he made sure that his "transfers" were well guarded. Only a few soldiers knew exactly what was going on, all of them being sworn Knights of Wisdom.

Not receiving word from Davis month after month bothered Blackwell. He thought about the amount of gold that the Blackwells were supplying The Confederacy, with little recognition. He also realized that Samuel and Thomas received no credit whatsoever. So, he began to hide small portions throughout his trips, literally burying ammo boxes of gold along the routes, keeping cryptic treasure maps in his field bag.

Blackwell convinced himself that he had become the most over-ranked soldier in The Confederacy, which angered him. He believed they had purposefully forgotten him, and he started dressing "out of uniform." Of course, it wasn't the first time that he had done this. So, it bothered him little. Rumors started after soldiers noticed Blackwell's mix of attire. Some thought him eclectic; some thought him deranged. Either way, most kept their distance from him.

In September of 1863, Blackwell received a letter from George Bickley. It was a well-written letter, asking how

Blackwell and his family were faring through "these trying times". This letter included a blessing to all those in the South. Blackwell had not seen it often, but he knew exactly what this letter was. That night, he deciphered the letter in his dimly lit quarters.

The deciphered message asked that he travel alone to Chattanooga, where he would meet with F. J. and J. B.. They would give him a package to bring back to Blountville and another courier would eventually collect it. Bickley, believing Blackwell to be one of the most informed generals in the Confederacy, asked for an "update".

Blackwell scoffed at this, as his resentment was growing. He had already planned to travel to Richmond to confront Davis, but decided to do this one thing for The Wisdom beforehand.

On September twenty, Blackwell boarded the train from Blountville to Chattanooga. Traveling through Rogersville, and staying in the train car, felt odd to Blackwell. He could not recall the last time he had not disembarked at the Rogersville train station. At one point, he even thought he had seen Samuel in Confederate uniform at the station, then erased the thought. Traveling to Chattanooga, Blackwell fell into a somber. Again dreamed of Sarah, and again killed all in the camp. Awakening before he could make it back to her bound body, he regained his composure and quickly made his way to gather his bag, prepared to exit the train in Chattanooga.

Blackwell left the train station and headed for The Railroad Hotel. While the Crutchfield House was a larger hotel, Blackwell believed his colleagues would stay somewhere less conspicuous. He stepped into The Railroad Saloon and immediately saw two familiar faces. Frank James was playing poker and John Boothe stood at the bar, obviously flirting with a "parlor lady". Seeing Blackwell, Boothe quickly excused himself from his flirtation.

Meeting Blackwell halfway across the room, Boothe extended his hand. "General Blackwell. It is good to see you, sir."

"You, as well, John. How's the "acting life"?" Blackwell asked, believing that Boothe would understand the underlying meaning.

They walked together to a table in the room's corner. Sitting down, Boothe replied. "Acting has proved to be one of our greatest assets, my friend. We are currently working on a play whereby the key person disappears. He doesn't die, he's just held captive until a little recognition is at hand. I understand you have become quite the investor in causes as such."

Blackwell grinned. "I don't know the details. I just know that I can support the bigger one. If the smaller ones benefit the "greater", why then, I believe I support those as well. Speaking of which, I understand I am to pick up a package here and take it back. I assume to Richmond?"

"Let's get you in a room, then we can discuss the package" Boothe offered.

As was done before, Boothe had rented four rooms at the end of the hallway. Stepping into the furthest one, with Boothe in tow, Blackwell asked. "Who's in the fourth?"

"That's Frank's brother, Jesse. He's a young one, but isn't afraid of anything. A bit of a wild card, but Frank swears by him, and claims that he'll keep him "in check"." Boothe divulged.

Blackwell walked to the washbasin, poured water, and lowered himself to wash his face. While washing his face, there was a knock at the door. Boothe let Frank James and another young man in. As Blackwell was drying his face, he heard the young man say, "He don't look that tough."

Blackwell turned to the men. "Frank. It's good to see you." Blackwell said while walking towards them. "…and the one with the big mouth, I understand is your brother?"

Blackwell's comment noticeably bothered Jesse, but Frank laughed. "Blackwell, it's good to see you too. Yeah, "big mouth" here is Jesse, my brother. Frank confirmed. "He-…"

Interrupting Frank, Jesse spoke. "Frank says that you've killed upwards of twenty men, mister. I say that's bullshit!"

Blackwell chuckled. "Well, I must agree with you, Jess. Twenty is a little low."

Jesse's face scowled. "Low? Bullshit! How many?"

"I stopped counting, young man. After one, it really doesn't matter. Hell is waiting for you. I suppose I could count the scratches on my knife. That'd probably be half, but it's not something that I'm proud of. Let's talk about why I am here, gentlemen." Blackwell stated as he walked towards his leather duffle.

"I ain't done talkin' to you, old man!" Jesse proclaimed.

Blackwell looked over his shoulder, and quickly noticed Jesse's hand on the butt of a revolver, tucked in his waistband. Almost without thinking, he drew his Bowie knife and threw it at the boy's head.

Jesse did not flinch as the Bowie spun past his head and stuck into the door. Grasping the revolver, Jesse pulled the gun. But something caught his eye. Just inches away from his head was the handle of the Bowie knife. On that handle, there were too many scratches to count. Fifty, seventy-five, maybe a hundred scratches, just on one side of the handle.

"Stop this, men!" Boothe exclaimed.

Jesse settled the revolver back into his waistband, and claimed, "You missed."

Blackwell looked sternly at the young man. "No, I didn't. You wanted to know…and I didn't want to add another scratch."

Frank broke out into laughter, pulled the knife from the door, and handed it to his brother. "Here, you want to give it a try? Put it in that door, close to where the General just did".

Jesse spun the knife in his hands, looked over the blade, and then the handle. "No, I'm good. Sorry I doubted you General."

Noticeably relieved, Boothe headed for the door. "Frank, Jess and I are going to get the package. Would you please pour the General a bourbon."

Returning just two minutes later, Boothe and Jess carried in a medium-sized travel trunk. Setting it on the floor of Blackwell's room, Boothe pulled a key from his pocket and held it out to Blackwell. "No need to look inside, but there's enough to support almost any effort the Confederacy should endeavor." Boothe revealed.

As he accepted the glass from Frank, Blackwell nodded to him, and then looked at the young man. "You all have been busy, haven't you?"

"Robin Hood would be jealous, General." Frank exclaimed.

Boothe started again. "General Shelby will have two soldiers on the train with you going back. You won't know who they are, but they are there to protect this package. Do you know Albert Pike?"

"If you are speaking of Brigadier General Albert Pike, I do know him." Blackwell replied.

"If you didn't already know, he had his fill of the fucking Indians. Davis asked him to go back to the

Oklahoma Territory and Pike resigned. But, he remains loyal to the cause. You'll meet up with Pike in Richmond. Go to the Spotswood. Pike'll find you there. Do not let this trunk out of your sight, General." Boothe instructed.

Blackwell looked perplexed. His brow tightened and his voice raised. "Pike was in Oklahoma? What the hell was he doing there?"

Frank and Jesse James had moved toward the door, but hadn't opened it.

Blackwell's interest in Pike confused Boothe. "Jefferson put Pike in charge of getting the Indians to join the cause. He was up there recruiting Cherokee, Creek, Choctaw soldiers. Pike's been doing that for the last year and a half. Quit a few months back. He's mainly focused on getting money in the hands of the Confederacy now. He's a good man. K.G.C. big time." Boothe explained.

Blackwell was beside himself with anger. Why did Jefferson Davis send General Pike to the Oklahoma Territory instead of him? Regaining his composure, Blackwell extended a hand to Boothe. "John, good luck with the "acting". Not sure when we'll meet again. I'm coming up on my last years, and patience is growing thin. Keep a bridle on them two." Blackwell nodded towards the James' brothers. "That young one's gonna be trouble."

"You too, General." Boothe replied. Walking out, he thought about Blackwell's comments.

That night, before laying his head down, Blackwell unlocked the trunk. Inside was jewelry, coins, and paper money from both the Confederacy and the United States. He lifted the trunk. Heavy, but he could handle it. He laid out his clothing for the morning and moved the rest to the trunk, then locked the trunk.

Aboard the train the next day, Blackwell noticed the two travelers seated behind him. Obvious KGC soldiers. He settled in for the long ride back to Blountville, and then on to Richmond. Resting off and on, he kept an eye on the two KGC soldiers behind him by watching their reflections in the windows. He saw them eventually sleep, as did most of the passengers.

Reaching Rogersville brought comfort to Blackwell. But then he noticed the Confederate soldiers. He knew Rogersville well, and there were too many soldiers here,…something was wrong.

Waving the brakeman down, Blackwell stood. "What's going on? Seems our stop is long? Blackwell inquired.

The brakeman looked nervous. "The next stop has been taken by the North. The Conductor is talking to the station to see if it's safe to proceed. To be honest, Sir, I'm stepping off. I'm from Georgia. They might hang me just for being from the South. If I was you, and you was from the South. I'd get off."

"Brakeman, isn't the next stop Blountville?" Blackwell asked.

"Yes, Sir" the brakeman replied.

The brakeman moved on, and Blackwell rubbed his chin. Standing, he looked back at the two KGC soldiers. They hadn't moved. Eyes closed, and motionless.

***

Blackwell reached the valley as the sun was going down. He could already see the moon rising. Noticing the red "tint" across the valley, he could tell that there was going to be a Blood Moon that night and drove the wagon to the barn. Seeing the miners washing up in the lake, he knew that he'd hadn't missed dinner. He knew that Samuel and Thomas would be helping Oos prepare dinner for all and hoped that Cufee and Juba were with them. Then again, it didn't matter to him. Blackwell retrieved a large leather saddlebag from the tack room of the barn. Standing in the back of the wagon, he moved all the jewelry, coins, and money from the trunk to the saddlebags. He then slid the saddlebags to the rear of the wagon. After climbing down, Blackwell dragged the saddlebags over his shoulders. He shifted a little, then started across the field, and up the side of the south mountain.

Returning to the barn two hours later, Blackwell saw Samuel had already tended to his horses. So, Blackwell headed for the house. Samuel, Thomas, and Moon Dove were on the front porch.

"I figured that was you. Same wagon that you borrowed from the blacksmith last time. Didn't figure you'd be coming back so soon. Fraid we've only got a little good stuff for ya." Samuel stated.

Blackwell stopped. Looked at Samuel, then at Moon Dove, and back. "Tell me something Samuel. You seem to trust Moon Dove. But you realize she can be just as savage as the rest, don't you?"

Moon Dove stepped off the porch and started for the old cabin.

"I'm no arguing with you Unc. But, we all trust Oos here. If it weren't for her, we'd have prolly starved to death." Samuel expressed.

"Sorry Samuel. That was a cheap shot on my part. I frankly don't like the fact that she knows about the gold. That's all." Blackwell made clear.

"They all know, Unc. Hell, they've been mining now for many years. They know what gold is and they really don't see the value in it. But they do know that it is here." Samuel explained.

"How long you staying?" Samuel inquired.

Blackwell stepped onto the porch and pulled a flask. "The North took Blountville while I was in Chattanooga. Not sure what happened yet, but I figure I'll find out. Be here a few weeks. Thomas, you up for helping me find out what happened in Blountville?"

Samuel immediately interrupted. "Uncle William! You said…Thomas..--"

Blackwell held his hand up. "We have to take two wagons into town tomorrow so I can return the blacksmith's. I just want him to ask around. That's all. If Rogersville is turning, it wouldn't be good for me to be poking."

***

Samuel was at the mine entrance when he saw Blackwell and Thomas coming across the valley. Curious, he called back to Moon Dove. "Oos, I'm going to meet up with Unc and Thomas at the house. You okay up here?"

"Uh-Huh" Moon Dove called back.

Meeting them as they rode up, Samuel grinned. "What'd ya find out?" he asked.

"I found out that Thomas is too good at getting information. I had left Carter in charge, Colonel James E. Carter. Five thousand of Foster's men attacked them. Carter and my men retreated towards Kingsport. Many got separated, now dispersed all over Hawkins and Sevier counties. There's a quiet occupation of Knoxville by the Union right now. But apparently, Carter had let some know that there was going to be an effort to take Knoxville back. We're in a damn "hornet's nest" right now. It might be best to collect a small group here, in the valley. Then try to join the Knoxville campaign. It sounds like General Longstreet will lead that campaign and I know his tactics well." Blackwell explained.

Thomas chimed in, "And they was two dead men on the train yesterday. Uncle William said they was sitting right behind him." Thomas said excitedly.

Samuel, appearing frustrated, raised his voice. "You mean to tell me we've got Yanks all around us, and you don't want me fighting? I don't understand Uncle! Hell, you just took your little spy into town! This ain't right! What the hell we gonna do if the damn Yanks come right through the valley?"

Blackwell realized he had created a situation that he needed to correct. "I'm sorry, Samuel. I know you want to fight, and the both of you have be diligent in your efforts here. Please hang on for a while longer. I personally know the war is going to come to an end soon. I'm going to tell you guys something that you have to swear not to tell anyone. You swear?" He asked.

Samuel and Thomas replied, "Yes, sir."

"The war is going to be over soon." Pausing, Blackwell contemplated how much he should really say, then decided that these two are his family, his most trusted people, and they needed to understand why he thought it better that they not get involved in the war. "There are "quiet forces" creating a plan. Lincoln is about to be kidnapped. Once this is done, the Union will have to come to "the table".

"All "the South" really wants is for "the North" to stop messing with slavery. Leave it be, and we all go back to being one happy family. It'll happen soon. But you bring up an excellent point. That being, what if Union forces come through here? If I create a small squad of soldiers to protect the mine and the valley, do you think you can keep them straight?" Blackwell quizzed, hoping that "the carrot" was enough to appease Samuel.

"Sure. Are you saying that I would be "in command" here?" Samuel asked.

Chuckling, Blackwell replied, "You have been for some time, Samuel… and when you are not here, Thomas is in command of the valley."

"and, then Oos?" Thomas asked.

Blackwell instantly pulled his head back. "What? No!...well, wait." he looked at Samuel's face, and saw the look of a man who needed reassurance. "I suppose you're right. Yes, then Oos." It was the first time that he had called her by that name. Waving the boys in, Blackwell whispered. "When this is all said and done, we'll be f…iilllllty rich. We'll have all the slaves that we want. We'll be able to sit back and watch everybody do everything for us. We'll build three mansions in the valley… and… and I want to watch YOUR children play in these fields." Blackwell suddenly remembered Sarah's words.

"This sounds great Uncle William. As much as I want to fight, your plan sounds better." Samuel smiled. "Can I at least have a rifle?"

"Absolute, Samuel. I'll give you a rifle, and I want you to have my revolver." Blackwell smiled. "His boys" were playing right into his hand.

Noticing Moon Dove's approach, Blackwell changed the subject and appeared more serious. "Thomas, you and Moon Dove get these supplies unloaded. Have Cufee or Juba cut the field down for tents. We're gonna have some visitors. You ready to cook for some soldiers, Moon Dove?" Blackwell smiled at his attempt to embarrass her. She touched Samuel's smiling face. Blackwell suddenly felt his blood boil with rage at her gesture towards Samuel, a clear acknowledgement she'd do anything for him.

***

Battle of Bean's Station – December 1863

A voice called General James Longstreet from his tent. The voice sounded familiar, but he couldn't quite place it. Surprised to see his old comrade, Longstreet wondering about the visit.

"Blackwell, my friend. You never change. Still dressing like a damn savage, I see. The last I heard, you took a hit at Shiloh. You appear to have bounced back. What brings you here?" Longstreet asked.

Blackwell shook Longstreet's hand and pointed to Longstreet's tent. Once inside, Blackwell un-rolled a map. "James, I'm still serving, but Davis doesn't seem to want to use me, as he should. I've been bouncing around East Tennessee." Not wanting to divulge his true camp location, Blackwell claimed to have a small militia "near Blountville" and that he had been wreaking havoc with the Union forces randomly. He explained his scouts saw that Longstreet's retreat from Knoxville was being followed.

Blackwell continued. "If you act tonight, you have a perfect opportunity to flank your pursuers. Their camp is just behind you, at Bean's Station. The calvary appears separated from the infantry. If you cut them in half, you'll take their entire calvary."

Longstreet stood for a moment, then called for the Sargent, standing guard. "Get me Humphreys, Martin, and Grumble. Immediately!"

Once all of the General's arrived, Longstreet asked Blackwell to repeat his findings. Blackwell also explained that he believed they should dispatch troops south and north of Bean's Station that very night, offering to guide the "North troops" because of the terrain, and his familiarity.

General Benjamin Humphreys doubted Blackwell's information. "General Longstreet, Let us scout this for ourselves. We'll leave at first light. If Blackwell is correct, then we can assess a strategy."

Longstreet had much confidence in his generals and thought it to be a good idea to verify the information. "Humpherys, do that and report back. By the time you get back, we'll have a battle plan."

Longstreet's decision obviously irritated Blackwell. "General Longstreet, this is a mistake. Two things will go wrong with this plan. One, you are giving them time for the infantry to catch up. And two,… if they see Humphreys, they'll be ready for battle."

Humphreys took immediate offense at Blackwell's analysis. "Certainly, you jest, Blackwell!…and it's General Humphreys, sir."

Blackwell rolled up his map and placed it back into the leather roll. Looking at Longstreet, he shook his head. "Good luck, James." He then started to walk out of the tent. Pausing, he looked back at Humphreys. "It's General Blackwell,…SIR!"

Disgruntled by the response that he received from Longstreet, Blackwell continued to lay low in the valley. He and his twenty-three-man militia kept coal supplied to Rogersville, and the Blackwells quietly collected copious amounts of gold, which they hid well.

Thanks to Blackwell's funding, the garrison at the valley was well stocked. All of Blackwell's men had rifles and revolvers, which was rare. With Blackwell's approval, even Samuel wore a Confederate uniform, which Blackwell himself "pinned" as Sargeant.

***

Fall 1864

After reading the letter, Blackwell called for Samuel. "Samuel, it appears that my "other" home has come under attack. A brother in "The Wisdom" is asking for help. I'll be taking twenty of our troops and heading to Franklin. We're going to meet up with General Forrest at Bull's Gap then move on to Franklin. You know what to do here." Blackwell instructed.

"Understood, General." Samuel replied.
Blackwell reached for his gloves, but noticed Samuel's

apprehension.

"Can I ask you a question, sir?" Samuel inquired.

"Certainly, Samuel." Blackwell offered.

"What ever happened to the war ending,…well, with Lincoln, the kidnapping, and all?" Samuel challenged.

"It takes time, Samuel. Complicated plans take time. It'll happen though." Blackwell said confidently.

"Very good, sir." Samuel soldierly replied.

***

Blackwell met up with General Nathan Bedford Forrest at Bull's Gap, but local skirmishes delayed their departure. Lucky for the delay, they were notified that General Sherman, with over fifty-five thousand troops, was heading directly in their path. Forrest, fearing the north route around Nashville may slow them with skirmishes, called a meeting with his war council, including Blackwell.

To ensure Forrest's safety, Blackwell's troops pledged to scout the northern route, mirroring the practices of the Indian Wars. Forrest saw this as a perfect opportunity to break Sherman's "rear guard", if the time was "right". Then they would eventually move on north, as advised.

Sherman's rear guard fell for the tactic and pursued Forrest's troops, thinking that they were retreating. In reality, they were just marching north as planned. Before Sherman's rear guard realized it, they were a day away from the original marching path and in territory randomly held by The Confederacy. Taking days to catch up, they lost over one thousand men and The Confederacy regained the supply line through Chattanooga.

Eventually reaching Franklin in late November, Generals Forrest, Blackwell, Cheatham, and Stewart met up with General Hood's twenty-seven thousand troops.

Blackwell saw the disagreement among the commanding officers. Believing that General Forrest was arguing the very points that he would, Blackwell asked to join the surgeons. He received no argument from the thirty-some generals, who already disputed every aspect.

On the day of the battle, November thirtieth, Blackwell regretted his decision to join the surgeons. Within hours, the Confederate Army suffered massive losses. The surgeons realized they could only help the soldiers that they believed would make it, and possibly get back into the fight. In the melee, Blackwell treated eleven Confederate Generals, all of whom perished.

Moving among the regimental hospitals, Blackwell could tell that the Confederacy was not doing well. At one point he was close to General Hood's command quarters. Covered in the blood of fallen soldiers, Blackwell was almost turned away, but one of Hood's commanders recognized him. "General Blackwell, are you hurt?" The young lieutenant asked.

"No, son. I'm a surgeon today. Can I bend the ear of Hood?" Blackwell requested.

"Yes, sir. Follow me." The lieutenant replied.

Seeing Blackwell covered in blood astonished General Hood. "Blackwell! What the hell?" He inquired.

"It's this bad, Sir. I'm only saving the ones who I think can go back into battle. We're all doing it. I've seen eleven of your generals go down. It's not good, sir. It's mostly hand to hand combat right now. I just helped a soldier who was stabbed with a pitch fork. I've not seen one break for us." Blackwell concluded.

Hood turned towards the melee. "We are not pulling back! You watch, We'll break those scoundrels, yet. Thank you for the update, Blackwell. I would like for you to assume a command point, but I have a hunch you'll just turn me down. Am I correct?"

Blackwell was shaking his head. "You don't need me getting back into battle, General. It's too late. You'll just bury me with the rest."

Turning away from Blackwell with formidable disgust, Hood said, "Very well. Return to the hospital. We are not giving up."

Blackwell began his rounds once again. As darkness fell, the stream of wounded did not slow. Many regiments continued the battle until nine o'clock. Blackwell continued to work on soldiers until midnight, when exhaustion finally took over. Blackwell told another surgeon that he was going to "sit down, for a minute". After finding a stump to lie against, he immediately fell into a deep sleep.

In his deep slumber, Blackwell saw Sarah. She was older now, but just as beautiful as he remembered. She came to him and reached out her hands. He took them. Looking up at him, she said, "No William. No." Not hearing any of the moans from the dying, Blackwell continued to sleep until a sudden jolt awakened him.

Two soldiers were attempting to lift him into a wagon. Blackwell cried, "Stop! What are you doing?"

The soldier carrying Blackwell's legs dropped them. "Oh shit! This one's alive. He ain't dead Josh."

The other, helping Blackwell to his feet, asked, "You okay, Sir? You have a general's coat on. Is you a general?"

"Blackwell, General Blackwell, I--" Blackwell was cut off by the young soldier.

"Cain't be. General Blackwell got kilt last night. I dun heard it from Corporal Miller. Said he died fighting." The young man proclaimed.

Blackwell, baffled by the soldier's belief, waved them both off.

Walking among the bodies strewn across the fields, he eventually came to rest on a log, by a creek. He noticed the movement towards the city of Franklin, though missing the report of gunfire. Confusion set in.

"Those guys actually thought that I was dead." Blackwell told himself. "If I was dead, then nothing would stop me from traveling on to Oklahoma. Getting Sarah back…and killing the savages who took her." His mind raced.

Removing his coat, he looked across the dead and quickly saw what he was looking for…someone his size, with a beard, and approximate age as himself. He pulled the man to the creek, where he traded clothing with him. Then, pulling the man back to the battlefield, Blackwell looked around,…nobody even noticed.

Blackwell started westward. Having changed clothing once again, into a more civilian appearance, he knew he could work his way to The Oklahoma Territory easily. He was sure that he could steal a horse, and all supplies needed. It had been years, but he had the skill-set.

The next night, Blackwell lay by the campfire and drifted off. He saw her again. Older, and beautiful. But this time, she was wearing a buckskin dress. Sarah again reached out. Blackwell again took her hands. "No, William. No".

Waking from the dream, Blackwell sensed that something was wrong with what he was doing. He also got the feeling that Sarah did not, or would not approve. He sat awake the rest of the night contemplating his life.

As the sun rose, Blackwell acknowledged his actions had triggered every "bad situation" in his chaotic life. He looked down at his hands. They were folded together, and he immediately thought of "prayer". Blackwell felt "William" coming back.

***

It took just over three months for William to return to Hawkins County. He was tired and had forgone the thought of finding Sarah. He supposed that is what the dreams were telling him this. Riding into the valley, he saw two young men helping Thomas with a wagon and a terrible feeling came over him. Riding up, William saw confusion on Thomas's face. "Uncle William?" Thomas said.

William smiled as he climbed down from his horse and turned with outstretched arms. "Come here, Thomas. I could use a hug."

Thomas ran to him. "But, but, we buried you. I don't understand. How have you come back?"

"That wasn't me. Unfortunately, that was a man that just happen to look like me." William laughed, while Thomas and the other two continued to stare. "When did you bury me? I don't suppose anyone came, did they?" William added.

"No, Sir. Just me an' the boys." Thomas divulged.

"Samuel,...Samuel wasn't there?" William inquired and then saw the color drain from Thomas's face.

"Uncle. A lot of bad things happened since you left. Oos, and the Indians are gone. Cufee, and Juba too. They were all in the mine and it collapsed. Me and Samuel tried for days to get to them, but we couldn't. Samuel was not the same for weeks an weeks. When a regiment came through in December, he went with them. They were heading to Petersburg. Eventually be part of Lee's Army." Thomas explained.

William could already feel it. Samuel was gone. He knew it. His gut told him so. The big guys were easy targets. Besides, taking down a large man was essentially like taking down two. William thought, "If only I had spent more time training him." He then saw the young man in front of him.

Slowly lowering himself onto a log beside him, William reached up and massaged his forehead. "This is all my fault. I did this." He mouthed.

"You okay, Uncle William?" Thomas asked.

Crossing one arm under the other, lowering his head, and placing his palm on his forehead, William thought for many minutes. When he looked up, the two helpers were walking across the valley and Thomas was leading one of the horses to the barn.

"Thomas." William called out.

Thomas stopped and turned.

"Can we talk tonight? I need to tell you some things." William explained.

"Sure, Uncle William. I'll gladly sit down with a ghost and yuk it up." Thomas smiled and gave a bit of a wink. He then turned and proceeded to the barn.

For the next four evenings, William told Thomas of the many sins that William believed he had carried out for his country, some for The Wisdom, and some that he couldn't even explain. William told Thomas about the gold that he had hidden. He gave Thomas the maps, and then he spoke of John Boothe, detailing the intent to kidnap President Lincoln. Now, William believed he needed to stop this "madness".

"Thomas, I'm going to go to Washington… and I am going to tell them about the plan to kidnap Lincoln." William divulged

Thomas had listened intently for four nights now, and he always respected his uncle's opinions. But it was time for him to speak. "Uncle, you can't! If they find out who you are, they'll arrest you. They might hang you! Please, No!" Thomas pleaded.

William laid his hand upon Thomas's. "Son, I want my legacy to change for the better. I need to do something "good"." William grasped Thomas's hand. "I've caused death and despair to so many. This farm, this land,…is now yours. I only ask that you do not follow my path. If I'm lucky enough to accomplish my task, and not die, I'll then track down your father and ask for forgiveness. I'll leave in the morning from Rogersville, but need to stop by the old Emporium, and post a "For Sale" sign. I will leave you with a deed for the homestead and for the Emporium. There'll be a key to the Emporium in my cabin." William concluded.

They both sat in silence until Thomas stood and walked away.

The following morning, William woke very early in order to be gone when Thomas woke. William made his way to Rogersville, and to The Emporium. Doing as he said, William opened the door to The Emporium one last time. Looking around made him smile. It reminded him of his "good" years. Helping others and enjoying the boys. He went upstairs and found the fine painted sign that he had traded for so many years before. Hanging it on the inside of the window, his job was complete. Stepping out and locking the door, he looked up at the "For Sale" sign, touched the window, and quietly said "goodbye".

William boarded the train and sat down. Not long after sitting, he saw two men come his way. He thought he recognized one, but the other he did not. When they sat directly behind him, he knew exactly who they were.

***

Thomas woke, went to stoke the fire, and start coffee. He looked towards the bedroom that Uncle William had rested in. The loneliness was gone for a short period, but now it was back. Sitting down with his coffee, he picked up the ten maps that Uncle William had left on the kitchen table. Flipping through them, Thomas read the notes. William had very detailed locations for each of the stashes. Once he reached the last map, he stopped and smiled. He counted one, two, three, four, five, six, seven, eight, and nine. One map was missing. For some strange reason, this made Thomas happy.

***

"Did you think you'd get away with it?" The young man asked.

"Someone intercepted me. You know that. I've stashed most of it for you to recover. I filtered the rest into the cause." William replied.

"There are two guns pointed at your back, and one at your head, Blackwell. Don't even think about pulling that pig-sticker. Where is the stash?" The older of the two asked.

"Blountville. The next stop. I jumped from the train, just before the stop… It's there." William claimed.

"Why should we believe you?" The young man challenged.

William pulled a tattered piece of paper from his pocket and held it up.

The young man quickly snatched it. "Why don't we take these few cars, then jump with Blackwell at the same place, Frank?" The young man asked.

"Too much attention, Jesse. I don't want to be on-the-run as soon as we arrive. Hey, Blackwell. How far back from the train station?" Frank asked.

For a moment, William regretted leaving all of his weapons at the valley. But then he remembered his objective and knew the consequences. "Maybe a mile. You can walk it easily." He stated.

Jesse laughed. "Dumb Fucker, You's goin' with us."

Before the train came to a stop, Jesse moved beside William. Holding one of his two pistols on him, Jesse frisked William for his weapons. "Where you got it? I know you got it somewhere."

"I do not." William replied. He then smiled, which made Jesse James uneasy.

This visit to recover one of "the stashes" hadn't gone as planned. But William was improvising, hoping the two thieves would not find Thomas one day. He hadn't actually told Thomas about the large deposit of gold or the saddlebag of "James bounty" that he'd thrown in the crevasse, near the cliff. He hoped that Thomas or one of his children would find it one day. Until then, it would be safe there. William hoped that the amount of gold in this "stash" west of Blountville would satisfy the James brothers. Then, he'd move on to the District of Columbia.

"Almost there." William said calmly.

Although both of the James brothers had their pistols aimed at William, he seemed to be in complete composure.

***

Jesse grumbled that he was sure they had walked five miles.

"That stone wall over there,… and those oak trees,…they're all on the map. Now let me please be on my way." William requested.

"Hell no! You're digging, bitch!" Jesse snorted.

William stood there for a moment, blinking his eyes, and looking at the two men. Holding up one finger, he walked over to a dead oak tree that had not yet fallen. Reaching into a section of the tree that had long rotted out, William pulled out a wooden shovel that was still in surprisingly good shape. When he turned back, he was facing three pistols. Two in Jesse's hands, and one in Frank's. Arms raised, appearing ready to shoot, they both let out a sigh of relief. William remained calm.

William dug in the ground for no more than twenty minutes before his shovel struck a trunk. After cleaning out the dirt from around it, he then struggled to lift the box from the hole, but did manage to get the box pulled from the ground.

"You're going to have to shoot the lock. That was my plan." William touted.

Jesse raised one pistol, but Frank yelled, "STOP! No Jess!" Frank was holding his free hand up towards Jesse. "It could be dynamite. Get back."

Frank and Jesse took twenty-five paces back. Then Jesse let off four rounds directly at the trunk lock.

William hadn't moved away, as they had. He looked down at the trunk. Amazingly, Jesse had put all four rounds into the lock from twenty-five paces. William walked over and kicked open the top. As the James' walked up, they smiled.

"There, you have what you came for. I'm leaving" William stated.

"Sure, Go." Jesse replied and began to laugh.

William did just that and began to walk away. As William was walking away from them, he felt something that he'd never felt before, euphoria. The trees faded, and faces began to appear. He saw Sarah, Jefferson, Albert, his brother Jonathan, Samuel, Thomas, and many, many more. All friends, both alive and dead. William felt comfort when he heard the report of the pistols. He saw the blood mist in front of him and splatter on the ground. He kept walking…and kept hearing the guns. William began to stumble, finally fell to his knees and collapsed forward.

William opened his eyes and raised to his feet. There was a bright light, and two people walking towards him. He squinted. The first was Samuel, and the second was a young Albert Johnston. "Wha,…What are you two doing here?" William asked.

Samuel smiled that big old smile that had always made William chuckle. "We wasn't gonna leave you behind, Unc."

"It's time to go, my friend." Albert affirmed. "It's a long way. But we'll all make it…together." He promised.

Chapter 16 –

"All Grown Up"

What started as a hobby evolved into a career for Tad. Initially dabbling with 3D printers at home, Tad found himself private labeling improved 3D printers online. With strong contacts in Taiwan, his business grew rapidly, becoming one that supplied 3D printers across North America and five other countries.

Three years went by amazingly fast. Zephyr established sales offices in ten states, with headquarters in Johnson City, Tennessee. While many companies were struggled, Tad hit a niche market that prospered.

After spending months in Taiwan negotiating, Tad returned to the U.S. feeling as though he'd just partnered with Hewlett-Packard. Selling his company to a firm that dominated the European market. The company wanted to keep Tad on for five years, at which point he would receive the final ten of the thirty million dollar buyout offer. Of course, this was contingent on consistent profit.

Selling Zephyr was hard for Tad. But he couldn't pass up the offer. Besides, the thirty million dollars gave him the opportunity to start something new. Something that became even more of a passion.

Tad started X-Caliber in Johnson City as well. Initially intended to be a development company for drone defense at the local level, they quickly found themselves working with Border Patrol and the DOD contracts. Keeping with the initial intent, Tad's team kept the primary technology available for local needs too. Local law enforcement, bank security, school protection, as well as a few others.

Adam Roberts, Tad's right-hand man at X-Caliber, kept things "rolling" when Tad was away. He had been with Tad since Zephyr and was lead designer of all the drone projects. Adam knew that Tad had spent essentially "years" working "on business", and often encouraged Tad to take personal time to do things he enjoyed.

"Bro, you have got to get out of here and enjoy yourself." Adam explained. "Go over to Pigeon Forge and ride at that new mountain bike park. Take someone to a concert in Nashville. Go see that place in Rogersville that you always tell me about. Do something, but don't spend another weekend here. I am seriously tired of coming to work and finding you working out back."

Tad's answer surprised Adam. "Camelot. You mean Camelot, not Rogersville. But you know what? You're right. I do need to get away. I fact, since your dumb ass doesn't want me around, I'll leave today. How's that suit you, mister smarty-butt?"

Laughing, Adam replied. "Good. Take that adolescent humor with you too. I got this boss…and for God's sake meet someone, please. I'm sick and tired of trying to fix you up. Caroline and I have run out of friends for you to turn down. Go! Go, have fun. Adam insisted.

***

Tad woke up early Saturday morning at a bed and breakfast on the north side of Rogersville. With his mountain bike strapped to the back of his SUV, he had come two days before.

After a hearty breakfast, Tad unloaded the mountain bike from his Land Cruiser and filled up his bladder-pack to set out for a long ride towards Camelot.

Traffic was light and Tad absorbed the majestic views of the beautiful mountains of East Tennessee. Twenty minutes into the trek to Camelot, he rode past a farmhouse. As he rode by, he slowed because he noticed an odd-shaped structure extending out from a barn.

He rode gingerly by the farm-front property, staring at a structure that he eventually realized was an old train car. The roofline and the end of the car were all he could easily see. Tad thought it odd that the roof, while deteriorating, appeared to have wooden slats.

"Hmm?," he thought, as he continued peddling towards Camelot. The mountains and scenic ride slowly faded from his mind. The "possibilities" of that train car filled his thoughts. Curiosity was getting the best of him, so he turned back.

He pulled into the farmhouse driveway and found a tree to prop his bike against. Tad walked up to the front door and knocked. Nobody came, so he knocked again, this time calling out, "Is anybody home?" Still, no one came. So, he walked back to his bike.

Standing there, straddling his bike, looking at the strange structure from, he wondered whether he should walk over and investigate. Just as he was about to step off his bike, he heard a voice.

"Can I help you there fella?." An older man came out of the side door of the farmhouse.

The man looked to be well into his seventies or eighties. He wore over-alls and a white undershirt. He had shoulder-length gray hair that was unkempt and the weathered face of a man who spent his entire life outdoors.

"Oh, hey." Tad said. "My name is Thaddeus. Thaddeus O'Banion. I own some property over at Camelot." Tad stepped off his bike and set it back against the tree.

The man grinned. "You mean Pressmen's Home… I ain't heard nobody call it "Camelot" in some time. What's got ya visitin' your neighbors?" the man inquired as he slowly moved down the walkway towards Tad.

Tad watched him walk. He was skinny. Hard to "read". Tad thought, "Wow, that old guy could be ninety." But the old guy still walked strong.

Tad met him where the walkway gave way to the gravel driveway. The old guy put out his hand. "Nice to meet you, young man." The old man said.

The old man looked at him with cautious curiosity. Tad continued, "I was out for a ride and noticed that strange structure sticking out of your barn, and well, curiosity got the best of me. What is it, if I might ask?"

The old man looked in the direction that Tad was pointing and walked that way. "That's an old coach car from when the railroad came right through here. Rail's gone now, and that old car ended up being given to me by my uncle. If you're really that interested, come on over here and I'll show it to you." The old man explained as they walked towards the train car.

Tad was smiling. It was exactly what he thought it was, and he was eager to see it. As they reached the end that was extended past the barn, Tad spoke up. "Sorry sir, I didn't catch your name?"

The old man stopped and turned around with a smile. "The name's Thaddeus too. Well, it was when I was born anyway, Thaddeus Wiseman. Folks round here call me "Pappy". Hell, I might even be your neighbor over there at Camelot." Pappy said, waiting for Tad to reply.

Tad thought for a moment, a bit confused, and then realized that Pappy might be one owner of the lots sold by his mother and father in nineteen seventy-three. He almost asked, but then thought it might be better to remain somewhat anonymous for the time being. So, he inquired, "Oh yeah, how's that?"

Pappy's face looked stern. "We all got swindled. That damn Camelot crew moved in and we all thought we was gonna have us a Country Club right here in Hawkins County, with a golf course, swimming pool, and a lake. Not that I'm a golfer or play tennis, but I loved the horses, and The Stable. It was just like outta the TV shows. Seemed like a good idea back then. But it never got done. The fancy developer died, and no one finished it. Back then there was at least fifteen hundred of us who bought land out there. When Lafferty,…Lafferty, that was his name, well when he died, rumor was the whole damn place got stuck in the courts. For years that ole judge hem-hawed around and we all got screwed. Some of us paid cash and we own those lots outright. Others just had money down. Most of those reverted back to Lafferty's estate, I think that's what I heard. To this day, I'm not sure who owns what out there." Pappy explained, shaking his head in disgust.

Unfortunately, Pappy was correct. Tad was glad he hadn't said too much. He now realized that it might be better if locals didn't know who his father was, for fear that some might want retribution for Camelot's demise. Tad knew there was nothing he personally could do about it. But it might be better to leave that discussion for another day.

He decided to explain his ownership as "acquiring" the Pressmen's Home property, as opposed to inheriting it. At least for now…"Wow, that's interesting. I'd heard part of that, but you're the first person I've met who owns out there."

Tad stepped up to the rear of the train car. Looking at the coach, he continued, "I actually acquired about sixty acres out there. I have the old Pressmen's Home buildings, the lake, and land around it. I guess I own the church and cemetery too. Not completely sure what I'm going to do with it, but it was too good a deal for me to pass up." Tad explained. But then thought it might be better to change the subject away from "Camelot". "Tell me about this old train car Pappy." Tad said as he walked into the barn.

Pappy's eyes gleamed the way an old man's do when he gets to tell a story. "Well, this old car ran on the track that came across the north side of Rogersville from roughly eighteen fifty to about nineteen seventy, when they re-routed it to the south side of Rogersville. My uncle worked for the postal service back then. That's how the mail got transported. When they decommissioned the track, they was a dozen or so of these cars in different places between here and Knoxville. Some of them was eventually stuck with no way of gettin' them off the track. So they just gave them away to people that would take'em apart for the wood and steel, and some had the means of movin'em, like me. I was gonna fix it up and let Ethel turn it into a diner…For years she'd ask me, "When you gonna start working on our diner?"…I guess I never got around to it." Pappy trailed off and looked out of the barn.

"That's a great idea Pappy. You SHOULD do it! You could put it out there on your property at Camelot and maybe we could lure some folks to come out and fish at the lake." Tad exclaimed with a mischievous grin.

Pappy and Tad climbed up to see the inside of the train car. The walls and benches were all wood, and in fantastic shape for something that had been sitting here for many years. There were cast-iron sconces and other black cast-iron accessories scattered about the cabin. There were brass accents as well. Tad thought it looked astonishingly good. Except for a couple of small farm crates and a field mouse nest or two, it was empty and Tad had no problem imagining it as a bed and breakfast, or diner for that matter.

"Pappy?…how long you had this thing?" Tad inquired.

"I guess, 'bout fifty years." Pappy replied. "Hmm,…yep, got right after them folks at Camelot shut down that place."

Tad suddenly felt guilty about his desire to have this train car. Pappy seemed like a good man, and Tad was sorry that his father had been involved in the "Camelot bust" way back then. He thought about it for a few moments while Pappy continued his tour of the ancient relic of days gone by. "Pappy, can I help you get this thing turned into a diner for Ethel?" Tad asked.

Pappy stepped back, looked down the length of the train car and sighed. "I'll tell you what Tad, Ethel would've loved to seen this a diner, but she's been gone now for over ten years. If you got the inkling, take 'er. Just make sure you name it Ethel's…, not Mel's!" Pappy grinned and looked back at Tad. His eyes welling up, he continued. "She'll be right here if you want 'er".

Tad, a bit shocked and saddened, dropped his head. "Mister Wiseman, I gotta be honest, sir. I was stopping by because I wanted to see it, but I also thought maybe you'd sell it. I had a wonky idea of putting it at Camelot as a bed and breakfast"…,but now you got me thinking about the diner idea and I like it." Tad stated, in an honest effort to make Pappy comfortable.

"Son, my days are already numbered. If you actually think that you could turn this old chunk of iron and wood into Ethel's Diner, why, nothing would make me happier. She'll sit right here till you're ready. How's that suit you?" Pappy asked.

"I don't know what to say Pappy." Tad replied. "I'm not sure, how soon I'll be able to move it. It might be months from now. Besides, I think I want to get a pole barn put up over there so it can be worked on, out of the weather."

"Not a problem Tad. Why don't you come in the house for a cup of coffee and I'll sign something that says it yours, cuz lord knows, I could keel over tomorrow." Pappy laughingly replied.

The next four-mile ride to Camelot had Tad's head filled with idea after idea. He wondered if that's what it was like for his mother and father so many years before. He quizzed himself, "Why did they "run"? Why didn't they try to finish Camelot? Why didn't they see if Lafferty left the estate to them?…Why did Lafferty's assistant, Jean Ranier, hide the will for so long?"

As he rode down Pressmen's Home Road, he imagined the golf course, and all the homes that should be here. Just as he got to the old tradesmen's building, his cell rang. It was his sister, Liz. "Hey Sis, your timing's good. I just pulled into Camelot. I rode out here on my bike and you wouldn't believe what I just bought?"

"Dynamite?" Liz replied.

Tad laughed. "No, I got an old train car. It's a mile and a half down the road. We're gonna do a bed and breakfast" or diner at Camelot."

Now Liz was laughing. "What the hell? Yep, you've lost it!" Liz replied.

Tad stood over his bike talking to his sister and didn't even notice the police cruiser that had pulled into the overgrown gravel drive.

As he finished up his call with his sister, he heard someone call out. "Hey there buddy. This is private property. You can't be back here." An officer said as he walked up to Tad.

Tad laughed. "Yep, sure is. It's actually mine officer. If you want to see it, I have a copy of the deed right here in my bag?" Tad explained, trying to set the officer's mind at ease.

The officer acknowledged with a nod, and Tad swung his backpack to the side. Out of the front pocket, he removed an envelope that he had prepared, just in case this happened.

"Wow!" the officer replied. "You're the first person I've ever seen on this property who has permission to be here. He flipped through the pages and paused. "If I could see some ID, I'll leave you to your business". The officer said as he shook his head and continued to look at the deed.

Tad reached for his wallet and pulled out his driver's license. As he handed it to the officer, he said, "Yeah I figured someone might question my right to be here."

The officer looked at the driver's license, handed it back and said, "Mister O'Banion, I hope you understand. We gotta kick somebody off this property about every month. Mostly hunters and poachers. I didn't figure you were either of 'em, on a mountain bike."

Tad wondered if he came off "rude", being prepared with paperwork and all. Besides, he wanted to be friendly to the local law enforcement, so he thought, " I better clean this up." "Officer," he paused as he looked at his name on his lapel. "Officer Williams, I might owe you an apology, I didn't mean to come off rude by having that paperwork ready. I appreciate you guys and everything you do. Please call me Tad." Tad claimed.

The officer smiled. "Not a problem, Tad. Not a problem at all. You made it easy for me. It's actually Deputy, but call me Nick. Nick Williams." The deputy extended a hand to shake. "Looking at that deed, it looks like you haven't owned the property long, whatcha gonna do with it?" The deputy asked.

Tad put his license and paperwork away in his backpack and pulled out a small hard case. He held it up and said, "I guess, for now, I'm going to explore."

Tad opened the case and pulled out a small device. What was in Tad's hand was a quadcopter drone. It was approximately the size of a two-inch cube. Tad held it up and inspected it. It had multiple lenses that shifted when Tad pressed a green button.

"At least until I can bring out something big enough to cut that lock off of that steel door." Tad said as he continued to inspect his toy.

Nick smiled. "I got you, boss." The deputy said.

Nick walked back to his cruiser and popped the trunk. Reached in and pulled out a large set of bolt cutters. As Nick walked back, Tad shut down the drone, returned it to its case. He then affixed the case to his belt loop with two Velcro straps that were on the top of the case.

"We gotta carry these cuz of them stupid "school shooters". We need to be prepared. Tad, you ain't gonna complain if I cut that old rusty lock off, are you?" The deputy asked.

"Have at it Nick! No complaints out of me." Tad replied.

Nick and Tad walked up to the side of the building closest to the overgrown drive. There was a steel door behind a fabricated security gate. Nick cut off the first lock and swung open the rusty security gate. The steel door had a deadbolt and also a padlock hasp, with a lock. Nick grabbed the handle of the door and pulled. The movement of the door showed them that the deadbolt wasn't locked.

"You gonna come back out here and lock this back up?" Nick said as he cut the second lock. Tad didn't reply. He was too excited to see what was inside.

Nick swung the second door open. The wind whistled loudly inside the building. Tad looked at Nick. "You first, you got the gun," he said.

Nick laughed with apprehension. "It's your building." He grinned.

Tad pulled a flashlight from his pocket, turned it on and went through the door. It smelled musty and of another strange odor. As he walked into a hallway lined with doors, he turned back and saw a stairway that he'd passed.

Nick was with him. He had pulled his own flashlight. "You know Tad, if there's a bear in here, I'm shooting you in the leg and take off running." Nick said so seriously that Tad almost wondered if he was serious.

"Actually Nick, I'm glad you said that. That little drone that I have actually has FLIR." Tad said, referring to Forward Looking Infrared Radar. "It'll look through the walls and a floor or two. I can run it down the halls and tell if there's any warm bodies. However, it doesn't pick up the cold ones, and those are the ones that eat your brain." Tad smiled as he started down the hall. "I'll be right back."

Nicked stayed put, flashlight shining down the hall. Tad walked down the hall, clearing cobwebs as he went. He looked into the first few rooms. Not much to see; an old desk, shelves with a few books and the carcass of a small animal. But that strange smell… it reminded him of something.

After Tad cleared the third room, he returned to Nick with the small drone and cell phone in hand. He looked up at Nick and said, "You're gonna like this."

Tad opened an app on his phone. "This is pretty slick. I can toggle between 1080k, standard infrared, and FLIR with this app. It's not even out yet. You'll probably see it within a year. We developed it for the DOD and law enforcement. We call it "The Sentinel". You do NOT hafta put your life in danger with this little critter! Yes, before you ask, this is what I do."

Tad set the small drone on his open palm and hit the green button twice. The drone came to life and lifted from his palm. Tad then took his phone with both hands and slowly flew the drone down the hall. As Tad hovered the drone down the hall, he would randomly stop and toggle through the infrared and FLIR.

"Dude, that's the "cats ass!" Nick exclaimed. "You make these for military and law enforcement?" He asked.

Tad smiled and pressed another button on the screen. After he did that, he just held the cell phone and watched the drone continue down the hall, randomly stopping to hover and toggle through the camera views. "It's on autopilot now. I had it in "teach-mode" a minute ago. So now, it'll keep doing that down the hall until it comes to the end of the hall." Tad explained.

After the drone returned and landed on Tad's hand, Nick said, "Holy shit!…Hey, listen, I have to call in real quick. I'm getting a poor radio signal in here. I'm gonna run outside and do that, but I want to see more of this. Let me check in and clock out for lunch. I'll be right back. This shit's crazy and I wanna see all of it I can, if that's alright with you?" The deputy asked.

Tad shut down the drone and followed Nick to the door. "Sure,…glad to have your company. Especially if I run into that bear!" Tad said with a wink.

Tad watched as Nick went to his cruiser and climbed inside. Standing in the doorway, he could clearly smell the distinctive odor. It reminded him of a time that he had tried so hard to forget. That distinctive odor.

Tad slowly brought back the memories of the time when he and Brett had come upon a bad car accident. It was long ago, Tad fourteen, and Brett seventeen.

They had been at work together on a Saturday. Brett was inside working on machinery and Tad was outside mowing the lawn. Tad had just gotten off the old Sears lawnmower when he heard the roar of a muscle car revving up and flying down the road.

***

Summer 1980

They did it all the time. The road was one and a half miles long and straight as an arrow. Hot-rodders used it to make runs with their muscle cars, and surely raced at night. Tad saw the Mustang zoom by the shop so fast that he actually walked towards the road to see how far down it was by the time he reached the road to see it. As the disappearing Mustang came into view, Tad saw it suddenly twist sideways, the wheels catching the blacktop, and then the car rolling. Tad counted one, two, three, four, before the hot rod came to rest in the ditch.

Tad ran back towards the shop as fast as he could. As he reached the door, Brett met him.

"What was that?" Brett exclaimed.

"Quick, get the medical kit from the wall. There's a car down the road! It rolled!" Tad screamed.

Brett knew Tad was not joking, unlike so many times before, and went straight for the medical kit. He handed it to Tad and grabbed his keys from his coat. They ran out the door to Brett's old International pickup truck. Brett jumped into the driver's seat, and Tad jumped in the truck's bed. Brett started the truck and dropped it into gear. With his foot on the accelerator, spinning gravel, they hit the road squealing.

Coming upon the Mustang, they could see that the devastation was immense. The car was actually sitting on what was left of the tires, with the rear of the car in the ditch. Blood covered the destroyed windshield, and there were two motionless bodies in the car. Tad jumped out and rushed to the car with the medical kit. What he saw next would haunt him for nights to come. He hurried around the car, hesitant to attempt to open it, for fear of what he would see inside.

Tad was confused. He could hear the hissing sound of the radiator, as well as many other strange sounds. But then again, it was also eerily quiet. He set down the medical kit and looked at Brett.

Tad wasn't sure what to do. As he looked to Brett, alluding to his confusion, Brett said, "Open it up!, what are you waiting for?"

Tad slowly reached for the handle and instantly pulled his hand back. Brett immediately grabbed the handle and pulled hard, fully expecting it not to budge. But it did. It opened fully, and a body covered in blood fell out. Tad felt weird. He was dizzy and nauseous.

Brett barked, "Tad! Open the kit and get bandages out!"

Tad did as he was told, but all of his senses went numb. He focused on opening the larger bandage packs, but he suddenly felt as though he was in a tunnel and dropped to his knees.

Suddenly he heard Brett bark, "Tad! Pull your head out of your ass and help me turn him over". Together, they gently turned the body over. It was a man in his twenties or thirties. His eyes were open, and he was breathing, but he was not moving. There was a faint gurgling sound as his chest quickly rose and fell. His face had apparently slammed hard against the windshield many times, which severely lacerated the left side of his face.

Brett said, "I'm not sure what to do, but I don't think we should move him and maybe get some of those bandages on his face." Tad did as he was told, and Brett circled around the car to try to open the other door. It wouldn't budge.

There was another man. He was lying down on the front seat, also motionless. Brett came back to the driver's side and said, "I think we should get him out of there. Since this thing rolled a couple times, it could be leaking gas and could catch on fire."

"Four times," Tad said. "Four times. I watched it flip four times." He continued.
Suddenly, the man lying on the ground sat up. Tad and Brett both jumped back as the man looked at them in confusion.

"Aw shit!" he exclaimed. "James, you're all right man. Come on, let's go down to Randy's and get them to tow this back to his house before the cops come." The man said in shock, not comprehending the severity of the accident.

Brett, astonished that the man was even alive, spoke up. "Listen bud, you've been in a nasty accident. Your car flipped four times, and you're in shock. You need to lay back down and wait for the ambulance."

The man focused on his friend in the car, but he slowly turned his head and looked at Brett. "Man, could you give us a ride over to Randy's? It's just down the street. We're fine." He said.

As Brett continued to try to talk the man into understanding the dire situation, they were in. Just then, the man in the car, James, moaned.

"What should I do Brett?" Tad asked.

Brett replied, "I got my hands full with this guy. See if you can get that other dude out of the car…and I couldn't budge that other door."

Tad didn't want to get into the car. There was blood everywhere. On the seats, the dashboard and it had even puddled on the floor. Tad thought, "I'm going to ruin my clothes just trying to get this guy out." But he gingerly climbed into the driver's seat, anyway.
Shattered glass was everywhere. All of it "tempered" glass. So, someone would have to bounce off of it or get pulled across it for it to cut the skin. Neither of which Tad planned on doing.

Tad was on his knees in the driver's seat and leaning over the top of "James". Looking over James, he could now see that James possibly had more severe injuries than the driver's. Although they really didn't know how bad the driver was. James's right eye was out of its socket, and his ear looked like it had been put in a blender. James had a bone protruding from his forearm. By the look of his pant leg and the dripping blood from it, Tad believed that another break was at his shin. James moaned again as nausea came back to Tad. He thought, "What is that smell? Is that gas?...No, Maybe battery acid?...No. Oh God, that's blood! I actually smell blood!" Tad coughed and felt vomit rise in his throat. He didn't want to vomit on the man, so he turned his face towards the back seat. He tried hard not to vomit and kept his mouth shut. The warm vomit filled his mouth and he swallowed hard. Back down it went, but again he coughed, and he could feel and smell the nasty vomit. He spat, feeling better that he hadn't "full on" puked in that car. He turned back to James and said, "Help is coming, man."

With Tad helping the guy in the car, Brett finally convinced the driver to lay back down. Brett began laying more bandages onto the driver's face and neck. The bandages quickly saturated with blood. Brett noticed the gurgling sound was louder, and just as he realized it might be better that the man sit up. Just then, a car came to a screeching halt on the road. A curvy young woman jumped out and said, "Did this just happen?"

Looking perplexed, Brett replied. "Well, yeah!" The woman, shaking herself out of a bit of shock, asked, "Did anyone call an ambulance?" as she herself dropped to her knees, to assess the situation of the man on the ground.

Brett wanted to tell her about the man's gurgling immediately, but answered her question instead. "We came from that shop, down the road. My brother, Tad, saw it happen and said they rolled four times. As we ran out of the shop, I yelled at my uncle to call an ambulance. I'm guessing he did, and we can ask him in a minute. I see him jogging this way right now. Oh, and just so you know, this gurgling sound that he's making when he breathes…it got worse when I laid him down." Brett explained.

The woman helped the man on the ground sit back up. She slowly peeled back some of the blood-drenched bandages so that she could continue to assess the damage. She looked at Brett and said, "You're doing good. Can you get behind him and keep him sitting up?"

"Sure." Brett replied. "Are you a paramedic?" He asked.

"Yes." She replied, "Well, I'm going to be. Not yet. I'm still in school for it. I'm Jane. What's the kid doing in there?"

Brett, repositioning himself to support the torso of the driver, looked up at Tad, who had been talking to James a moment ago. "He supposed to be getting that guy out of there, but we can't get the other door open. We were afraid that the car might blow up." Brett replied.

Jane stood and went over to Tad. "Hey, Honey. How's it going? I'm Jane. You want to let me in there to look at him, I'm a paramedic." She said.

Tad was eager to trade places, and as strange as it sounds, thankful that he didn't vomit in the back seat. Jane was pretty. Not thin, but not heavy either. In a way, he felt embarrassed that he hadn't gotten James out. So, he spoke up as she crawled in just as Tad had. "He's pretty messed up. Worse than the other dude. His eye popped out and he's got bones sticking out in his arm and leg." Tad said, with a bit of confidence, suddenly hoping that the young woman was impressed.

Jane looked over James for a moment and turned to look at Tad. "Good assessment kid. Can you ask that other boy if there are any tourniquets in that med kit?"

Feeling bashful, but "proud" that Jane complimented him, Tad quickly hustled over to the medical kit. He knew what a tourniquet was. They had just covered them in "Health Class". Rummaging through the medical kit quickly, and hoping to impress Jane again, he realized there were none. He stopped and looked back at Jane while shaking his head. Her inquisitive expression changed to one of concern.

"Do you have a belt on, boy?" Jane called back to Tad.

Tad quickly unbuckled his belt and took it back to the young woman inside the wreckage. He handed it to her and called back to Brett. "Brett. Do you have a belt on?" Tad asked.

"No." Brett replied.

As Jane put the belt on the leg of the man in the car, their uncle came jogging up to the crash scene. "You dumbasses left without me." He shouted.

To which, Brett blurted out, "Did you call an ambulance?"

Breathing heavily from the impromptu sprint, the boy's uncle looked around at the carnage. "Whoa! These guys really fucked up. I didn't know it was this bad." The uncle exclaimed.

"Did you call for an ambulance!" Jane interrupted.

"Yes, yes, I did." The uncle replied, seemingly in shock himself.

"Listen, I need to keep pressure on this tourniquet, but the boys brought up a good point. If I can release this hood, can you see if there looks to be anything that would make us want to get far away from this car?" Jane said to the uncle.

The boy's uncle walked over to the front of the car and looked at the crushed hood, and replied, "My guess is that it'll open from out here, if it'll even open." He looked around and found the latch. Pulling it, the hood popped loose. The hood fully opened with a squeal, and he looked around in the engine well. After almost a minute, he came out from around the front of the car. "The battery had already come loose, and I don't see any gas leaking. I'll check out the gas tank, but that funny smell is the battery. It's busted open." He said.

"It's blood." Jane said, "That smell is blood. You smell the iron in the blood. We learned it at Paramedic's School."

Tad was handing Jane some gauze bandages, and she was wrapping the passenger's head, when she suddenly stopped. "Oh my god!" Jane screamed. "James,…Todd, is that you? She said as she turned back to look at the man that Brett was supporting. The man attempted to look up, but the blood-soaked bandages covered his face and eyes. "Todd Miller, is that you!" she screamed again.

To that, the man replied. "Yeah, can you just run us down to Randy's house? I'm fine." He slurred.
"I know both guys! Dammit, where's that ambulance! Are you sure that you called?" Jane exclaimed.

Sirens sounded as if on cue, and an ambulance turned onto the long stretch of road. Tad continued to hand Jane gauze bandages until the ambulance abruptly stopped in front of the car.

Two paramedics jumped out. One came to Tad's side and dropped to-a-knee between Jane and him. "You okay son?" he said as he looked at Tad, himself now covered in blood.

"Yeah, I'm fine, we were just helping. These two guys flipped this car and she, well Jane, stopped to help too." Tad replied.

A fire truck had now arrived right behind the ambulance, and one of the paramedics was pulling a gurney and backboard from the rear of the ambulance.

The "quiet" had stopped. There were firefighters climbing off the firetruck and pulling all kinds of gear out of compartments all along the truck. A police car sped by and blocked the end of the road, a quarter of a mile away.

Looking at Tad, "Okay, you did good buddy, but we got it from here. Step back, get away from the accident." the paramedic stated.

The other paramedic had already asked Brett to step away and was preparing to slide the driver, Todd, onto a backboard, when Tad closed the medical kit, latched it, and stood up. "This is ours," Tad said solemnly, and walked towards Brett's pickup truck.

The adrenaline rush had worn off. Tad felt sick and dizzy. He could not get the smell of blood out of his mind. Walking backwards slowly, he and Brett climbed into the cab. Brett had stopped the lifted International quite far into the ditch. So much so that the police temporarily stopped him to make sure that he was not involved in the accident.

Brett slowly backed through the ditch until he could pull back onto the road. Their uncle was talking to the police and firemen, so they turned the truck around and headed back to the shop.

It was a couple of years later when their uncle would tell them that Todd and James had stopped by the shop, to thank him for saving their lives. Brett's response was one of astonishment. He quickly replied. "You didn't do shit!" But Tad's "image" was instant nausea. The memory brought back that putrid.

Their uncle, short in stature, grinned and said, "Hey, I made sure that car didn't blow up…and I had to give a police report. They were racing on the road, right? And the car they were racing didn't even stop. Hell, that other car probably bumped them. The cop found what looked to be blue paint on the bumper. I'm sure that other car stayed far from our road after that."

Tad's brow furrowed, and he was squinting. "That's not what happened at all." Tad said. "There wasn't another car. I saw it all." Tad said as Brett shook his head and walked out the door.

Tad's uncle held both hands up, as if gesturing, "what do you want?". Tad stood there for a moment, then turned and walked out to join Brett walking to the parking lot.

"He's an asshole, Brett." Tad proclaimed.

Brett laughed, "Yeah, I know. He's an asshole." Tad laughed too and climbed into the passenger side of the International.

As they left the shop and drove past the very place of the accident, Tad remembered Jane. He closed his eyes. He just imagined her. She was pretty,…and he still kinda had a crush on her. How could such a tragic day prompt such emotions? He didn't know it, but he did like remembering her. It was the only thing about that day that made him smile.

***

Back at the Tradesmen's building, 2021

Hearing Nick say, "I'm back, did I miss anything?" snapped Tad out of his little trance. Remembering that fateful day in nineteen eighty always made him nauseous.

"No. I was, um, just calibrating the Sentinel and got sidetracked." Tad explained as he tucked the little drone into the case on his side.

Nick had brought back a sandwich in a sandwich bag and had clipped a water bottle to his tactical vest. He held up the sandwich. "You want half? It's PB and J?" Nick said, attempting to share his simple sandwich.

Nick was likeable, Tad thought. The predisposition that an officer of the law being curt, or flat out rude, was quickly dispelled after meeting Nick. With the "cobwebs" shaken from his head, Tad replied. "No thanks, Nick. Appreciate it though. Besides, that weird smell kinda turns my stomach."

Nick tucked the sandwich into a pouch that he opened on his vest. "What is that, Tad? It smells like acid or metal. Maybe electricity? Did you have the power turned on out here?" Nick asked.

Tad walked down the hallway. The same one they had previously searched with the drone. Nick followed as Tad spoke. "It's coming from the elevator shaft. It,…it smells like blood."

When they got halfway down hallway, there was a large double sliding door, slightly ajar. The doors were massive. Hanging on brass rollers with large in-laid copper plates, and windows in the upper half. Each door had a long, vertical brass handle mounted on it. Tad grabbed hold of the handle and pulled to the side. Both doors slid apart to expose an old elevator. Tad thought it was rather large for an elevator. He stepped in and walked to the far side. There was a lot of overgrowth outside, but he could see out the front of the building. He could see Nick's cruiser through the windows of the elevator shaft. The elevator was very large and "industrial" looking.

Nick had stepped into the elevator and was looking around as well. "You suppose it's safe to be in this thing?" Nick asked.

Tad walked over to the gap between the hallway threshold and the elevator. There was every bit of a three inched gap. Tad pulled a small flashlight from his pocket and clicked it on. Getting down on his knees, he leaned down and shone the flashlight through the gap. "It definitely goes down at least one, maybe two more levels. I can't tell if that smell is coming from below, or above. I guess it doesn't matter right now though." Tad said, looking over his shoulder at Nick.

As Tad began to get up, he bumped the edge of the threshold with his flashlight. Losing his hold on the light, it fell through the gap. "Shit!" Tad exclaimed.

Nick got down on his hands and knees to look through the gap as well. "I see it down there. The light's still on." Nick observed.

The two of them stood up. "I'll get it later. It's a rechargeable Streamside. When I get it, I'll recharge it and it'll be as good as new. Let's get back to checking out the floors." Tad urged.

"Are we going up, or down?" Nick asked as they both stepped out of the elevator.

"I think, up." Tad replied.

"But your flashlight is down." Nick explained.

Tad paused. Something didn't feel right about going "down". He couldn't explain it, but Tad felt that he wanted to check out the lower levels on his own. "Up seems easiest. More light. I want to check out the lower levels when I can bring some lighting with generators." Tad replied.

Nick headed for the stairwell near the open door they had originally come through. "Okay then, Let's get that little "hummingbird" back in action. You only got me for another forty-five minutes. After that, you won't have anyone to push down and run, when you run into a bear." Nick said, grinning over his shoulder.

Tad paused and looked back. "The gap" at the elevator was lit up from the illumination of his flashlight below. A pink tint though. Tad kept walking, but thought, "That's odd".

Once Nick and Tad reached the second level, they both observed that the floor layout was different. There was a set of double doors halfway down the hall, just before the elevator shaft. Before that, the layout appeared to be similar, with offices and rooms on each side of the hallway. Knowing he could pause the "program" that they had taught the Sentinel on the first floor, Tad walked to the approximate location of the hallway that they had been on the floor below. He pulled out his cell phone and started the Sentinel app. He then pulled the drone from its nest and held it in his open palm. Tapping a few buttons on the cell phone app, the drone came to life. It lifted from Tad's hand and hovered. As it hovered, Tad again grabbed his phone with both hands and started the program.

The drone slowly traveled down the hall, stopping at each doorway, and scanning the rooms. Tad intently watched the cell phone screen. Nick walked behind him, opening each door afterward, and shining his flashlight inside, taking a quick assessment of what was there. One door was locked when Nick tried to open it. He jiggled the handle and pushed. Nothing. It wouldn't budge. He moved on.

When they reached the double doors, Tad paused the program. The drone hovered approximately five feet off of the floor while Tad pressed a series of buttons. The drone beeped, and a red light flashed. Nick had just caught up to Tad and said, "Clear! Well, except that one office door that was locked."

Nick looked curious. "You see anything on your "hummingbird"?" he asked.

Tad furrowed his brow and looked at Nick. "Sentinel, Nick. It's a Sentinel. Get it right, or I'm not going to donate one to your department." Tad said with a grin.

Nick chuckled. "Okay then, …Sentinel it is."

The drone continued to hover as Tad opened the double doors. Nick followed him and propped the doors open with the door stoppers on the bottom of them.

The new room was big. It extended the remaining half of the building, and up another floor. It had larger vertical windows approximately every five feet. Along the front wall, where the elevator shaft was located, there were more doors. But beyond those, no other doors could be seen. Tad turned back, held his hand under the drone and shut it down. Tucking it away, he returned to Nick as they walked into this immense room. There were old printing machines of all sizes in the room and stacks of printing plates scattered about. Some stacks almost five feet tall.

The machines looked like dinosaurs in a museum. Standing majestically, frozen in time, from long ago. Nick had his flashlight out, so Tad followed him. They wandered through the aisles of dinosaurs and stacks of ancient plates. Tad picked a plate up and blew the dust from it. The plate appeared to be copper with a lead backing and a piece of wood mounted to it. The image on the plate was a "reverse image" of what would be printed from it. This one showed an old train and mentioned Rogersville. Most of the printing plates were of this similar form. A few didn't have the wooden board "backer", but most did.

Nick was the first one to speak. "Dude, this is sick." He said as they continued to look around the room. "What do you suppose is in those rooms?" Nick asked as he pointed to the row of doors along the front wall. Some of them being double-doors.

Without hesitation, Tad replied, "Those are the labs. The rooms where they'd make these plates." Tad now remembered this place.

Tad felt relieved. "That smell, like blood. It's the copper plates. It may be the lead, or a mix both. I'm not sure. But that elevator door is open, and I think it was coming from here." Tad explained.

After a few more minutes of looking around, Nick holstered his flashlight and they headed back down the hallway. Tad felt comfort with the deputy's company for the remaining upper floors, and he also knew Nick was intrigue.

As they passed the locked office door, Nick said. "That's the door that is locked. Don't know if you're gonna have a locksmith out here, but I know someone who can pick anything."

Tad stopped and dropped to his knees in front of the lock. He pulled out his phone and took a picture of the keyhole. As he stood back up, he started walking again. "I'll get it open. Picking locks is a hobby of mine too." He touted with a grin.
Nick shook his head and followed Tad to the stairwell.

The third floor looked like the second, except the end of the hallway had windows, looking into the "dinosaur museum" below. Tad asked Nick if he wanted to try out the Sentinel. Without hesitation, Nick wanted to give it a shot. Tad prepped the drone and put it into a hover at the start of the hallway. He held up his phone and showed Nick the basics.

"Since we "taught" it already, the only thing that you need to do is to watch the screen for anything "not normal". The screen will cycle through the normal, FLIR, and infrared cameras. When it pauses at the doorways, it's scanning forward, then left, then right, then up with all of those cameras. It knows to stay five feet off the floor. If you want to pause it, hit the yellow button. To proceed, hit the green button again. You can also pause and cycle through the cameras yourself, with the buttons on the left. If you want to try that, just pause it halfway down the hall and I'll walk you through it." Tad explained.

Nick took the cell phone from Tad and positioned himself behind the drone. "Oh, here, use my flashlight."

Nick said as he pulled it from the holster and handed it to Tad.

Nick was intently watching the cell phone cycle through the cameras. Tad couldn't tell if Nick was excited or just resolutely focused, but Nick's face never changed expressions. He just kept staring at the screen. As they worked their way down the hall, Tad did as Nick had been doing previously, and opened each door, shone the light and took a quick peek that all looked "okay". Tad was sure that Nick was too focused to remember to pause The Sentinel. When they got to the end of the hallway, the drone stopped, and just hovered.

Startled, Nick said, "Did I do something? It just stopped."

Tad came out of the last office doorway and replied. "It's done. You scanned the whole thing. What did you see? Anything?"

Before Nick could reply, Tad put the palm of his hand under the hovering drone and made a clicking sound with his tongue and roof of his mouth. The drone lowered to his hand and shut down.

"What the heck was that?" Nick exclaimed.

Tad laughed and replied. "That's something that I've asked that we add. My guys are fighting me a bit on it, but some form of it will be in the production version. It's a "command". Like you would give a dog. I just told it to shut down. With an AI version that we are working on, you'll be able to talk to the Sentinel, and tell it what you want it to do. The one that I'll get to your department won't have it yet, but we should be able to add it in the future."

"Are you seriously going to give us one of these?" Nick asked.

Tad tucked the drone back into its pouch and started back down the hall. As they both walked, Tad explained that they already had a few of them in select departments. A SWAT team in Los Angeles, a fire department in Montana, and the Border Patrol has a hundred of them,…although two of those have been shot down by the cartels. Tad told Nick how impressed he was with Nick himself and asked that Nick and the Sheriff visit him in Johnson City, where he would prepare a unit for especially for their department's use.

Nick couldn't contain his enthusiasm but also thought that he should check in. He keyed the mic on his shoulder. "Hawkins Dispatch, Deputy One-Three-Two-Two checking in." Nick said.

"Copy that, Nick, I got you, but ain't you on lunch?", the dispatcher replied.

"Yeah Carrie, I am. I'm still out at the old Pressmen's Home with the new owner. I took lunch to walk through this old place with him. This guy, Mister O'Banion, has a sick military drone that he's been using to inspect the property. He says that he's gonna give the department one. I wanted to tell the Sheriff about it." Nick stated as he walked to the stairwell to head up to the fourth floor.

"Copy that Nick, gimme a minute to tell the boss", dispatch replied.

Tad was already halfway down the hallway when Nick arrived. "Hey, you started without me!" Nick said as he hustled to walk right behind Tad.

This hallway looked like the last two, which made them both curious about what was at the end of the hallway. Could it be another "dinosaur museum"? Or something more interesting? Just as they got to the last doorway before the double doors at the end, Tad stopped abruptly. He was staring at the screen and cocking his head. Nick looked over Tad's shoulder. He could clearly see a heat signature in the last room. It wasn't the size of a person, but bigger than any rodent, or coyote, for that matter. It was not a skinny animal either.

They were both thinking it, but Nick said it first. "What the hell is that?" Nick said, not even realizing that his hand was now on the butt of his gun.

"Could be a bear. Looks about the right size. A little small, but I don't know what else it could be." Tad took manual control of the Sentinel. He turned it in multiple directions and kept looking at the screen on his cell phone. Then he grinned. "Deputy, here's what were gonna do. Put your gun away. You can't shoot that damn bear." Tad said, and then he started poking at the buttons on his phone.

Nick spoke with authority. "Tad, I don't feel like getting mauled by a bear today. I'm gonna shoot it." He explained as he unholstered his firearm.

"Nick, I want to keep what I'm about to tell you a secret. Can you do that?" Tad asked as he eased the drone close to the closed door.

Nick was shaking his head. "Tad, I just met you man, please don't do something stupid." Nick replied again with authority.

"Nick, the Sentinel has the ability to blow that bear to pieces. This is the military version, and I can't have everyone knowing that I have such a weapon. You okay with me using it?" Tad asked as he reached for the door handle.

Nick was shaking and surprised at how calm Tad appeared. For a moment, he thought, "This guy acts like he's done this before!".

Suddenly, the Sentinel was in the room with the bear, and Tad pulled the door back shut. Expecting to hear the blast of this strange weapon, Nick never heard one, but he saw the image on the screen appear to blow to pieces. Large pieces of heat signatures went in all directions.

Nick's mind raced. "What on god's green earth did you shoot that thing with?" Nick asked. Then he noticed something. The smaller heat signatures were still moving, and some were disappearing. Possibly even out a window? It finally hit him when Tad started chuckling. Nick blurted out. "You asshole! I believed you! How'd you know?", He challenged Tad.

As Tad laughed, he kept looking at the screen and finally said. "The show isn't over Nick. That sow racoon is huge. Most of the babies ran off, but she's staying put. I say, we let her be and leave the fight with her for another day. What do you think?"

Nick was walking away, shaking his head. "I can't believe you! I was shitting and didn't know what to do." Then Nick burst out laughing. He was bent to his knees laughing when his cell phone rang.

Nick stood up, collected himself, and answered, "Hey boss. Sorry,… I'm still laughing at something that happened out here at Pressman's." Nick paused while the Sheriff spoke.

"Hey Nick, I'm not sure what you're up to but your voice tells me you're having too much fun. What's this Carrie tells me? You bought some expensive military drone from a gypsy? Please enlighten me." The Sheriff requested.

Nick was walking back towards Tad, who was still using The Sentinel to check out the room with the raccoons. "Tad, Hey Tad. Would you mind if I put you on the speaker phone with the Sheriff?" Nick asked.

Without turning around, Tad replied, "Sure thing. Give me two minutes to get The Sentinel out of this room without getting rabies."

With that, Nick began pacing the hallway, explaining his initial meeting of Tad, and how he decided to take his lunch hour to assist Tad with his building survey.

Within a minute or two, Tad had the drone back in his hand and joined Nick's side. "Sheriff, I'm putting you on speakerphone and want to introduce you to Tad O'Banion, with X-Caliber, in Johnson City." Nick said as he put the speakerphone on.

Tad spoke up. "Sheriff Evans, it's an honor to meet you sir. My name is Thadeus O'Banion. I'm the owner, and founder of a company in Johnson City that works for the D.O.D. and other assorted law enforcement agencies. I brought out one of our latest gadgets with me today. Basically, to do some reconnaissance on a property I own over in Camelot. Deputy Williams was kind enough to assist me, which I'm very grateful for. We often pick sites to test out our toys and, in appreciation, I'd like to invite you and your deputies over to J.C. to see our facility. I'd like to offer your department one of our Sentinel drones. It's not much bigger than a Rubik's Cube with features that would allow you to use it to save lives. You'd essentially become another test site, if you want to call it that. It's safe, I promise you that. The Border Patrol started using a hundred of them last year. What do you say, Sheriff?"

There was a brief pause, and the Sheriff spoke. "Nick, Is this legit? Have you been using one out there at Pressmen's Home?" the Sheriff asked. Nick smiled. "Boss, I've actually flown this thing. This thing can see through walls, and in any direction. Once you teach it what to do on one story of a building, it'll repeat that on the next, and the next. It's sick." Nick, touted as the Sheriff interrupted.

"Mister O'Banion, I'll be blunt. What's the cost and what's the catch?" the Sheriff asked.

Tad stood there for a moment, pondering how to reply and decided that honesty was the best answer. "Sheriff, The Sentinel is a military grade drone. While it's technically still experimental, there are over two hundred and thirty of them deployed all over the United States. Mostly with the Border Patrol. The beta's run approximately five thousand dollars. But, we're already being told that we've saved multiple lives. It's like this Sheriff, Nick impressed me, and I'm hoping that he's representative of you and your department. I have plenty of friends in Johnson City law enforcement, but I wouldn't mind having a few over here in Hawkins County. I own all of the old Pressmen's Home property and I wouldn't mind having you guys keeping an eye on it. What do you say Sheriff? It's a "win" all around." Tad concluded.

Another long pause from the Sheriff then he spoke. "Mister O'Banion, we'll check on your property just as we do for all business in Hawkins. I can't do any big favors, but we'll certainly keep an eye, as you said, on it. My guys would love to go on a "field trip" to see your company. I hate to sound cliché, but have your people get in touch with mine and let's get something set up for us to come over. I appreciate your time Mister O'Banion, and Nick? Good job today,…but get back to work."

Nick smiled and replied, "Yes sir, I'm on it."

Tad was already walking over to the double doors on this last floor, as Nick put his cell phone in his chest rig. Tad pushed open the double doors without even putting the Sentinel into action. The last room was a large cafeteria-meeting room and kitchen. The kitchen still had pots and pans in stainless steel cabinets. Most of them open and in vast disarray. Tad and Nick weren't nearly as enthusiastic as they had been and spent little time looking through the final rooms.

"You had enough, Nick?" Tad asked.

"Yep, I gotta get back on my route, Tad." Nick answered, and they both walked through the double doors and down the hall.

Once outside, Nick asked, "So, you said you're gonna come back later today and lock up that door, right?".

Tad walked over to a dead tree and broke off a small limb. Then went over shut the door and gate, shoved a piece of dead limb in each hasp and threw the rest of the limb on the ground. "There, that'll keep our little racoon family safe until I come back out later. Gonna be dark, but I have another flashlight in my truck back in Rogersville. I appreciate you Nick, and hope to see you over at J.C. here real soon."

Nick was standing with his cruiser door open and was ready to step in, then he stopped. Looking back at Tad, he said, "Tad, If your heading back to Rogersville, I can actually give you a lift, if you want."

Tad looked at his Garmin watch. Looked up at the clouding sky and replied. "I think that I'll take you up on that Nick. I appreciate it."

"All our cruisers have bike racks, cuz some guy was as cool as you, and donated e-bikes to our department." Nick explained.

Tad wheeled his mountain bike over to the rear of the cruiser, where Nick was prepping the rack. Nick lifted it in place, and secured it to the rack. He looked the mountain bike over and had to ask. "This is an e-bike too? But it looks more like a mountain bike than ours. What is it?" Tad double-checked the power was off on the bike and replied, "It's an Ibis, Oso. Great bikes. The guys out in Santa Cruz make one of the best out there. What's the make of the departments?"

"Ours are LeMonds. I guess the owner was a famous racer, at one time. They're headquartered in Knoxville. You'll often see them from here to Knoxville."

Tad laughed. "famous racer huh?... Greg LeMond only won the Tour de France three times." Tad claimed.

Nick shrugged his shoulders and keyed his mic to let Carrie know he was giving Tad a ride back. Then he pointed at the front seat for Tad to sit in. Nick had to move some things around before Tad could sit in the passenger's front seat. Then they climbed in, belted up and backed out of the drive.

On the way to Rogersville, Tad explained to Nick that he was going to put a few towers out at "Camelot", as he called it. He explained that these are another product that they make for the C.B.P. They're portable towers that extend up thirty feet, with automated lighting, cameras, a cell reception repeater, and a "garage" for a Sentinel. Called "The Sentry", they can work together with other Sentrys, using an A.I. program that will allow them to track movement for five hundred yards, and further, if the program calls to release the Sentinel. The A.I. will assess an object's size, movements, and mannerisms to allow it to decide if the object is a threat, and whom to contact, like the police, fire department, or landowner. The Sentry can even identify whether an object has a weapon and what type of weapon. Tad said that he would have The Sentrys programmed to notify himself and the Hawkins County Sheriff's department in three warning codes. "Possible Trespasser" would be a "mild threat" and may not need cause for attention. "Possible Threat" would be someone like a hunter who shouldn't be on the property. The Sentinels might be deployed and the department may want to follow up. "Eminent Threat" would be someone that appeared to "threaten" the property, like a vandal, an arsonist, or worse. The Sentinels would be deployed and would actively surveil for up to two hours.

While Tad explained his intentions with The Sentrys, Nick interrupted, "Dude, you're freaking me out. Pressmen's Home has been a "ghost town" for fifty years, and you're suddenly making it "Fort Knox". What's out there that's so important?"

Tad thought, "My reply better be good. This kid's rattled'. He paused for a moment, then spoke, "Listen Nick, I'm not a hundred percent on what I'm doing with that property, but I'm thinking that I want to do something kinda nice out there. I really don't want anybody fucking it up, and I have the ability to stop it. I know about The Manor fire in the nineties. That was arson. With you all's help, I can put something nice out there like a bed and breakfast or something, with the lake and trails, and have it be a nice place for visitors. That's all! I just happen to have the means to make it safe, Nick."

Nick looked apologetic as he pulled into Tad's bed and breakfast gravel drive, near Rogersville. "I'm sorry Tad. You're right. If I had that property, and the means to make it safe, I'd do the same. Sorry for the insinuation." Nick apologized, looking back at Tad as he opened the patrol car door.

In the following weeks, Tad was busy at Camelot every weekend. He'd set up five Sentrys and was thinking about putting one on top of the tradesmen's building, but decided to leave that effort for another day. He had not been back in the tradesmen's building since he and Nick Williams had checked it out a few weeks back, and Tad had a weird feeling about the building, anyway. Every once in a while, he'd get a whiff of that acrid smell, and the hair would "stand up on his neck". Besides, he thought, "That "momma sow" needs a place to take care of her babies". He saw no sense in evicting them just yet. Tad really did have a soft spot for animals. A soft spot that went back to his younger days in Tennessee.

He remembered Poochie joining him and Brett on their many adventures in the mountains of Pigeon Forge.

May May always warning them, "You boy's gonna run into a bear, or sumtun worse one day, and I ain't gonna be dere to stop it. You keep dat Poochie close. He gonna be all dat gonna save you one day." Tad wondered how many times Poochie might have saved them. But then again, he always felt safe in the woods. Well, at least in East Tennessee. He wasn't sure why, but he did.

The Sentrys had been doing the job. There had been a couple of visitors to the property; one person was caught poaching, another caught camping, and then there was the young couple caught having sex in their car at midnight one weekend. That one stirred up a bit of controversy, as the girl was the niece of the pastor of Stone Mountain Baptist Church. The pastor was just beginning to stir up a "stink" when his niece divulged she was already pregnant. The matter was dropped immediately.

Tad saw the deputies almost every day that he was on the property. He'd quit staying at the bed and breakfast in Rogersville and started staying in a small trailer that he'd bring over each weekend from Johnson City. He'd park it behind the lake, next to the tradesmen's building.

Not far from his camping spot he'd had a local fencing company install an eight-foot-tall, chain-link fence all the way around the tradesmen's building for added safety. Tad was fairly confident that no one was bothering any of the buildings, but now that they were all fenced, and the Sentry towers were in place. There was a Sentry to the east of his camper, and another to the west. There was no safer campground in Hawkins County.

Nick had made it a habit to come by and hang out with Tad from time to time. Sometimes when he was off the clock, Nick would come by at dusk with a six-pack of IPAs. He and Tad would sit by a campfire and tell each other stories about their youth. Eventually, Tad felt comfortable enough to tell Nick about his early years at Camelot. Tad's reflection of the property surprised Nick. Tad made him swear to "keep it to himself", as he didn't want any adverse attention.

One Friday night, Nick stopped by and noticed Tad on a backhoe, clearing and leveling an area on the front side of the lake, between it and the road. Tad was spreading gravel when Nick honked. Tad drove the backhoe over to Nick's car, stopped, and shut it down. Still sitting on the tractor, Tad called out, "Hey Nick, whatcha up to?".

Nick opened the door of his Jeep and held up a bag of groceries. "I've got fixins for some subs, if you're up to it?"

Tad held up five fingers and barked back, "Gimme five to ten minutes and I'll call it a day. I think you know where most everything is. If you want to toast the bread, start a fire and I'll be over soon."

With that, Tad fired the backhoe up and started back to the front of the lot. Within a few minutes, he'd spread much of the gravel and the sky was beginning to darken, so he drove the backhoe around the lake and parked it behind the trailer. After climbing off and putting the key inside the trailer, he walked over to the new well-pump that he had installed and began to pump the handle.

Nick walked over. "Hey, you got a well!", he said.

Tad was lathering some soap on his hands and rinsing in the pail hanging from the well-pump. "Yep, they came out and drilled it Monday. I was afraid that they might leave big ruts, so I had East Tenn Rental drop off that backhoe. Ended up not needing it and decided to start working on the pad for Ethel's Diner, which is another idea I have that you're gonna hafta keep quiet about for a while." Tad said, while walking back to the trailer for a towel.

"Oh boy, here we go again. What does Tad have going through that crazy brain now?" Nick laughingly stated.

Tad came out of the trailer with two beers and a notebook. He handed one beer to Nick, set his own beer down on the picnic table, and opened the folder. Tad flipped through the paperwork in the folder, looking for something in particular. Then he finally stopped and pulled out a drawing. It was an artist's rendering of a train car with a hip roof canopy built over it, and a fluorescent sign above that read "Ethel's Diner". Tad passed it across the picnic table to Nick.

Nick took a drink of his beer, set it back down, and picked up the artwork. As he slowly looked over the drawing, his brow furrowed. "What the heck are you up to Tad?...Wait a minute, Is that…?" Nick began to ask, but Tad interrupted him.

"Yep, that's Pappy's train car. It's going to become Ethel's Diner, right here in Camelot. It's going before the zoning board next week. Between us, if it passes, which it should, I'll be able to move it down here next month. It won't be open until next spring, but my long term plan is to eventually expand it into a larger restaurant." Tad explained.

Nick started shaking his head, "How are you going to get it down here,…and, and, are those other train cars on this side of the lake?" Nick asked.

Tad looked down at the artwork with Nick. "These are going to be replicas of the same car. Well sort of…They'll have authentic wheels and bogie side-frames. The roofs will look almost identical. But the rest of it will be a fabricated house. The insides will look somewhat authentic. But they'll be brand new rentals. I found a company over in Asheville that agreed to partner with me on the design and build them. The first ones will be here, but I can't tell you how many other people are already interested in them. We could actually put them all across the U.S.. As for getting the flagship, Ethel's Diner here, I've got something lined up. But we'll need a police escort. You know anybody?" Tad inquired.

Nick laughed and stood upright. "Let's fry up some of this meat over the fire and toast the bread." He replied.

After they ate, Nick went back to his Jeep and brought back a cherry pie. Tad gave him a "thumbs up", then raised the campfire grill for Nick to set the pie on. Nick set the pie down with both hands and quickly pulled them away, blowing at them. He grabbed a folding chair and sat near the fire. Tad did the same. They sat there without saying a word for five minutes. Just watching the fire. Eventually, Tad picked up a stick and poked the fire. "Did you ever go down and get your flashlight?" Nick asked.

Tad sat back, looking perplexed. "Flashlight?" He replied.

Nick laughed. "The one you dropped in the elevator shaft of the "Racoon Mansion". He replied.

Tad's eyes opened wide. "Oh hell. I forgot all about that. I'll go after it eventually. Maybe tomorrow. I was pondering putting a Sentry on the roof. We have another version we could bring up to the roof in pieces. Maybe I'll go down and look for it when I get around to the rooftop Sentry." Tad said, then stood and went into the trailer.

While Tad was gone, Nick looked back at the tradesmen's building. Squinting his eyes, he thought the building must have been kind of "trendy", for the time. Sure, it showed ages of neglect. But it had a modern look about it. It kind of looked like an office building. Well, with a huge elevator shaft built right in the center of the front of the building. The elevator shaft protruded out from the rest of the building face and had the same windows as the rest of the building. If Nick didn't already know that it was an elevator, he thought that he probably wouldn't have guessed it was one. But there was something kind of ominous or foreboding. As Nick squinted, he could almost swear he saw a dim light emanating from the first floor. He re-focused his eyes and realized he was mistaken. It was just the reflection of the reddish moon.

Tad exited the trailer with some more paper plates, a pie knife, two forks, and two more beers. Setting them all on the picnic table, he looked at Nick and asked, "So what d'ya think about Ethel's?".

Nick finished his beer and came over to help Tad get the cherry pie off the campfire grill. "Tad, I don't know where you come up with this shit, but I think Camelot likes that you came back. For a minute, people in Rogersville thought you were gonna turn this into some kind of private hunting ground. They saw you were putting up eight-foot fencing and the rumors started flying all over town. The Sheriff and the deputies did their best to dispel it, but we really didn't know what you were up to either. You've really cleaned up around the lake, and when they hear about Ethel's, I think that you'll find quite a few people warming up to you." Nick explained.

Resembling two little boys who had just been given a pie as their dinner, they both cut large pieces and sat down to enjoy a piping-hot slice of "heaven".

Between bites, Nick asked, "Whatcha doing for power? Did you already get some of it back on?"

Tad laughed, "Oh hell no. I'll have new service ran for Ethel's, but the rentals will have electric generators with solar and wind turbines. They'll have propane for heat and hot water. But I don't plan to run any service to them."

Nick looked over his shoulder at the tradesmen's building that sat just a hundred yards away, then back at

Tad. "I coulda swore I saw light over there a while ago." he said.

Tad, eyeing the rest of the pie, spoke without even looking at Nick. "You're seeing the reflection of the fire or sometimes the moon off of the lake. I've seen it too. It's a full moon tonight. That's when you see the reflection the most. That's what you're seeing." He eyed the pie. "Whatcha think, finish it?"

Nick looked at the pie, shrugged his shoulders and said, "Hell, why not. I'm only running in a 5K tomorrow." Nick dished the rest of the pie onto their plates.

The second half of the pie was eaten much slower. They both talked about their own favorite pies. Cherry was Nick's favorite. He claimed his grandmother made the best cherry pie in Hawkins County, possibly the best in East Tennessee. When it was Tad's turn, Nick made a "sour face" as Tad explained his was the rhubarb pie that his mother-in-law used to make. Tad said there was rhubarb on the property and he was going to make sure that Ethel's carried Nelda's Rhubarb Pie.

While they were both cleaning up the picnic table and around the campfire, Tad asked Nick, "You serious about running a 5K tomorrow?".

Nick was packing the trash in a bag so that he could take it with him. He could feel Tad's interest and took his time to reply. But eventually, "Yep, Hawkin's County Annual. If you wanna join us, all the deputies not working are running. We'd love for you to join us."

Tad cocked his head and closed an eye, obviously contemplating the offer.

"Meet us at the station around ten. We're walking over to the park from there. Then, Cindy's got us covered at The Blue Dog for lunch. You can clean up at the station, before lunch." Nick glanced at his cell and flipped through a few screens.

Tad walked over. "Ya know what Nick, I think the 5K might just be the right place to let people know about Ethel's. That'll put the pressure on the board, too. You okay with that? I don't want any favoritism from the local law enforcement." Tad said.

Nick gave an "Awe shucks" kind of head sway and body swing. "I suppose we'll let ya tag along. Ya think you can keep up?" Nick asked.

Tad laughed. "Maybe…If you'd get outta here and let me get my beauty sleep. I'm no spring chicken, like you!"

Nick chuckled and climbed into his Jeep. "See you in the morning, "Slow Poke"." He snickered.

Tad's eyes widened. "Hey, wait, no fair! You've already given me a nickname that I haven't earned it yet!" Tad exclaimed and held up his hand. "Thanks for dinner Nick, I appreciate it, and will obviously repay sometime. Be careful driving home."

As Nick was backing his Jeep to turn around, it blocked Tad's view of the Pressmen's Building. As Nick drove down the drive, and the Jeep cleared Tad's view, he thought he saw a light in the elevator shaft. On the first floor. Tad blinked his eyes and quickly convinced himself that he was imagining it.

***

Tad pulled into the Sheriff's Department parking lot at nine forty-five. He saw a few of the deputies stretching out front and knew all of them by name. Shawn Baker, Jim Rhoads, Matt Josefik, Kimberly Foxx, and Carrie Upton, the "dispatcher".
Tad got out of his truck and opened the back door. He got a

water bottle, closed the door and started walking towards the gang of deputies.

Kim hollered out. "Hey Tad, rumor is that you might be an honorary deputy today. Is that true?".

Tad chuckled, "Well Kim, you know what they say about rumors, right?"

"What's that?" Kim replied.

Tad spoke back, "Everyone knows you can't disprove a rumor. That's why I'm starting one about you." All the deputies laughed, even Kim.

"You can't start a rumor bout me that ain't already been started, deputy!" Kim chided back.

The deputies continued to laugh, stretch and warm up. Tad did the same and asked, "Where's the guy responsible for my aching body later today?"

The deputies again laughed. Shawn, who was probably the least mischievous of the bunch and answered. "Nick ran out to the Sheriff's house to get you a department running shirt. Beth has an embroidery machine and they're putting your name on it. You gotta look good, if you're gonna be sworn in Mister O'Banion." Shawn said.

Again, the gang chuckled and Tad thought to himself, "This can't be good!".

They all stretched for another five minutes before two cruisers pulled into the lot. One was Nick and the other was Sheriff Evans. Nick parked, but Sheriff Evans pulled along side Tad and rolled down his window. "Hey Tad, I had nothing to do with it. Just want you to know that." The Sheriff said.

Tad, already knowing something might be up, looked at the Sheriff and replied, "Yeah, I know Sheriff. You really need to get better help around here."

Sheriff Evans laughed and looked at his watch. "Hey come inside, I got to swear you in before you all head over." Evans said.

Tad looked back at the group of deputies. They were all standing by the walkway up to the department entrance, waving Tad over.

***

Tad held up his right hand, with his left hand on a Bible. Trying not to laugh, as the rest of the deputies were doing while he repeated the Sheriff's words. When done, Deputy "Slow Poke" was sworn in. The Sheriff even gave him a badge number and honorary badge. Tad was now ready to join the ranks, and for his first official duty…probably come in last in a 5K run for the department. He enjoyed every bit of the camaraderie and thanked them all.

Just as he was giving Kim a hug, Nick spoke up. "Let's mount up boys! We got us a race to win!" Double-taking and noticing the evil stares from Kim and Carrie were enough of a warning that he knew that he "did wrong". "Ok, I got it girls. How bout let's mount up, deputies?" he asked, with an unhinged crook to his neck. The affirmation from Kim and Carrie gave them all the "go ahead" to head out the door.

Rogersville Municipal Park was across Highway 11W, just down from the Sheriff's Department. They all jogged into the park, looking like soldiers at bootcamp, with Tad bringing up the rear. People filled the park, which the town had decorated for the day. Many people appeared ready to run, and many others were there just for the festivities. There were bounce houses, booths with antiques and art, and food trucks setting up all over the park. The

Junior Reserves Officer's Training Corps Honor Guard was presenting the colors in front of a small stage. Behind them, on the stage, were the local governing body of Rogersville and Hawkins County.

Tad looked around, taking notice of how everyone appeared to know each other and how friendly it all seemed. The atmosphere buzzed with merriment, as people shared smiles and laughter. Rogersville had a warming small town feel, yet big enough to put on an event like this. He really enjoyed being there and was glad that the Sheriff's Department welcomed him in. He knew there was more he could do for this little community and considered the ways to contribute beyond gifted drones.

Tad saw Nancy and Rob, both on the zoning board, together on the stage. He approached them, feeling that the moment was perfect. "Nancy, Rob, good to see you guys." Tad said.

As Nancy turned around and read Tad's shirt, she burst out laughing, and it took her a moment to compose herself. "I'm sorry Deputy, I just had a goofy image that took over. Please proceed Deputy Dog." With that, she and Rob both chuckled.

Tad stood there with a grin, and then chimed in, "You do know that you are talking to an officer of the law, don't you?" Tad said with a chuckle of his own.

"How the heck did they talk you into this, Mister O'Banion?" Rob inquired.

Tad quickly replied, "Please Rob, call me Tad, and I'm not completely sure how I got talked into it. But it sure looks like the deputies are having fun with it anyway. It's all in fun, and I'm happy to oblige. They're good people. Oh, hey, I wanted to mention to you two that I'm submitting a request for a zoning variance and permission to put Pappy's old train car down on my property, by the lake. Pappy and I worked out a deal and I'd actually like to do that next week, if possible. Look over the proposal and let me know what you think. My lawyer should have dropped it off yesterday…Oh, and call me anytime, if you have any questions."

Rob spoke. "I glanced at it yesterday. I see nothing wrong with it, but I'll give it a better look and get back to you. It's interesting that you got Pappy to give that old thing up. But he'll sure be glad to see you put it down on the property right next to his uncle's old place. It's gone now, but his uncle owned a stable down there for years. What am I saying, Pappy worked it for years, too."

Tad looked confused. "Wait, what?…when did Pappy work there?" Tad questioned.

Rob looked at Nancy, then closed his eyes, and cocked his head. "Kinda before my time, but I'm guessing round the late sixties through the seventies. Maybe eighties." Rob replied.

Now Tad was really confused. How did he not remember Pappy? "He's not Pop from way back when is he?" Tad asked.

Rob replied instantly, "Oh no, that was his uncle. Pappy went by Nick back then. His real name is Thadeus, but he got the nickname "Nick" from the bullet ricochet that took a bit of his ear off, when he was hunting. In fact, Nick Williams is Pappy's great-nephew. Named after him."

This was quickly becoming more than Tad could process before running 3.1 miles. He decided to close the conversation for now and get ready. "Thanks guys, gotta run!". Tad comically stated.

Tad turned and jogged over to the deputies. Some were again stretching and warming up. Others had stopped to talk to various people they knew. Tad's mind was now racing.

Mayor Weaver was following a few organizers around and was pinning numbers on the runner's shirts. As he came to the deputies, he exclaimed, "Now deputies, you know that it's not righteous to be bringing in a "ringer" at the last minute, right?".

They all laughed, and Carrie thought to introduce Tad. "Mayor Weaver, this is Tad O'Banion. He is a runner that we drafted from Johnson City. Don't let the name and badge number fool you. He's the real deal. So, all those ringers that you brought in have got their work cut out for 'em". She said with a grin.

Tad was shaking his head in disagreement, but the Mayor was now looking at him. "Deputy, not sure who you're trying to fool, cuz I know whom Mister O'Banion is and I also don't know what you are talking about regarding "my ringers"." The Mayor said, extending a hand for Tad to shake.

Tad did so and kept shaking his head. "Don't believe Carrie sir, she's just trying to get your goat. It's an honor to finally meet you." Tad said.

It was obvious from the organizer's agitation that the Mayor needed to keep pinning numbers on runners. So, they all made cordial acknowledgments and the group moved on.

Carrie explained, "The Mayor actually does bring in ringers for the city Police department, that's what's funny. Then Sheriff Evans has to hear about it for the next three weeks. It's actually bullshit that he even said that! Nick, you're the one who's been training. Did you get down to an eight-minute mile?" She quizzed.

Nick smiled and bent over at the waist. As he was bent over and stretching, he affirmed, "I don't know if I can run it the whole way. But I have run an eight-minute mile."

Tad was stretching just a few yards away and listening. Appearing indifferent, but feeling the need to give

Carrie and Nick some reassurance that "anything is possible", Tad spoke up. "Nick, I used to run eight-minute miles all of the time. It's how I trained. I've run close to a seven-minute mile in a 5K before. The only trick is not to bonk. It's easy, I'll set the pace, you just relax, stay behind me and relax. Completely disregard what is around you. Just look at my back and relax. During the race, I'll prompt you for when I think you need to make your move. When I do, I want you to pass me, and run a seven-minute mile. If you've been training, you've got this. Just look at my back. Relax and listen to me. You good?"

When Tad stopped talking, he realized that all the deputies were listening intently with mouths slightly open in confusion.

"Who the hell did you bring here Nick? A spiritual coach?" Kim askeded.

"That's Mick. He's my trainer." Nick joked.

Nick was on the ground when Tad explained "his" strategy. While the rest of the deputies looked at each other in disbelief, Nick stood up and walked over to Tad. "So, you can win this, can't you?" Nick asked.

Tad shook his head. "No Nick, none of us needs to win this, we just have to beat the Police Department's ringers. If you've really been training, I can help you cross before any of those ringers. That's a "win" in my book. Whad'ya say kid?"

By now, the deputies appeared ready to take on the world, exchanging "high fives" and "fist bumps" as they headed for the starting gate.

Approaching to the crowd of runners at the starting line, Tad noticed the "ringers" in the front. Nick immediately wanted to go to the front. Tad grabbed him by the arm and again coached. "Listen to me Nick. You have to listen. I need you to stay relaxed and watch my back. Just watch my back and relax. Just Reelaaax. I'll get you in position. When I tell you to go, I want you to give it everything you've got. If you stay relaxed and watch my back, you'll be ready to pounce. If you watch them, you won't. Relaaax. We don't need to be up there with them. You want to be about twenty-five yards behind them. I kinda want to put some runners between us. I don't want them to see you coming until it's too late. Okay?" Tad asked.

Nick nodded. With the look of a fighter going into the ring, Nick's face became expressionless. He was already focusing on Tad and the rest of the deputies filed in behind them. Most were smiling, but Nick… and Kim focused on Tad. She had been quietly listening to Nick's trainer as well.

The mayor eyed his ringers as he raised the starting gun. Slightly before he pulled the trigger, the ringers led the pack of runners down East Main Street. The crowd erupted as the runners took off, and soon there was a steady stream of runners flowing down Main Street. Tad quickly found a crease he liked and Nick tucked right in behind him, then Kim behind Nick.

As they ran through the downtown section, throngs of people cheered and called out to fathers, mothers, brothers, sisters, spouses, and more. But then Tad heard it. As they passed the Masonic Temple, the cheers became loud and one came from a bullhorn. "You got this Rogersville Pee Dee! They're already falling back. You got this one in the bag boys." The voice rang out.

Nick immediately responded by telling Tad they needed to go faster. Tad replied, "Don't listen to them Nick. They're trying to get in our heads because we're actually gaining ground. Stay right where you are. Ignore the "barking". Be relaxed and ready when I tell you to. Are you relaxed Nick?" Tad asked.

Nick slowly answered in a bad Rocky imitation, "I'm good Mick, just let me go!"

Tad smiled and thought, "Wow, that's way before Nick's time"…and they ran on.

They turned onto Houston Street, and then onto Stanifer. Even though the police had cordoned off the route, the street width was not friendly for passing. Tad, Nick, and Kim were slowly gaining on the front of the pack. They could actually see the jerseys of the ringers when Tad realized the ringers had given way to the "phenoms" who show up to every 5K.

Tad had run in many marathons, and there was always a group of men, and women, that seemed to be Olympic athletes. Many years ago, he took offense to them because they made a seven minute mile look like a joke. He eventually realized that these people needed competition and even a 5K was something that they could use to gauge themselves against others. Tad learned to embrace the joy of the small wins.

As they came out onto Lee Highway, Tad could feel the relief of more running space and also that infamous burn that he'd get in his quads around the two-mile mark. Once it passed, Tad normally felt like he could run all day, and at times, damn near did. But that was a few years back, so Tad was relying on Nick,… and now it appeared Kim could be "a golden child too". He had been listening to Nick's breathing. It was fast and steady, but not labored. If the kid had been training, they might just beat the ringers. He noticed the ringers had picked up their pace. Expecting it, he adjusted as well. Tad called back, "How you doing Rock?", in his best Burgess Meredith voice.

Nick replied, "Ready to go Mick. Lemmy go!"

Tad chuckled, "Soon Rock. Soon."

Just as Tad finished the last "soon", one of the ringer's feet got tangled up in another runner's feet. The both of them tripped and took two more runners with them to the ground.

Immediately, Tad said, "I gotta stop and help these guys."

Before he could say another word, he heard Kim from right behind him. "Nope, I got this. Unless you're a better EMT than me, which wouldn't surprise me, I'm the one stopping. Get your ass in gear boys and win this thing!" she shouted.

As Tad and Nick ran away, they heard Kim say, "You go get 'em Rock! Whoever the hell that is!"

They both chuckled, and Tad said, "We're close Nick. I need you to put something in your mind now. You ready?"

Nick hesitated, then said, "What is it, Tad?"

Tad was already putting the image into his own mind. "Nick, what I need you to do is think about NASCAR."

Nick thought, "that's a bit odd", and then said, "Uh, NASCAR?"

Between the stumbling of the runners and the bit of acceleration that Tad had put in place, they were now a mere ten to twelve feet away from the remaining ringers.

"Yeah Nick, they're gonna block us if we go right at 'em. That's why we're gonna fade right and we're gonna close this gap. When I say "now", I want you to slingshot past me on the right. I promise you that you will feel like there is no wind, and nothing stopping you. It'll almost feel like you're being pushed. You run hard and steady all the way to the finish line. You ready?" Tad exhaled.

They moved to the right, just as Tad said they would. Nick realized that this was smart because the next turn was to the right, and then again, to the right, into the park. Before he could shake that thought, Tad barked, "Now!"…and Nick strode to the right of Tad. He was correct; there was no wind, and he could feel a push from behind. Nick felt as though he could outrun everyone, but then remembered what Tad said. "Hard and steady". Nick set his pace. A fast pace. There was less than half a mile left, and as he was turning into the park, he saw a young man vomiting on the side of the roadway. He continued to run "Hard and Steady" to the finish line, where he slowed and jogged after crossing.

Nick was spent, but amazingly, not many runners had already crossed the finish line. He guessed maybe six or seven. He wanted so badly to win this race and felt disheartened. That was until Tad jogged up and lowered his head between his legs.

"You won kid. You did it." Tad said while bending over.

Nick looked over at a few of the "phenoms", then said to Tad, "I didn't Mick, I couldn't beat them." Nick said.

Tad stood up and grabbed a water from the young lady handing them out to the runners. "You weren't going to beat those guys, Nick. They're on another level. The battle was with those guys over there." Tad pointed at three men, all exhausted and clearly looking at them in disbelief.

Tad and Nick caught their breath and circled back to the finish line to watch scores of runners came across the line. Runners of every age, color and gender. A man in a wheelchair crossed and raised his arms as a small crowd erupted in cheers. Some runners crossed, looking surprised, some with big smiles, but most just raised their arms in triumph, which showed that they had "finished". They watched an older blind runner cross with his hand on the arm of a young lady, possibly his granddaughter, or just a neighbor trying to do something good. Tad thought of Pappy, and how nice it would feel to get "Ethel's Diner" up and going.

A local country band played behind them and they could hear the festivities getting louder. By now, most of the deputies had joined them, but Tad and Nick were intent on staying and watching for one special runner…and then they saw her. Not running, but jogging, behind a wheelchair, and in the wheelchair was none other than the "ringer" who had gone down… the one Kim wouldn't leave behind.

Kim saw Nick and Tad and swerved the wheelchair toward them. As she and her new friend crossed the line, all the deputies raised their hands and pumped their fists.

Kim stopped by Nick and Tad. "Nick, Tad, this is Brenden. He says that he's not in pain, but that's adrenaline talking." Kim said as she patted him on the shoulder. Brenden reached over his shoulder, grabbed Kim's hand and smiled. "It's nice to meet you guys. You've got one special deputy right here." He said.

Kim squeezed his hand and smiled back at him. "Listen guys, I need to get him over to the EMT tent just in case he needs to go to the hospital. I may go with him, so y'all may have to do The Blue Dog without me."

As Kim pushed Brenden towards the ambulance, Tad and Nick looked at each other perplexedly. Nick said, "Okay, that was interesting. I think Juliet just met Romeo, and where the hell did they get a wheelchair?"

Unbeknownst to Nick and Tad, when Brenden went down, a few other people stopped to help besides Kim. A state trooper came over from a barricade with a med kit. Kim was wrapping Brenden's ankle when Jeff Randal strolled up with a wheelchair. Jeff is a well-known local, who was pushing his eighty-year-old father in the race. Seeing the situation, Jeff's father stepped up from the wheelchair and offered it up to Brenden. Jeff's father offered to walk the rest of the race, but the state trooper wouldn't have it and offered to drive the elderly man over to the park and get him situated to watch Jeff cross the line. Jeff's father accepted and left with the trooper.

While Kim was wrapping Brenden's ankle, he asked. "Why'd you stop? You had us beat. I'd been turning back and watching you from time to time and you didn't even look "winded".

Kim didn't look up, but smiled and replied. "The Chief brings you guys in every year, just for this race. That doesn't relieve me of my duties as a deputy or EMT. Besides, you're kinda cute and I want to beat you fair and square. When you get healed up, come on out to the Spartan Camp and I'll show you how we race there." Wincing a bit, Brenden returned, "You've got yourself a date, deputy."

The runners kept coming for another ten minutes, but eventually gave way to the walkers, so the crowd in the park grew, and the deputies re-grouped. One by one, Shawn, Jim, Matt, and Carrie congratulated Nick. "You did it brother." Shawn said.

Nick looked at Tad and laughed. "I couldn't have done it without Mickey. Pretty sure I'd have "bonked"."

Carrie chimed in, "Pretty impressive from behind. That little "slingshot" thing looked amazing. I've never seen it anywhere, but NASCAR. Didn't know it would work like that."

Nick rebutted, "Tad knew. He knew how it worked."

Tad shook his head. "It doesn't. Well kinda." he stated. "That was mostly in your head Nick. There's not enough draft for you to really slingshot. But you believed you could…and to be blunt, you surprised me. I wouldn't want to guess what you ran that last mile. But it was fast." Tad explained.

Just as they began to walk back to the station to shower, the Sheriff met them on the street. From his cruiser he called out. "Great job guys! All of you. Nick, I just got off the phone with the Police Chief. He's quite humbled right now, and four hundred dollars lighter. Ha, Ha. He said that they were watching the trackers on a notebook and you ran an average of seven-point-two. He said the he may hafta recruit from Knoxville now, but I think you and Kim may hold your own for a few years." The Sheriff proclaimed. As the deputies gathered around the sheriff's cruiser and listened to him, the radio came to life.

"Hawkins Oh-one, what's your status? Hawkins Oh-one, what's your status?" The radio squawked. The Sheriff replied, "Oh-one, ten-ninety-eight, whatcha got Sabrina?"

Sabrina Hua was another dispatcher for the Sheriff's Department, along with Carrie Upton, Serena Roman, and semi-retired Kay Longford. The four of them covered the dispatch solely for the Sheriff's Department. This made things rather "casual" at times, often speaking "freely" on the radio. Sabrina squawked back, "Sheriff, Dennis Mansel wants us to swing by and check on Pappy. He said he has coffee with Pappy every Saturday morning and Pappy didn't walk over this morning. He said he went over and looked in, but didn't see nothin' wrong. Do you have time to run out there?" she asked.

"Ten-four Sabrina, I'll head out there right now." The Sheriff replied.

Nick right away spoke up. "I'm going too, Sheriff!"

As he came around the car to sit in the front seat. "No, no, no Nick! Since I probably can't talk you into taking a shower first, you get to sit in the back." The Sheriff exclaimed.

Tad and the rest of the deputies stepped back with concerned looks on their faces. Nick climbed into the back seat as the Sheriff got back in the front. The crew of deputies closed back in on the Sheriff's open window before he pulled away. "You guys did great today. Go have an excellent lunch. I'm sure everything's fine with Pappy. He's old, but ornery. We'll catch up with you at The Blue Dog."

The rest of the deputies, including Tad, returned to the station, showered, and dressed to go into town where The Blue Dog was preparing a table for them. Carrie gave Tad a new Hawkins County SWAT team shirt and a duffel bag with the same insignia.

Excited about his new togs, stowed his running gear and joined the crew.

Shawn and Matt had dressed in their patrol uniforms, so Tad assumed they had to work soon. Jim wore a similar shirt to Tad's and a pair of blue jeans. Carrie had a clean "Sheriff's Department" running shirt and a tight pair of jeans with many holes in them. Tad, with his SWAT shirt and a pair of jeans, fit right in and appeared to be "one of them". He even commented so. To which, Carried reminded him he was actually a "sworn in" deputy. They all laughed at this, and Tad wasn't sure what that really meant.

They all reminisced about the race, explained many idiosyncrasies of the department to Tad, and of course, expressed concern for Pappy. But they eventually left the station, bidding farewell to Sabrina on the way out and loading into three cars. Two cruisers and Carrie's little SUV.

***

The Blue Dog is just three minutes away, in downtown Rogersville. It's a cute place. Rustic but inviting, with a bar along one side, the rest filled with tables for patrons throughout. Above the bar, hanging from the ceiling, an electric train runs on continuously on a track, over the patrons' heads. At the end of the bar, past the hall to the kitchen, is a stairway that leads up to a large balcony, overlooking the entire restaurant.

Cindy Blackwell, the owner of the Blue Dog, had a table on the balcony set for six. Tad had only been in here once before, but never paid attention to the pictures on the walls. Old black and white photos covered the walls. Some pictures were so old that the very frames that housed them had to be valuable. There were photos of coal miners, houses, train cars, horse-and-buggies, and many of people that Tad assumed were famous Hawkins County history. On the back wall of the balcony area, high above, there was a larger photograph of a Civil War soldier. He looked important, and Tad guessed him to be an officer...possibly Robert E. Lee. The old military officer mesmerized Tad until he finally broke the hypnotic state. Taking a seat with the deputies, Tad sat positioned so he was looking up at the photograph that intrigued him.

Cindy was by their side before they all sat and greeted them with a cheery "Hey guys, what can I get the winner's today?"

The deputies all looked at each other and then back at Tad. Tad looked back in surprise. "Don't look at me, Miss Daisy. You was riding right there with me." Tad said.

Matt interceded. "Alright Cindy, what did the Sheriff tell you?" he questioned. Cindy smiled.

"Oh, it wasn't the Sheriff, it was the Police Chief. He said that his department got their asses "handed to them" in the race. He canceled their reservation and said for y'all to have a round "on him". So, what'll it be?" Cindy asked.

While everyone was celebrating, like a bunch of high schoolers, Tad, trying not to be obvious, but was noticing

Cindy's attractiveness. She was probably thirty-five to forty, auburn hair, lightly tanned, with freckles across her cheeks. Built like what Tad would call a gymnast; she appeared to perform as she melded with the gang of deputies. Shaking off the fixation, his mind returned to the camaraderie, occasionally glancing at the ginger who had taken Tad's mind off the Civil War officer watching over them.

After they all finished their fist-pumping, high fives, and "churning-the-butter", the gang ordered drinks. Tad was chatting with the everyone when Cindy returned. She served their drinks and took their lunch orders. Before she left, Tad asked her a question about the pictures on the walls, and when he got to the soldier's picture, she explained, "That's my great-great-great uncle, William Blackwell. He was a General for the Confederate States. Went to West Point with Jefferson Davis and became a doctor. Our family actually owned the property right out there by you, back during the Civil War."

Tad's chin dropped, his head pulled back and his eyes widened. "How'd you know I own property out there?" He asked.

Cindy rolled her eyes upward and held her palms upward. "Tad, every eligible "Southern-Belle" notices when a "Damn Yankee" comes to town."

Tad was beginning to blush, but before he could respond, Carrie chimed in jokingly, "Easy there, Southern-Belle. That Damn Yankee is a duly sworn-in officer, his department comes first."

Matt, Shawn, and Jim looked at each other. "Oh boy, it looks like Nick just lost his bromance." Matt claimed.

"Wait what? Y'all, full stop. I'm married. Well widowed. But I'm not Nick's "bromance"…and", Tad paused and grinned. "Oh hell, maybe I was. But I sure didn't know it!" All of them, including Cindy, were shaking their heads in agreement.

Cindy turned to walk down the stairs and said aloud, "But, it sounds like "available" to me." Then kept walking.

Tad was glad that the subject had changed and their food came quickly. All were famished, but conversation was lively. Each deputy took their turn asking Tad about his company in Johnson City. They asked questions about the Sentinel drone Tad donated, about the towers on Tad's property and why Tad kept referring to the property as "Camelot". Tad, in turn, told his new friends about his plans to place Pappy's old train car on the property and turn it into a diner. Everyone thought it was an interesting idea but expressed concern about patronage, as the place was a fifteen to twenty-minute drive from town.

Jim explained, "It might be hard to only have the deputies as patrons." and they all laughed.

When Cindy returned to clear dishes, Shawn asked her, "Hey Cindy, Tad's talking bout putting a diner out at the old Pressmen's Home. You know anybody he could talk to who'd know anything about food service?"

Appreciating Shawn's lead, she replied, "Oh, I can think of someone.", then winked at Tad.

Carrie let out a loud "A'hem" as Cindy went down the steps carrying more dishes than any normal person could handle.

Just as Tad was going to change the subject again, Matt and Shawn's radios squawked. They both lifted an earpiece and listened. As they listened, their faces went from concern to eyes closing and heads lowering.

Matt raised his head and looked at Carrie and Jim. "Ten-fifty-five, ...Pappy's place". Matt said.

Carrie and Jim both shook their heads and looked down too. Tad was confused, but suspicious.

"What's ten-fifty-five?", he asked.

It took a moment for anyone to answer, but Carrie finally spoke. "The coroner's been called. Pappy's gone." She paused for a moment and then spoke, "It's gonna kill Nick. Pappy was like his grandpa."

Tad wasn't sure what to say but thought mentioning Ethel might be appropriate. "Guys, Pappy's with Ethel now. They deserved to be together,…and now they are. She's been waiting for him for a long time."

One by one, the deputies sighed and shook their heads in agreement. Their lunch celebration was finished on a sorrowful note and prompted them to leave.

Carrie drove Tad back to the station. He thanked everyone and promised to visit the station more often. He waved goodbye and started to leave the lobby when Carrie said, "Hey Tad, I'll walk out with you. I'm leaving too."

All the deputies were extremely cordial, so Tad thought little of it. That was until he saw Carrie's "walk". She had changed her gait, now walking with a bit of a skip in her walk. She rocked her shoulders and kept looking at Tad with a "half-grin". He hadn't noticed how pretty she was previously. With her blonde hair pulled back in a ponytail, Tad guessed her to be about the same age as Cindy. Reaching his Land Cruiser first, he jokingly asked which Jeep was hers.

Turning to the small row of Jeeps, Carrie smiled. "That's my sweetheart right there." Carrie said, pointing at a teal Rubicon.

Feeling awkward, since Carrie hadn't walked towards her Jeep yet, Tad asked. "Any benefits of being a deputy, now?"

Flirtatiously, Carrie replied, "You can come use the gym any time that you want. You won't get any more tickets…and" Carrie paused, looked down, then back up at Tad. "and you get to see me any time you want."

Now feeling very uncomfortable, Tad decided that he should go. "You be safe out there, Carrie."

Carrie cocked her head. "You too, Tad.", and winked.

Chapter 17 –

"Goodbye, Old Friend"

Tad sent a consoling text to Nick, but did not see or hear from him until the day of the funeral. The Stone Mountain Gap Baptist Church hosted the funeral services, including visitation, a brief service followed by a procession to the cemetery. The gravestone read "Nick "Pappy" Wiseman". Tad chuckled, as he realized might be the only Thadeus in town now, and the only other one he knew didn't have it on his gravestone.

After the interment, everyone was welcomed back to the church for refreshments and to share memories of Pappy. Tad hadn't planned on staying, but decided to stay since he had gotten to know Nick fairly well. Once inside, Tad found himself with the deputies and was sitting down with a glass of tea when Nick came up.

"Thank you all for coming. Pappy loved you all. Not sure I ever told any you this, but he talked about every one of you." Nick offered.

Tad felt uncomfortable, and kind of out-of-place. But Nick made him feel better with what he said next.

"Tad, …Pappy musta liked you. Cuz he left you a note. It's dated a couple weeks back and it claims that you bought the train car for a dollar from him. The lawyer has it now, but I took a a picture for you." Nick held up his phone with a picture of a handwritten note.

To Thadeus O'Banion,

Tad, I was pleased that you grew up to be someone special. We all knew that it had to be hard for you. But we also thought that you were tough and would make it. Your brother was tough too…and a natural on a horse. Pop really hoped to see him come back, but your family was obviously fighting some demons. I pray the rest of your family is well. You made me remember Camelot in its glory, even if it was gone in the blink of an eye.
It was nice to hear you mention Ethel kindly. I appreciate that.

To Whom It May Concern, Thadeus O'Banion purchased my old train car for one dollar. Paid in full. I was the owner, and now he is the full owner of the "old train car in the barn".

Tad, I hope you find comfort in that old car. Even if you don't get it done, know that Ethel and I will smile down upon you. I'll be remembering that little boy who walked down from the cottages every day.

God Bless,
Pappy Nick Wiseman

When Tad finished reading it, he looked back at Nick. They both had tears slowly rolling down their faces. Tad shook his head as if to clear "memories" and looked at the others.

"What'd it say?" Carrie asked.

"It says that I own the old train car. That's what it says." Tad replied, and he looked back at Nick. Nick, realizing that Tad did not want to explain more, shook his head in agreement.

"We found it on his bureau, along with a couple other hand-written notes. One to his son, whom he's actually with now, and one to me. He had a will, but with the letters it looks like he wanted to get a couple things straight before he passed. The coroner says that he did have cancer but he died of a heart attack in his sleep. He went peacefully. Auntie Ethel has her Nick back." Nick explained. "He left me everything but the train. I guess there's really nobody else. So, after the lawyer gets everything straight, I guess I have a farmhouse to fix up. Sorry about your luck Tad, but you're on your own with that silly diner that you're building. Oh, and by the way, I need that old train car off of my property by next Friday."

The group broke out in laughter and drew suspicious glares from other tables.

The deputies continued to reminisce and make the visitation upbeat, which Nick knew would put a smile on Pappy's face. As the visitation grew to a close, Tad stopped by Nick.

"Nick and Ethel's" Tad said to Nick.

Nick looked confused. "I'm not sure I'm following you there, Hoss. What's that mean?" Nick inquired.

"The diner. It's going to be Nick and Ethel's", Tad replied.

"I like that Tad. Thanks for everything, man. It was a good day. Pappy is happy." Nick said, as he stretched out his hand for Tad to shake.

Tad slapped his hand away and put out both arms for a hug. They briefly embraced, Tad patted Nick on the shoulder, and left.

As Tad walked out the door, Nick watched him and thought about Pappy. He tried to see Pappy as Nick, out in Camelot…and the little boy who Nick knew so long ago.

Nick smiled, and whispered, "You did right by him Pappy. He'll do right by you. I know it."

The following weeks were busy. The board approved a preliminary building permit for Tad to move the train car down to Camelot and to have a shelter built over the top of it. Essentially covering it except for the sides, front and back. This served two purposes. It allowed Tad and the contractors to work on the car pretty much anytime, and second, it was to be a permanent structure to protect the train car after restoration.

Before installing power, Tad had presented the plans to the zoning board for the addition of a commercial kitchen on the west end, at the rear of the car. This would allow most of the patrons to have a clear view of the lake and block their view of the old tradesmen's building.

Nick came by often, both during work and not. He'd been working on Pappy's house and planned to move into it soon. Pappy's house was just a mile and a half away from Camelot, so Nick coming by with a meal every once in a while was pretty convenient for Tad. Nick noticed Carrie doing the same. He found himself asking her if it was "his night" or "hers"? She laughed it off and blushed.

There were periods of time that Tad couldn't be there at all. He had to travel for work and asked Nick to keep an eye on the place. Nick watched over it like it was his own. In fact, he reminded Tad that he now owned some of the old lots that Tad's father had sold so long ago.

After a few weeks of travel, Tad was astonished to see how much work the contractors had completed on "Nick and Ethel's", when he returned to Camelot one Saturday morning. To Tad, it seemed like he had been gone for months. The contractors built the roof with red tin and it was big enough for a small outdoor patio in front of the train car. It had a tall gable roof that gave the image of a portico to the train car. But it didn't take away from the train car's nostalgia. The train car was still the focus. Tad closed his eyes and imagined where he would put the Nick and Ethel's neon tube sign.

The carpenter Tad hired was almost complete with the woodwork inside of the train car. Initially, he gutted it, pulling out all the seats and tables, then he refinished all the base wood. He refinished the original seating and re-positioned them into booths along the front of the train car. All new windows adorned the car, which Nick must have taken upon himself to approve. Tad liked it and had no qualms about Nick's decision.

As the interior refinishing was wrapping up, with a few mechanicals, HVAC, and sprinkler system completions then the car was complete, they could move on to the kitchen.

Either Nick or the carpenter had found someone who knew how to refinish the car's roof-shingles. So that was well under way. Tad smiled and was impressed. Walking around, looking at the workmanship, his cell rang. Tad saw the number and realized that the people in Asheville must have been busy too.

"Is that you Darren?" Tad asked after he pressed "speaker" on his keypad. Darren Ratliff was the owner of The Mouse's Retreat, a custom tiny-home builder in Asheville. Tad had convinced them to partner with him in designing and building tiny-home "train car" replicas. These would be the rentals that Tad planned on placing around the lake.

Darren replied, "Yes sirree. How you been Mister O'Banion?"

"Busier than a mosquito at a nudist camp, Darren. I just got back in town. I'm over at "ground zero" right now, looking at a beautifully restored train car. You should drive over and see it some time. It's looking pretty good. There's still a whole kitchen addition to be built. But hopefully they approved that while I was gone. I'm hoping that your call means that you've got some designs for me to look at for the rental units?" Tad asked. "Oh, and stop calling me Mister O'Banion. It's Tad."

"I sure do, Tad. In fact, we've made some panels to show you, and I think we can knock that timeline down quite a bit if we can base the inside on one of our existing designs. I have one built right now, here in Asheville, if you want to see it?" Darren inquired.

Tad finished up the call by scheduling a visit to Asheville the following Tuesday. He was looking forward to relaxing a bit but noticed the piles of dirt and large pits that had been dug over by the fence of the tradesmen's building. He walked that way when a sheriff's cruiser drove by and honked. Tad turned to wave and saw that it had stopped and was backing up. He expected Nick, but a female stepped out of the cruiser. For a second, he didn't recognize the driver, but then realized it was Carrie.

"What in the world are you doing on a patrol Carrie?" Tad inquired.

"Dispatch was getting boring. Besides, a few of us wanted to step up patrols out here, while you were gone, Tad." Carrie replied, with an bashful looking grin. "Sure is looking pretty good. We'll be having dinner at Nick and Ethel's rightly soon, I reckon?" Carrie quizzed Tad, with her head tipped forward, eyes up, as if expecting the correct answer to her liking.

Tad smiled. "Aren't you the persistent one?" Tad proclaimed as Carrie walked toward him. "If you have a few minutes, I'll show you how this is going to look before the end of the year." Tad continued.

Carrie paused, made a comment on her radio and looked back at Tad. "I'm actually off of work in ten minutes. So, show me where the bad guys are buried, to be official.

Then, I'll clock out and you can give me the real tour." Carrie said, with a wink.

Carrie had stopped by many times before. But those had been brief visits, just to bring Tad a meal. This time, it appeared she was going to take full advantage of Tad's offer, even though she had just finished a third-shift patrol.

Tad walked her around the lake. He told her about the future train car rentals. He explained that the groundwork that was in process over towards the tradesmen's building was for a septic system. It had to be a minimum of one hundred yards away from the lake. They stopped at the picnic table next to his trailer, and Tad held up a finger as he stepped into his trailer. He came out with two cold water bottles.

As Tad handed one to Carrie, she asked, "Whatcha gonna do with the old building? Tear it down?"

"I'm not really sure, Carrie. I haven't even been in there since Nick and I checked it out, months ago. Tearing it down seems a shame, but I suppose that'll probably be the right thing to do." Tad mused. "Some part of me wants to remember it the way it was. But another portion tells me its life is over." He explained.

Carrie looked puzzled. "What do you mean *remember it the way it was?*" she asked.

Tad realized that he "slipped" and needed to clear that up. "Well you can imagine what it looked like back in the day, can't you? This was all a bustling campus. There was a hotel across the road and Nick's great uncle had a stable right over there." Tad said, pointing down the road a bit. "I mean, those days are gone." He insisted.

They continued to talk for almost an hour. Carrie had called in to clock out, but now she could feel the effects of the "third shift" taking its toll on her, as she felt tired.

Tad noticed it and thought it would be best if she got some rest.

"Deputy, I appreciate the company, but you've had a long night. You've got to be beat, and here I am running my mouth. Get on outta here and come on back when you've got time to stay a while." Tad suggested, hoping that his offer was kind, but not overtly forward. While Carrie was nice and very attractive, he really was not ready for a relationship.

"Tad! The next time you refer to me, as "deputy", instead of Carrie I'm gonna sock ya!...and, how bout tonight? How bout I fix you a home cooked meal? I'll bring it out here since you won't take me out for a nice one." Carrie smiled, cocked her head, and shrugged her shoulders.

Tad felt like he'd met his match. He then noticed her dimples and knew that he couldn't say "NO". He thought for a moment and replied. "Alright Carrie. You got me. But you have to promise me you'll go home and rest before you cook. This is not a date though. Understood? I don't want Nick mad at me."

Carrie looked elated and giddy. "Sure thing. Rest and then cook. Got it. Say six ish? And Nick is not my boyfriend! I don't know why people say that."

"Rest, eight hours!" Tad demanded.

Carrie was already heading to her cruiser and held up her right arm, with her thumb high in the air.

Tad watched Carrie back out and pull away. In his mind, he told himself that he needed to go get a tablecloth, better dishes, and clean up the inside of his little trailer. Then he shook his head. "What are you thinking Tad? It's just a friendly dinner, with one of your friends from the Sheriff's department…but the tablecloth and dishes are probably a good idea."

Tad worked around Camelot until around two, then he ran over to Rogersville to grab a quick lunch, and then stop at Walmart. On his way, he thought about Carrie. Her dimples. Her smile, and how "forward" she was with him. Then something bothered him about her,…he didn't like her patrolling. He liked the thought that she was safer at the station, dispatching. Then he realized that he'd been in town almost a day and hadn't talked to Nick. He pulled out his phone and dialed "Deputy Nick".

Nick answered his phone with a, "You've reached the cell of Deputy Williams. I'm unavailable right now, but if you're calling to donate to my college fund, or me personally, then by all means say so".

Tad laughed, "Nice Nick. What are you up to this fine day?"

"Heading out to Walkers Church Road. Theres four cows on the road. I guess I'm a Livestock Agent now…Like them boys out there at Yellowstone." Nick described. "You back in town?" he asked.

"Yeah, I am. Do they really have Livestock Agents in Tennessee?" Tad inquired.

Nick laughed. "They sure do. But they're different than the ones out west. Less about cattle rustling, and more about making sure that people are taking care of their critters. They make a whole lot more than me too. Maybe I should go into that!?…Hey, you wanna do chow tonight?"

Tad unknowingly scratched his head, but realized where this might lead. "No, I can't. I kinda already have something planned. But I wanted to catch up with you today or tomorrow. Nick and Ethel's looks great, and I know that you've been keeping that rolling. I want to pay you something for your help."

"It's Carrie, Isn't it. You're leaving me for Carrie…and you're trying to pay me to go away. I can't believe you!" Nick said jokingly. "I don't want any of your damn money. All I did was check in on the projects."

"Bullshit, you kept the carpenter rolling, you took care of the windows,…AND, got the sewer guys going, on your own. And, okay, it is Carrie. But, it's as friends hoss. That's it". Tad defended.

"Just bustin' your balls, man. Tomorrow's prolly better. By the time I get off today, you'll be sitting by the fire, holding hands with your little lady." Nick chuckled.

Tad shook his head. "Alright. That's enough. How about a late breakfast at the Blue Dog? I'll have Cindy save us a table upstairs. You good for ten-ish?"

"The man is sleeping in, after his date with the deputy, and then going to see his other girlfriend the next day for brunch. I've heard it all now!" Nick laughed as he turned onto Walkers Church Road.

"I'm hanging up, Nick." Tad chided, rolling his eyes, with a scowl.

Tad made his run to Walmart, and then stopped by the Blue Dog to ask for a table the next day. Cindy wasn't there, which made Tad more comfortable, especially after Nick's accusations.

As Tad drove back to Camelot, he started thinking about the septic system plans for the rentals and "Nick and Ethel's". His mind wandered back to the digging that had begun the day before. He could see the hole, the fence, and then the tradesmen's building in his head. Then it hit him…where is the septic for the old building? Is there one he could tap into? Probably not; way too old. But are they getting ready to dig right into an existing system? He hadn't gone to the basement of the building yet, but thought that he better…before Monday.

Chapter 18 –

"First Date"

Tad was spreading the tablecloth out on the picnic table when he looked up at the old train car that had recently transformed. He stopped and thought for a moment. "Maybe dinner in the train car?", and folded the cloth back up. Then thought again, "No, that might seem romantic. Best to keep it a little less "wooing" and stick with the picnic table. Tad quickly laid out the tablecloth and started a campfire. He put up the tiki-torches that he'd also picked up at Walmart, then lit them.

At five forty-five, Carrie's Jeep pulled onto the gravel drive that led to Tad's trailer. She slowly drove back, looking for Tad. Tad normally would be out. Especially if he was expecting a guest. Not seeing him around, her senses heightened. She reached into her console and pulled out her Sig Sauer P365. Slide checked for a round and then checked the safety. Carrie opened her door and stepped out. Grasping her pistol with both hands, bringing it to "the low ready", she slowly stepped towards Tad's trailer. She looked around. Saw the tablecloth, the fire, and tiki torches. She smiled slightly. Carrie knocked on the side of the small trailer. "Tad, you in there?"

Carrie remained vigilant. Tad's Land Cruiser was here, but "No Tad".

She called out. "Tad, you out here?!"

No reply. Now Carrie was officially "spooked". Considering a call for a deputy, she thought she'd try one more time. This time she shouted towards the tradesmen's building. "Tad, Tad, you out there?!" she announced.

"Yeah! Coming. Sorry." Tad replied.

Still holding her pistol "at low ready", Carrie watched as Tad came at a slight jog from around the tradesmen's building.

As Tad jogged up, he suddenly stopped and looked at his watch. He pulled out his phone, opened an app and entered a series of numbers.

Just as Tad did that, Carrie heard a "whizzing" sound and looked up. Two drones were flying overhead and then sped out of view.

"What the hell, Tad?" Carrie exclaimed.

"Sorry, Carrie. I was over there looking for the septic system and didn't realize that it was almost six. Hey, you're early…and "packing". Am I in some kind of trouble deputy?" Tad asked.

"You will be if you call me "deputy" one more time." Carrie replied. And what's with the damn hummingbirds? I didn't even see them up there until you stopped and did something with your phone."

"They saw your gun, and were defending me…well kind of. The cameras on the towers saw the gun and deployed the Sentinels. I think I stopped them in time, but we may get a visit from Hawkins County's finest. But, I think I caught it before they reported you." Tad explained.

Just as he finished that comment, Tad's cell rang. He answered. "Yeah Adam, I think I know what you want. All good here."

"Boss, the call center lit up like a Christmas Tree from your Sentrys. Who's the little lady with the gun? The Sentinels determined she wasn't a threat." Adam reported.

"She's actually a Hawkins County Deputy. They're all entered in the database, so they wouldn't have taken her out." Tad claimed, winking at Carrie.

Relieved, but still a little edgy, Carrie had lowered her pistol and started back to her Jeep. Tad was still on the phone, but heard Carrie say clearly, "At least the drones wanted to take me out."

Carrie was pulling a box from the rear seat of her Jeep when Tad came up.

"Here, Carrie. Let me get that." Tad offered, with his arms out.

They each carried a box over to the picnic table, and Carrie set out a few food storage containers. It was obvious to Tad that Carrie had a plan, and he decided it was best to let her set dinner up. Then she suddenly stopped. "Do you want to eat now, or wait a bit? The meatloaf is pretty hot and could cool down for a bit." Carrie asked.

Tad held up his hands. "I'm good to wait. You tell me when, and we'll eat. You want something to drink? I stopped and got a red wine, a white wine and some beer...I have sweet tea or water too."

"Beer...or whiskey! Either will do. You actually bought red and white wine?" Carrie quizzed Tad.

Tad walked toward the cooler by the trailer. "Yeah, I wasn't sure what you drink, and wanted you to have something you like." He pulled out two beers, grabbed a couple of koozies and returned to the picnic table.

As Tad handed Carrie a beer, she cocked her head and asked him, "Can those drones really take someone out?"

Tad did not immediately reply, but instead looked up, head cocked, wondering how to answer without garnering some skepticism. "Come, walk with me by the lake and I'll explain."

Tad and Carrie walked along the back side of the lake as Tad explained that there are military and civilian versions of the Sentinels. The DOD and CBP have units that can explode with onboard ordnance. The civilian versions don't have this feature, but do have a "Wasp" mode that could keep a perpetrator busy trying to fend off the drones.

"What version do you have here?" Carrie asked.

Tad smiled. "Well, wouldn't you like to know?...Just kidding. These are NOT the military versions. These are kind of a hybrid. The Sentinels do not have ordinance, but they would certainly make you miserable if they thought you were a threat. They're even connected to me."

"How so?" Carrie inquired.

"When I'm here, they monitor my heart rate. If it were to raise suddenly, or worse, they'll come to me immediately to investigate."

"That kinda ruins my plans there dude." Carrie said with a wink.

Tad's eyes widened, and he twisted his lips. "Um, I have an emergency "shut down sequence" that I can do on my watch. It's all good."

They stood there for a few moments, looking at the lake and the surrounding scenery. Tad picked up a stone and skipped it across the lake.

"It's pretty safe out here isn't it?" Carrie asked.

"Unless there's a sniper that the cameras didn't pick up, which I doubt, it's probably the safest place in Tennessee." Tad replied. "Let's head back and see how your meatloaf is doing."

As they walked back, Tad felt Carrie's closeness. She was walking right next to him. Much closer than when they walked along the shoreline. He wanted to grab her hand, but the feeling was also uncomfortable. His mind raced, and he thought of the Sentinels. He glanced at his watch. It had been twenty minutes…and his heart rate was fine…and a cross between a "crush" and paranoia was taking over. He closed his eyes for a moment and cleared his head. All was gone.

Tad stumbled but caught himself quickly.

"Did you just learn how to walk, Tad?" Carrie laughed.

Tad laughed too. "I suppose. Kind of caught up in the moment."

"Oh? How so?" Carrie quizzed a now blushing Tad.

"Well, Um. Never mind. I'll get us another beer and set the table. Let me know what you need help with." Tad said.

As Tad went to the cooler, Carrie looked at her cell phone. By the time Tad had opened the bottles, had them in Koozies and got to her side, she was holding up her smartphone. "Sixty percent chance of rain, big fella. What now? In your trailer?" Carrie asked.

Tad turned his head and looked at his trailer. "Oh hell no. That thing's the size of a closet. Even if it was immaculate, I sure as heck wouldn't take a first date in there." He declared.

"First date?" Carrie popped back at Tad.

"No, I'm sorry. You know what I mean." Tad defended.

"Okay, Loverboy. What about Nick and Ethel's? Looks ready for patrons to me...or at least move the picnic table under the cover." Carrie exclaimed.

Tad looked over at the old train car. "Well, I'd hafta get permission from Nick or Ethel first."

"They said yes, let's go! Help me box everything back up and let's head over there." Carrie whispered, like she didn't want the "owners" to know that they were breaking into the restaurant to have a candlelight dinner.

Tad and Carrie packed up the two boxes and carried them over to the old train car. With the cloud cover and the sun setting, it was fairly dark in the train car. After they set the boxes down, Carrie turned and pulled Tad close to her. She lifted herself on her toes and kissed him, just once…and then settled back, turned and started taking items out of the boxes.

"What was that for?" Tad questioned.

"I know that you're not ready…and I understand that. That was just letting you know that I'm here when you are." Carrie smiled, without turning and looking at Tad. "Why don't you run back and get that tablecloth, before it gets wet."

Tad sprang into action, and Carrie smiled again. On his way out of the train car, Tad flipped the light switch, and the car lit up. He stepped out and jogged over to the picnic table.

When Tad returned, he had the cooler and a small device that looked kind of like a lantern. He set the cooler down, laid the tablecloth over the table next to Carrie and then turned on the lantern, setting it on the table behind them.

Carrie watched him without looking up, and then asked, "Is that a little candlelight for dinner?"

"Oh, no. It's to keep the mosquitoes away." Tad replied. "they're actually starting to get a little feisty, this time of year. That thing is made by another company that we've partnered with. This one is small, but will keep mosquitoes away for about twenty feet. I've got some prototypes coming that they think will keep them away for a hundred feet…no more spray." Tad explained.

Carrie asked Tad to sit as she divvied out portions of meatloaf, mashed potatoes, and roasted Brussels sprouts. The portions were way more than Tad would normally have taken, but to be polite, he accepted the portions Carrie served.

While they ate, they talked about Tad's business and Carrie's career in law enforcement. She expressed a desire to change careers but wasn't sure what she wanted to pursue. She explained she had thought about nursing, but she didn't think that she'd be able to handle all the "downsides", as she put it. When asked what those were, she simply said, "not at the table".

Carrie asked about Camelot, but Tad kept his explanations to "current day" but did divulge that he heard the area was called "Camelot" at one time.

After they finished dinner, Carrie pulled a cherry pie from one of the boxes. "I made this today, so please just tell me it's okay. I was going to -".

Tad interrupted her. "Wait a minute. You were supposed to go home, and get some rest. There's three to four hours of cooking here!

"Yeah, well, first impressions, you know." She rebutted.

To that, Tad replied, "Carrie, dinner was fabulous. But I did NOT want you making a big meal for me. I'd have been fine with dogs and mac n' cheese. I would rather you had gotten-"

This time, Carrie cut Tad off. She held one hand up and in an "Irish accent" she said, "I don't want to hear it, Mister O'Banion. It took me all of an hour to prep all of this, and another half to post prep, afterward. I got a full six and a half hours of sleep, which is more than I normally get.

So, don't cha be complainin' bout nothin', when you got your bangers n' mash there fella."

Still holding her hand up, Carrie was pointing at Tad's face. He paused for a moment and burst into laughter. "That was pretty good, Carrie. You might actually pass for a "lass" from Ireland. Well, a pretty blonde one."

"Maybe I am a "ginger", there lad." Carrie chimed. She winked as she set out two plates of cherry pie.

They picked at the pie for half an hour, discussing the history of Hawkins County. Tad's knowledge of the area surprised Carrie. He knew all about the old days of Presmen's Home, and even some history clear back to the Civil War. She knew Davy Crockett's parents and grandparents lived in Hawkins County because his grandparents were buried in Rogers Cemetery, right downtown. But, Carrie didn't know that they had been killed by Indians, or how much influence the Indians had with the settlers.

Tad continued to tell Carrie about Andrew Jackson's persistence in "routing" the Native Americans from the Carolinas, Tennessee, Georgia, and Florida. While cloaked in the misconception that it was being done "for the settlers". He explained that many speculate the real reason was coal, gold, granite, and other natural resources that the "new" Federal government desired.

Tad divulged that by the time the government got around to moving the Cherokee, it was 1838. Over the next few years, the government forced one hundred and twenty thousand Cherokee from their homelands and thousands died during the walk to Oklahoma.

Carrie was listening and couldn't believe she didn't already know about the sad Cherokee history, and Jackson's "ethnic cleansing". She always thought the Cherokee "just lived" around East Tennessee, not realizing the majority of them were driven out. She even knew a couple of people who are Cherokee. So, her heart kind of hurt for them.

"Tad, there are Cherokee in East Tennessee now. Heck, there's a reservation South of Gatlinburg. Did they come back?" Carrie asked.

Tad buckled his chin as he lifted his lower lip. "Yeah, some came back. But some never left. There were many who were already friends with the settlers. I'm sure there were small bands who stayed. As long as they "laid low", I'm sure that most of them were left alone. Not everyone agreed with the "Cherokee Removal Act". In fact, your own Davy Crockett didn't and he was a U.S. Senator."

"Wait, Davy Crocket was a U. S. Senator?" Carrie questioned.

"Yep, and he died at the Alamo in 1836." Tad replied.

"Wait, you said the said that the "Tears trail" was in 1838?" She quizzed.

Tad smiled at her, impressed that she caught the disparity of the dates. "It was. You think political or government action moves slowly now…imagine back then? It took years for shit to take place. How about we clean up and sit out by the fire. I'm pretty sure the chance of rain has passed."

They packed the remaining food in the boxes for Carrie to take back. Tad explained, it was better than putting it in any trash cans, for fear of drawing in rodents or bears. After they had everything put away, Tad set two chairs beside the firepit. Purposefully setting them three feet apart, but on the same side of the fire. He wanted to make a point, but not overtly put so much distance between them that they were talking over the fire pit. He was pulling two beers from the cooler when Carrie returned.

"That should probably be my last one. Unless, of course, you have a guest room?" Carrie inquired with a grin.

Tad laughed. "No. Not yet. But I may after a couple months. The guys over in Asheville have a prototype little-home that they want to show me early this week. I'm hoping that they can make one for me first. It'll sit right here, where my camper is." Tad pointed around the lake. "Then one over there, and there, and there." He finished.

"Not really what I meant, but okay." Carrie paused. "Let's try this…will you have a spare place for me in your cabin? Or do I have to sleep in one of the other cabins?" She said with eyebrows raised flirtatiously.

With the look from Carrie, Tad quickly changed the subject. He came back to Hawkins County decades ago. Attempting to paint a mental image of Nick's great-uncle's stable, he talked about the barn, the horses, and his favorite, the ponies.

Pointing in the direction past the tradesmen's building, Tad explained. "Right over there, was "The Stable". Nick's great-uncle was called "Nick" by everyone around here. He served the county by running the stable, being a farrier, and eventually being a mentor to a lot of young cowboys just like his uncle." Tad closed his eyes.

"When was that?" Carrie asked.

Before Tad could think clearly, he answered. "Nineteen seventy-three".

Carrie didn't ask. She figured Tad would explain more when he wanted to. She just looked in the direction that Tad had pointed and tried to imagine a large stable, the riding rings, the hay bales, and the young cowboys.

Just then, something caught her eye…a light. "Tad, Did you leave a light on over at the tradesmen's building?" she asked.

Tad had turned back around, but quickly responded. "There's no power. Can't have a light without power." He replied. Then, looking in the direction that Carrie was staring, he squinted.

"Sure looks like a light to me." Carrie responded.

Tad stood up. Turning towards the building, he then took a few steps. "What the hell…" he said.

Carrie sensed that something was wrong and immediately jogged to her car. When she returned with her pistol, Tad was stepping out of the trailer with a Ruger Mini-14 and holstered pistol. Attaching the holster to his belt, but not removing the pistol, they both stepped behind the trailer, blocking the view of them from the building.

Tad and Carrie checked their weapons by first checking their safeties, and then sliding each slide and magazine back slightly, looking for a round. Then Tad asked, "Don't suppose I can get you to stay here, can I?"

"Not a chance, Cowboy." She made clear.

"Okay, that gate has remained locked since they put the fence up. I unlocked it about twenty to thirty minutes before you got here. But I was over there. So, whoever is over there went while we were eating. I'd rather we stick together, so stay by my side. We'll approach from the East side of the building. Do you have your badge?" Tad asked.

"No. It's in the car, but I can get it." Carrie replied

Tad snickered, which set Carrie at ease a bit. "Hang tight." He whispered.

Tad went back into his trailer and came back out wearing his Sheriff Department SWAT shirt, with a badge in hand. When he reached Carrie, he handed her the badge and said, "You hold this. I'm not sure how to present it." He admitted.

Carrie smiled. She put the badge in her back pocket and double-checked her safety. "You look pretty good in that shirt, by the way."

Tad smiled back at her. "You ready?"

"Yep. Let's go, Cowboy" she replied.

They stepped out from the rear of the trailer and approached the building slowly. They both stepped carefully, so as not to make loud sounds. After roughly a dozen steps, Tad held his hand up in a fist. They both stopped.

Tad lowered his Mini-14 and raised his watch. Pressing a sequence of buttons on his watch, he looked at Carrie and whispered. "Something's wrong with this." he stated. "I heard one of the Sentinels fire up, and I sent it back." He explained quietly.

Carrie looked a bit confused. "What's wrong with that?" She whispered.

"The Sentinels and Sentrys didn't pickup anyone going into the building. They should have launched and notified me while we were eating. It doesn't make sense." Tad explained.

Tad again looked at his watch and toggled through a few screens. Shaking his head, he looked back at Carrie. "Everything checks out, it's just weird. Let's approach slowly"

Tad and Carrie hunched down and continued towards the building. They could clearly see the light emanating from the lower level of the building. They circled to the rear of the building, but on the outside of the fence. Tad randomly checked Carrie's face, which was surprisingly focused. He found her attractive, even when serious. Her forehead glistened slightly in the bright moonlight. He was a bit surprised. She was calming him. Not the other way around.

They came to the gate, and it was closed, unlocked, just as Tad had left it when Carrie arrived. Tad slowly slid the latch and gate ever so quietly. Tad, noticing Carrie's observance of any movement behind them, smiled.

After reaching the side door, Tad whispered. "I've got to unlock two locks, then swing this gate open, then unlock the door. It's obvious that they didn't come in this way. It's going to make some racket. I would expect them to know that we're coming. If you want to, just look for "squirters". If you see anything, announce yourself and take cover…Okay?"

Carrie held up a thumb and took a few steps back so that she could see most of the long sides of the building.

Tad unlocked the gate and swung it open. "Squeeaak", it sounded as Tad bit his lower lip. He then keyed the door lock and slowly opened the entry door from the side. Protecting himself, should someone be on the other side of the opening door.

Carrie leaped from her position and ran to the front of the building. She didn't announce herself, which confused Tad. He circled around the front of the building, Mini-14 "at the ready".

"What did you see?" Tad whispered

Carrie hunched over and slowly lowered her pistol from an "aimed" position. "I thought I saw a shadow. But I think that my damn eyes are play tricks on me."

They stood there for a moment looking around…nothing.

Tad waved for Carrie to join him and they headed back to the side entry door. They stopped at the entrance. Tad reached down and turned on the light mounted on the Mini. He reached into his pocket, pulled out another light and handed it to Carrie.

Together, they entered, taking positions, like they were soldiers clearing a building in Afghanistan. As they worked their way down the hall, they realized that the light was actually coming from the lowest level. A basement. One that Tad had never been to. They retreated back toward the entry door and saw the steps that led downstairs.

Tad again held up a fist, and they stopped. Tad looked back at Carrie, pointed a thumb at his chest and made a walking motion with his fingers. Carrie realized she was to "cover" him from above, while he descended the stairway.

Tad slowly proceeded. When he reached the landing, he looked up at Carrie. She could barely make him out, but he appeared to wave her down. Once she was by his side, he mouthed, "Again". He descended the last section of stairs and disappeared from Carrie's view. For a moment, her heart raced, and then she saw his flashlight return. He waved her down.

Two solid metal doors were at the bottom of the steps. Tad reached for the handle. It turned, and he pulled. Tad and Carrie noticed the smell immediately. It was the same sweet, acrid odor that Tad had detested just months earlier, and so many years ago. It smelled like blood.

Tad and Carrie entered a long open basement, with larger boilers that looked like monstrous spiders. Their long legs extending across the ceiling. As they moved forward, they passed old lockers and a few old desks. They tip-toed towards the center of the building,…where the light seemed to come from. There was a drainage grate on the floor, appearing to extend the length of the building. They could hear liquid draining through it, and Tad felt he had to check. He kneeled down and shone his light in the drain. For a moment, he thought the liquid looked discolored, but then focused. It was water. There was a slight odor of iron and sulfur. But it was water.

They crept to an area in the center of the building, favoring one side. The area had two large sliding doors, and Tad immediately knew that this was the doorway to the elevator shaft. Tad gestured for Carrie to watch "their six", and he slung the Mini over his shoulder, to his back. He grabbed the large latch and released it from its hold. As he opened the door, he saw the light coming through.

Tad stepped into the elevator shaft, and his jaw dropped open. In a dry pit, about three feet down, was a flashlight. It was on, and lying where it had fallen many months before. It was Tad's.

Carrie whispered. "You good?" But Tad did not answer.

Again, Carrie whispered, but this time a little louder. "Tad, ARE YOU GOOD?!?"

Tad shook himself out of his trance. "Yeah, Um, Yeah. Come on in here." He muttered.

As Carrie entered, Tad was clicking the flashlight on and off. He stared at it as though it were stuck to his hand.

"Did you find that down here?" Carrie quietly asked.

"Yeah, I did. It's mine". Tad affirmed.

Carrie was looking at Tad intently. He looked confused. "Was that the light? I mean, the light that we saw outside?" She inquired.

Tad was shaking his head. "I don't understand. How could it be on? I dropped it down here when I was with Nick, months ago."

Carrie's mouth dropped open. Then she closed her mouth and squinted her eyes at Tad. "Wait a minute. You're fucking with me. You dropped that down there on purpose…when I got here, didn't you!!"

"No, I didn't. I swear." Tad denied.

Carrie looked bitter, but not necessarily angry. "You better watch it, Deputy. You are quickly going from "my crush" to "asshole of the year"! I'm not sure I follow WHY you did this, but scaring the shit out of me is not something I enjoy. Just saying."

Tad's face remained aghast as he looked at the flashlight, clicking it on and off. He continued to look at it until Carrie said, "Listen, Tad, I don't mean to be rude, but I've got an early morning. You can stay here and play your games, if you want. But I'm heading home. I had a nice time. Well, until about 15 minutes ago. Thanks, and call me when and if you're not in the mood of messing with people."

Suddenly Tad shook his head and realized what Carrie was saying. "Carrie, stop. I apologize. I must have accidentally dropped this when I came through here earlier, like you said. I just don't remember dropping it. I don't want you to go. I am sincerely sorry!"

Carrie appeared ambivalent. Her expression changed from short anger to a half-smile, so that only one dimple appeared. She lowered her head and gave a sort of "pouty" look back to Tad. "Okay, I don't have an early morning planned, either. What do you say if we just go back and curl up in a blanket, by the campfire?"

Tad felt better. While still confused himself, he didn't want Carrie angry with him over something out of his control. "Sure. Let's go back and talk about Hawkins County." Tad said, conceding.

Carrie put her hand out to help Tad up from the pit. But, just as he was about to step out, he noticed a small round "something" over in the corner. He pulled the ghostly flashlight and shone it in that direction. There, in the pit, with crumbled concrete fallen around it, was a box turtle shell. Tad suddenly felt the need to pick it up. "Hold on, Carrie. There's something over there." He insisted.

Carrie scowled as Tad walked over to the turtle shell and picked it up. "Oh hell, this little guy is in here. As lifted the shell to look into the "portal", a small head popped out and Tad could have sworn it smiled.

"Hey there, little fella. How'd you get down here? Tad said out loud. He then turned to Carrie and said, "Here, we've gotta get this fella out of here so he has a chance to make it. I don't know how he got in here, but he won't make it long without food and water."

As Carrie smiled and reached for the turtle, a mouse ran across the pit, up Tad's pant leg, up his shirt and across his outstretched arm. By the time Tad and Carrie realized the motion, the mouse was already on Tad's forearm. With a quick flip of his arm, the mouse went flying. "What the hell was that?!" Tad cried out.

Carrie laughed. "It was just a little mouse, Deputy. Nothing to be afraid of." Carrie proclaimed, a bit mockingly. She set the turtle on the concrete floor and reached back out for Tad. Once pulled up, Tad and Carrie checked themselves to make sure they hadn't dropped anything. Tad verified his pistol was holstered and reached over his shoulder to check the position of his rifle, slung across his back.

Even though the moon's brightness illuminated the basement, and their eyes had adjusted, Tad pulled out his flashlight and shone it to the floor. The turtle was walking away from the pit, towards the drainage grate, and the mouse was running circles around it profusely.

"Check this out Carrie." Tag said. "I've never seen anything like it."

"Wow." Carrie returned. As they watched, the two animals appeared to play. "Should we leave him?"

"No. The mouse will be fine, but that turtle won't make it but a couple days down here. Let's take him up and set him outside. If we leave him inside the fence, he's probably got a better chance, and I'll get him some lettuce and make him a little area to get some water tomorrow."

Tad didn't notice, but Carrie had a big smile and was looking right at him as he picked up the turtle and started across the basement. Her disdain for Tad's previous actions had completely dissolved and now she saw a person caring for one of God's creatures. She was smitten, smiling all the way through the basement and up the stairs. As they ascended the stairs, the water in the basement's drain took on a red, then pink hue, but neither of the humans noticed it.

Once outside, Tad set the turtle down, closed and locked both the door and entry gate. "He'll be fine out here. I'll have Brooks Brothers make a small pond over there for him… and yes, Carrie, I'll put some food and water in the basement for his friend." Tad smiled too.

They left the fenced area, and Tad locked the gate behind them.

Returning to the firepit, Tad put a couple of logs on the fire and went inside the trailer. When he came out, he no longer had a rifle or sidearm, but emerged with a wool blanket. He outstretched the wool blanket and asked Carrie to turn around. She stopped him.

The blanket was beautiful. Based in white wool, the blanket had a cross-hatch pattern of black, with coral-colored strips from end to end. Carrie stood there looking as Tad kept it outstretched. He knew what she was thinking,…the same as he did when he first saw it.

"Turn around Carrie." Tad said. She did so, and Tad laid it over her shoulders. "It's Cherokee." He explained.

"It's beautiful. I almost don't want to use it. Don't you have a sleeping bag, or something for both of us?" Carrie inquired, still standing.

Tad chuckled. "No sweetheart. I don't." knowing full well he had a couple of sleeping bags in the trailer.

Tad sat down in one chair by the fire and patted the chair next to him. "Come young Cherokee princess. Sit and smoke peyote with me." Tad said in a Native American dialect.

"I'm not a princess,…"squaw" maybe, but not a princess, Carrie replied, as she sat in the chair and pulled her legs up to her chest, then covered herself with the wool blanket.

"No offense, but technically your neither." Tad smiled. "Squaw is actually offensive to the Native Americans, and the term princess was mis-applied by the settlers who tried to apply European royalty titles to the daughters of tribal chiefs. I prefer "princess" from the mere fact that it infers that you are special, which you are." Tad finished.

Carrie sat there smiling and shaking her head. "Full of chivalry, but he won't lay with me, by the fire."

Tad smiled, then looked up at the sky. The clouds had cleared and the moon was large. It gave off such a bright light that Tad could see clearly across the Camelot valley. Tad liked the thought "Camelot Valley".

"Camelot Valley Train Station?" Tad announced.

"What?" Carrie replied.

"Camelot Valley Train Station. That's what we should call this area when we get all of the rentals down here." Tad proclaimed.

Carrie grinned. "We? You know you keep saying "we"?"

"Don't get your doeskins in a bunch, there princess. "We" refers to me, Nick, you, and everybody else who is helping me to make this happen." Tad retorted.

Still grinning, Carrie winked. "You said "we".

Tad, believing that he was going to lose this battle, did not reply. Only grinned himself. Then, Carrie got up and moved her chair right next to Tad, climbed back into it and laid her head on Tad's shoulder. They sat there watching the fire until the burning logs were small, Tad asking Carrie if she was awake a few times, until she finally didn't answer.

Tad's mind wandered. For a moment, he thought perhaps he was also asleep. His mind went from the flashlight to the tradesmen's building, the *dinosaur museum*, and the basement. He remembered going there when he was a child. He remembered his imaginary friend,…what was her name? As he continued to look at the fire, he heard the coyotes off in the distance. Yelping and howling, as they often do.

Tad was not afraid of the coyotes. The Sentrys would notify him if they were close, which he didn't think was imminent, anyway. As the fire crackled, and the night was clear, he thought he saw a coyote across the lake. But it was bigger, and heftier. A wolf? It appeared reddish.

The red wolf stood across the lake looking at Tad. They stared at each other intently. As if in a trance, the creature mesmerized Tad. But fear was not what he felt. Almost the opposite. Safety is what he felt. Safer than when the Sentrys were active. "Oh shit." Tad thought. "I never turned the Sentrys back on after we came back to camp."

Tad raised his watch slowly, so as not to wake Carrie. He slowly pressed the buttons on his watch to bring the Sentrys back to life.

He looked back at the red wolf. It was sitting, still looking at him. But then slowly stood, turned, strode away, and disappeared.

Tad watched the fire and Carrie comfortably wrapped in the Indian blanket for a while longer. He finally looked at his watch. "Eleven seven. Probably oughta get this princess home.", he thought. Looking down at Carrie, she had maneuvered her way to the point she was almost in Tad's lap. Tad felt comfortable and, for just a moment, he thought maybe they could just sleep right there, but knew that the fire burning out would bring a chill to them both.

"Hey princess. It's time to head home." Tad quietly said.

Carrie rustled, murmured, and snuggled closer to Tad.

"Come on Carrie, time to head home." Tad tried again.

This time, Carrie didn't move. Just stayed curled up like a little Native American Princess, protected in the night by red wolves.

Tad sat there thinking. "What now?" he wondered. "I guess I take her home."

Tad slid out from under Carrie, threw a couple of logs on the fire and went to his trailer. Coming out, he again had his sidearm as he walked over to Carrie's Jeep and moved the boxes to the back seat, so that the front seat was vacant. He then went over to Carrie and picked her up, cradling her like a child.

When they got to Carrie's house, Tad went in and took a quick look, so he could take her directly to her bedroom. He then returned to the Jeep and carried her into the house. When he laid her in her bed, she rustled and murmured. As he removed her boots, she mumbled, "You staying?"

"No sweetie, gotta get going." Tad replied.

He slid her clothed legs under the sheet as she curled into a ball, on her side. He spread the wool blanket over her and touched her cheek. "Definitely a princess", he thought. He closed the bedroom door, went to the kitchen refrigerator and got a bottle of water. He then went out the front door, locking it before he left. Tad then began walking home to "The Camelot Valley Train Station".

Chapter 19 –

"Making Pappy Proud"

Tad was sitting upstairs at the Blue Dog Saloon when Nick came up. "What's up chief?" Nick asked.

"All good. How bout you?" Tad replied.

Nick shrugged his shoulders. "Oh, you know. Catching bad guys, and fixing houses." Nick returned. "How'd your date go with Carrie? Did you guys-"

"Date with Carrie! What the heck, Tad! Breaking my heart before I even get a chance!?" Cindy exclaimed, while she stood there with two menus in hand.

Tad put up his hands in front of himself, palms out, and stuttering. "Wha, Wait, she just brought me some dinner. Um, I made it clear that we're just friends. We didn't do anything but sit by the fire."

"That's more than dinner, Deputy! When do I get to bring you dinner and sit by the fire?" Cindy retorted. "Tonight?"

"Um,…Yeah, I guess. Friends only, right?" Tad replied defensively.

"Be there round six. What's your favorite?" Cindy returned.

"Um, anything. I don't care." Tad stammered, now looking at Nick, who was sitting down with a huge grin.

"The normal for both ya?" Cindy asked.

Nick and Tad replied, "Yeah, sure."

As Cindy walked back to the stairway, she stopped and smiled back at Tad, whose face looked lost and confused. After she descended the steps, Tad looked back at Nick. "What the hell was that?"

Nick let out a laugh. "That right there is the starts of the next big Hawkins County cat-fight. Ain't been one here for 'bout five years…and just happens to be the same two jealous felines."

Tad shook his head from side to side. "What the hell did I just get myself into?"

"Those two been fightin over men for years. They both grew up here and the only time that they didn't fight over a man was when they were both married. But, even then, it seemed that they were still jealous of each other." Nick picked up his water and took a drink. "Them are two peas in a pod. Prolly oughta just marry each other and be done with it. Carrie's patrolling tonight, so this should get interesting."

Tad rolled his eyes, looked up and turned his hands, palms up. "Oh great. This is how I go. Shot in East Tennessee, defending the honor of one woman against another." Tad declared, now chuckling himself. "Okay, before I die, I need to talk to you about "The Camelot Valley Train Station."

"Let me guess. Now you want to build a train station and revive an old railroad track you found somewhere. Is that a good guess?" Nick questioned.

Tad squinted one eye. Shaking his head, he looked at Nick as if he had just done something wrong. "What's the matter with you? I don't own a railroad track!" Tad then smiled. "Yet!...your wrong, but I like the idea. The Camelot Valley Train Station is what I want to call the old Camelot area. You now own some of the land out there, the land that you inherited from Pappy, right?"

"Yep, and I'm buying a little more. The Blankenship's and the Miller's properties. Where you going with this? I know you, and you've got an angle you're working." Nick claimed.

Tad grinned. "Not an angle, Nick. A partnership. I already own the land where the old stable was. We build that same thing there...a horse stable. We hire or lease it out to someone who wants to raise and train cowboys. After we plop these tiny home rentals all over the valley, we build hiking and riding trails throughout. Partner with me on this Nick and we'll make bank."

Now Nick had a puzzled look. With one brow raised and the other squinting, he looked at Tad for a moment, then finally spoke. "You'll let me in on the rentals?...and you'll rebuild Pop's Stable?" He asked.

"Yep, we'll make it legal. We'll create an LLC, and I'll sell that stable land to the LLC for a dollar. You keep your plots of land, I keep the lake and property around it, but give exclusive right to any tenants at The Train Station. Heck, I'll tell you what. We'll buy the old hotel property and build a train station there. Use it for a museum, library, ice cream parlor, something.... They will come, Ray. They will come for reasons they don't even know. But they will come, Ray. What do you think?" Tad excitedly asked.

"You kinda lost me there Tad, but I'm in. Let's do this!" Nick claimed.

Cindy came up with two Italian subs and more water. As she set down the plates, no one spoke. Then

Cindy broke the silence. "Ya'll are up to somethin', I can sense it. Ya ain't said a word since I come back up. I was expecting somethin'. But you two are suddenly all clammed up."

"Just saving the world, Cindy. Starting with Hawkins County first though." Nick avowed.

"Lord knows we need it." Cindy looked at Tad. "You needed anything else, Cowboy?"

Nick looked down at his plate and grinned as Tad replied. "No, I think we're good Cindy."

Cindy turned, and as she walked away, said, "The subs are on me boys. Anything for Hawkins County's finest."

"Why does everybody keep thinking I'm a deputy? That was all a joke." Tad sighed.

Nick was shaking his head when he answered. "Eh, technically you were sworn in, and that means you actually ARE a deputy. But, that is not what she meant about you."

As they ate their meal, Tad and Nick continued to discuss The Camelot Valley Train Station. They bounced ideas off of each other and Tad quickly realized his offer to partner with Nick was a wise choice.

Nick liked the idea of building a faux "Train Station" on the grounds of the old hotel. He thought a better use of the place would be a gym or possibly a pool. Tad lit up with the thought and said, "why not both?"

They finished up eating and were walking down the stairway when Tad asked Nick to join him on his visit to Asheville the following Tuesday. Nick ecstatically replied, "Of course partner. Oh, hey, you never asked me where my properties are."

Tad replied, "I already know", but was interrupted by a call out from behind the bar. "Six o'clock, Cowboy! It's a date!" Cindy shouted.

Tad and Nick both gave a wave to Cindy, and Nick waved to someone else he knew at the bar. They walked out the door and to their cars.

Stopping short of his Land Cruiser. Tad turned back to Nick. "Nick, you ever seen a red wolf?"

"No. They're long gone. Nobody's seen one around her in over a hundred years. Why, did you see one?" Nick asked, almost mocking Tad.

Tad smirked and kept the grin. "No. No red wolves Nick. I'll see you Tuesday."

"Field of Dreams." Nick called out as he opened his cruiser door.

Tad chuckled. "Right", he affirmed.

Chapter 20 –

"Second First Date"

Nick spent the day on patrol, but thought of nothing but "The Camelot Valley Train Station". Meanwhile, Tad returned to Camelot and changed into a pair of hiking pants and boots. He strapped on his Osprey hydration pack, grabbed a machete from the rear storage, and headed down the drive.

The Manor, the old hotel, sat directly across the road from Tad's property. Vandals burned it down in the nineties, and kudzu had overgrown the foundation for decades. Tad could not see the foundation clearly but knew it was there.

As he hacked his way through the invasive vine, he thought about a friend out west, Arrow Brooks. Arrow was a bronc rider, turned botanist, turned entrepreneur. He had developed a weed control chemical based on organic compounds. Every golf course in the world used some form of Arrow Brook's products. Tad wondered if Arrow would have an interest in controlling the vine that had taken over the southeastern states. If anyone could do it, Arrow could.

Tad continued cutting through the vine and eventually cleared a path to the old hotel's foundation. He examined what he could and felt reasonably sure that he could convince the board to let him build.

Then Tad looked further back on the property and resumed cutting away at the vine. Feeling like Hiram Bingham, looking for the lost city of Machi Picchu, Tad continued hacking at the mass of vines. After another seventy-five feet, he saw the vine indentation. He cut up to the edge of the indentation and again kneeled. Pulling vines away, he spied "the city"…the pool that his mother had installed fifty years ago.

Tad had just finished cleaning up in his outdoor shower. While Tad didn't mind showering outside, he looked forward to the day when he could shower in his new tiny-home, which he hoped was just a few weeks away.

Cindy found him partially dressed and shaving when she pulled into the drive. She pulled her Jeep up to the camper and stepped out.

Tad came out from behind the camper, barefoot and shirtless, with a towel, wiping away the remaining shaving cream. He had on a pair of khaki shorts and sandals, but was still unkempt from the shower. "You're a little early, aren't you?" he asked.

"Better than late. Don't you think?" Cindy replied.

Tad snickered. "That's right. My father-in-law used to say, *You can call me anything. Just don't call me late for dinner.*" He disappeared behind the camper, but Cindy followed.

"Look at you, Tarzan. Bathing in the great outdoors. If I'd known that, I'd have come half an hour earlier. Cindy grinned. She walked over and opened the shower curtain to peek inside. "Wow, plenty of room in here. Enough for two." She claimed.

"What is up with you East Tennessee women? You all drive Jeeps and have to be the most forward in the nation." Tad said as he folded up the outdoor sink and gathered up his few shower essentials. He threw his towel over his shoulder and started around the camper. "Let me dress and I'll help you. Gimme two minutes." He said.

"Do you need help?" Cindy asked as Tad stepped into the trailer.

"No Cindy, I don't need help dressing. I'll be right out." Tad retorted.

"My competition is looking pretty good." Cindy announced loudly.

"What? Is Carrie here already?" Tad replied from inside the camper.

The comment obviously offended Cindy. But not enough to be upset. "No goofball. I'm talking about your little diner. Can we take a look at it later?"

"Sure. If you want, we can eat in it." Tad added.

"Sweet! I'll be the first patron of your diner!" Cindy exclaimed.

Tad was stepping out of the trailer, fully dressed. He had put on a pair of jeans, and a button-up shirt, left untucked, and a pair of cowboy boots. "Well, not exactly. I had dinner last night in there." Tad said, knowing it was going to create an interesting conversation.

Cindy quickly took the bait. "That hussie! Just dinner?" she queried, a little enviously.

"Just dinner Cindy. Just dinner with a friend, just like I'm having with you." Tad rebutted.

"Well, we'll see about that. You want me to pull down by the diner?" Cindy asked with a grin.

"Unless you've got some place to be, I was gonna have a drink and take a walk first. Can I offer you anything?" Tad inquired.

Cindy came over to the cooler that Tad was opening and looked in. "A cold beer would be great."

For a moment, Tad thought he was re-living "Groundhog Day". Except this time, it was a different woman. As he had done the night before, he got out two cold beers, opened them, and placed them in koozies. Handing one to Cindy, he said, "Come, walk with me."

As they walked down the back side of the lake, Tad explaining the safety features of the Sentrys and Sentinels. He explained they had a recent update that allowed him to travel around the property with a guest and they would not take action unless initiated by Tad, via watch or phone. What he didn't tell her was that this revision was just programmed and installed today.

Cindy had driven by this place many times and didn't realize how beautiful it really was. "You're in a *bottom* right here, pretty much secluded, except for those few houses over there. Pretty cool. Who's mowing it for you? It's well kept around the lake."

Tad looked around. "Yeah, I like it. I have some boys from down the road mow it every week. They've hauled off probably thirty dump truck-loads of brush. Hell, once we get the rentals up and going, I'll have to hire some people full time. Why'd you ask?"

"My brother has a lawn business. Dumb fucker couldn't keep a job till he started doin' his own thing. Now he loves it." Cindy explained.

They continued to walk around the lake. As they came to the northeast end of the lake, where the large creek feeds it, there was no apparent way to cross. Tad showed Cindy a small path that led into the woods a bit, where there were a series of large boulders that they could step across. Once around the end of the lake, they headed back.

Halfway back, Cindy asked, "What about the old building? What are you going to do with that?"

"You mean "buildings". There are actually four, if you count the church. I'm not sure just yet. They've been here so long, and have a unique history."

Cindy stopped and looked around. "Where's the church?"

"It's back there. Further off the road. It's in the worst shape. The others aren't too bad. I had the fence put around that one." Tad said, pointing to the tradesmen's building. "The sanitarium and admin buildings already had fences that the state put up years ago. I guess I oughta do something about the church pretty soon. But I'm afraid that it'll catch on fire if I walk into it. Will you go check it out for me?" Tad asked with a chuckle.

Cindy tipped her bottle up and said, "Honey, that church will fall down if I get within a hundred feet of it." She giggled herself. "We'd better get back, or we'll be eating cold brisket."

Tad nodded. "Yep, we'll be back in a jiff. I can see the diner already. You made brisket?" He quizzed.

"Sure did, It's your fave, ain't it?" Cindy asked.

"How'd you know that?" Tad picked up the pace.

"Listen boy, you spend some time with me and you'll soon find out that I read minds and know exactly what you want. Then you'll find out that I can give you everything you need. A LOT more than that little "missy" down at the department." Cindy proclaimed.

Tad grinned. "How the heck did you two ever get to be so jealous of each other?"

"We used to be best friends. Up until Carrie stole my boyfriend in our senior year of high school. Jeremy Blake and I were in "L" "O" "V" "E", and that little bitch started hanging out at his house. Before I knew it, they got caught in the Blake's hay loft." Cindy alleged.

Tad stopped walking. "Cindy, don't take this wrong, but, if he was in the hay loft with Carrie, then he wasn't "in love" with you. Just sayin. Besides, that was ten years ago. Ya'll oughta be over it by now…and it sounds like Jeremy lost you both anyway. So move on and make amends." Tad started walking again.

"You little sweetheart, you. "Ten years ago". You know it was a lot further back than that, and sadly Jeremy died in Afghanistan. He said that we broke his heart. He joined and was gone. He used to text us both. He was a Navy Seal and got blown up over there. Maybe that's why I'm mad at her. Maybe he'd still be here if she wouldn't have moved in on him?" Cindy whispered.

Tad slowed his walk and stopped. He reached for Cindy's hand and faced her. "Sorry Hon, I didn't mean to go there. I'm sure that Carrie is full of remorse, and I'm sure that she'd love to be your best friend again."

Cindy was looking down, but suddenly looked up at Tad and said, "Fuck that! I'm stealing her boyfriend this time!" Cindy dropped her empty beer, put an open palm on each of Tad's cheeks and gave him a big kiss.

When Cindy finally set the heels of her boots down, Tad didn't know what to say. He looked astonished. She squeezed his chin and winked at him.

"Don't look so surprised, there cowboy, there's plenty more where that came from!" Cindy announced as she picked up her beer and began to half-jog towards the train car.

Tad stood there for a few seconds and then ran after her.

After they got to the train car, Cindy stopped. "What, can't keep up?"

Tad replied, "Wait a minute, little lady. I didn't see you in that 5K."

Cindy laughed and went to the door of the train car. She attempted to open it, to no avail. Then Tad pulled out his cell phone, opened an app, and with a few keystrokes, the lock made a low growling noise. "Try now", He claimed.

Cindy did so and walked in. "Nice. Perfect place for a romantic dinner. Kinda missing a kitchen, but I'll figure something out. I'll go get my Jeep."

"What do you need me to do?" Tad asked.

"Get me another beer…and music. Come up with some music." She commanded.

Cindy backed her Jeep down to the train car and was unloading the boxes when Tad came back. "Beer Ma'am?" Tad said as he was setting down a small speaker. "What music do you like?" he asked, as he noticed Cindy had brought her own tablecloth and dishware.

"Surprise me. I like surprises." Cindy said without looking up. The evidence of years of practice were present. Cindy spread the tablecloth out and set the table. Tad thought it odd that Cindy had picked the same table that Carrie had the night before. He wasn't sure about the music, so he just started his "workout playlist". Cindy spun around as the music started. "Lazy Eye, are you kidding me? One of my favorite songs, lover. Takes me back a few years. What else you got in there?"

Cindy put her arm around Tad's waist as she looked at his cell, slowly scrolling through the music. "K, O, L, love them…You've even got some country mixed in. I like it. Send me that playlist. I'll play it at the Blue Dog… I'm almost ready." She tipped up on her toes and gave Tad a quick kiss on the cheek.

Tad made no gestures in return. He wasn't quite sure what he thought of Cindy's affection. In some ways, it made him feel good; in others, he thought it was overbearing.

Cindy pulled a bottle of wine from the box. "Can you open this for me, sweetheart?" she asked.

Tad looked at the label. "Brunello Di Mantalcino. Well, you do read minds, don't you. Not sure if I like the Brunello or the Rosso better. Although, I really don't drink wine that often."

"If you'd rather have the Rosso, I brought a bottle of it as well." Cindy offered, grinning.

"Did you really?" Tad asked as he looked in the box. There was another bottle, but it was the Brunello as well. Tad realized that he'd been tricked and shot a glance back at Cindy.

"Chip, Chip cowboy. Dinner is getting cold." Cindy urged.

Tad returned with a cork pull. He opened the bottle and poured into the two wine glasses that Cindy had placed out. Before he could place his napkin on his lap, Cindy had her wine glass raised. "Thank you for inviting me over to your estate Mister O'Banion!"

Tad raised his glass. "The honor is mine, Miss Blackwell. The honor is mine."

Chapter 21 –

"Imaginary Friend"

Tad and Cindy were sitting by the fire when the Sheriff's cruiser came down the drive. They had finished dinner and had just cleaned up.

Just as with Carrie, Tad had initially positioned the camp chairs apart from each other, but Cindy immediately moved hers right next to Tad's. The sun had gone down, but there was still plenty of light. So, Carrie could clearly see the two of them sitting next to each other.

Carrie stepped out of the cruiser with something in her hand. She was holding something from underneath and it was wrapped with a ribbon.

As Carrie walked towards them, Tad stood up and walked towards her. "Hi Carrie, I thought you might come by." He said as they met by the drive.

To Tad's surprise, Carrie tipped up and gave him a quick kiss. "I brought this back. I slept like a baby in it. How'd you get home after we fell asleep anyway?"

"Carrie, stop. We didn't fall asleep together. You fell asleep by the fire and I drove you home. I was a perfect gentleman. Put you to bed, locked up your house and

walked home. Thank You for bringing my blanket back."
Tad replied as Cindy crept up behind him.

Cindy slipped her arms around Tad as he stood there
talking to Carrie. Carrie, in turn, pointed out the note that
she had left on the wool blanket. Wrapped under a silky
ribbon was a note that read, "Thank you so much for the
great time last night! Carrie", and with her signature, was a
lipstick kiss. Cindy lifted herself and peered over Tad's
shoulder.

"Nice, Bitch!" Cindy announced.

Carrie, noticeably offended, barked right back.
"Excuse me, but I should be the one calling you a bitch.
You're doing it again! You always do this when I lay claim to
any-."

"Girls, Please!!" Tad interrupted. "This is
ridiculous…and probably my fault. I should never have
accepted either offers for a meal. My bad, and I will fix this.
I will not be dining or anything else with either of you again.
Understood?!?"

Both women appeared to want to speak, but Cindy
started first. "She's the one who showed up here, Tad. Why
should I have—"

"Stop! We are adults. I have made myself clear.
Carrie, I apologize, but I'm asking you to leave…Please."
Tad requested. "We can talk later, but right now all of
Hawkins County is hearing the Cat-fight that I was warned
about."

"I suppose you're right Tad. Besides, arresting her
for D and D probably wouldn't be good for her business."
Carrie threatened, with her thumbs locked under her tactical
vest.

"Deputy, Please!" Tad exclaimed

Carrie's head dropped, as did her hands. "You're right, Tad. That was probably uncalled for. Sorry,…Cindy. Sorry to both of you. I'm being a butt. I think I'm gonna go sulk somewhere. Maybe I can find a drug dealer to beat up."

They chuckled, although Tad didn't like the thought of Carrie even approaching a drug dealer.

Carrie walked back to her cruiser and stopped before turning around. "If you hurt him,…I'm gonna beat the livin dog shit outta you. Just sayin." Then she opened the door to her cruiser, stepped in, and backed down the drive, never really making eye contact again.

Tad and Cindy didn't say a word. They just strolled back to the chairs by the fire and sat down. Tad placed his palm on his forehead and lightly clasped his fingers, rubbing his temples. He sighed. Cindy curled her legs up in the chair and watched the fire.

After a few minutes, Cindy spoke. "How did she die?"

"Pardon?" Tad replied, hoping that he had misunderstood the question.

"Your wife. What happened?" Cindy inquired.

Tad sighed. "Trigeminal Neuralgia took her." He paused. "It might be the worst affliction on the planet. Well, definitely for those afflicted. It's horrible. If you could imagine the worse migraine possible and then someone stabbing you in the face with hot, electric knives…and it doesn't go away. That's T.N.. People ask, "did she suffer?" Hell yeah, she suffered…and there's no damn cure. Of all the shit my company has invented, that's actually the thing we should be working on. Saving the lives of those suffering."

Cindy was looking at Tad intently. "Why don't you?"

"Why don't I, what?" Tad replied.

Cindy sat up in the camp chair. "Why don't you find a cure?"

"Not in my wheelhouse." Tad said, appearing to be annoyed over the conversation.

"And you never had kids?" Cindy asked.

"Just the three little girls that are in heaven with her." Tad now tearing up.

Knowing the subject needed to change, Cindy thought it best to honor Tad's late spouse. "She must have been one hell of a woman."

"The best ever." Tad muttered.

They both sat there for twenty minutes. Not speaking, just looking at the fire. Cindy finally stood up. Brushed ash off of her jeans and started collecting her things.

"I'm gonna go, Tad. Sorry for screwing everything up tonight. For what it's worth, I enjoyed your company….and , eh, Sorry about your wife." Cindy walked towards her Jeep.

Tad didn't get up or look away from the fire. But he did speak.

"Me too, Cindy. Me too." He whispered and let her leave on her own.

After Cindy left, Tad got up, went into the trailer and came out with a glass of ice and a bottle of bourbon. Setting them both on the picnic table, he opened the bottle and poured a half glass of bourbon. He then took it and walked back to his chair.

He sat there for thirty minutes, staring at the flames as they danced in the glass of whiskey. His face was still. Motionless. He'd move the glass down and look from above, at the depth…and thought of the despair that often followed it.

As he held up the glass, watching the ice melt, he noticed the shape, visible through the glass. The shape of a wolf. He lowered the glass, and there, just twenty feet away, was the red wolf.

Tad watched the wolf as it appeared mesmerized by his own stare at the magnificent beast. He almost forgot about the whiskey that he had yet to taste. Then Tad reached out with the glass and poured it into the fire. As the flames erupted from the sudden fuel, the wolf's glare softened. When the flames subsided, the wolf was gone.

Tad stood. He no longer wanted to wallow in despair. He took a deep breath. "Thank you, Ellen", he whispered under his breath.

Tad, standing with his back to the camper and tradesmen's building, picked up a bucket of water that he kept near the fire, and doused the flames. The embers crackled and spat. He felt a sense of calm he'd not felt in a long time. Possibly, not since Ellen was beside him. A sudden chill crept up the back of his neck.

Tad slowly turned his head, and there by the fence was the red wolf. He turned and walked towards it. He was not thinking of danger. He was curious about what the wolf meant. As Tad closed the distance, the wolf watched him…and when Tad was within fifteen feet of the creature; it leaped and strode around the building, out of sight. Tad stopped and waited for it to return, then noticed the pink hue emanating from the lower level of the building, right where the elevator shaft rose.

Tad wasn't sure why, but fear was farthest from his mind. He walked around the building but didn't see the wolf. The moon shone brightly as Tad unlocked the fence and approached the side door. He unlocked the gate and side door. But, as he attempted to open the door, it struck something. He looked down, and there on the ground was the box turtle he'd released from its prison just the night before. But the turtle didn't retract. It was standing and looking up at Tad.

Not knowing why, maybe for comfort, Tad stopped and picked up the turtle. He cradled the little guy with one folded arm and entered the building. Turning at the stairwell, he descended without hesitation.

As he stepped onto the basement floor, he saw the drainage grate glowing pink. But it slowly dissipated into darkness. Slowly stepping through the basement with some caution, Tad still was not afraid. After all, he had his protector with him. His friend, the turtle.

Tad walked to the center of the room and stopped. Looking around, he saw nothing. He stood there for a few moments and just as he was preparing to walk back to the steps, the liquid in the drainage grate started to bubble.

The liquid took on a color that disturbed Tad,…crimson. The sweet, acidic smell emerged from the well. Although unable to move, Tad felt no fear. What he did feel was the turtle's legs moving, so he looked down. The turtle was looking up at him, and again, Tad could have sworn he was smiling.

Tad stood there, motionless, as the liquid slowly changed from crimson to red, and then to a pinkish color. The liquid began to rise in one particular area of the drain, moving around the grate, and then reforming. It continued to rise, and formed a shape, almost humanoid. And then, like the fog clearing from view, the shape gained detail. That of a young lady.

The young lady was beautiful, with dark braided hair. Her skin appeared soft and pure. She wore a Native American deerskin dress. Her arms formed from her sides, and all but her feet became well defined. She slowly moved toward Tad as he stood on the drainage grate.

Tad was transfixed and watched the being come towards him. She stopped just a few feet away and reached up, touching his face. The caress was comforting. She had an aura around her. Bright pink. She then reached down, caressed the turtle and said, "Willow".

Unexpected words came from Tad's mouth. "Moon Dove?"

"Yes, Little Warrior?" she replied in a Cherokee dialect long forgotten.

Tad understood her. "Is this really Willow?" Tad asked.

"Yes, Little Warrior. I kept your friend safe. He comforts me." Moon Dove replied.

"Bu-, but how? He would be fifty years old". Tad inquired.

Moon Dove smiled. "I knew you would return, Little Warrior. The wind, the river, the red wolf, told us of your return to save us."

Just then, Willow, swung its legs energetically, and Tad saw the mouse hopping down the cement floor. Tad kneeled and set Willow down. He watched as the mouse and turtle re-united in obvious affection.

Tad stood back up and faced Moon Dove. "I'm dreaming, aren't I?" he asked.

"No, Little Warrior, you've come to save me, and the others." Moon Dove continued, "You must take us from the river of blood, and release us to the river of light. I have little time, now. The great clouds take me away. Please come to see me during the next full moon. I'll explain then."

Moon Dove slowly disappeared back into the drainage grate. But before her shape disappeared, Tad heard, "Hee Yah Golv Kwoh Dee" clearly.

Tad watched the pink hue gradually disappear, as memories of Moon Dove returned to his mind. He smiled and thought, "It turns out that my friend wasn't "imaginary" after all…or, have I just lost my mind?"

He watched Willow and the mouse play a bit more and looked at his watch. Two thirty-three. "Whoa, where did time go. I better get some rest." He told himself. He almost picked up Willow but looked at the two playing and thought Willow was fine right where he was.

Chapter 22 –

"Let's Just Be Friends"

Tad woke at seven. Though he'd only had about four hours of sleep, Tad felt like he had slept eight to ten hours. He was refreshed. His memory of the night before was as clear as when he had met his old friend again, just a few hours ago. He believed what he saw and used his phone to find out when the next full moon would be visible. After recording it and saving a "reminder", he decided to go for a run.

As Tad ran, he kept saying a phrase in his head… Hee Yah Golv Kwoh Dee. Hee Yah Golv Kwoh Dee. "What did that mean?" he asked himself. "I need to know." Tad ran northeast on Ninety-four and turned on Laurel Branch Road and kept running. He felt the burn, but also the glide that was coming. As it kicked in, he picked up the pace.

By the time Tad had circled back and came up on the old train car, he was right at nine miles. He glanced at his watch. It had been an hour and ten minutes…whoa! That's less than an eight-minute mile. He walked over to the spigot by the trailer, pulled up the lever, released the secondary valve and took a drink. The water tasted good and reminded him of days gone by. As the water continued to pour, he raised his head and closed his eyes. He turned and could clearly see the golf course in 1972. He could see the stable and the hotel. Tad stood there soaking it all in until he heard the crackle of gravel and tires slowly rolling. He opened his eyes. Cindy was pulling up the drive.

"Did'ya go for a run?" Cindy mocked as she stepped out and walked up to Tad.

Tad, sweating and shirtless, raised an eyebrow and snickered.

Cindy continued, "Hey, listen. I'm really sorry about last night. Carrie and I were both out of line. But, I was really out of line. Then I started asking questions that were none of my business. You were right about everything, and I'm going over to Carrie's after this to apologize. I want to give you your space and let you know that I'll be glad to just be your friend. Feelings aside, I'm happy knowing that is what you want."

Tad felt something he hadn't felt in decades. Like she was "breaking up" with him. Break-ups are tough. Sometimes, your very heart feels as though it's being ripped from your chest. But those feelings rarely last long, and end the end, it's usually for the better. Fortunately for Tad, this was not the case. He was actually relieved that Cindy was talking so rationally. Maybe too relieved?

"It's quite alright Cindy. All of it. You even gave me a little time to remember Ellen, which was good. I appreciate that." Tad explained.

Cindy was smiling, which pleased Tad. "Looks like you may have drowned your sorrows, there cowboy." Cindy pointed at the bottle of bourbon on the picnic table.

Tad turned and looked and laughed. "Yeah, I tried… filled the glass, set it down and just looked at it till three A

M. Then I dumped it in the fire, and went to bed. Guess them days are really over."

Cindy walked up to him and gave him a light kiss on the cheek. "Tell you what, cowboy. I'm here if you ever need me. Even if it's just a shoulder to cry on, you got my number. But, I'm letting you be." She gave him a slight hug, turned and started towards her Jeep. She opened the Jeep door and stopped. She smiled at Tad. "Oh, and I guess we'll see what your playlist does to my business this week." Cindy winked and stepped in.

Tad waved as Cindy backed down the drive. "Hee Yah Golv Kwoh Dee" he thought.

After cleaning up the campsite and taking a shower, he locked things up and headed to Johnson City.

During the drive, he called an old friend. "Arrow, old friend, how you been?"

"Most days, pretty good. Some days, pretty bad. I guess them damn broncs really do have the last laugh. How you been my brother?"

Tad replied, "Doing much better. Drinking a whole lot less. Seems the cryin' comes with the drinkin', ya know?" Tad paused. "Listen, I have this thing going on over in East Tennessee.—"

"Yeah, I know. All the fancy D O D stuff." Arrow interrupted.

"No, No. Not that. I've got some more shit going on. Remember the place called Camelot that I told you about?" Tad asked.

"Yeah. The place when you were a kid? Where your brother was becoming a cowboy, and you did nothing but ask you nanny to wipe your ass?" Arrow chuckled.

"Yeah, Asshole. Same place... Well, as it turns out, Liz and I inherited some of the land and I'm setting up a little get-away place for folks to come and relax." Tad rebutted.

"You and Liz, what about Ole Brett Maverick?" Arrow inquired.

Tad swallowed hard. "Arrow, Brett passed a few years back."

"Bro, I am so sorry. I didn't know. Was it bad?" Arrow asked.

"No. He died like a cowboy. Froze to death in his own back yard. The dumbass came home from the VFW on the coldest night of the year and lost his keys. By the time he had gotten a spare from out behind his house, he was done for." Tad explained. "He was supposed to work for me the very next day. When he didn't show, I thought "Oh boy, Is this how it's gonna start?" Little did I know, the next call would be from the Sheriff. It sucked."

"I can only imagine." Arrow muttered.

"Hey, you still huggin' trees and saving the world with your inventions? I got some trees that need saving." Tad described. "This damn kudzu has taken over East Tennessee. Hell, it's taken over about six states. I need something safe to kill it off. Something biodegradable. You up for the task?"

"Ya know, I might already have something close. I'd need to do some testing on it. You're not the first person to bring this up. You're just the first that's forcing it on my radar. How about I fly out in a couple weeks and take a look? I'll send out some samples beforehand, if you can store them for me. Then I'll come out and do a little testing a week or two later. I can't promise anything, but we can catch up, and who knows, maybe you'll make me another five million." Arrow chuckled.

Tad smiled. He hadn't seen his friend in many years. "Sounds like a great plan. Send samples to my plant in J.C.. I'll text you the address. Oh, and Arrow, do you happen to know what "Hee Yah Golv Kwoh Dee" means? I think it's Cherokee."

"I don't…and it doesn't sound Tsalagi,…but could be. I might know someone here, but if it's eastern, you may be on your own. I'll call her, but the Cherokee Nation right there should be able to translate. Who said it to you?" Arrow inquired.

Tad pondered how to answer this. "Another old friend, old friend. We'll see you in a couple weeks. We can talk then."

***

Tuesday came quickly. Nick drove over early, so they were on the way to Asheville by eight. When Tad pulled into the parking lot, his face lit up. The lot, full of tiny homes, had one that resembled the train car back in Camelot. Nick exclaimed "Whoa!"

They stopped the Land Cruiser right beside it, both almost jumping from the vehicle. Both were smiling as they walked around the outside of the brand new train car, looking at every detail.

It wasn't long before Darrell came out of the building, pushing open a large sliding door to the main building. Through the open door, Tad noticed two more of the train-car tiny homes being built inside.

Darrell walked up to Tad. "I had them set this one out here yesterday. I wanted you to see it when you pulled in. Besides, we need to let it get rained on and make sure there's no surprises with this funky roof. The inside's not done. I wanted you to decide on that. But we can finish it this week. We still haven't gotten the approval from Hawkins County yet for the foundation requirements. They're kinda waffling on the whole "Semi-permanent" structures thing."

"It looks great Darrell. Better than I had imagined. The train-trucks look perfect. They look like they're ready to set on the track." Tad stopped and pointed at Nick. "Oh, Sorry. Darrell, This is Nick. Nick Williams. He's my partner at Camelot. He'll be buying a few more of these from you yet this year."

Nick reached out to shake Darrell's hand. "I don't know about a few more, or when, but I love it. I'll just have to sell a property first. Then maybe I can buy one."

"Bullshit, I'll get you a loan Nick. It's not a problem. Darrell, look at your schedule and let us know when you can build five more…and as for "semi-permanent" structures, they're not." Tad explained.

"Hawkins County wants them attached to a foundation, or the lots are technically a campsite. Darrell rebutted.

Tad was shaking his head. "That's what they are. The only difference being that I want these sitting on top of the water, sewage, and electrical…and if they want them attached to the ground, we'll screw them down like we do with the towers. Anchored with four five-foot screws, and this baby ain't going nowhere. I've already gotten our patented anchoring approved as "permanent-structures' in Texas. I'll talk to the Hawkins County zoning board, or Tennessee state officials, if need be."

"Can we check out the inside?" Nick interrupted.

Darrell waved them towards the building. "Sure. Let's go in. We have some options set out for you to look at."

They walked into the large open bay building, where an assortment of tiny-homes were under construction. Closest to the large door were two train-car-looking tiny homes that were slightly smaller than the one outside. Another appeared to be under construction at the other end of the shop, slightly bigger, like the one outside.

"We'll need more locomotive trucks." Darrell, referring to the train cars' steel wheel assemblies. "I'm guessing you can get more?" he asked.

"Yep. I can get you as many as you need. The cleanest ones I can get are out of Arizona. I'll get a hold of them and get eight sets in route in a couple weeks." Tad replied. Which prompted another strange look from Nick.

They followed Darrell to the stairway at the end of one train-car. Darrell explained the stairway could fold into a ramp for wheelchair access, explaining that a conversation with Tad had prompted the idea.

As they stepped into the tiny home, they quickly noticed the partially finished walls. One with a panel of white composite and another with a faux wooden composite panel. The ceiling was finished in an off-white panel, with an exposed heat duct extending from one end to the other.

"What do you think Nick? Old school wood, or new-clean white?" Tad challenged.

"Wow. They both look great." Nick paused. "I'm thinking bedroom and living space in wood. Bathroom and partial kitchen in white. But this is your baby. What do you think?"

Tag held up a thumb in agreement. "I agree. The bigger ones will have another small room with a full mattress. Make that room white, to make it look bigger. I see the accent lighting. It looks awesome too. You've really outdone yourself Darrell! Do you really think that you can have these ready in a week?"

Darrell looked at the calendar on his cellphone. "I can get the one outside, and one of these, over there next week. The other two in three weeks. When do you want the next five?"

Tad looked at Nick. "That depends. When do you think you can have your four lots ready Nick?"

"Whoa, wait a minute, bro. I don't even know if I can get a loan right now. Let alone get the lots ready." Nick made clear.

"I told you Nick. We're partners. I'll help with a loan and the rentals will pay for themselves by the following spring." Tad turned back to Darrell. "D-man, eight to ten weeks sound doable?...If so, I'll wire you a down payment on them later today."

Darrell gave a nod of approval.

Tad and Nick took some pictures and were on their way.

Not two minutes into the ride back to Johnson City, Nick started in. "You really think that I can swing this?"

"Of course I do. Nothing ventured, nothing gained." Tad contended. "I've got some ways to get you a great interest rate, and I'll get the lots prepped. Well, I mean the company will."

"What company?" Nick asked.

"Camelot Valley Train Station. Don't you listen to anything?" Tad questioned. "We'll start an LLC...partners, like I said. You haven't gotten cold feet, have you?"

Nick just smiled that big grin and shook his head.

Chapter 23 –

"Maybe More"

Nick and Carrie drove down to escort the train cars to Camelot. When they arrived, Tad was waiting with the same smile that he'd seen on Nick's face just a week before. The lots had been prepped, approved, and within three hours there were two new train-cars in Camelot.

After a few pictures, and a christening ceremony that Tad asked Carrie perform, the lights were turned on. For a moment, Tad thought, "Wow, these look better than the original." He had to remind himself that the "original" was over a hundred years old.

As Tad, Nick, and Carrie admired the new train-cars, a familiar face pulled in the gravel drive. Cindy climbed out of her Jeep with a handful of longnecks and hollered out a "Yee-Haw". Rambling on about taking someone to the "train station", Nick and Carrie laughed.

Tad didn't follow the comment, but noticed that Cindy gave Carrie a hug first. This made him smile as he shot a glance at Nick.

Nick's confidence was on a "high". "Celebrations are aplenty, there little lady, but two of us will hafta come back when we're off and get the cruisers home. If you and

Tad wanna hang out for an hour, Carrie and I will come back with some barbeque from The Blue Dog. What'dya say?"

"I'll call it in Nick!" Cindy suggested. "Devon just made a batch of collard greens, and I'll tell him to bake some rolls right quick. It'll be waiting for you, when you get there!"

Nick and Carrie followed each other out, and Cindy turned to Tad. "Well cowboy? Gonna show me the new ranch?" She said in jest. "Wow, they look good! Coming up the road, I thought one was Nick and Ethel's. Please tell me you ARE moving into one of them?"

"Well, yeah. That's the plan. But first, Cindy, I want to thank you. You hugging Carrie made my day. Way better than these damn rentals. It seems like everything I touch gets less and less civil. But you two give me hope." Tad described. "Thank you, from the bottom of my heart!"

"Oh, stop being all gushy, cowboy. Hell, she and I actually hung out last night at The Blue Dog, after I closed. We had a great time and I think we're on the mend. Besides, nothing like a "break up" to bring two people together, huh? Truth be told, I think she's got a thing for ole Nick. But keep that to yourself" Cindy confided.

Tad smiled. "That's funny. I thought those two were a little overly-friendly today. Well, I just hope that all are happy. That's all I care about. Come one inside and take a look at my little abode."

Tad showed Cindy through both of the new train-car rentals, as well as the kitchen that was being built onto the back of Nick and Ethel's diner. He explained he thought that they might have the diner open before winter. To which Cindy exclaimed. "I'll tell you what. If I see you talking to

Devon, I'll wup you and all your fancy little drones!" she said laughingly.

Devon was the chef at The Blue Dog Saloon. Originally a chef in Dallas, his life took a down turn when he got hooked on drugs. After spending three years living on the streets of New Orleans and Atlanta, he finally went into rehab. Cindy found him washing dishes and cooking in Knoxville. After hearing his plight, she offered to let him stay in the apartment above The Blue Dog and become her chef. Everyone in Rogersville claimed that The Blue Dog Saloon and Restaurant went from a three-point-five to a five-star restaurant overnight. Cindy, not one to be shy, touted that it was her "plan all along."

Tad laughed. "No, no. It's a diner right now. It'll be a minute before it becomes a five-start competition to The Blue Dog. Besides, isn't competition good?

Cindy raised her long neck and leaned into Tad's face. She lifted her bottle quickly. Bumping the bill of his baseball cap back on his head. "Just, watch it, there fella!" she whispered. Leaning back, she smiled.

Stepping out the back of "Nick and Ethel's", Cindy waved Tad to follow. "It's gonna be a nice night, let's get the picnic table set for some vittles." As she set the table, Tad opened another beer for each of them. "When you gonna furnish them? The rentals." Cindy asked.

"I'm actually picking up a box truck in the morning and heading to East Knoxville. Not sure what all I'm getting, but ready to give it a go. At least, that's the plan." Tad explained. "Hell, all I really need is a fridge and some towels right now."

Cindy stopped and turned to Tad. "Pick me up."

"Pardon?" Tad quizzed her.

"I said, pick me up. I need to take a day off, and I think it'd be fun to spend someone else's money for a change. Besides, I really think that you need the help. Otherwise, these things will look like an Army truck. Like your camper." Cindy continued. "Pick me up on your way to get the box truck. I won't charge much. I promise."

Before Tad could answer, they saw Nick's Jeep pulling in the drive. Cindy called out, "I hope you got more beer! We done drank all that was here. What'd ya'll do for an hour and a half, anyway?"

"Cindy!" Tad chided.

"Oh, stop. They know I'm kidding." Cindy declared. "Over here, guys. Bring it all over here."

The four of them took turns preparing their own plates and sat down. Nick by Carrie and Tad by Cindy. Tad sat down last and took note to the new seating assignment. As they ate, they talked about The Camelot Valley Train Station. Nick explained he owned four lots up, behind the old hotel foundation, which became a prelude for Tad to describe the new "Train Station" concept he and Nick had discussed. The girls thought the idea of a gym and bike rental was an "okay" idea. But they thought a small retail store that sold trinkets and knick-knacks should be included in the plans. Nick and Tad both rolled their eyes.

After dinner, they wandered from train-car to train-car, continuing their discussion about the property and the future. While walking to "Nick and Ethel's", Carrie asked, "What'cha gonna name them, Tad?"

"What? Name what?" Tad retorted.

Carrie stopped and put her hands up. "Every good rental cabin has a name. What are you gonna name them?"

"Wow. I hadn't thought about that. But, Camelot originally had areas named that related the story of King

Arthur. Maybe the Lancelot Suite, or the Guinevere Suite? Merlin, and etcetera." Tad polled the three.

"Car, …not suite." Cindy replied, "Cabin doesn't fit either. It's got to be "car". Don't you think?"

"That's it!" Tad exclaimed. "The cars shouldn't have names. They should be numbers. Like "Car 1985". Each train car will have a specific number. We can name the area that they are in with the "Camelot names" that Cindy came up with. Similar to the way they were in 1973."

"What's the number of your car Tad?" Cindy inquired.

"Twenty-two. It's Twenty-two." Tad suddenly looked solemn.

"Why twenty-two?" Cindy asked.

Tad sighed. "It's Ellen's father's favorite number."

Cindy smiled, raised her beer, and spoke aloud. "I like it! Train car Twenty-two it is!"

They continued talking about names for the rentals, ideas for the "Train Station", and even a potential stable that Tad had previously told Nick about. Nick loved the idea,…it was one more thing that brought the memory of his family back.

Nick struggled, trying to understand why Tad was helping him so much…and others too. He slowly realized that Tad was connected to this place in some strange way and he wanted company. Nick wanted to know more, but figured Tad would tell him when he was ready.

The four eventually made their way back to Tad's campsite, where Tad proposed a campfire and started building the base. Carrie and Nick said that they were going to his Jeep to get a blanket and two more camp chairs.

"How long does it take to get a blanket and chairs anyway?" Cindy exclaimed. "They've been gone ten minutes." When she looked back at Tad, he handed her a pair of night-vision binoculars. "Hey, thanks!" she chirped, and set them at her eyes.

Tad put his hand out. "I shouldn't have done that, Cindy. Give em' back.

Cindy kept looking through them and smiled. "Okay, fine." She said as she handed them back to Tad. He clicked them off and set them on the picnic table. Cindy was grinning from ear to ear.

"I'm not even going to ask what you saw." Tad stated.

"You just did." Cindy responded. "And it's just what we thought."

"Good for them." Tad replied. "Want another beer, Cindy?"

"You bet. I ain't working tomorrow! Cindy exclaimed.

"That's what you think." Tad smiled.

A few minutes later, Nick and Carrie returned. Nick set down two camp chairs together by the campfire. Cindy moved a couple of chairs to the other side for her and Tad, while he opened four cold longnecks and passed them out.

While Tad was sitting down, Carrie asked, "Them damn hummingbirds ain't gonna attack us, are they?"

Tad and Nick both laughed. "No, they'll leave you alone. They just got another update yesterday and now know who you are. The A.I. can tell that it's you by your gait and movements." Tad explained. He then looked at his watch, took it off, and threw it over to Carrie. On the watch face was the dialog, "Visitors – Carrie Upton – Cindy Blackwell – Nick Williams – CLEARED SAFE".

Carrie looked up at Tad with an odd look, kind of curled her lip and shook her head. "That's a little freaky. Kind of Big Brother-ish. Don't you think?"

Tad took a drink and proceeded to defend himself. "I guess that depends. This is my home, while I'm here. Don't you have a video doorbell?" Carrie nodded in agreement.

"Well, I just happen to have a better video doorbell." Tad contended.

Carrie threw Tad's watch back and tipped up her beer, looked at Nick and smiled. "Damn thing probably caught us by the Jeep."

Cindy spoke up. "Oh, it did. You two little lovebirds."

Nick blushed, but felt the need to say something. "Yeah, um, I guess you two figured it out. Or maybe your A.I. did. But Carrie and I kinda think we're gonna see where things go. It might be best if we keep this between us for now, if y'all don't mind."

Cindy stood up, walked over and hugged Carrie. "I think I can speak for Tad, and I, both…that's great news…and we know nothing about it. Right Tad?"

"Yes ma'am." Tad replied. "I wish you all the best." He stated as he raised his beer. The other three followed and clinked their bottles.

As they sat there talking by the fire, the subjects changed from rentals to "The Train Station" and back to rentals. Cindy thought it would be okay to tell Carrie and Nick that she was going to help Tad pick out furniture the next day and even claimed that Tad was paying her to decorate. She invited Carrie to go as well, but Carrie declined.

When Tad got up to get more wood for the fire, Carrie commented, "It looks like your light is on over at that building again, Tad."

Tad dropped the wood that he was carrying and quickly took steps in the direction of the old building. After about ten feet, he realized Carrie was joking with him. "You got me there, Carrie." He admitted as he returned to pick up the wood that he had dropped.

As he was picking up the wood, Nick, Carrie, and Cindy all looked at him perplexed. Nick whispered, "What the heck?", but they all stayed quiet.

While Tad put a few logs on the fire, Nick asked. "Hey Tad. Did you ever go back through that building? Or get into that locked office?"

Tad pulled his flashlight from his pocket and shone it under his chin, as if to create an eerie countenance. "Been in there a few times, but frankly forgot about that office. You all want go over and see what's in there?"

"Let's do it!" Cindy proclaimed.

Carrie set her beer between her legs, held up both hands. "I've been down this road before and Tad will scare the shit out of you. I'm warning you both."

"Oh come on! Let's do it." Cindy rebutted.

Tad had stepped into his trailer and come back out with an LED lantern and a couple of flashlights. One of them being the flashlight that he had dropped into the elevator shaft a few months before. He handed them out and tucked a small pouch into his back pocket.

"What was that, Tad!!" Carrie barked.

Tad pulled it back out. "It's my lock-pick set. I'm not out to spook you again, I promise…Well, unless there's a dead body, or something in there." He grinned. "Come on, let's go see what's been locked inside the old office for fifty years."

The four of them walked slowly over to the fence gate, where they found it unlocked. "That's weird. I thought I locked that." Tad stated and grinned.

"You're a dick, Tad. Here we go again." Carrie avowed.

They continued over to the side entrance, where Tad unlocked the gate and then the steel entry door. Tad slowly opened the steel entry door. "Creeeeak", the door cried.

Tad looked back at the three behind him. Cindy was close, and he realized she was holding the back of his shirt. Behind her was Carrie, who was shaking her head and mouthed, "You better fucking not". Behind Carrie was Nick, carrying a Glock 43 that he must have had at his appendix carry. They all looked like the "gang" from Scooby Doo, ready to catch the next "perpetrator". Tad smiled and felt safe.

They ascended the stairs to the second floor, and Nick pointed towards the door that he remembered not budging.

Tad tried the handle,…nothing. He put his flashlight in his mouth and pulled out the small leather case. Unsnapping it, he pulled out a specific pick. He then manipulated the pick through the lock while keeping pressure on the handle. Within thirty to forty seconds, the pressure on the handle released, and the door lurched forward.

Tad uprighted, took his flashlight from his mouth and pushed the door open. "Creeeeak". One by one, each of the four stepped in.

It was an office with a large desk. There was a bookshelf along one wall, and three pictures hanging on the other.

Cindy was close to Tad's side, and Carrie by Nick's. Nick had re-holstered his Glock and was shining his around the room.

Tad and Cindy walked over to the bookshelf, which was mostly empty except for one section that still had fifteen to twenty books. Tad reached up to pull one book down, but it didn't fold out from the spine as you would expect. He tried another book. It didn't budge either.

"Tad, check out these people. Who do you think they are?" Nick questioned.

Tad and Cindy looked over. "Headmasters, maybe? Or union leaders, maybe? I know that the Pressmen's Union left here in the mid-sixties. They initially gave this building and the buildings next door to the state. The state turned the other buildings into a sanitarium again. But, as far as I know, nobody ever used this building. My guess is that this is the headmaster's or Union President's office." Tad offered.

Cindy was holding Tad's shirt and had been quiet since they unlocked the door. "You mean to tell me that this office has been locked up for roughly sixty years?" she asked.

Tad laid his hand over Cindy's "death-grip" on his shirt. He could feel her trembling. "It's okay, Cindy. You're here with two Hawkins County deputies. And besides, if there was anything to be afraid of, we'd already know about it by now."

"Three", Carrie said, "Three deputies, and a dozen of them screaming hummingbirds…I'm guessing Tad's right, we're safe."

Tad shook his head and rolled his eyes, as he always did when any of them referred to him as a deputy. But he appreciated Carrie's reassurance, and he also felt as though Carrie really was trying to calm Cindy down.

Tad and Cindy returned their attention to the books on the bookshelf. Tad tried another couple of books, and they didn't move. "You notice anything odd with the books?" Tad questioned as Nick and Carrie were now at their side.

"They don't move?" Nick replied.

"No, look at the titles. They're all classic novels and literature. Why would those be in a headmaster's office?...and, even if the headmaster was into classic literature, why'd he leave em?" Tad furthered.

Tad shone his light on the dust-covered floor, and then back at the bookshelf. He went to the side of the bookshelf and pulled. The bookshelf moved. "How'd you move that?!" Nick exclaimed. "It has to weight three or four hundred pounds."

Tad pointed to the floor. "See those marks? This bookshelf is on wheels. Move out of the way girls. Nick and I are going to try and move it out, and I don't want it falling on you."

Tad and Nick positioned themselves, one low, and one high. They both pulled and the shelf slowly swung away, pivoting from the far corner, where it was hinged.

After they had moved the bookshelf perpendicular to the wall, Tad shone his light towards the space behind the bookshelf.

In the wall, right in front of them, was a large safe. Standing nearly six feet tall, it had a large locking mechanism. The large handle and dial extended beyond the wall. "Hall's Safe & Lock Co. Cincinnati" it read across the front of it.

Tad shone his light on the back of the bookshelf, where they could see the hollow wooden box feature that normally covered the safe locking mechanism and appeared as books from the front.

Tad turned back to the safe, kneeled and blew at the ancient locking mechanism. Dust bellowed in all directions, looking like a miniature atom bomb had just exploded from the front of the safe.

Once the dust settled, Tad attempted to turn the wheel to open the locking mechanism. It would not turn. He then kept pressure on the wheel and attempted to turn the combination dial. The dial would not turn either. He bent down and looked at the keyhole next to the dial. "Ain't happening tonight kids." Tad contended.

"Can't you just use your lock picking gadget thingy?" Cindy decried, "You got us all worked up and now your gonna just let us down?" she continued.

"That's what he does. Get used to it." Carrie said with a grin.

Tad shot a look of disagreement towards Carrie. "I'll call Adam tomorrow and ask him about it. He's the one who got me into picking. He's "cracked" safes before, but I'm not sure that he's seen anything this old." Tad returned.

Nick stepped up and tried the dial and spindle. "Is it jammed up? From sitting here for so many years?"

"I don't think so. I think there is a key to let the combo dial loose." Tad replied.

"Hey! Maybe it's in the desk." Nick exclaimed.

Tad went over and pulled the old wooden desk chair away. He opened the drawers one by one and looked through them. They were all empty. He then got down and looked underneath the lap drawer. Nothing. "Outta luck on that one." He claimed.

What Tad didn't say was that he noticed the two upper drawers seemed to be shorter than the rest. At this point in the evening, he thought it might be best to come back in daylight and investigate on his own. "Guys, can y'all do me a favor and keep this to yourselves for a bit? I really don't want someone claiming that the safe is theirs, or even somebody getting the bright idea that they can break in here and have a go at it. Okay guys?" Tad requested.

Nick spoke up first. "No problem partner. Just remember we's partners, though." He said, overtly smiling a big grin.

"Until we find out what's going on here, I'm mums the word." Carrie said, joking as though they were part of a group of cartoon sleuths.

Cindy was shaking her head. "I don't know there, cowboy. It'll cost ya."

"I appreciate it, guys. You all know that. This was a fun night, but I've got to head to Sevierville in the morning." Tad said.

"We, …not you. Don't forget your sidekick, there cowboy!" Cindy barked back.

Tad looked at Nick and Carrie. They both were grinning and held their hands up, shrugged their shoulders, then laughed.

***

Later that night, Tad woke. After making sure that Cindy was still asleep, he slid on some boots and went back over to the building. Again, picking the lock of the old office door, he opened it and went directly to the desk. He pulled on one drawer that he knew was shorter than the rest. It resisted a little, but eventually broke free. As Tad shone a light into the back of the drawer "pocket", he saw a hole. Reaching back, he put his finger in the hole and pulled. Out came another drawer that was hidden behind the first. Removing it, he saw a sliding wooden cover, and slid it open.

Shining his light into the drawer, there were two large coins. Dumping them into his hand, Tad then inspected them. One had a five-pointed star, with a circle around it. Each point touched the circle. The other side had the Latin word "Unitas" and what appeared to be a K, G, C in script. Each letter appeared on top of the next.

Inspection of the other coin revealed an owl with spread wings on one side and a crested shield on the other. Words seemed to be inscribed, but they were too worn to see. Tad put them both in his pocket.

Tad returned the drawers and then pulled the other "short" drawer. After a little resistance, it finally pulled free. Again, he saw a hole at the rear of the pocket. He pulled the hidden drawer and looked inside. There lay the thing he had expected to see…a key.

When Tad returned to the camper, Cindy stirred and mumbled. "Wha…what are you doing?"

"Just feeding Willow, hon." Tad replied.

"What?" Cindy asked

Tad smiled. "Nothing, Sweetheart. Back to sleep. We have a big day tomorrow."

Cindy laid her head back down and patted the vacancy next to her. Tad slid out of his jeans and climbed in beside her.

The following morning, Tad sat there drinking his coffee, looking towards his bed. Cindy was curled up in the comforter, still sleeping. He felt guilty, just as he knew he would. Though he knew Ellen would not want him to. The guilt hurt and he felt he betrayed her.

Cindy stirred. "Hey cowboy, you got one of those for me?" she asked.

Tad shook the thoughts from his head. "Sure do ma'am." Tad replied and loaded up a K-cup into the coffeemaker. "I'm afraid, we don't have any of that fancy creamer and stuff, out here on the range. So, you're gonna hafta take it like us cowboys."

"I took me a cowboy last night, so I'm sure I'll be just fine with no creamer." Cindy parried. "You gonna make me use that cowboy shower, or you gonna come over and take a shower at my place?"

"That'll work. Then we gotta get over to pick up the box truck. Are you sure that you're good with wasting your day, looking at furniture for my rentals?" Tad asked.

Cindy popped out of bed. She was just wearing one of Tad's t-shirts. She sauntered over to him. Standing on her tip-toes, she kissed him on the forehead, then his nose, then his lips. Cupping his face with her hands, she said, "I'm looking forward to it, goofball!"

They showered at Cindy's and picked up the box truck promptly at eight-thirty. Tad had chosen several furniture stores, based on the furniture he thought they might carry. He was hoping for something durable and fit the motif of the train cars. Bringing Cindy turned out to be "god-send", as she was quick to give Tad a "thumbs-down" with several items he considered. But she eventually picked out furniture that Tad agreed was perfect. He doubted that he could have made such quick decisions without her.

By two-thirty, they had everything that he thought they would need, except the appliances. So, they stopped on the way back and bought those as well. The store would deliver those items the following week. Tad, realizing that he would be back in Johnson City, mentioned that he'd have

Nick at the rentals when those items were being installed. But Cindy offered meet the installers.

"I don't think that I want you there." Tad claimed. "Most of these young guys look like male strippers, and you might go home with one of them."

"Wow, already a jealous side? I like it." Cindy refuted. "One last thing we need to get before we get back…sheets, pillows, and a new comforter for your cozy little home. I'm not sleeping in that overland trailer again."

Tad didn't argue. Just smiled and climbed into the box truck.

Of course, Nick and Carrie came over on Sunday to help assemble and arrange all the furniture. Impressed with the furnishings, Nick did offer to be available for the appliance installs. But Cindy quickly cut him off and explained that she would be there. After leaving, Nick and Carrie grinned to each other, as they had noticed that one bed had already been assembled and "made-up" before they got there.

Chapter 24 –

"The Cavalry Has Arrived"

Tad picked up Arrow Brooks the following week in Knoxville. As they traveled back to Camelot, Tad filled him in on his latest endeavor. Arrow was intrigued and said his people were already working on a potential organic herbicide that might just help Tad's war with the Kudzu.

Tad had met Arrow almost twenty-five years earlier, when Arrow was doing a college internship at the same company. Tad had gone out-of-his-way to invite Arrow to go boating with his friends. Arrow ended up spending most weekends with the group, and before long, he was friends with them all. That's where Arrow met Ellen, Tad's then-girlfriend, and Brett, Tad's brother. Arrow was intrigued with Brett's obsession with speed and daredevil antics. He often said, "It was Brett who made him want to ride broncs".

Strangely, with a master's degree in biology and plant science, Arrow developed a passion for the world of bronc and bull riding. Tad and Ellen visited him in Oklahoma often, and had even seen him ride in Amarillo, Nashville, and Cheyenne. He was a nationally ranked rodeo professional until a bronc actually stomped on his neck in

Fort Worth, which stopped his career cold. After seven years, three cracked vertebrae, and notable spinal stenosis, but still able to walk, Arrow finally quit riding broncs. He refocused his energy on plant biology. Then, his connections with farming investors and Native American Tribes quickly put him in opportunities that provided substantial contracts. Within three years, Arrow and his team had developed over fifty patents related to plant biology.

Through all of his work, he became very close to the Cherokee Nation and had many ties to the governance. It also didn't hurt that his wife was Cherokee as well. This is where Tad's admiration for the Native Americans, especially the Cherokee Nation, grew strong. Tad had visited eastern Oklahoma many times and had befriended many Cherokee during his visits. Tad actually introduced Arrow to Salali, who eventually became his wife. Known to most as Sally, she grew up in strong Cherokee tradition and graduated from Northeastern State University, a predominantly Cherokee college.

"How's my girl?" Tad asked.

"Your girl tends to piss off every U.S. Congressman west of the Mississippi, these days." Arrow replied. "I was going to bring her but was sure that I was staying some shitty little camper, like usual. Am I right?"

"Really bro? Is that what you think I do to you?" Tad refuted. "Hell no. Call her and bring her out. You've got your own place while you're here. So, tell her to saddle-up. We could use her help designing The Stable."

Arrow shook his head. "Oh No, if she knows you've got horses, she'll leave me and move in with you! We sold that little ranch and moved to Tulsa two years ago. She's not liking it. She wants her horses back."

"Move out here. You can't get any closer to the Cherokee land than right here. I'll GIVE you land to build on." Tad offered.

"You said WE. You got a little lady here in East Tennessee?" Arrow quizzed.

Now, Tad was shaking his head. "I was referring to Nick, the deputy I've mentioned. And don't bring up the little lady part in front of he or his girlfriend, Carrie. It's complicated and needs some time to settle."

"Let me guess…your old girlfriend?" Arrow asked.

Tad cocked his head. "Well, not really. We went out a week ago and things got, well…wait, why am I explaining this to you. Just be nice to everyone and no peyote, or shit could get even weirder."

Laughing, Arrow started in. "Wait, you went out with this girl just a week ago, she left you and now she's with Nick, right?"

Tad, realizing that he could not skirt the subject, replied, "Okay, it gets a bit worse. There were actually two girls that I went out with. Carrie was the first and then Cindy, also a good friend,—"

"What the fuck Tad? Same night?" Arrow laughed.

"No, No, No…the next night, and don't interrupt me again. Those two have been best friends on and off over the last twenty-five years. I was getting ready to be the next obstacle, so I stopped it. Besides, I immediately felt guilty anyway." Tad defended.

Arrow slowly dropped his head. "Yeah, about that brother…Sally and I can't tell you how sorry we are. About Ellen and Brett, both. You should have sent someone to tell us. We'd have come immediately."

Tad became defensive. "I know you would have. But you two were in the middle of the Amazon and all your research would have stopped. Maybe completely. Ellen would NOT have wanted that…and frankly speaking, I'm not sure why I didn't tell you about Brett. He was drinking quite a bit and caught in a legal battle that was killing him as well. I guess…I'm the one that should be apologizing. I'd take you to see him, but he's up in Ohio, buried right next to his best friend, Mike. How about we change the subject?"

Arrow shook his head in agreement. Then Tad started telling Arrow about the D. O. D. business and how much it had grown, explaining all of the devices and equipment that X-Caliber had implemented throughout North America. Tad told of the continued advancements and updates to their equipment due to A.I.. He even explained that he needed to register Arrow as a "friendly" when they arrived, or the Sentinels might "take Arrow out". Arrow laughed, but shot a glance back and looked a bit unsure.

Tad reminded Arrow of the short time he had lived at Camelot as a child and how it had changed. He explained he wasn't sure what brought him back, but that he knew he needed to be there.

As they come into Rogersville on Highway 11W, Tad mentioned, "I want to introduce you to someone, here in town, before we head out to Camelot."

Tad parked near the Blue Dog Saloon and said, "We can grab a beer here."

As they walked in, "Just Another Girl" was playing over the sound-system. Tad thought, "Well isn't that appropriate."

Tad pulled a couple of chairs out at a table and sat down in one. Arrow took the other. Out of the kitchen came Cindy carrying what looked to be six different orders. But she headed straight for Tad.

Cindy paused for a second to say, "Hey there cowboy, you must be new around here. I'll be right back to get ya whatever you want." Cindy winked.

"Really? Auburn? Tan? Freckles? You really do want my wife, don't you?" Arrow teased Tad. "I thought you said you ditched this trouble? Son, you are a glutton for punishment!" Arrow declared.

"Cindy's a good girl. She moves a little fast, but IS a good girl. And you're right, if I hadn't met her, I was probably going for Sally…again!" Tad teased back.

As Cindy approached, Tad tried to introduce Arrow, but was quickly shut down.

"You the "Injun" come to steal my man from me for a bit?" Cindy asked of Arrow.

Arrow quickly rebutted, "No ma'am, I'm here to claim what is rightfully mine, and my people's. Which is most of East Tennessee. Y'all got till sundown to pack up and leave. Else, there's gonna be some scalping going on."

Tad sat there with his hands over his face, head down.

Cindy smiled. "I like you "Injun". Please don't scalp this one, he needs to keep that hair. Even if it is turning a little gray. Name's Cindy Blackwell. Owner of this establishment and owner of the alter-ego that has a thing for this here cowboy."

Arrow looked puzzled. "Alter-ego?"

"Yes Sir. The smart one, Cindy, knows to stay away from this cowboy. But the half-witted one, Sindy with a "S", can't seem to stay away from him." Cindy continued. "He ain't all bad, I suppose." Cindy, bumping Tad's shoulder with her hip.

Tad shook his head. "Stop, both of you. Can we order? Miss Sindy, with an "S"?".

Cindy and Arrow laughed.

After lunch, Tad and Arrow drove to Camelot. As they drove down Pressmen's Home Road, Tad explained what the place looked like in 1973. When they pulled onto the gravel drive, they saw three pickup trucks and multiple men working on the kitchen expansion to Nick and Ethel's. Tad pulled past the trucks and around the lake, passing his little trailer and the first rental train-car, finally stopping at the second, slightly smaller one.

"There you be. Your own place to stay. So put Sally on a plane, cuz I need to talk to her about The Stable." Tad urged. "These are brand new, but the one out front is a hundred years old."

Arrow stepped out of the Land Cruiser. "Bro, this is dope. And you're putting more of these out here?" Arrow asked.

Tad had stepped out and came around the vehicle. Pointing, he explained the plan. "Yeah. Probably five, maybe six more around the lake. Then we'll have another twenty or so scattered around the properties. Up there where all the Kudzu is, we plan to build a faux train station. It'll really be a small novelty shop, ice cream parlor, and a gym. Maybe a bike rental. There will be a pool behind it. We'll have horse trails and separate bike trails. That new gravel road you see, over there, goes up to Nick's land. He'll have five rentals up there yet this year. Come on let's get your gear unloaded and maybe walk over to the Train Station to check things out."

Arrow looked around and pointed to the old building. "That's the old Pressmen's Trade building that you told me about?"

"Yeah, we'll have time to check it out while you're here. It's a pretty crazy thing to see." Tad expressed.

They unloaded Arrow's luggage and three Pelican cases of lab equipment, putting them all in the new rental train-car. After checking out the rental, Arrow joined Tad by the camper, where Tad was stoking the smoldering embers of a campfire.

"Party last night?" Arrow inquired.

"Just the normal crew. Nick, Carrie, and Cindy." Tad replied. "Brother, I can't thank you enough for coming out East, but am I crazy to think that you can clear this damn invasive weed?"

Arrow looked at Tad directly. "I should know in a couple days. My guys said that they think they might be on the right path. We use A.I. as well these days and this shit goes real fast. I'm guessing that you know that though. Oh, for what it's worth, this is like a vacation for me. I'm happy to be here, my friend." He said with sincerity.

They spent the afternoon walking from the future site of the Train Station then back to the campsite. Arrow had taken samples and set up all sorts of laboratory equipment. With beakers, chemicals, and a microscope, he when to work until Tad urged him to stop.

"The guys working at Nick and Ethel's are getting ready to break for the day. If you want to get cleaned up, we'll go back into town and meet up with the gang. That alright with you?" Tad asked.

Arrow came up from looking into the microscope. "Sure thing. Give me a hand moving this stuff back to my unit, and I'll clean up."

"Do you just want to use the camper as a lab?" Tad inquired.

"If you don't need it right now, that'd be perfect." Arrow replied.

They moved all the lab equipment into the camper. So, Arrow could make the camper his own mobile lab while visiting. Tad even offered to move it across the street to be closer to the evasive weed, but Arrow claimed he needed the walk. Besides, the "damn stuff" was growing on the side of the tradesmen's building, anyway.

After getting the lab basically set up, Arrow went to his train-car, called "14", while Tad made one more trip over to the old train car to check on the guys there. Observing that there was not very much work to finish it out, it was obvious to Tad that their work would conclude in just a week, or possibly two. Thinking about it for a bit, he realized he needed to prepare a small parking lot and get going on a sign. He walked outside, to the front of the train car. He imagined a neon sign.

The sign would have a distressed look, and be written in a font that would resemble something from the forties. Maybe neon, maybe not. He could see it above the covered rooftop. Not sure if the county would allow it, at least the omage looked good in his head.

"I've also got to get a cook, hmm." He thought. "Actually, I probably will need someone to manage the properties." Knowing that he was going to be there for a few days, he considered asking around.

Arrow came walking up. "That little place is sweet. Way better than any tent…which is where I thought I was staying. Probably a little safer too, huh?" Arrow referred to black bears he thought were prevalent in East Tennessee.

"Oh. That reminds me." Tad pulled out his cell phone and took a picture of the front of Nick and Ethel's, and then turned to Arrow. "I need to video your face and then you walking back to the truck. I can upload it to the

Sentrys and they'll create a profile of you while you're here. Then they'll leave you alone."

"The towers?" Arrow asked.

"Yep. And the attack drones they release." Tad jokingly replied.

Arrow shook his head. "I never know when you're kidding anymore."

Walking to the Land Cruiser, Tad was looking up and wondering whether to tell Arrow he was serious. Tad thought, "maybe it's better that he doesn't know."

***

As they pulled up to the Blue Dog, Tad saw Nick's Jeep. Stepping inside The Blue Dog, Tad heard yet another song from his playlist and saw Cindy behind the bar. She pointed upstairs, where they found Nick and Carrie looking their way.

Tad climbed the, now very familiar, stairs. Arrow in tow.

Introductions were brief, as Nick and Carrie had already heard a few stories about Arrow from Cindy.

"So, you were an actual rodeo rider?..." Carrie inquired. "I'm assuming that Tad was a clown?"

Arrow chuckled. "A rodeo clown is technically a bullfighter. Tad isn't fast enough for that. And, Yes ma'am, I was a bronc rider for seven years. I loved it. But, it takes a heavy toll on your body and I was in it for way too long. I'm just waiting for a wheelchair. So, I got out and put that hard-earned degree to work" Arrow winked at Tad.

"How long you in town for?" Nick asked.

"Don't know. Maybe a week, or two. Tad's putting me up in one of those cool little train cars, up the road a bit.

I hear you're in on that action, with Tad?" Arrow challenged Nick.

Cindy came up the stairs as Nick and Arrow continued their conversation. She had water glasses for everyone and a folded piece of paper under her arm. After setting down the waters for everyone, she walked over to Tad, unfolded the paper, and laid it in front of him.

Tad looked down. "What's this?"

"It's your menu for the diner, dummy." Cindy replied. "Devon put it together this week. He says that he's made most everything on it, and would be happy to show "your chef" how to perfect them."

Tad paused to read through the menu as Nick, Carrie, and Arrow continued their conversation. Cindy stood by, watching Tad's expressions.

"Hon, this looks awesome! I want to order off of this menu right now. I thought your said—"Tad was interrupted.

Cindy blurted out. "Oh stop. You don't have a clue what you're doing out there and it'll go under in a month if I don't help. Unfortunately, I have a stupid *thing* for you, and feel compelled to help. Stick to this menu and the diner will do fine."

By now, Nick, Carrie, and Arrow had stopped talking and had taken an interest in the conversation between the two.

Tad passed the menu to Nick.

"Wow. This looks great. But I don't see beer or alcohol on here." Nick declared.

"Bite me, Williams!" Cindy said as Nick laughed.

"Devon is making six of the eight sandwiches on there, right now. Y'all hafta try some of each and let me know your thoughts. I'm pretty sure they'll all be "five star".

But let's see which one of ya's dumb enough to give em' four stars." Cindy concluded.

Cindy gave Tad a kiss on the top of his head before she started back down the steps. Halfway down, she stopped and turned back. "Oh, and talk to Carrie about someone to run Nick and Ethel's. She's got someone in mind."

While Cindy was walking away, Tad looked at Carrie. "What the hell is it with you people around here. You into reading minds or something? I was just thinking about this shit a half hour ago."

"We do." Carrie laughingly replied. "The Knights of the Gold Circle host seminars once a month where they teach us to read minds. But if I tell you any more, I'll--"

"Have to kill me. I got it." Tad interrupted. "Do you really know someone who could run the diner?"

"Yep. My niece. She graduated from culinary school and wants to come back to Rogersville because her boyfriend won't move to New York. She'll be in town in two weeks. I'll hook you two up." Carrie offered.

"Sweet. Thanks Carrie. That'd be awesome. Sounds like I picked the right people to hang out with in Rogersville." Tad replied. "Even if they are in a secret society, that sacrifices sheep."

"Goats." Nick claimed, without even looking up, while the rest broke into laughter.

The four of them finished their lunch and all seemed genuinely impressed with the six sandwiches Devon had created for the diner. On their way out, Tad stopped to talk to Cindy.

"Hey Sweetheart, Arrow and I are going back to Camelot. Are you coming out?" Tad asked.

"Yeah, I'll come out for a bit. But, I don't want to get in the way of you two "catching up"." Cindy replied.

"Bullshit. Come out. I want you there. I enjoy your company." Tad said.

Cindy was looking down, washing glasses in the bar sink. Without looking up, she said. "We'll see, I've got to close, and open tomorrow too."

"Please come out if you can." Tad said. Then turned to catch up with Arrow, who was holding the door for him.

Cindy kept washing the glasses, with a wide smile.

Chapter 25 –

"Going Back, Way Back"

Over the next week, Tad tried to stay at Camelot as much as possible.

Arrow had the area looking like a crime scene. Yellow "police tape" cordoned off different areas of testing. Overturned buckets with black marker writing identified the dates and times of the spray and soil sampling. Arrow pulled soil samples from each area every day.

Tad left Arrow to his business. He had his hands full preparing the diner. The zoning board approved the gravel parking lot, the sign's size, and its location, so Tad was pleased. He asked Darren in Asheville to build the sign based on the design Tad had described. Darren said they would bring it with the next two train-cars the following week.

Carrie's niece, Gail, turned out to be the perfect person to manage the diner. In her late twenties, she had changed to a culinary career after deciding that her banking career was "boring". She met Tad at the diner and planned to order supplies the following week.

Cindy came out to visit almost every day, often staying the night. She met with Gail and asked her to come to the Blue Dog to train with Devon. This gave Cindy a little more "free time" at Camelot and she even found herself on the tractor, mowing. She had donned a flannel shirt, tied at the bottom and Tad's straw cowboy hat.

Tad and Arrow both chuckled as Cindy rode by.

"I'm getting close, Tad. If this works out well, my company is going to patent it. You want to be listed as an inventor as well?" Arrow inquired.

Tad was smiling, watching Cindy mow. "That girl cracks me up. I think she's trying out for a country video."

Arrow looked up from his table by the camper, and at Cindy again. "Yeah, she's a hoot. Inventor, Tad? I'm having my lawyer file the preliminary, next week. That'll give me six months to make it perfect. I've driven around and talked to a lot of people about this stuff. There's a fortune to be made, just with the state. If you want in, I'll list you as an inventor. Cut you in for ten percent?"

Tad looked at Arrow with a stern face. "Ten? I was thinking fifty percent!" He exclaimed.

"Kiss my ass, dipshit. It's five now." Arrow rebutted.

"In all seriousness, Arrow. I don't need a thing. It's your baby. I'll just be thankful if you can get rid of it." Tad said.

"Oh, I'll get it *gone*…and the poison ivy too. I didn't even tell you that, did I?" Arrow declared.

"That would be sweet, bro!" Tad agreed.

"Ten, it is." Arrow said with a wink.

Tad walked away from Arrow, and toward the diner. The Brooks Brothers were putting the finishing touches on the gravel parking lot and Tad wanted to see how the kitchen was coming, so that he could report to Gail later in the day.

He pulled his smartphone from his pocket and checked the weather. "Hmm,…full moon tonight." He thought.

The lot for the diner looked great and the subs working inside claimed they'd be finished by "days end". Tad called Scott, his new friend at the zoning office. Final inspections could probably happen in a couple days. He imagined that they'd be able to open in just a week or two. The excitement was overwhelming.

The next night, Cindy did not stay. Tad and Arrow sat by the campfire and reminisced. Calling it an early evening, Arrow excused himself to return to train-car 14, and call Sally.

Tad sat there until he saw Arrow enter his unit. Then he stood and started toward the tradesmen's building.

***

He was in the basement for over an hour before the water under the drainage grate started to change color and bubble. He hadn't noticed them before, but Willow and the mouse were by his side.

As Moon Dove slowly appeared before him, he felt warm. Not a bit of fear.

It took almost ten minutes for her to appear clearly, Tad knelt down and picked up Willow. Before Tad could stand, the mouse leaped onto Willow's shell. Tad stood up slowly.

Tad spoke. "Moon Dove, I want to help. I don't know what to do."

"You do, my warrior. You just don't understand yet." She said in her ancient dialect.

Tad understood her clearly.

"Will you come with me?" Moon Dove asked.

"Will I come back?" Tad asked.

"I will bring you back, my little warrior." She affirmed.

Tad felt he needed to set Willow and the mouse down. After doing so, he saw that Moon Dove's arms were stretched towards him with her palms up.

Tad laid his hands in hers.

Tad immediately saw a bright light, and all around him, colors of red, and purple swirled. The basement vanished from his view.

Eventually, the colors of green and brown turned into a landscape. Tad was outside of the building, and he thought he recognized the valley. It was Camelot, except much different. He could see a log cabin and horses. He felt himself walking across a field and saw a man dressed in a gray uniform. He recognized it. It was the uniform of a Confederate soldier. He could not control his motions and looked down at his body. It was the body of a young Native American woman. It was Moon Dove's body. Tad appeared to be "along for the ride".

"How many today, Moon Dove?" the soldier asked.

"Sgo-hi." Moon Dove replied.

"English! Moon Dove. Speak English!" the soldier commanded.

"Ten." She replied.

"That's not enough, and you know it. We need fifteen...and the gold rocks?" he questioned.

"Yes. I put gold rocks in place you told me. We found much today. It is why we only make ten carts of black rock. I no think we ever make fifteen carts, General Blackwell." she insisted.

General Blackwell looked down, clenched a fist, and then opened it. Swinging his arm across his body, and then back, he struck Moon Dove with the back of his hand.

She fell to the ground.

As Moon Dove looked up, Tad wanted so badly to punch the General in the groin. But Tad could not move. He could only watch.

General Blackwell glared at the young woman. "Damn you! Your tribe is counting on you! Do you really want me to tell you father, "The Big Chief", that you failed the tribe?!? I promised your father that I would take you to the Oklahoma territory myself, once you, and your clan finished here. Don't you want to see your father?" Blackwell barked.

Moon Dove did not rise. She stayed on her knees and looked up.

"We need to be moving out, within a week, so the coming days had BETTER be fifteen black rock, and two to three gold. Do you understand?!?" Blackwell declared.

As Moon Dove slowly rose, the General walked over to another soldier. They had a brief discussion, then the soldier mounted a horse, and rode off. Moon Dove walked to a small cabin, opened the door, and stepped in.

Eleven Native Americans had already lain down to rest after a full day of digging coal and gold for the Confederacy. They were almost lying on top of each other. Many were still covered in coal dust. As Moon Dove stood there, Tad heard the deep cough that he guessed was what some call "Black Lung".

Moon Dove opened the door again and stepped out. She looked across the valley. Soldiers were preparing to leave the camp with large wagons pulled by enormous horses. Clydesdales, Tad believed. He saw Blackwell walking toward a mine entrance. He recognized the spot. It was where the tradesmen's building was. But it was obviously not built yet. He guessed Blackwell was going to the place where Moon Dove put the gold rocks.

She also walked toward the mine entrance and entered. She slowly worked her way through the catacombs until she was standing next to Blackwell.

Both stood looking down at a large pile of gold and coal, Blackwell spoke. "You're damn brave to come in here with me. I should ravage you, like your people did to my sister, Cecilia, and sweet wife, Sarah. But, I need you to keep these damn savages working until we depart. So, consider yourself lucky!"

Moon Dove said nothing. Again, Tad wanted so badly to punch Blackwell.

"I'll get this gold moved. You need to come back here in two hours and blow out all of the candles. Tomorrow better be fifteen carts. Understood?" Blackwell quizzed Moon Dove.

Just then, a large young man came around the corner. "Hey Unc, Oos. I'm back." Samuel said

A startled Blackwell replied, "Oh, hey, Samuel. Moon Dove and I were just talking about how well they're doing. She said that they'll get fifteen carts tomorrow."

Moon Dove shook her head and walked away.

As she was walking away, Tad's vision waned. The darkness of the mine faded, and the colors of red and purple returned. He could hear Moon Dove's native tongue, then everything went dark.

Chapter 26 –

"What a Trip"

Tad woke up in a hospital bed. Cindy, sat in a chair, arm stretched out, holding Tad's hand. With her head lying on the bed, she appeared to be sleeping.

Arrow was in a chair in the corner of the room. He was asleep as well.

Tad grasped Cindy's hand, and she moved. Slowly raising her head, she shouted. "He's awake!" She grabbed his hands with hers.

Arrow jumped out of his chair and came to the other side of the bed.

"What the hell am I doing here?" Tad inquired.

"I'll get the nurse." Arrow said.

"Wait. Stop. What's going on Arrow?" Tad asked them both.

Cindy was beginning to cry and wouldn't let go of Tad's hands.

"Bro. You've been in a coma for two days. I found you unconscious, and they Care-Flighted you here. How do you feel?" Arrow asked.

Tad looked at them both in astonishment. "I feel great. I mean,…uh, I feel fine. Can you sit me up?"

Cindy talked while raising Tad's bed. "We were planning to fly you to Knoxville. The doctors have all been baffled and haven't been sure of a prognosis. They originally thought that you had Locked-in Syndrome, but then you kept saying random things. Three different doctors have seen you and all three said different things…Traumatic Coma, Hypoxic Coma, PVS. They all admitted that they've never seen this. What do you remember?" she finally asked.

Tad thought for a moment. He remembered everything. Visiting Moon Dove, the trip to the past, General Blackwell, the native's abuse, and the mine. He remembered being in the cave with Moon Dove and walking away from Blackwell. He thought it better to NOT explain all of it to his friends. At least for now.

"Well…I went to check on Willow. Make sure he had food and water. Then I must have fallen and hit my head, or something." Tad explained.

Arrow put his hand on Tad's leg. "Tad, you have no contusion, or anything. They even did a full-body MRI. No tumors, bleeds, nothing. They thought maybe you took something with fentanyl in it, but no traces of that either. Does anything hurt at all?"

"No. I'm telling you, I feel great. I mean, I feel better than normal. Even my back and shoulder don't hurt and they always do." Tad chuckled.

Arrow looked curious. "What's up with your back and shoulder?"

"Oh, hell. They always hurt. Screwed my back up thirty years ago, and got a labrum tear a few years back in my shoulder. It hurts when it rains. Listen, I feel fine. I wanna get out of here." Tad declared.

As Tad was pulling the bedsheet down, a nurse walked in. Her eyes opened widely. "No, No, don't do that Mister O'Banion."

She went to his side, picked up the "call button" and pressed it.

The speaker squawked. "Yes. What do you need?"

"Call Doctor Woods. The patient is awake. I repeat, the patient is awake." The nurse announced.

She turned to the two visitors. "Listen, I'm going to have to ask you guys to wait outside. At least until the doctor sees Mister O'Banion. Can you do that?"

Arrow and Cindy looked at each other. Cindy kissed Tad's forehead, and they both went to the waiting room, down the hall.

Once they got to the waiting room, Arrow looked around and saw no one nearby. "Okay, I've got to ask, Did you not notice Tad?"

Cindy shook her head in agreement. "He looks ten years younger. The gray in his hair is literally gone…and I think he looks,…well, bigger." She quietly claimed.

"Yeah, I thought the same. He looks like he did when he trained seven days a week. One doctor actually asked if there was a chance he was on steroids. I don't know, Cindy, but he definitely does not look like the same guy that we saw three days ago. He seems mentally fine though." Arrow whispered.

After about an hour and a half, Doctor Woods came to the waiting room. "I'm baffled. Tad seems fine. I want to run more tests, but he's refusing. Hell, he's in there putting on his clothes. I'd love to keep him, but it's going to be up to you two. Watch him for the next few days and, by any means necessary, bring him in if you see anything out-of-the-ordinary. I have both of your numbers. If we find anything abnormal in the blood samples, I'll call one of you. Good Luck."

As the two started back towards Tad's room, Arrow stopped for a moment. Cindy said, "What's wrong?"

Arrow paused and said, "Oh, Nothing." And as they continued down the hall, he thought about that morning. Just three mornings ago, at three AM, Arrow heard howling. He stepped from his train-car to investigate. What he saw seemed strange.

A red wolf near the tradesmen's building was howling at the moon. Something in Arrow's head told him to make his presence known. Once he did, the wolf circled to the back of the building and out of sight. Arrow felt the need to pursue the wolf. His native heritage believed the wolf to be sacred and he felt no fear. So, he went.

When Arrow circled to the back of the building, he saw the open gate and eventually found Tad in the basement. He carried Tad out of the building and called 911. Of all people, Carrie answered. She immediately dispatched Care-Flight.

Before they saw Tad again, Arrow decided to keep this portion of the night to himself. He had a weird feeling that the wolf had led him to Tad and that meant something greater.

As they approached his room, Tad came walking out. "I've got to stop at the counter, but we're outta here. Thank you guys, for being here, but I want to get to Camelot. I've got a million things running through my head and need to process them." Tad revealed.

"I haven't had a shower in two days dude. I'm checking out, when we get back. Cindy, on the other hand, kept showering in your room. Even though they told her she couldn't." Arrow said.

"Fuck em, I needed a shower." Cindy blurted out.

"Have you two been in my room since I got here?" Tad asked

"Yeah bro. Leave no man behind. Right?" Arrow affirmed.

Cindy grabbed Tad's hand as they started towards the door. She looked up at him and smiled. "I swear, he's taller." She thought.

Cindy and Arrow received no fewer than five calls each during the ride to Camelot. They had driven Tad's Land Cruiser to the hospital, but Tad would not let them drive to Camelot. He drove faster than normal, but he seemed "in control". Cindy sat in front with Tad, and Arrow purposefully sat right behind Tad. Cindy looked back at Arrow many times during the ride home.

"What's up with you two? You keep looking at each other, and it's freaking me out…Arrow, you got a thing for my girl?" Tad asked.

"You mean the girl, who looks like my wife?" Arrow retorted.

"Touché, there brother. This one's mine though. Speaking of which, why don't you fly Sally out for a couple days?" Tad inquired.

Arrow was swaying back and forth with Tad's driving. "She's already on her way. She booked a flight, after she found out about you. She'll be here in a few hours. I'm gonna take a quick nap and run to Knoxville to get her. Cindy, do you need to go home, or to the Blue Dog?"

"No. Devon and Gail have been taking care of the Saloon, and I have clothes at Tad's. I'm gonna stay with him, and make sure he's following "doctor's orders". You go on and get Sally. I want to meet my twin." Cindy smiled and looked back at Arrow.

It was already dark when Arrow came back with
Sally. Tad and Cindy were sitting by the campfire, drinking a
beer. Tad stood and walked toward the Land Cruiser as they
pulled up.

"How's my girl!" Tad shouted, with his arms open.

Sally threw open her door and ran to Tad, arms
wide. She leaped into his arms and embraced him.

"I thought we lost you, my love." Sally proclaimed.

Cindy was standing, with a confused look on her
face.

Arrow walked toward Cindy and held his hand up.
"It's okay. They do this shit. They think it pisses me off. But
it's all for show. How's the superhuman?"

"I hope this shit wears off soon. He's like a damn
rabbit, Arrow. He can't stop moving, and his testosterone
has to be through the roof. I'm just waiting for him to
"crash". Then I'm going to sleep for a day." Cindy muttered

Tad and Sally came toward the campfire, arm in arm.
After introductions, Cindy spoke. "Damn girl, you could be
my twin."

Sally looked Cindy up and down. "Yep, Cherokee.
I'm guessing twenty-five to thirty percent."

Cindy chuckled. "I like this girl. She ain't been here
but ten minutes, and already insulting me. Sally, my blood's
about as "non-Indian" as one can get. Hell, my ancestors ran
the injuns outta here." Cindy replied.

Sally closed one eye and cocked her head. "Don't say
Blackwell girl, cuz that's an Indian name."

Cindy's jaw dropped open. Then she squinted a gaze
at Arrow. "You, shithead. I just got set up. Didn't I?"

Arrow held his hands up and shook his head,
obviously acknowledging that he had nothing to do with the
conversation.

Tad interrupted, "Before someone gets scalped, let's all get a beer and take a walk. I want to show Sally around."

Tad jogged over to his train-car and disappeared.

Arrow looked at Sally. "I warned you… Just help us keep an eye on him."

"Cindy, I apologize, if I insulted you. That was not my intent. But, I got a weird feeling when I saw you, and "Blackwell" just came out. I've got Blackwell in me." Sally got out before Tad came jogging back with four open longnecks.

After handing them out, Tad grabbed Sally's hand and said, "Come, let me show you around."

Tad and Sally walked off together, leaving Arrow and Cindy by the campfire. They looked at each other and started laughing.

"Arrow, are you telling me everything about how you found Tad?" Cindy asked.

"Cindy, if there was more that I could add, I would. Maybe he drank one of my "solutions". If he did, he could be Doctor Jekyll or Mister Hyde." Arrow replied.

Cindy chuckled. "Oh shit. Which one is he now?"

They both laughed, and Cindy started walking towards train-car 22.

"Where you going?" Arrow asked.

Cindy stopped and looked back. "Getting the keys to the diner. Tad'll want to show it to Sally. And I want to see what Gail's been doing with it anyway."

Arrow jumped off the picnic table he was sitting on. "Hey, I'll join you. I got a feeling that Tad's gonna keep Sally busy for a while."

Cindy didn't turn, but said. "If she comes back absolutely worn out,…you'll know why." …both of them laughed.

***

Over the next few days, Tad's energy levels seemed to subsided to something "more normal", although he constantly commented on "how good he felt".

He soon started getting calls from Adam, from Johnson City. Since Tad had been away for a couple of weeks, Adam had made some decisions of his own. One was landing another twenty-million dollar contract to supply Sentrys and Sentinels to Canada. Tad was pleased and impressed that Adam had negotiated the contract for him.

"I hope that you're good with it, because I started another development project for us. Do you remember those guys from MIT. The ones with the micro-drones?" Adam asked one afternoon.

"Yeah, I do. What about it" Tad replied.

"They have drones almost as small as a mosquito now. They can only fly for about fifteen minutes, but they're essentially disposable. I believe, with our AI interface, these little guys could leap-frog each other, and go much further. Using them in a collapsed building, car accident, or other small area, could be a massivebenefit. If we upgrade our software to include them, we will have subscriptions from every municipality out there. What do you think?" Adam proposed.

Tad's face lit up. "Dude, I love it. Stay on it. Send me a contract proposal for the MIT guys… Hey, wait! Could they fly into a keyhole? Could you crack a safe with them?"

Adam paused for a while. "Not sure. You still want me to give that safe a "go", there bro?"

Tad was excited. "Yes. I found the key that releases the tumbler dial. So, come on over anytime, and let's see how good a safecracker you've become. In fact,…are you doing anything this weekend? It'd be awesome if we could all be together when it's opened."

"Sure. It'd be fun. I'll come over Saturday morning. Nine-ish." Adam confirmed.

Tad had thought long and hard about the safe, and what might be in it. Gold? Coins? A dead body? He understood why no one had ever moved it. Hell, it probably weighed three tons. But he didn't understand why it was locked shut, with the tumbler key hidden. The more he thought about it, the more he convinced himself that it had to be empty. But, still, he had to know.

Chapter 27 –

"If it Weren't for Those Pesky Kids"

By Saturday morning, Tad had somewhat lost interest in the safe. That was until Adam showed up at nine AM.

Tad thought he heard a vehicle come up the road, but hadn't heard one pass. He looked across the road, past the diner, and saw Adam's Tacoma. Easy to identify with the rooftop tent, and "decked out" in overland gear. Tad looked back at Arrow and waved. Arrow, in a white painter's suit, was finishing up the last spray test of "Sample Twenty-two", waved back.

Tad walked up behind Adam, in front of the diner. "How 'bout some flap-jacks fella?" Tad claimed.

Adam jumped. "Oh shit dude. You just scared the crap out of me. You snuck up, like a damn panther. Don't do that!" Adam sputtered.

"Sorry. I seem to have a bad habit of scaring people a lot lately. Did you bring everything you need to crack that safe?" Tad asked.

"I think so. Well, I brought everything I have, and remember, I'm a rookie. Dude, did you dye your hair?" Adam said, with an odd look.

Tad snickered. "Yeah, long story. Let's walk over to my place to look at a few things, and I'll reach out to Cindy and the gang.

Adam grabbed a couple of Pelican cases from the back of his truck and followed Tad to train-car 22. Once inside, Tad handed Adam some documents and pulled out his phone. Adam began looking through the documents while Tad dialed each member of the "cartoon sleuths".

Cindy was immediately on her way, but Carrie and Nick couldn't come until lunchtime. Tad explained that they'd start without them but wouldn't open the safe until they got there. They both said the same thing…"Go ahead and open it."

When Tad got off the phone, Adam looked up. "These all look good. Signed, and notarized. I'll get them sent over to the Canadians, and we'll keep things rolling. How you hanging in here, since your stroke?" Adam asked.

"Never felt better, and it wasn't a damn stroke!" Tad emphasized. "I've got them baffled right now. I'd rather keep it that way."

Arrow knocked on the door.

"Come on in!" Tad shouted.

Arrow cracked the door and poked his head in. "Oh, Hi Adam. We've talked on the phone, but never met. I need to jump in the shower. I'm sure Sally wants to come along too. I think I know where it is. If you guys want to go on over there, we'll catch up." Arrow explained.

"No worries. We'll catch you over there." Tad replied.

Adam was still looking over the documents, and asked, "Not that I really give a shit, Tad. But it's okay for us to crack this safe, right?"

"I already checked that out. I asked our lawyer about it, and he says that I own everything on the property. Including mineral rights." Tad replied. "Good, or bad. I own what's in that safe."

"Bad?" Adam said. "What could be bad?"

"A body." Tad replied.

***

Tad again picked the lock to the office and opened the door. He and Adam entered and set Adam's cases on the desk. Adam looked around the room and appeared to be in awe.

He finally stopped and looked at Tad. "Where's the safe? Did somebody take it?"

Tad walked over to the bookshelf, released the latch, and pulled it away.

"Oh, hell yeah!" Adam avowed.

Tad removed a key from his pocket, inserted it into the keyhole beside the tumbler dial, and turned. They saw the dial move slightly.

Tad then spun the dial and turned to Adam. "Your turn." He said.

Adam put a set of earphones around his neck, set a magnetic pickup, and attached a long arm to the lever. Adam started listening and moving the dial methodically, making notes on a small pad of paper.

Tad figured that he'd give Adam some "space", and walked to the hallway. Taking out his phone, he called Cindy. "Hey, hon. We're over at the old office, Do you want me to come out and get you?" he asked.

"Tad, you don't know it, but I tagged you. I've got your longitude, and latitude. Pretty sure that I can find you anywhere on earth." Cindy laughed. "I'm good, babe. I see Arrow, and Sally. I'll join them and be there in a hot minute." Cindy promised.

Tad walked down the hall and propped open the double doors to the "museum". Imagining the fossils coming to life, Tad could see a day when this building was full of vocational students of all ages. A forgotten time. The dinosaurs that may have actually started the industrial revolution. He could see the teachers and students in their lab coats, with a full suit underneath. Well, minus the jacket. But, nonetheless, sweat dripping from their noses. He wanted so badly to walk to the front window and look across the campus, at the majestic "Manor Hotel".

Just then, Tad heard the creak of a door and the sound of footsteps. After seeing so many strange things since coming to Pressmen's Home, he stood there in the dark corridor, waiting for the next foreboding appearance. Would it be General Blackwell himself?

While prepared for anything, Tad was pleased to see Arrow and the girls appear at the end of the hall.

"Down here guys." Tad shouted.

As they approached, Cindy slowed. She knew better than to trust that Tad wouldn't pull a prank. She had heard about what he did to Carrie that one night, and Cindy wasn't prepared or interested in any such shenanigans.

Arrow had been here with Tad the week before his incident and was sure Arrow had toured the tradesmen's building. He knew Sally would find the place interesting…and he was right. Sally's face lit up. She walked around all the machines and laid her hands on the stacks of printing plates. She picked one up and moved to the sunlight. It was the image of "The Madonna", The Virgin Mary. Sally looked at Tad.

"If you want it, it's yours. Not sure how you'll get it home, but take it." Tad insisted.

As they walked around the room, looking at the "dinosaurs", Cindy stayed by the double doors. Not afraid and perfectly content watching the rest explore.

"There's other interesting rooms, but this one's the best." Arrow explained to Sally.

"I guess we'd better check on Adam. He's probably been at it for a half hour now, and he hasn't come to find us." Tad suggested.

They all walked down to the office. Adam was sitting in the old desk chair, working away at the safe.

"How's it going? Can we help with anything?" Tad inquired.

Adam stopped and pulled the earphones from his head, then wrote a few numbers in his notebook. "I'm not sure. I think I found the driver gate, and I thought I found wheels two and three. But the damn thing won't open. I think I've opened harder, so I'm pissed." Adam paused. "One thing that's weird is that the dial goes to one-thirty. I've never seen that before."

While Tad, Arrow, and Cindy were listening to Adam, Sally was walking around the room. She stopped at the large photographs. One by one, she lifted them off of the wall, and inspected them.

"Cindy, This fella here is a Blackwell. It says "President". Of the Pressmen's Union, I'm guessing. He look familiar to you?" Sally asked.

Cindy walked over. "I don't know him. But I suppose I could be related. This was his office. It obviously got cleaned out. Not sure why they left the pictures."

Suddenly Tad turned. "Let me see those!"

Tad pulled out his Benchmade knife, knelt on the ground, and cut into the dustcover of the large photo of Blackwell.

He fully expected to see a combination written somewhere…there was nothing. He quickly moved to the other two photos…same thing.

Adam and Arrow looked at each other and curled their chins and lips. "That would have been pretty cool, Tad. Any other ideas, Sherlock?" Arrow asked.

As Tad stood, Nick and Carrie walked in, still on duty an in uniform.

"I'm not sure that we should be here if y'all are breaking into a safe." Nick jested.

"It's all legal deputy. I checked." Tad replied.

"Just joking, Fred. Velma and I are here to help." Nick jested.

Cindy introduced Sally to Nick and Carrie, while Tad sat down in the old wooden desk chair.

Adam explained the predicament for the newcomer's sake and was ready to offer to hire someone better than he at cracking safes. Tad sat rubbing his chin while Arrow looked around the room.

Nick broke the silence. "Well listen, we snuck away, and someone is covering for Carrie. So, we gotta get back. We'll both be off around four, if you want help with the body. Until then, you're on your own."

Nick and Carrie exchanged a cordial "goodbye" and departed. Cindy and Sally followed them into the hall.

Once in the hall, Sally said to Cindy, "I'm getting a weird feeling." She stopped and pulled out her phone. "You haven't checked to see if you're related to this guy?…What was his first name?" Sally inquired.

"It just says T.W. Blackwell. Union President. I can call my great aunt, she might know." Cindy responded.

Inside the office, Adam was on his smartphone, searching for ideas. Arrow was still looking around the room for anything that might give an indication of the combination.

Tad, sitting in the old chair, suddenly leaped from it. He darted to the desk and pulled out a drawer, inspected it, and set it on the desk. Reaching into the drawer slot, he appeared to tug hard. Appearing to be "Merlin" himself, Tad suddenly had two drawers where one once was. Tad had moved so quickly that he startled both Adam and Arrow. They stopped to watch his performance.

Tad inspected the second drawer closer than the first. The second drawer had a sliding wooden cover that Tad removed. He set the small drawer down on its side and inspected the small sliding door. He held it up to the light and angled it.

Arrow interrupted his inspection. "Tad. The drawer." Arrow pointed at the small drawer lying on the desk.

Tad picked up the drawer and turned it over. Stapled to the underside of the drawer, in the base's pocket, was a folded piece of paper.

Tad again pulled his Benchmade and carefully pulled the staples. Pulling the paper from the pocket, he slowly unfolded it and began to read.

Dear Sirs,

I am writing this to acknowledge my guilts, and attempt to reconcile with the Lord. I have spent most of my life in the service of those other than the Lord. For this, I am truly sorry. While most will remember me as a lifelong representative of The International Printing

Pressmen and Assistants Union of North America, my allegiance has actually been to the Knights of Wisdom and The Gold Circle. I have served The Wisdom for almost sixty years, after my own family recruited me many, many years ago. During this time, I have seen many an atrocity at their behest. Most of which were purely for monetary greed or megalomaniac visions that had been percolating for centuries. The secrecy that has been bestowed onto myself, and others, would divulge many of the atrocities that the world has witnessed. I, myself, regret and admit the very actions that I took that day, in Dallas, November 1963.

The Wisdom is now moving to New York, and I have seen the light. I must repent. Unbeknownst to them, The Union, and The Wisdom, will move without me. I have stayed behind to close the headquarters. I will return to Knoxville, to my home beside the FPC. This will be the combination of prayer and solitude that will fill my final days, as I attempt to sever this limb of The Wisdom.

May the Lord bless the souls who have been entombed by the actions of The Wisdom, and of The Gold Circle. I pray that all are freed.

> *Sir Theodore William Blackwell,*
> ~~*President*~~*, International Pressmen Union*
> ~~*Knight and Dame Commander*~~*, The Wisdom*
> *Follower of the Lord, Jesus Christ*

Tad finished reading, and looked up, realizing that Sally and Cindy had returned.

Sally broke the silence. "That's the guy in the picture. I just did a "search" for him a few minutes ago. Not much on the net about him. All you can really find, is that he was the President of the Pressmen's Union from 1946 until 1967. And I also found his gravesite in Knoxville in the cemetery for The First Presbyterian Church."

"I've got it." Cindy whispered. "We go to the cemetery tonight…like at midnight. Then we dig dear ole Teddy up. We get the combination from his pocket, and voilà, we open the safe and find the goods" She jested.

The timing was good, and everyone chuckled.

Tad looked back at the letter. "There's something odd about this letter."

"Like it's not real?" Arrow asked.

"No. It's written in a way that it doesn't sound right." Tad replied. "And the word combination is—" Tad paused. "Oh, shit!" he exclaimed.

Tad quickly pulled out his smartphone, opened an app, and began looking. After a moment, he looked up at Cindy.

Walking over to her, he cupped his hands on her cheeks, and said, "You're a friggin genius, you know that?"

Cindy looked at the people in the room. "He does this shit, and I have no idea what I just did."

Tad turned to Adam. "Adam, you said that you thought you might have had the first two numbers, right?"

Adam nodded.

"And they were thirty-five, and ninety-six, right?" Tad continued.

"Yeah." Adam acknowledged.

"I think I can give you the next two numbers." Tad said excitedly.

Adam looked up and cocked his head. "Well, I wasn't thinking that there were four. But yeah, some safes do have four."

Tad looked back at Cindy. "What did you tell me, when I called you earlier?"

Cindy looked confused and furrowed her brow. "That I can find you anywhere?"

"Yes! Anywhere!" Tad confirmed.

Still looking at Cindy, Tad raised his smartphone to show her what was displayed.

"No matter what latitude or longitude!" Tad announced.

"Oh shit!" Arrow interrupted. "It's the damn latitude and longitude of his gravesite!"

Adam quickly pulled the wooden chair back to the safe. He put the headphones back on, and said. "Give them to me."

Tad read off. "Thirty-five, ninety-six, eighty-three, and ninety-one."

Adam slowly rotated the dial. After the last number, he pulled on the lever, and it rotated with a loud "thunk".

Chapter 28 –

"The Stench of History"

Adam stood and rolled the chair away from the safe. He waved Tad over to open the safe.

Tad stepped towards the safe and paused. "Guys, if there's a dead body in here. We're just gonna plunder, and bury it out back, right?" he half jested.

No one laughed. Everyone just kept looking at the safe.

Tad grasped the handle and pulled hard.

The safe door slowly opened. A sweet acrid smell filled the room and everyone's eyes grew.

The safe was not a "walk-in" style like Tad had hoped. The interior of the safe had an open cavity at the bottom. The upper one and a half to two feet had metal shelves filled with books and manuscripts. Separate from the books on one shelf was a wooden box. Below the shelf in the open cavity appeared to be a stack of bricks covered by a linen cloth. Resting on top of the bricks was a large canvas bag and a rifle.

Tad reached in and picked up the rifle. It was a Lee-Enfield No. 4 Mark 1 sniper rifle, with a Weaver scope. He inspected the chamber and handed it to Arrow.

"You don't suppose that was-?" Adam started to ask.

"Yes. I do. He all but admitted it, in his letter." Tad interrupted.

Tad removed the ornate wooden box from the shelf and laid it on the old desk. The ornate box resembled a large jewelry box that had an opening lid.

Tad slowly opened the lid.

Lying on a velvet lining were two Wogdon dueling pistols.

"Hamilton-Burr?" Arrow asked.

"Doubtful." Tad replied. "I thought they were at a bank in Chicago. But I'll bet these have a story."

Tad left the case open and returned to the safe. He pulled a few of the manuscripts and opened them.

"Damn, these are from the Civil War. Albert Johnston?" Tad questioned.

"He died at Shiloh. They say that it may have been a completely different war, if he hadn't died there." Adam explained.

Tad laid several of them them down on the desk. Adam picked one up, gently opened it and leafed through the pages.

"Wow, he mentions Pittsburg Landing in here. This might have been his last manuscript." Adam exclaimed.

As Adam continued looking through the old manuscripts, Tad returned with the canvas bag. He opened it, looked in and poured its contents onto the desktop…jewels of all shapes, sizes, and colors.

"Charles G-U-I-T-E-A-U?" Adam quizzed. Spelling out the last name.

Sally quickly searched for him on her smartphone. "He killed President Garfield in eighteen eighty-one."

"Holy Shit." Adam expressed. Then he saw the jewels on the desk, he said again. "HOLY SHIT!"

Tad went back to the safe. He dropped to one knee and pulled the linen cloth from the bricks.

There, lying at the base of the safe, were eight gold bars, or "bricks". He slid one so that he could get his fingers under it to lift. Looking surprised by the weight, he lifted a brick and then set it back in place.

"Shit, That's got to be close to thirty pounds." Tad claimed.

Tad stood, turned and sat in the old wooden desk chair.

Rubbing his chin, Tad said. "Might have been better if it was a body that we found. I'm not sure what to do."

"I thought you said the lawyer's got you covered? You said that anything found on the property is yours." Arrow said.

Tad remained seated and looked around the room. "Yeah, but there are answers here. Answers to events that the people should know. Not to mention, there's the whole secret society shit that probably shouldn't be a secret. I'm not sure what to do."

Sally, always one to point out the rational side of things, spoke up. "Tad, it's pretty obvious that no one knows this is here. Otherwise, it'd already be gone. I would highly suggest that this be kept secret and that you take some time to secure all of it. After you've had time to think about it, you can make a better decision."

Tad stood and returned to the old desk. He began putting the jewels back into the canvas bag, while Arrow grabbed the linen towel and dropped to a knee in front of the safe. Adam picked up the old rifle and came to Arrow's side. Covering the gold bricks, Arrow took the rifle from Adam and set it inside of the safe.

As Arrow stepped away, Tad returned with the canvas bag and manuscripts. Setting them inside the safe, Tad asked, "Can you all keep this to yourselves? At least until I figure out what to do?"

Cindy spoke first. "It was empty, as far as I'm concerned. In fact, I won't even bring it up to anyone. I'll tell Nick and Carrie, it just had a few trinkets."

Adam followed. "Same Bro. No reason to even talk about it."

Sally acknowledged by closing her eyes and nodding.

"I know nuth-sing!" Arrow chided, in his best "Sargent Schultz" impression.

"Thanks guys. At the end of the day, your all part of this…and I'll make sure each of you reaps any benefits. Hopefully not any curses." Tad insisted.

"Okay, that was a little spooky!" Cindy protested. "How bout we all go to the Blue Dog, grab an early dinner, and have a beer?" She inquired.

"Sounds great. Head that way in ten?" Arrow asked all.

Adam looked at Tad. "Shut 'er back up?"

Tad nodded.

"Okay, I need about twenty minutes to double check you can get back in here, then I'll be ready." Adam clarified.

"If ya'll want to go on down, I'll help Adam, and we'll be down in twenty. Meet at the campfire. Oh, and the damn "media" better not be out there, when we come out!" Tad jested.

Arrow, Sally, and Cindy snickered, and exited the office.

Sitting at the picnic table, Arrow was looking at the screen of his smartphone.

"There's a friggin fortune up there!" Cindy claimed

"Well over ten million dollars. Possibly twenty. Each gold brick is over a million. The jewels, the manuscripts. Shit there's at least thirty million dollars up there." Arrow whispered.

"There's nothing up there, you two. Nothing." Sally corrected them. "We made a promise. Stop talking about it."

Cindy and Arrow looked at each other and acknowledged that Sally was correct.

Chapter 29 –

"Good Deeds"

The coming days brought a bit of chaos to Camelot. Nick placed two more train-cars on his lots above the old hotel foundation. Nick and Ethel's received it's fancy sign. Gail continued working at the diner to prepare for its grand opening the following week. Arrow completed the solution that seemed to kill off the kudzu and poison ivy, while harming no other species of plant or animal in its proximity.

Tad had fortified the old office in the tradesmen's building and installed a security system. When asked why he included cameras in the basement, Tad just laughed and said that he "wanted Willow to feel safe".

After Arrow had killed off most of the kudzu over at the old hotel property, he let Tad know that he and Sally needed to return to Oklahoma.

Tad had enjoyed having his good friends here and didn't want them to leave. "Any chance, I can get you two to stay? There are worse places to retire, you know?" Tad urged.

Arrow chuckled. "Yeah, I know. But Oklahoma's home bro. Maybe we can come out and spend some time a little more often though." He promised.

"I'll always have a "car" here for you, my friend." Tad said, meaning the train-car units that were beginning to pop up all over the properties.

The next day, Cindy and Tad drove their two friends to Knoxville. As they walked to the terminal, they paired up just as they had when Sally arrived. Tad was with Sally and Arrow with Cindy.

"You'll keep an eye on my boy, won't you?" Arrow asked Cindy.

"Of course I will Arrow. You have my number. Call me any time." Cindy insisted.

Noticing that Tad and Sally were talking and had gotten a bit ahead of them, Arrow lowered his voice. "Um, Cindy? Listen. This is going to sound a little strange. But, if you see a red wolf out at Camelot,...follow it. It might be telling you something."

Cindy, looking bewildered, replied. "Ah, sure. Is this an "Indian thing"."

"Yeah, I think it is. Thanks." Arrow said and then hugged Cindy.

After their "goodbyes", Tad and Cindy stayed and watched their friends disappear into the Terminal.

"Watcha thinking cowboy" Cindy asked.

"I'm thinking that I may have the best friends on earth." Tad replied.

"Well, I hope that includes me?" Cindy smiled flirtatiously.

"Oh, I suppose so." Tad claimed, with a grin.

Cindy "fake punched" Tad in the gut. "let's get back to the ranch, cowboy. I want to see if Gail needs any help."

"I thought the diner was my place." Tad commented.

"Yeah, well, you suck at being a diner owner. So, somebody has to run it." Cindy claimed with her own grin.

Upon returning to Camelot, they noticed ten cars in the diner parking lot. Tad pulled in and parked there as well. "Look's open to me! Let's check it out!" Tad exclaimed.

Gail had a "soft opening" for friends and family to come in and sample the food. Nick, Carrie…and even Devon were there to make sure that everything was correctly prepared and served.

Tad and Cindy sat down in the booth with Devon.

"Who's running The Blue Dog?" Cindy inquired.

"I'm only going to be gone for an hour, boss. Josie has things under control…and, Gail is flat slammin' it here. She good. She good." Devon proclaimed. "Order the jambalaya. She tweaked my recipe, but it is G-U-D, good!"

Tad laughed. "Hey, sweetheart. I need to go check on Adam while he's here today. He's up at Nick's properties putting up another Sentry. Will you get me something and I'll meet you back at "22" after a bit?"

Cindy was smiling right when Tad said "sweetheart". "Sure, Honey. Go play with your toys." She replied.

Taking longer than Tad expected, he didn't get back to "22" until almost two hours later.

Lying on the kitchen table was a note.

My Love,
There's jambalaya in the fridge. I've got to close The Blue Dog tonight. Come by if you want. I'll prolly stay at my place tonight, cuz I hafta open tomorrow.
Cindy

She signed it with a heart and X's and O's.

After reheating it, Tad sat down at the table to eat some Nick and Ethel's jambalaya, and think about the contents of the safe.

After finishing the meal that Tad thought was phenomenal as a leftover, he sat back in the recliner and dozed off.

Waking after just ten minutes, Tad sat up. He had made his decision.

He walked into The Blue Dog at eight PM.

"I was beginning to think that someone stood me up!" Cindy stated as she got Tad a longneck.

Tad sat at the bar, picked up the beer, and guzzled a quarter of the malt beverage down.

"Dang Cowboy! Long day on the range?" Cindy asked. "Did you get everything "squared away" with Adam?"

"I hope so." Tad replied

"What do you mean?" Cindy said while setting drinks on the serving tray.

"Oh, Nothing. Hey, did you ever say anything to Nick, and Carrie, about the safe? I feel kinda bad not coming clean with them over it." Tad divulged.

Cindy finished making a drink, set it on the tray and lifted the tray up to her shoulder. "They asked, the next day. I told them that there was nothing in it but a bunch of old trinkets. If you want to "come clean", go tell them. They're both working the late shift tonight…But, I'd knock first." Cindy winked and headed off toward the patron's tables.

When Cindy returned, she saw Tad had finished his beer. "Ya want another, or a whiskey, there cowboy?"

"No, I'm good. Thanks. Since you're going to your house tonight, I think I'm going to run over to JC, and catch up on a few things there." Tad replied.

"Okay,…tell that girlfriend in JC that I'm coming for her…she may get an ass wuppin' from this little ole thing in

Hawkins County." Cindy winked again, but this time she spun Tad's chair around and kissed him.

"See you sometime tomorrow, Babe. Whether you like it or not!" Cindy said, as she flipped up Tad's ball cap with her finger.

Tad squeezed Cindy's hand, smiled at her, stood, and walked away.

***

It was after midnight when Nick and Carrie arrived at her house.

Pulling into the driveway, Nick brought up the subject that Carrie despised. "So, when are you going back to school Carrie? You keep saying that you will. But you haven't talked about it in weeks,…and I know that the new semester has already started." Nick questioned.

"Nick, I've got to save some money first. I know you don't like when I patrol, but the Sherrif said that I can keep that to "as needed". I'll start back next semester…Maybe." She protested.

As Nick unlocked the door with his own key, he argued, "I can't stand this Carrie. What if I help pay for your school? The rentals will be up-and-going soon. I know I can swing it." Nick continued.

Stepping into the livingroom Carrie spoke. "Nick! What the fuck!"

From the living room, they both could see into the kitchen. Lying on the kitchen counter was a large brick of gold.

"Oh shit! Do you think its real?" Nick asked as they approached the shiny object.

"Nick, the alarm was turned off. Who do you know that would break into my house, turn the alarm off and leave something like this?" Carrie challenged.

"I'm friggin jealous! It's obvious that "whoever it is" still has a thing for you. I wish I could give you a bar of gold!" Nick laughed.

Carrie turned and pushed Nick. "Oh stop!...hell, there's probably one at your house too!"

They suddenly looked at each other. Without saying a word, Nick handed the keys to Carrie. He picked up the brick of gold, and out the door they went.

After finding the very same thing at Nick's house, they both had questions. With both bricks of gold in the car, they headed towards Camelot. As they discussed the situation while driving, they changed their minds. "Let's talk to Cindy first. She might know what's going on." Nick suggested.

Pulling into Cindy's drive, they noticed the lights on and were confident they wouldn't wake her. They left the bricks of gold in the car and went to Cindy's front door and knocked.

Cindy came to the door sobbing. She unlocked the door, opened it, and walked towards the kitchen.

"What's wrong Cindy?" Carrie asked.

Cindy pointed toward the brick of gold on her kitchen counter. She began sobbing and tried to speak. "Th-, That asshole left me this, and I-, I can't reach him. He's gone to JC, and his phone goes to voice mail."

Carrie put her arms around Cindy. "Cindy, hon. He did the same for us. It's okay. He's okay. He probably just wants us to chill." Carrie consoled Cindy. She then realized \ that Cindy's tears were both joy and frustration that she could not reach Tad.

Cindy's sobbing slowed. "Well, I hope mine is bigger than yours. Right?" Cindy choked back a laugh, while still sobbing.

***

-In Johnson City

When Adam got home from Camelot, he noticed a strange duffle bag in the back of his truck. "What the hell", he thought. He lowered his tailgate and reached in. It was heavy. He pulled it to the tailgate and unzipped the duffle. His jaw dropped open as he saw the gleam of a large gold brick.

Tad returned to Camelot around three o'clock the next day. Cindy and Carrie were at the diner and came to Tad's Land Cruiser as he stepped out. Cindy walked up to him, slapped him, then grabbed his face with both hands and gave him a big kiss. After she did this, she stepped to the side and Carrie did the same.

"Are we doing this again?" Tad chuckled. Cindy grabbed Tad by the neck and kissed him again.

As before, Carrie did the same.

"Stop! Both of you! I get it. Please stop. I'm afraid that I can only handle one of you." Tad laughed.

"And, it's going to be ME!" Cindy chuckled.

"Over to 22, both of you. We need to talk…and stop kissing me!" Tad ordered.

Once inside "22", Tad explained to Cindy and Carrie that he had decided to share a portion of the findings with each of them, including the Brooks'. "I'm going to do the same with the jewels. I just have to figure out how to do that." He explained.

"Jewels? What Jewels?" Carrie asked.

Looking at Carrie, Tad explained that there were jewels and jewelry in the safe as well. Again, he asked for their confidentiality.

"Arrow was right. I have to be very careful. In essence, I need you, and Nick, to forget that you know anything about the safe. In fact, it is empty now. So, as far as you know,…IT WAS EMPTY. Understood?" Tad asked.

As they both agreed, there was a knock at the door.

Tad opened the door and let Nick in. Nick was carrying his brick of gold, wrapped in a towel.

Nick set it on the counter. "I can't take this, Tad. You've already done too much for me. I appreciate it, but can't."

There was dead silence. Then Tad spoke. "Adam already tried the same shit, Nick. It's done. I've made my decision. Heck, the girls seemed fine with it. I appreciate you all being grateful. That's all I really want." Tad finished.

"Except I'm having sex with him!" Carrie blurted out.

"Me too!" Cindy followed.

"Can I have sex with him?" Nick asked, and they all burst into laughter.

While laughing, Tad held up his hand. "Seriously though, Nick. There's nothing in the safe, and that's all you need to know. Understood?"

"Got it, partner! Well, it looks like I won't have any trouble furnishing my units, or paying the bank back…and Carrie, looks like you'll be signing up for the next semester at E-T-S-U or Knoxville" Nick said.

Carrie smiled and nodded in agreement.

"I think that I'll pay off The Blue Dog, hire some additional help, and spend a little more time out here, in

Camelot…If that's okay with you, there cowboy?" Cindy questioned, looking at Tad.

"Sounds good to me. Maybe there's another "case" we'll need to crack. Velma, Shaggy, and Daphne up for a drink at The Blue Dog?" Tad asked.

They all nodded, and headed out the door.

Chapter 30 –

"Another Trip"

The Camelot valley remained busy throughout the subsequent weeks, and fall would be approaching soon. While Tad had not opened his units up for rental yet, Nick had. Nick's four units kept a steady stream of renters. Nick had bought ten more lots and had already committed to six more train-cars from Darren.

The original eight train-cars were in place. Four of Tad's, by the lake, and four of Nick's on the North ridge. With four more coming for Tad, and six more coming for Nick, Camelot would soon look like the "train station" that they had imagined. Nick was already pushing Tad for a construction timeline for the "station".

Clearing the kudzu revealed the charred foundation of the hotel and the pool that was built in 1973. Although Tad was hoping to keep his mother's pool from '73, the local experts said that the pool would need to be replaced. Tad and Nick agreed that this was a better option anyway. Now they could include an in-ground hot tub that they were sure the guest would use.

Tad asked Nick to plan trails throughout the ridges. If they stayed on the original "roadway easements", the county would allow them to be considered "county roads" if graveled. So, Nick worked on the trail plans and even found space on top of the "South Ridge" to clear for a "picnic area". "Guinevere's Landing" would be home to a shelter, and restrooms. It would be a good resting spot for hikers, bikers, and horseback riders.

Cindy made good on her promise to hire additional help at The Blue Dog. Which meant she spent more time at Nick and Ethel's, and of course, and train-car 22, just a hundred yards away.

Carrie enrolled at Tennessee College of Applied Technology, with intentions of becoming a "Licensed Practical Nurse", and possibly transferring to UT or ETSU, to continue with an RN. Sheriff Evans fully supported Carrie's new career path, and agreed to reduce her to a "part time" status. He even wrote a letter to the college hoping her "work experience" would account for college credits.

Tad talked to Arrow and Sally about his intended "gifts" to them, but both refused the offer. Tad was explicit, so they finally caved. They promised to visit in the fall and said that "further discussions as to the percentage of ownership" would be required at that time. Tad just laughed.

Tad found himself spending most of his days and nights in Camelot. He had asked Adam to be a fifty percent partner in the business in Johnson City. To which, Adam argued that he could not afford to buy "half" of the business. Tad was quick to ignore Adam's contention and had the paperwork drawn up by the lawyers, anyway. Essentially, day-to-day operations would be run by Adam. There would be monthly meetings, whereby Tad would have a say, but beyond that, Adam's ownership was earned by his management of the company…which was booming.

The diner stay quite busy. Tad had considered having the parking lot paved, but decided that the gravel gave the place a "homier vibe".

So, Tad focused his energy on "The Stable". that he had promised months before. As always, the county zoning board had to approve the plans. After the second meeting. He wasn't sure if they would agree to the "Barndominium" that he proposed, but Nick's appearance with him seemed to "sway" their approval. Tad hoped to build the structure throughout the winter. When completed, he and Cindy could move from train-car 22 the following summer. They needed more space anyway. Cindy had already converted the spare bedroom into her walk-in closet, her western-wear from Wiseman's filling the room. Tad made sure there was a large walk-in closet in the barndominium plans.

Just the talk of horses brought a smile to Cindy's face routinely. She purchased a western saddle, and the smell of leather heightened her anticipation every time that she stepped foot in 22.

The days were getting shorter and Tad noticed the moon had been "waxing gibbous", which meant a full moon in just two days. He began to think about his approaching visit with Moon Dove.

When Cindy opened the door to train-car 22, Tad was at the table. He had the "The Stable" plans spread across the table and was writing notes on a legal pad.

"Hey babe. Whatcha doing now?" Cindy inquired.

"I added a larger patio area, with an outdoor kitchen,… and a wine cellar. I'm wondering what the board might say, since I've already been back to them three times." Tad looked up at Cindy's smiling face. "Oh, I need to run to JC on Saturday. I'll probably stay there. Why don't you work on getting your house ready to sell? I'll be back Sunday, and we can go down to Bull's Gap, to look at those foals that you found."

Cindy's face lit up. "Really? Where would we keep them until The Stable is done?" she challenged.

"We'll find someplace close, hon." Tad replied.

Cindy hustled over to Tad, pushed his chair back, and plopped down in his lap. She took off his hat, kissed him on the forehead, then on the nose, then lips, as had become her "go-to" thank you.

Still sitting on his lap, Cindy said, "Okay, I'll stay at my house Saturday night. But you get right back here Sunday, because I'll have a special gift for you."

"Oh yeah? Will it be wrapped?" Tad asked.

"Not in much." Cindy smiled flirtatiously and then leapt from his lap.

She bent over and gave him another kiss. "I've got to run into town. Do you need anything?" Cindy inquired.

"If you want to pick up a nice wine for dinner?...in fact, get two. We need to start our cellar collection." Tad winked and patted her on the rump.

✳

Tad left for Johnson City early Saturday morning. He didn't wake Cindy, but stopped for a moment, to enjoy her beauty, as she slept.

As he walked into the plant, a few unfamiliar people waved to him. "Hi Mister O'Banion".

He walked into Adam's office. Previously Tad's office, Adam had adorned the walls with mounted heads of boar, deer, and a large bison.

"Holy Shit, where'd you get that?" Tad asked.

Adam stood from his desk and came around to meet Tad. "I found that on-line. It's pretty old. I had it cleaned up and repaired. I had the local game warden come in and check the origination of it, last week. It's a little intimidating over the conference table, don't you think?"

"Yeah. I like it." Tad commented and sat down at the conference table.

"What brings you over here, on a Saturday? Am I getting fired?" Adam jested.

"Yep." Tad chuckled. "Nah. I just had to get away. I'm meeting McKee for lunch and I thought that I'd swing by here." Tad looked around his old office. "I saw plenty of new faces out in the plant."

Sitting across from Tad, Adam replied, "I think we're right at a hundred. Probably be double that next year. Canada doubled their purchase orders this week. I'm going to need close to twenty people "in the field" by spring. Oh, sorry, "WE" will need them—"

"It's okay Adam. It's essentially your business. I'm runned off. R-U-N-N O-F-T." Tad gave his best Appalachian voice.

Adam walked Tad around the plant and introduced him to a few of those "new faces". Seeing all the Sentrys being built, made Tad nod in approval. He stopped counting at thirty. "Ya think I can sneak two or three into your production schedule, Adam?"

"For you?...maybe. I'll check with the boss." Adam chuckled.

After the tour, Adam followed Tad to the rear of the building, where Tad had parked his Land Cruiser.

"You still looking for a FJ55?" Adam inquired.

Tad cocked his head. "Nah, I kinda like the new ones. Hell, I might drive one back to Camelot tonight." Tad grinned. "You're doing a good job here Adam. Keep up the good work…and think about the day that you want to buy out the rest of my shares. Mind you, I'm NOT giving that part to you."

Adam looked down. "Brother, I can't thank you enough, for what you've already done. I promise to keep 'er afloat. And we'll ride this thing as long as we can…or until we get a massive offer from Elon."

They both chuckled, and Tad raised a thumb in approval.

Tad spent the rest of the day having lunch with his friend Dave McKee and then visiting the dealerships, looking at new Land Cruisers. In Kingsport, Tad saw a brand new Traildust Land Cruiser, loaded with options. Driving it off the lot, Tad smiled as he headed towards Camelot.

By the time he got on the road, it was starting to get dark. He didn't want to arrive back at Camelot too early because he wanted to make sure Cindy was not there. This situation could foil his plans to visit Moon Dove. So, he "detoured" a few times, but eventually pulled into his drive around nine-thirty.

Parking his new Land Cruiser in his usual spot, he stepped out and looked out to the valley. It had changed so much. But he could also remember what it looked like when Moon Dove showed it to him. Anticipation was growing within him.

Tad went into 22 and got a beer. As he sat at the breakfast table, his mind wandered to the last time he had seen Moon Dove. "Was she okay? What became of General Blackwell?" he thought. "Hee Yah Golv Kwoh Dee" he said aloud and furrowed his brow.

At midnight, Tad started towards the old building. As he circled to the back side of the building, he saw the wolf. With no fear, he walked toward it and as he passed it, his hand reached out to stroke its fur. The wolf appeared content with Tad's passing. Not slowing his stride, he continued into the building and down the steps.

Tad saw Willow and picked him up. The mouse ran up Tad's pant leg and bound to Willow's shell. Tad remained calm and waited.

As Tad stood on the drainage grate, the liquid changed colors, once again. Slowly to pink, then orange, then blood red. Moon Dove took shape in front of Tad.

When her body had full definition, except her feet, she spoke in her native tongue. "*Little Warrior, I missed you. I know you returned safely. I could see you through the wolf's eyes. I watch over you often, my warrior.*" Moon Dove divulged.

Tad replied and spoke the same tongue. "*Moon Dove, What happened to you? What happened to the General?*" He asked.

Moon Dove looked down. "Your friend. The Ah-GAY-yoo-tsah that has been in the valley often, she shares the same blood as Blackwell. But her heart is pure. Unlike the General's. I will take you to see why I am trapped here. Your friends, Arrow, Sally. They can free us. Please, my warrior, free my soul, so I may travel down the river, and blow in the wind."

Tad looked confused. "Do I need to bring them here, so that you can meet them, Moon Dove?"

"No, My Warrior, I should only take you on one more quest, or your body will become young, and you will live too many Blood Moons. Like Willow. After this journey, you will know what to do. Are you ready, my warrior?" Moon Dove asked as she reached out.

Tad laid his hands in hers.

Tad immediately saw the bright light, and the colors of red, and purple. Again, the basement vanished from his view.

Eventually, the colors of green and brown turned into the familiar landscape. They were looking across the valley from the opening of the mine shaft. General Blackwell was across a field, reading a letter handed to him by a scout. Suddenly, he started barking orders to multiple soldiers. "Get loaded up. We've got to march within the hour. We have brothers in need!"

Blackwell folded the letter and attempted to tuck it into his belt, but it fell to the grass below.

Once the General was out of sight, Moon Dove walked down the field, and picked up the letter.

It read:

General Blackwell,

I understand that you and your men have recently returned from battle. Forgive me, but it is imperative that you join with me to travel west to Franklin. Union troops are mounting, and I fear they plan to try Franklin, once again. I have sent this scout forward. If you could meet us at Bull's Gap at nightfall, we will march to Franklin together. We will meet up with Cheatham and Stewart's Corps along the way.

Your Brother,
General Nathan Bedford Forrest
KOW, KGC

Through Moon Dove's eyes, Tad could read all of it, but did not speak.

Moon Dove walked back to the mine entrance, but stopped when she heard the General. "Moon Dove, Stop!"

She quickly folded the letter and slipped it into her pocket.

The General came quickly. "I need you to help me move any gold that you have mined today." He commanded.

"I do not know where you take it, General." Moon Dove replied.

"Come, I'll help you." He insisted.

As they entered the mine, the General stopped to pick up a couple of leather satchels. "Will it fit in these?" The General inquired.

Moon Dove replied, "Yes. I believe so." And they walked into the mine.

***

Outside the mine, the camp had quickly become chaotic. Soldiers were running in every direction. Some loaded their personal "haversacks", some loaded trailers, others hitched the horses.

General Blackwell emerged from the back of the mine with Moon Dove following him. They were both struggling to carry the heavy satchels as they inconspicuously navigated their war across the edge of the valley.

They walked through a gap in the woods that led to a ravine. After a short distance up the ravine, Blackwell stopped and set down his satchel. Moon Dove did the same. The General, took a large limb and pulled the honeysuckle to the side. Picking up the satchel, he crawled under the honeysuckle, where there was a crevasse, on the far side of the bush. Moon Dove followed him into the dense foliage. The General, took each satchel and tossed them into the crevasse.

"All of the gold is down there?" Moon Dove asked.

General Blackwell replied with an ominous stare. Moon Dove nodded.

They left the ravine and out the gap in the woods. Halfway back to the mine shaft, the General stopped. Unsure what to do, Moon Dove stopped as well.

The General looked agitated. "I need the biggest day yet, from your people. You go up there and keep them working until I come and get you. Do you understand, Moon Dove?"

"Uh huh." she replied.

Moon Dove walked up and into the mine. Tad watched as she told her people that the General expected "much from them". They looked exhausted already. She did not want to tell them, but she knew the General and his troops were leaving. She figured one of two things was going to happen. Either the General would take them to Bull's Gap, or they might release them, hoping to recapture them upon return. The threat to her family regarding the gold, lead her to believe the latter.

Outside the mine, a rough-looking Sargent approached General Blackwell. "General, what are we doing with the Indians?"

"Sargent, I want you and one of your most trusted to stay behind. An hour after we're gone, blow both entrances with dynamite." Blackwell instructed.

"With them in it?" the Sargent asked, with no look of doubt.

"Yes. I don't want them to ever come out. You understand? Then haul ass, and catch up with us at Bull's Gap. We'll be there for the night." Blackwell clarified.

"Yes, sir!" The Sargent saluted.

The troops assembled quickly, as they had done so many times before. While many Confederate corps had "lost" much of their discipline for "military formations", Blackwell's men knew he expected them to march "in rank", and assembled as such. They marched out of the valley and headed to Bull's Gap.

Moon Dove was picking as hard as she could. She needed to rest and to get a drink of water. She walked over to the water pail and picked up the ladle…empty.

Moon Dove, being the leader, always kept water in the pail. She had gotten so busy trying to help that she failed to replenish the life-giving liquid. She picked up the pail and started down the mine. As she approached the entrance from the inside, she saw the Sargent.

Confused about why he was stacking wooden boxes within the mine entrance, Moon Dove called out. "Soldier, can I speak to the General?"

The startled Sargent turned and drew his sidearm. "What the Fuck! You're supposed to stay inside the mine, damn you!" he hollered.

Moon Dove remained confused and walked towards the soldier. She saw the fuse lying on the cave floor as he raised his pistol.

Moon Dove dropped the pail as she heard the report of a forty-four caliber revolver echo loudly.

Tad screamed, "Moon Dove!" but only Moon Dove heard him.

Moon dove stumbled backward. She felt cold and looked down. Below her was a bright red puddle of blood. She turned and stumbled towards the inner tunnels of the mine. After a few steps, she again heard the deafening sound. She stepped two more slow steps, then fell to the ground.

Within the tunnels, all had stopped working. They looked at each other in bewilderment. Suddenly, an explosion brought the mine down.

***

Tad again awoke in a hospital bed. This time, he expected it. This hospital looked far different. A much bigger room, and Tad could feel multiple monitors connected to his chest and head. As before, Cindy was by his side, but no one else. As he attempted to rise, he felt the tug of something pulling his head back.

Cindy quickly stood up from a chair, next to the bed. "You did it again, Cowboy." She whispered.

"Where am I?" Tad inquired.

Cindy put her hand on Tad's. "We flew you directly to U-T-M-C this time. No lay-over in Rogersville for you. Your head is restrained. They have E-E-G sensors connected to your head and are all freaking out here. They've watched your body heal over the last three days, and they can't figure it out."

"And you? You seem awfully calm. You know I haven't put any of my worldly possessions in your name yet, right? Tad jested.

"Yep. You're back." Cindy chuckled. "I had help, Tad. I don't understand it, probably never will. But Arrow, and Sally had researched it when they went home…and…and Arrow told me about the red wolf."

"Tad, Arrow and Sally are here. They just went to get something to eat. They brought someone with them. Um…an Indian "shaman". Cindy explained.

"Native American, or Cherokee I'm guessing? What did they say?" Tad asked.

Cindy sighed. "They seem to think that you're being haunted by a spirit. The Shaman says that you've been on sort of "vision quest", and that a pure spirit has made you younger. Tad, I'll find a mirror somewhere, but you look younger than Nick."

Tad squeezed Cindy's hand. "Nothing a little gray dye won't fix, honey. Besides, I've got a "thing" for older women." He said and winked.

Just then, the door swung open. Leading Arrow, Sally, and the shaman into the room, was a doctor. He was discussing the tests that they had planned for the evening and didn't even notice Tad's awakening until he saw Sally's face light up. Sally ran to Tad's bedside, and kissed him on the forehead.

Cindy smiled a sarcastic grin. "Hey, Indian girl… Enough!" She scolded.

Arrow chuckled. "You're back, Ke-mo-sah-bee. How was your trip?" he asked.

The doctor immediately interrupted. "Mister O'Banion, or should I call you Mister Benjamin Button? How do you feel?"

Tad raised his arms and felt the sensors on his head. "I am perfectly fine. Please ignore my friends. They get jealous sometimes. I just seem to age more slowly than they. But that's because I take care of myself. They do not." He smiled at them.

"Mister O'Banion, I'm Doctor Patel. Since you have been here, you body has been in overdrive. We don't know why yet, but your healing and growth ability has somehow heightened by a factor ten. I have a few colleagues who would like to meet you. A couple of them are coming into town this afternoon. We'll make you as comfortable as possible, but we have a brain scan scheduled for this evening, and a few other tests to run before we know what is causing these seizures. Would you like some Jello, or water?" The doctor offered.

The shaman walked to a chair along the far wall from Tad's bed. He sat down and began to mumble and chant. His voice was very low, but Tad was listening to him, over the doctor.

Suddenly, Tad interrupted the doctor, addressing the shaman. "Tsu—s-qua-ga-e-hi shv-no-yi e-do-hi nv-da wesa."

The shaman stopped chanting, and the others looked at Tad in astonishment.

The shaman returned. "My son, if it is Moon Dove, you are a very lucky man. Legend is that she is lost and cannot find her way."

"Can you free her?" Tad asked.

"Yes. If what you say is true, I can free her." The shaman replied.

"Ooookay, this is beginning to sound like an exorcism, which I want no part of. Mister O'Banion, the nurse will be in to take your vitals, have you sign a couple things, and get you anything that you need. I'll be back, with a few colleagues this afternoon, and we'll discuss your condition then." The doctor stated as he patted Tad's leg.

"My clothes. Have her bring my clothes." Tad announced.

The doctor chuckled and rolled his eyes. As he was walking out, Tad said, "I'm serious!"

Sally was still at Tad's bedside, with Cindy on the other. Sally looked at the shaman, and back at Tad. "Tad, this is Gray Feather. He is from the Cherokee Nation. After Arrow and I told him about your last, um, episode, Gray Feather said that he felt we should come. He thought you might be in danger. Can you tell us why this "spirit" might attack you?" Sally asked.

"She's not evil. She didn't attack me. She's my friend. I've known her for fifty years. She needs our help. She's trapped." Tad told them.

Tad stopped and put his hand to his forehead. Closing his eyes, he mumbled. He suddenly opened his eyes and said, "Gray Feather, If I can take you to Moon Dove, can you free her? Can you send her to the river, and the wind?" Tad asked.

"Yes, I believe I can, my son." Gray Feather answered.

"And the others who died with her?" Tad asked.

"Yes. If their souls are ready, I can set them free." Gray Feather replied.

Twenty minutes later, a nurse came to Tad's hospital room. Not a single person was there…including Tad.

Chapter 31 –

"We Belong To The Land"

"Think you got a big enough rental, Arrow? I noticed that you even found one with Oklahoma plates. Nice!" Said Tad, from the back seat.

Arrow, driving the Jeep Grand Wagoneer, looked in the rear-view mirror at Tad. "Um, well, we drove. Sally was pissed at first. But Gray Feather claimed that the spirits said you were "fine". Besides, I already saw you pull this stunt once before."

Sally was looking back at Tad, who was shaking his head at Arrow's snide comments. "You're an asshole, Arrow. Can we stop somewhere and get me some clothes? I'm friggin starved too." Tad requested.

Arrow smiled and looked at the Cherokee shaman next to him. The shaman smiled back.

During the ride from Knoxville to Camelot, Tad borrowed Cindy's phone and called Adam. "Hey Bro." *-long pause as Adam speaks-* "I'm fine. I promise! I'm telling the truth, dude. Yeah, stop, listen for a minute…You know the new drones that you are working with? The tiny ones? Yeah, can you take tomorrow off and bring a couple dozen over?...and I'm assuming you can fly them, right?...Good, be here at eight. Thank you, brother. Yeah, bye."

Cindy picked Tad's arm up and over her. She laid her head on his chest. "What's that about?" She asked.

"Hee Yah Golv Kwoh Dee." Tad said.

Gray Feather turned to look at Tad. "Very old language."

The shaman turned back.

"What does it mean?" Arrow asked the Shaman.

"They are under you." Gray Feather replied.

When they arrived in Camelot, Nick was waiting for them. In his uniform, he was sitting on the picnic table. "Ya'll haven't seen the likes of a Thadeus O'Banion, have you? There's a BOLO for him. Even the Sheriff laughed, when he asked what the BOLO was for. They said he escaped from the hospital. I just laughed and told him that was a long time ago." Nick chuckled.

Tad climbed out of the backseat and walked up to Nick. Nick gave him a hug and said, "Damn good to see you, partner!"

"You too, my friend!" Tad replied.

Introductions were made with Gray Feather, then the explanation that Tad had been on a version of a "vision quest", which prompted many questions. Tad attempted to explain much of what he knew, but didn't go into the details of "who" was responsible for the deaths of the indigenous. He just referred to them as soldiers. When asked where Moon Dove and the others were, Gray Feather pointed at the old Pressmen's Building.

"You already know, don't you?" Tad asked the old shaman.

"I do, my son. I will need to stay there tonight. I will begin at nine o'clock, and must be alone until the morning. Can that be arranged?" The shaman quizzed.

"Of course, Gray Feather. Anything you need." Tad confirmed.

They continued to discuss the events. Again, Tad explained much of what he had witnessed. He held back any reference to the person responsible, and the gold. He talked about the few years that he "played" with Moon Dove when he was young. Tad explained he didn't know about the healing power, or the effect that the journeys would have on his body. Gray Feather confirmed that the effect was "most likely" not a continued regressive state. No Bejamin Button Syndrome. He believed Tad would age normally. His body just happened to be twenty to twenty-five years younger, now. Sally and Cindy chimed in and said "This is bullshit! How can we go on one of these journeys?"

***

They talked, laughed, and almost cried until dinnertime. Gail expected them at the diner and had booths prepared.

Carrie joined them for dinner, and they updated her on the events. At first, she didn't believe them. She thought they were all "messing" with her. Then Tad stood and came over to sit beside her. She touched his face, his chest, then ran her hand down his shoulder and arm. She then turned to Cindy. "Screw you, he's mine!" Carrie claimed.

All seven erupted into laughter.

The laughter and camaraderie made Tad feel good. But then he thought of Moon Dove.

Tad returned to his seat and addressed Gray Feather. "Sir, do you really think that you can free Moon Dove? They all need to be freed."

The old shaman put his hand on Tad's. "My son, their bodies are holding their spirits from the river, and wind. The ritual I will perform tonight should allow their spirits to transcend. Have faith and say goodbye tonight."

Tad smiled. "Gray Feather, Salali, Arrow. Would you mind if we go back to the campfire. Could you show us how to prepare for a Cherokee funeral?"

Arrow spoke. "We'd be honored, if all of you would join in."

Gail hustled them out of the diner, Nick excused himself to change clothes, and the rest went to the campfire.

They moved the vehicles far from the fire pit and Arrow began building the logs for the fire. He spoke with Gray Feather for a moment and asked Sally to join him in gathering some specific timber.

Gray Feather unloaded his luggage from the Wagoneer and went to the train-car that he was offered. When he came out, he was dressed in a deerskin leather shirt, a breechclout covering his loins, and buckskin boots. He wore necklaces of shells, turquoise, and turkey spurs. He also wore a simple headdress, with feathers pointing down in the back.

Gray Feather called Sally over in Tsagali, the Cherokee language. He spoke to her in Tsagali. After some instruction, Gray Feather walked toward the old Pressmen's building, and dropped to his knees. He held up his arms and looked up to the sky. He began chanting. "Oya kay Sa loy yak ah…" he continued the chant.

After Nick joined them, Sally proceeded to sit each person on the ground, positioning each of them so that they were facing east. She explained that on her cue, they would rotate around the fire and face the west, where the sun sets. They all took the position that Sally instructed, as she walked off.

Arrow was lighting the fire when Sally returned. He saw what she was carrying and prepared them. "Guys, Sally is going to paint your faces…It's going to smell a little funny, but it is safe,…it's natural. I think it's blue, for sorrow."

Sally did as Arrow said she would. She painted Arrow's face. He then painted hers. She then walked over to Gray Feather and painted his face as he continued to chant. One by one, the remaining group received face painting. Afterward, she returned to the campfire and took her place next to Arrow.

Tad felt extremely relaxed. He didn't know if there was something in the face paint, or the ceremony was relaxing him. He looked over at Cindy. She looked relaxed too…as did the others. He closed his eyes. With his eyes shut, he saw the clouds passing by quickly. Almost like a time elapsed film. He saw the hawk fly over. He felt as though he could touch the raptor. He saw the trees sway and heard the water trickling down the creek. Everything was so crystal clear.

Tad opened his eyes, and Gray Feather was directly in front of him, still chanting. From the corner of his eye, he could see that everyone had their eyes closed.

Gray Feather began to stomp and dance around Tad. "Hey Ky Yah Ts Yah Koh Ts Ky Yah…"

Tad again closed his eyes. This time, he saw Moon Dove before him. Eleven Cherokees were behind her. She was smiling, and said, in English, "Thank you my warrior. We will soon be free, because of you. I will always be with you. When the wind blows, when the water flows, I will be with you." Moon Dove closed her eyes, and reached towards Tad. He reached towards her, but everything faded away.

When Tad opened his eyes, Gray Feather was now dancing around the fire, chanting. Everyone's eyes were open. Sally stood, and everyone followed her lead. They rotated around the fire and faced west and sat back down.

Gray Feather danced between them for approximately ten minutes. Then he waved Sally up. She stood and danced similarly to Gray Feather. Then Sally waved Arrow up, and he too began to dance. One by one, they all called each other up, and found themselves dancing around each other and the fire.

The ceremony lasted twenty to thirty minutes, with Gray Feather closing the ceremony with arms raised and then dropping. His chanting stopped immediately.

Afterward, Gray Feather asked Tad, "Did you say goodbye?"

Tad smiled. "You know, I saw her…and the others. I said goodbye."

Everyone reported they felt a great "one-ness" with nature, and something special. Everyone except Cindy. She had tears running down her face.

"You okay, hon? Tad asked.

"Yeah. I'm fine. It's just all so sad." Cindy claimed.

Tad hugged Cindy. "Not anymore, it's not."

Tad wasn't sure of the etiquette, so he approached Arrow. "Hey Brother, Is it okay to have some beers, or that "taboo"?"

Arrow laughed. "If there is anything that the Cherokee can do, it's "celebrate". Yes, it's fine. I'll help you."

Sally set out the camp chairs, and everyone sat down. They all continued to talk about what they had seen. About what they felt and the closeness they currently felt with nature. Nick said that he felt like he wanted to "run through the woods naked". Tad replied, "That might be a bad idea. I think that the AI algorithm would probably cause the Sentrys to call the police."

They clinked bottles, toasting Moon Dove and eleven others, soon to be free.

Tad noticed Gray Feather and Arrow walking towards the tradesmen's building, and quickly caught up to them. "I'll get that gate, and door for you." Tad said.

As they turned to the rear of the building, they saw the red wolf. Tad and Arrow honored the wolf with a pause and head nod, but then moved on. They both recognized that the majestic beast was a symbol of "protection".

After they passed the wolf and entered through the gate, Tad removed his smartphone, tapped an app, and began scrolling. "Yeah, I figured as much." He noted.

"What's that?" Arrow inquired.

"The Sentry's can't even see the red wolf. I'm shutting it all down tonight, anyway." Tad said.

"Permanently?" Arrow asked.

Tad shot Arrow a surprised look. "Oh, hell no. Just until I know that they've all been freed."

Tad led them into the building, and down the steps. He explained how he would see Moon Dove, and the specific location.

The old shaman pushed back an old workbench, and Tad moved things away from the area. Gray Feather explained that this ritual must be performed privately. He closed his eyes and mumbled some Cherokee words. He abruptly paused and smiled. "Very good, warrior." Gray Feather whispered.

"Moon Dove?" Tad asked.

Gray Feather stared back at him with a grin. "No, but I can hear her. She calls you Little Warrior."

"She does." Tad replied.

"We must leave. I will return for the night. There will be smoke. Do not be alarmed. Let's go." Gray Feather instructed.

As they were all walking out, they heard Cindy yell. "Taaaaad?"

"Yeah, Hon?" Tad saw Cindy, about one hundred feet away, standing with Nick and Carrie.

"That big wolf, it's by the gate!" Cindy told him.

Arrow, Gray Feather, and Tad all walked by the wolf, and Tad stopped to stroke its head. "Yeah, I know. He's here for Moon Dove. He'll probably be gone in the morning." Tad explained nonchalantly. "If he's not, we can probably adopt him. Right?"

Cindy's reply was obvious by her eyes being wide open and her head shaking from side to side.

Not long after everyone returned to the campsite, Gray Feather gathered a few items, some logs, and departed for his private ritual. The valley was beginning to darken.

Tad stoked the fire with additional logs, and sat down with his friends. It suddenly seemed very quiet.

Tad felt sad, but happy. His "imaginary friend" would soon be gone. Free from her prison of a hundred and sixty years. He had said goodbye, but it still hurt.

Cindy was watching Tad and knew what he was thinking. She got up from her camp-chair, walked over to him, and sat sideways on his lap. She reached behind his head and pulled him to her. "You okay, sweetheart?" she asked.

"Yeah, just a little sad." Tad replied.

Looking in his eyes, she replied, "We all are, honey."

Trying to "break the silence", Tad mentioned Adam would be there in the morning. He explained Adam was bringing many devices that might just allow them to travel into the cavernous mine and possibly see inside.

"The micro-drones, right?" Arrow inquired.

"Yeah, I've seen them. They're tiny. Adam says they already used them for a mine collapse in South America. I'm hoping that we can fly them through the drainage grate, and to Moon Dove's resting place." Tad continued.

Arrow started to speak and stopped. "Ya,..you know, Tad. After tonight, we'll technically already — "

Tad interrupted, "You don't have to say it Arrow, this will be considered sacred and treated as such. No one will ever disturb them. Feel free to let the Cherokee Nation know…and I'll sign any documentation to support it. Moon Dove once told me, "No one owns the land." That "We belong to the land". Not vice-versa. I'll do whatever they want me to. It doesn't belong to me."

"They'll just ask that it not be desecrated." Sally intervened.

"It won't be. I promise." Tad replied.

"Hey, how you feeling Tad? The last time this happened you were a ball of energy. You're pretty "chill" this time." Nick questioned Tad.

"I don't know, I suppose I'm holding back a bit. It'll probably hit me here shortly." Tad replied.

Cindy's eyes got big, and everyone laughed.

Soon, everyone left the campsite but agreed to return in the morning.

Before Tad laid down at 22, he stood outside and looked back at the old tradesmen's building. He could see the glow of a fire and heard the chant of a Cherokee shaman. He smiled. "Goodbye, Moon Dove."

Tad awoke to the sound of Adam's rig coming up the gravel drive. Cindy didn't rouse. Tad slowly slid out of bed, put on some jeans, and stepped outside.

"You a late riser now, Tad?" Adam asked, handing Tad a coffee.

Tad was walking gingerly across the gravel. Without a shirt, Adam noticed the defined bulk that Tad's body had taken on. He also noticed that Tad was taller. "Thanks bro. Been an interesting three or four days. I'll fill you in on the details until the others come."

"The others?" Adam inquired.

Tad explained most of the events to Adam. Adam seemed astonished at first, but then "settled in" as Tad divulged his hopes of finding Moon Dove's resting place. In turn, Adam confirmed that there would be a good chance of finding her if there was "just a crack" for the mini-drones to enter. He explained they had used the AI algorithm to train the drones. Once he instructed the drones what to do and what to look for, they would do this on their own. "We'll just sit back and watch." Adam described.

As they stood there discussing the process, Gray Feather came walking up. He approached Tad and held out his hand. In it was a choker necklace made of assorted bone, stones, and beads. Tad accepted the necklace from the shaman, and held it in both hands, displaying it for the three of them to see. In the center of the choker was a red turquoise stone, with a carving...The carving of a dove, and the crescent of the moon encircling it.

"Moon Dove asked me to give this to you." the shaman explained.

"Is she gone?" Tad asked.

"No, Little Warrior. She will always be here. But she is free. You will not see her, but she is here, in the trees, in the river, in the lake. She is free, my friend. She is free." The shaman affirmed with a hand on Tad's shoulder.

Gray Feather set down his deerskin satchel, walked over to a camp-chair, and sat down. Within a minute, he was asleep.

Tad waved Adam to join him walking towards "Twenty-two". As they came to the door, it opened. Cindy stepped out. Covering herself with a Native American blanket. Tad thought, "how appropriate". She, barefoot as well, put her arms around Tad.

"What's that?" she asked.

"It's from Moon Dove. Gray Feather says she is "free" now. Somehow she gave this to him and asked him to give it to me." Tad explaining the necklace.

Cindy held it up. "It's gorgeous!" she exclaimed.

"Put it on." Tad encouraged.

"No, No. It's not for me. It's for a woman far stronger than me. But she did give it to you—" Cindy said.

"And I'm saying, put it on, Cindy. Moon Dove would want you to." Tad argued.

Cindy looked at Adam for support. But Adam held up both hands in defense.

"Okay, maybe later. I'm jumping in the shower right now. Gail's expecting us at the diner around eight-thirty." Cindy conceded.

Cindy walked toward 22, looking at the choker in amazement.

Adam said he needed to "need to answer a few emails", so Tad excused himself and went to shower as well. They all met back at the diner promptly at eight-thirty. Arrow, Sally, Nick, and Carrie arrived as well.

"I better check on Gray Feather." Sally announced.

Tad held his hand up. "I'd leave 'em. He looks exhausted. He's sleeping, out by the campfire."

Tad told them all about the necklace. Nick commented. "How the heck? Did it come from eighteen fifty?"

"Eighteen sixty-four, I believe." Tad told of the letter from General Nathan Bedford Forrest, and the journey to Franklin. He explained that he had looked up the battle, and that it was a disastrous loss for the Confederacy.

"What ever happened to General Blackwell?" Nick asked Tad.

Cindy answered. "He was killed. Shot and killed in eighteen sixty-five. He was found in a field in Blountville. Some say it was Indians. Some say robbers. Legend has it he was forced to dig his own grave."

All were staring at Cindy. Nick resumed. "Wow. That's crazy. Is that the guy, on your wall, at The Blue Dog?" he asked.

"Was." Cindy replied. "It was…It's no longer hanging there. I asked Devon to take it down."

Tad placed his hand over Cindy's and squeezed. She smiled back at him.

"Let's change the subject. Or, at least, lighten the mood. Listen, Moon Dove is free and we should all be happy. We're going to go exploring this morning,… with the help of Adam. Let's eat, and make this a positive day. Who's up for that?" Tad said.

Everyone agreed, as the waitress arrived at their table.

After breakfast, they met in the driveway, next to the sleeping Cherokee shaman. They agreed to let him sleep as Adam unloaded four large Pelican cases. Nick and Arrow assisted Adam with the cases, and started toward the old tradesmen's building, their excitement obvious by the haste of all. Cindy and Sally, holding hands while they walked, smiled widely.

Coming down the stairs, they could still smell the smoldering logs beside the drain grate. The men moved the old workbench and the girls found different objects for everyone to sit on. With a couple of chairs, a five-gallon bucket, and some antique stools, everyone could settle in for the "journey".

Adam opened the cases and Tad removed the heavy drain grate. Adam set up a couple of fold-out monitors, and other assorted equipment. Connecting everything to an inverter power-supply, the monitors came to life.

Adam opened the last case, which housed a few dozen miniature drones in clear cases. He pulled the cases, set them on the table, and opened the tops of them.

Standing over them, Nick exclaimed, "Holy shit, these are small. You mean to tell me they each have a camera too?"

"Yep. You'll see them in action pretty soon." Adam affirmed. "Hey Tad, Can I turn the Sentrys on?" He inquired.

Tad came over and joined the group around Adam. "Sure, I just didn't want them interfering with Moon Dove's ritual last night." Tad explained.

Adam was poking away at a small keyboard when magic happened. He picked up a stylus and said, "And here we go!". Then, pecking one last key with the stylus, one by one, the tiny drones took flight and hovered. Adam then pointed the stylus at the drainage tile and pushed a button, which illuminated an infrared beam. One by one, the drones took off and started heading down the tile. Everyone sat and watched as the monitors showed the inside of the drainage tile.

"I can view one, or multiples." Adam toggled a "hoy key", which suddenly split the monitor into twelve smaller views. He then toggled the view back to one,…the leader. "The AI is tracking their battery life. Once it determines that it needs to return, the leader will find a place to land. It will "rest" while the others return to charge. I can simply send another batch towards the leader, and they will get there much quicker, because they know where the leader is, and the path it took. I can also send a "charging drone" if any openings are big enough. I brought enough drones that we could probably travel a mile or so." Adam explained.

"How do they know what to do? Do they know what to look for?" Cindy challenged him.

Adam smiled. "They do. I put them into "cadaver" mode. They're looking for human remains. It could be as small as a finger bone. Their talking to the AI, so they know exactly what they're looking for. The leader is always trying to find the best path. If it finally determines that it's done, it can't go on, it will "pass the baton". The next "strongest" one will pick up, and become the leader." Adam continued.

They watched in amazement as the screen showed the drones coming to a crack where water was spilling from it. One by one they slipped through the crack and continued through a series of cracks and fissures in the rock, eventually coming to an opening. The opening appeared to be a tunnel in the mine. Everyone watched intently.

Adam stroked a few keys. "Deploying the *charging drone*". He revealed. It took to the air and down through the clay tile.

The screen continued to show a tunnel as the drones passed through it, eventually coming to a split. "Right, or left? Which way should we go?" Adam polled.

"Left. I think it's left." Tad replied.

"Left it is." As Adam poked a key.

Just minutes later, the drones came upon human bones. Four decomposed bodies. As the drones circled the bodies, Tad spoke. "No, none of them are Moon Dove. Move on." He instructed. Everyone looked at Tad in bewilderment. Tad focused on the screen.

The drones traveled another thirty feet and came upon eight more decomposed bodies. Seven surrounding one. The one in the middle, wearing her bloodstained deerskin dress…was Moon Dove.

Everyone sat there in silence. Tears fell from most, including Tad.

Suddenly, a voice from behind said, "She is happy, Little Warrior. Don't cry for her. She is happy." The Cherokee shaman said. He, too had tears slowly coming down his face.

"Bring 'em back Adam." Tad requested. He stood and walked to the shaman. "I can't thank you enough." Tad extended his hand.

Gray Feather grabbed Tad's hand and covered it with his other. "No, little brother. The Cherokee Nation thanks YOU!" The shaman was looking at Tad's face. "Moon Dove and your bravery have made you Cherokee. It will be written, Little Warrior."

The little drones zipped out of the tile drain and landed in their respective docking stations. Adam turned to Tad and asked, "What do you want to do, Tad?"

"Did you record that?" Tad asked.

"Yes." Adam replied.

"Give a copy to Gray Feather." Tad requested. "The Cherokee Nation will tell me how they would like the site marked. I'll get it secured. If you don't mind, I'd like to keep this to ourselves…at least for now. Gray Feather, Sally, Arrow, you do what you need to…and get back with me."

Nick and Arrow returned the grate to the flowing culvert in the cement floor. Tad then helped pack up the gear, while the rest left the basement.

Gathering outside of the building, Arrow explained they needed to head back to Tahlequah in the morning. Adam said he had to go back to Johnson City. Even Cindy claimed she needed to "take care of some things". Everyone solemnly broke and went in different directions. Tad remained standing, looking back at the tradesmen's building, the lump in his throat making it hard to swallow.

***

All had left except Gray Feather, Sally, Arrow, and Tad. After a long period of silence, Tad spoke, "I need to show you guys something. Can we go for a little hike?" he asked.

Agreeing, they followed Tad past the Pressmen's Home buildings, and to an area at the base of the mountain. Tad led them up a ravine, and to a section of the mountain with cliffs and crevasses. He paused a few times, appearing to orient himself, but then proceeded to a specific crevasse. He said, "Wait here."

Tad climbed into the honeysuckle and then to the edge of a crevasse. Positioning himself so that he could shimmy down the crevasse, he disappeared from their view. Slowly he descended until he reached the bottom. Once at the bottom, he dropped to his knees and dug at the soft soil until he reached rocks. He closed his hand over one of the "rocks" and pulled it from the loam. It was gold and stone.

From above, Arrow, Sally, and Gray Feather could not see what Tad was doing. They could hear his actions and looked at each other. Tad pulled a leather satchel from under the dirt. He dusted it off and inspected its deterioration. To his surprise, it was fairly "sound". He slung it over his shoulder and slowly ascended.

Once Tad was close to the top, he lifted the satchel. Struggling to get it up to the edge of the crevasse, it eventually landed with a "THUD". Breaking open, out poured a mixture of rocks, gold, jewels, and jewelry.

Tad climbed out of the chasm. Dropping to one knee, he did his best to push the "jewels" back into the split leather satchel. He gathered it up with both arms and crawled out from under the honeysuckle. Holding it out to Gray Feather, Tad said. "I want you to have all of this." Tad explained. "There's plenty more down there. I mean A LOT!"

Gray Feather inspected the stone. "I cannot take this, Little Warrior." He claimed.

"It's yours, please take it." Tad insisted.

"He can't, Tad." Sally interrupted. "It's *Blood Gold*, he can't take it."

"Moon Dove would want you to have it, Little Warrior. This, I know." The Cherokee shaman instructed.

Tad stood there looking down at the leather satchel. After a few moments, he dropped to his knees, crawled back under the honeysuckle and pushed the satchel of gold and jewels back into the crevasse. "Have it your way, but you're still taking some gold back to Oklahoma." Tad said with some sarcasm.

***

Riding in the back of the Wagoneer through Camelot, Tad looked up at Sally. She was driving. From the back seat, he suddenly felt young again. He looked down at his little legs hanging from the leather, and could see his mother driving the limousine. His brother sitting next to him, he saw the valley as it was in 1973. It felt good. He smiled.

Cindy was standing outside The Blue Dog when they arrived. "I've got our favorite spot reserved." She informed them.

Tad was the last to exit the Wagoneer. "Hey, Hon." He called out.

As he approached, Cindy looked him up and down. "Cowboy boots? I like 'em!" she exclaimed.

Tad walked up to Cindy. She lifted up on her toes and laughed. "I can't reach you anymore."

"Not a problem, Ma'am." Tad put his arms around Cindy, and picked her up for a kiss.

Arrow, Sally, and Gray Feather were standing in the doorway. Sally looked at Arrow. "He looks happy, Arrow." She said.

"He does." Arrow said with a smile.

Nick and Carrie were already on the balcony, drinking cold ones. Coming up the stairs, Tad immediately saw the outline of where the General's picture once hung.

Throughout dinner, Cindy seemed preoccupied and kept looking at the front door. She suddenly jumped up when she saw a particular person enter. It was a young lady, and she was carrying something. Thinking that it must have something to do with the restaurant, the rest of the group quickly lost interest. But, shortly after Cindy had descended the steps, she came back up, with the young lady.

"Everybody! This is Serena. Serena is one of the aspiring artists, at the gallery. She has something to show us. The young girl hoisted a framed portrait. A portrait of Moon Dove, in charcoal. A stunning image of a young Cherokee woman, wearing the very necklace that was given to Tad.

"My God. It looks just like her." Tad stood, looking at the art.

Cindy helped Serena set the portrait onto the edge of the table so that everyone could see it.

"How did you even- I mean, the necklace. It's beautiful. She's beautiful. Serena, I'm impressed." Tad said.

Sally and Carrie both had their hands over their mouths, while Arrow, Nick, and Gray Feather just smiled.

"Hey Cowboy, you want to help me hang it up where it belongs?" Cindy asked.

Tad walked over and picked up the framed portrait. Lifting it higher, he hung it where the portrait of General Blackwell had hung for so many years.

"Miss Blackwell." The young lady announced. "Your necklace."

Serena was holding out the "Moon Dove Choker".

Tad quickly stepped between Serena and Cindy.

Taking the necklace from the young girl, he turned and draped it across Cindy's neck. "Turn around, Sweetheart." He requested.

Tad connected the simple hooks and watched Cindy's face as she held back tears and smiled. The table began clapping. Cindy reached her arms around Tad and squeezed. Tad bent down and kissed her on the forehead.

***

Morning came quickly. Arrow and Gray Feather were loading the Wagoneer when Tad came out the front door.

"I guess y'all are getting ready to roll?" Tad asked.

Arrow walked over to Tad. Extending his arm, they clasped hands, and lightly hugged. "Yes, bro. But we'll be back. Sally and I were talking last night. We wouldn't mind buying one piece of property, here in the valley. A nice little "barndominium", and some horses might be a good second home."

Tad chuckled. "Yeah. There are worse places to retire…speaking of which, I've got something for you." Tad started back towards 22.

Tad emerged from the rain-car with a thirty-pound gold brick. He walked towards the rear of the Wagoneer.

Gray Feather stood with a confused countenance, and suddenly Arrow raised his arms. "No, no, NO!" He stepped in front of Tad.

Tad stopped. "Bro, I already gave it to you. You just didn't have a way to get it home. We talked about this…You can either take them, or I'm donating them to UT, in your name. And I swear, I will!" Tad asserted.

Arrow's arms dropped as he watched Tad load it into the back of the SUV.

"Come. Help me get the other two." Tad commanded with a nod.

"The other TWO?!" Arrow exclaimed.

"Yes. I'm giving the last one to Gray Feather. It's not "Blood Gold". It might be stolen from The Confederacy, but I think they can do without it." Tad declared.

Gray Feather stood emotionless. He watched as the two Cherokee warriors loaded almost five million dollars worth of gold into the Wagoneer.

After loading the third brick, Arrow looked at Tad. "You know that I'm just going to donate the money to Northeastern State, in your name." Arrow revealed.

"I don't give a shit what you do with it. I gave it to you three to do as you please. There's no way on God's green planet that I can repay you for what you've done. Thank you, my friends." Tad said.

Still emotionless, Gray Feather stepped towards Tad. He closed his right fist and covered his own heart. "Little Warrior, I know not a man that has the spirit as you. You belong to this valley, she watches over you. She will walk with you and keep you safe…Soon you will come to Tahlequah and officially become Cherokee."

Gray Feather then took his fist, laid it on Tad's chest, covering Tad's heart. "Dah-Nee-Tah-Gah". Gray Feather said.

Tad put both hands over the Shaman's fist, looked at him and repeated, "Dah-Nee-Tah-Gah".

Cindy and Sally had come out and were standing next to Arrow.

"What does that mean?" Cindy asked.

"Blood brother." Sally replied.

Chapter 32 –

"The Camelot Valley Train Station"

Tad stepped through the sliding door, and out onto the deck, overlooking the horse pasture. He watched Cindy as she brushed the majestic creature. All chestnut with black points, "Robino" was one of ten horses that Cindy claimed "belonged" to the valley. Even though she bought them all, she'd not say she "owned" them.

Tad thought she worked more than before. But Cindy claimed that "The Stable" wasn't work.

They'd built the "Barndominium" over the winter and lovingly named it "The Stable". Another was being built just down the road by the Brooks'.

The Camelot Valley Train Station was recently completed. Sitting atop the old hotel's foundation, it overlooked ten tiny home train-cars scattered around the lake. Nick owned another twelve on the ridges and had four more on the way.

Tad took a sip of coffee and looked out toward the lake. He saw two children in a paddleboat. He squinted his eyes. The coffee shop looked busy at The Train Station. Tad breathed in heavily. He could smell the hay crop, recently cut.

Tad closed his eyes and remembered. Seeing the little boy running down the hill, he smiled. With the mutt chasing him, Tad saw the little boy heading towards the Pressmen's Trade Building. He knew the little boy was going to visit his friend. Not an imaginary one. But, a loyal friend.

The Pressmen's Trade building, and approximately two acres behind it, was now registered with the federal government. Considered a Cherokee burial ground, was now "protected" and it would not be disturbed. Protected by a new stone fence and four Sentrys, the burial site would remain sacred for eternity.

When Tad came back into the house, he saw Cindy coming up the wide spiral stone staircase. "How was your ride, Hon?" he asked.

"Great! Nick's trails are awesome. I ran into a couple of hikers, and three people on mountains bikes. We've been pretty busy for our first season, don't you think?" Cindy inquired.

Tad set his coffee cup on the counter and walked over to Cindy. Putting his arms around her, he pulled back, but kept his arms around her.

Cindy grinned. "Yeah… I know. I smell. I'll take a shower. You think we've been busy? The rentals, and The Train Station?"

Tad kissed her on her forehead. "Yeah, we have. The train-cars are booked solid. I think that we're going to have to make the parking lot bigger at The Train Station soon. This is becoming a full time job and we're supposed to be retired…We need to talk about hiring more people."

Cindy pulled away from Tad. "Let's talk to Nick and Carrie tonight about that. Can you get "Moon Dove" out of the vault for me? I want to wear her tonight. She'll go perfectly, with a little outfit I bought for you to see." Cindy was walking away, but stopped, and looked back. "But, right now, I need to jump in the shower. Wanna join me, cowboy?" Cindy asked, with a wink.

"Lead the way, little lady." Tad replied.

***

Nick and Carrie had both resigned from the Sheriff's Department. Nick was managing his own rentals and creating the trails for hikers, bikers, and horseback lovers. Carrie was attending college full time.

Nick and Carrie had a slightly larger version of the train-cars on the peak of the North Ridge. Referred to as "Merlin's Tower", it was the highest point in Camelot. Nick said that they intended to build a home there, and move train-car 88 down to the valley.

***

Tad and Cindy pulled up to "88" around three PM. Their electric side-by-side, built by Adam's new company, "Send It", boasted over one hundred-fifty horsepower. Looking more like a military vehicle, Tad owned one-oh-two, the second one built. The vehicle quietly whined to a stop.

Tad and Cindy were already sitting on the front porch when Nick came out. "I CAN NOT hear you coming, with that damn thing." Nick asserted. Stopping to pull a beer from Tad's cooler.

"Yeah. It's pretty cool. Adam's probably going to slay it with those little guys. He already can't keep up with the orders." Tad explained.

Carrie stepped out of 88, walked over, and gave Tad a kiss on the head, and then did the same to Cindy.

"Enchiladas. I hope you guys like 'em. I'll put them in about four."

Cindy had a pair of cut-off jeans, a short-sleeve western shirt, a cowboy hat, boots, and her favorite,…the "Moon Dove" choker. She tipped her hat up and looked over her sunglasses. "Need any help, there sweetness?" She said to Carrie.

Carrie pursed her lips. "Nope, got it covered. You all just relax. Come on in. Nick's out back, on the deck."

Tad walked to the edge of the immense deck and looked out. "This view is insane." He claimed.

"Yeah. Probably better than I would have originally thought. It'll hafta do until I can get the time to think about the house." Nick replied.

"I'm glad you said that." Tad turned back. "Don't you think we should go ahead and start hiring people to do a lot of this shit for us? I mean, we're paying cash for the new train-cars already. I'd like to see all of us relax a bit. Maybe go on a trip, or two. Hell, I bought the Sprinter van, and we haven't done one single adventure with it." Tad grumbled.

"Adventure? What adventures do you want our company for?" Nick asked.

"Well, let's get the old gang together, and see if we can save another "Indian Princess". Or let's solve the mystery of Stonehenge. Something,…anything, just as long as we're not "working". Tad requested.

"I've got school." Carrie retorted.

Cindy lowered the hat back down. "Oh, shut up! You don't even need to go to school anymore." She jested.

Nick walked over, turned and leaned against the rail with Tad. "I suppose you're right. I'll get started on it…and it would be fun to go on a trip. Something besides Tahlequah, though. Somewhere where ten thousand people

ARE NOT kissing Tad's ass because he donated millions of dollars to their university. Huh, Carrie?"

"That new building at the university was crazy…and pretty cool that it was named after Moon Dove, …and General Blackwell. Well, actually his wife, I suppose. Sorry, Cindy." Carrie apologized.

Cindy stood. "Yeah, I think it's even cooler that I found out that Sally and I are related. I have a sister in Oklahoma I never knew I had." She walked over to join Tad and Nick at the railing. "On top of that, I officially became Cherokee. Well, the old General is probably turning over in his grave." Cindy grinned.

"I doubt it, Hon. My guess is that he's watching over us right now…with his arm around Moon Dove." Tad said, with a smile.

"Ya think?" Carrie asked.

Tad turned back and looked across the valley. "I do."

***

Four weeks later----------

Nick had interviewed over twenty people, hiring just eight. But, it was a good start toward the promises they had discussed a month prior. He laughed when he thought about the Mercedes Sprinter van Tad had put together. Tad recently had the exterior "wrapped" with a scheme similar to the vehicle driven by cartoon sleuths, that Tad often quoted. With swirling colors of blue and green, Tad had "Where Are You?" plastered on the sides of it. The van was sure to garner attention if they actually did any trips with it.

Carrie would soon be home from school. Well into her studies for an LPN, she said that she wanted to finish.

She wasn't in a hurry, but wanted to complete the program, just the same. She said she would probably just offer her services "in the Camelot valley". All thought it to be a great idea.

Nick called Tad. "Hey Tad. What are you guys up to on a beautiful Friday?"

"Hanging by the pool with Cindy. Watching cute kids having fun. How about you?" Tad replied.

Nick explained. "I hired eight people, Tad. Four start Monday, and four the following Monday. I got one I think we might promote to manage things fairly quickly. I don't know if you saw the text, but the Brooks' are coming in tomorrow morning, and will need to be picked up."

"We're on it, my friend. Why don't you and Carrie come down to the diner to join us for dinner tonight?" Tad asked.

"Carrie will be home soon. I'm sure she'll be up for that. Ya know, Tad. It's crazy, but just a couple of years ago, this valley…well, it was broken. And today people are enjoying it everywhere I look. It's all just a bit crazy. See you soon." Nick said, then hit the "end" button on his phone.

As they sat by the pool behind the "Camelot Valley Train Station", Tad reached over to Cindy. "Ya know,… sorry to paraphrase Lovely The Band, but,…at the end of the day, we're all just a little…broken. "

Cindy smiled, reached out and grabbed Tad's hand.

They sat there watching the setting sun. As it lit up the far side of the valley, both smiled at each other, squeezed the other's hand and said…"Broken."

Then, Cindy squeezed again, holding her left hand up to the sky, admiring the large pink-orange sapphire on her finger…She said, with a smile, "My love,…I'm pregnant."

Afterword

While this is a work of fiction, the land, the history, and many of the emotions are real. There are many unbelievable facts within *Echoes*. The local notoriety of the Crocketts, Pressman's Home, Camelot, and even much of the Civil War conspiracy are all true aspects of Hawkins County. Of course, there is much fiction as well. There are no caves, gold, or jewels hidden in Camelot. So please leave the forgotten place be.

Personally, it broke my heart returning to Camelot and seeing the decay. I was there as a young child and watched the effort that so many were putting into making it something grand. I watched my brother learn to ride horses there and I was the little boy walking around the clubhouse at some of the lavish parties. My memories of that little valley are special.

As for Moon Dove, she came to me in a dream and everything else just kept fueling her character. The abundance of Civil War history in East Tennessee inspired William Blackwell, and many of the characters of *Echoes* are based on friends and family. The rest just seemed to flow.

I always wanted to write a novel. When I was younger, I read a lot—mostly thrillers that made me think "Hey, I can do that", but I never put pen to paper. The amazing thing was that when I did, the thoughts and images just flooded in. I told a friend one evening "I have no idea what writer's block is" because I've never had it—not once. In fact, there are about 60 - 70 pages that I took out of *Echoes* before publishing.

I've obviously created characters that I may continue to write about. I'll certainly see what dream takes me in a new direction. But, for now, I hope that you enjoyed *Echoes*... and, like me, stay broken.

James Ryan